ISOLATION

ISBN: 978-1-7343846-0-4 (E-book)
ISBN: 978-1-7343846-1-1 (Paperback)

First Edition: December 2019.

Logo design by Looka.

Scorpio Writing, LLC
PO Box 68225
Baltimore, MD 21215

www.SurvivorsofJohanum.com

ISOLATION

Book One of The Chronicles of the Survivors of Johanum

Tiffany Aurora

Chris,
Make it a life well-lived.

Tiffany Aurora

INTRODUCTION

We know it now by many names, but in those days it was known by only one: Johanum.

The writer in me longs to describe it to you, but I'm afraid any such attempt would do you a great disservice. Johanum is not so much understood as experienced. So I will let the story speak for itself. I ask you only to reserve judgment.

To all who have walked in Johanum
May you find yourself among friends
For you are not, nor have you ever been, alone.

CHAPTER 1
Middlestan

It was not the day I had planned.

I was preparing for one of the biggest nights of my career. I was a tenure-track professor with reasonable popularity among my fellow faculty, but my students were not fond of me. Each spring, I ranked in the bottom quartile of professors on campus, thanks to what our survey responses labeled "mumbling, incoherent lectures."

I spent years searching for the one thing that would set me apart. I knew the answer would lie in research. I hated public speaking, and I was not terribly fond of students.

Six semesters back, I found my niche: Interplanetary strategy for military alliances.

Never mind that my own planet, Middlestan, had been the first to sign our solar system's peace treaty. By signing the Treaty, we gave up our right to bear arms and handed that exclusive right to the planet Bisurakhan. Bisurakhan is the most powerful and advanced planet in our solar system. Time passes more quickly there, and it gives them a strategic advantage. Middlestan must gain approval from Bisurakhan for any measures it takes to protect itself from invaders. Bisurakhan, for its part, bears responsibility for protecting itself and the other eight planets in our solar system. Their leaders make decisions and issue decrees from a tall, ugly tower called the Turris, located in the Capitol district Zawal.

Interplanetary strategy for military alliances. It was an unusual choice. Anything involving military force or coordination between planets was automatically tagged as "of interest" to our Curators, which meant loads of questions, lots of interviews, and seemingly endless amounts of paperwork. Curators are the men from

Bisurakhan who travel across planets to observe important developments and record them in our universal Logarithms, or Logs. They go where they wish, ask what they like, and you give them whatever information they ask for. That's just the way it is.

I knew my research choice was risky. But I needed something big if I was ever going to shake out of my miserable existence as a teaching professor.

So, I took a gamble. And I won.

Last week, all my research was published in the paper, "Future Alliances and the Planets that Build Them." By week's end, I was a small-time celebrity.

Leaders on the planets Cornersville and Kabira called to congratulate me. Faculty members at the university treated me with a new level of respect. It was a lot to take in. I enjoyed some of the attention. Some of it was pompous and ridiculous. But I enjoyed the feeling of autonomy that accompanied my new status. To me, that was the prize.

Dean Everett Corban summoned me to his office at the end of the week and handed me a letter from Bisurakhan's president, the Honorable Khalid Basjid. President Basjid was effusive in his praise as he congratulated the university on its homegrown talent. Then he closed with these words:

"I can't help but notice that Middlestan has neither need nor reason for producing such insightful material. It seems a bold move for a planet that could easily be eclipsed by the one it aspires to outmaneuver."

Dean Corban said the memorandum was the best entertainment he'd had in a long time. He promised me that the university would continue to fund my research as long as I promised to keep Basjid on his toes and give him plenty of reasons to send the dean more letters.

A reception was scheduled for tonight, preceded by a painful hour of networking in the lobby outside Barclay Hall.

Dean Corban himself would present the results of my research and the university's official statement of endorsement. I was a terrible speaker, and this was the dean's way of politely managing me out of the program.

I didn't mind. I had my prize. Sweet autonomy and a foreseeable end to public speaking.

A university driver pulled up to my house at 6:05. Black clutch in hand, I locked my front door and walked down the sidewalk to the street.

I arrived at the university fashionably late. I would have preferred to not arrive at all. I didn't mind listening to the dean summarize my research, but I was dreading the networking event. Events that encourage adults to pretend they're interested in you while asking questions that show off their own intelligence should really be eliminated.

"Welcome, Dr. Kanale! It's such a pleasure to see you here tonight!" An overly friendly student with a toothy grin had been placed at the door. He was happy. Too happy. He had been prepped to be nice to me, I could tell. In fact, I recognized him. He had been in one of my classes the previous year. He sat in the back the whole semester and snickered as I talked.

"Are tonight's events still scheduled to take place in Barclay Hall?" I asked.

"Yes, absolutely. And everything is in your honor, just as it should be. Now, in case you don't know, Barclay Hall is directly down that hallway, then to the right. You can just follow the signs."

"I know where Barclay Hall is," I said. I didn't care for his condescension or his fake smile. But it wouldn't do any good to get angry. Not tonight. I was so close to achieving my goal. I needed to let the little things go.

"Of course you know where Barclay Hall is. Forgive me. I'm just so excited to be celebrating you tonight, Professor. Your paper is truly groundbreaking."

"You read it, did you?" I asked.

He stuttered.

"It's all right. I didn't expect that you would," I said, letting him off the hook.

At least he had the decency to look embarrassed.

I headed down the hallway in the direction of Barclay Hall. It felt good to let a little offense go. Normally, I would have been annoyed. I might have written him up. But not tonight. Tonight, we would go our separate ways and not even think about each other ever again. I was on my way to a permanent research position. I wasn't going to have to deal with students much longer.

That thought made me deliriously happy.

The foyer outside Barclay Hall was full of lively conversation. My entrance drew an instant round of applause. I twisted my face into a forced smile.

Three history professors were standing near the doors as I walked in. They cornered me before I had a chance to escape.

"I don't know how many people noticed, but I thought you would want to know that your reference to the Peace Treaty on Page 32 contained an error." It was Dr. Butch Moody, a tall man in his fifties with a nasally voice and thinning hair. "You listed the signing date of the Treaty as the fifth day of the tenth month. But you failed to make any reference as to which planet's time signature you were using. If interpreted under a time signature other than that of Middlestan or Cornersville, your paper could be perceived as factually inaccurate."

It was an entirely unnecessary comment. All academics know the time and place when the Peace Treaty went into effect. In fact, young children across every planet learn those details in their earliest days of school.

I had overheard some of my students referring to Dr. Butch Moody as "Dr. Bitchy Mood." The nickname fit.

Dr. Catherine Cassidy spoke up. "It would also serve you well to name Quanderos as the signatory location in future papers, should you spend much time on the Treaty's history again." Her voice was as smooth as the long, manicured fingernails she waved excessively as she talked.

"I didn't spend much time on the Peace Treaty in this one," I answered, trying not to sound dismissive. It would do no good to alienate them now, even though I didn't like them. I tried to explain my reasoning without sounding annoyed. "I didn't think it was necessary to name Quanderos as the signatory location because it's common knowledge. As is the date and time when the Peace Treaty was signed," I couldn't help but add.

"And it is common knowledge for us, the well-educated," Dr. Cassidy replied, patting my arm. She came from a family of celebrated academics and had earned three PhDs herself. She never missed an opportunity to remind others how accomplished she was. "But you see, I like to encourage my students to read innovative research. They need to read the new stuff. They spend too much time pouring over our old dusty textbooks, and it's not engaging for them. Your research is exciting, if for no other reason than it's provocative and new."

I chose again to not be offended.

"Anyway, students these days know so little about our history," Dr. Cassidy concluded, voicing every history professor's biggest complaint about Middlestan's education system.

Dr. Moody nodded his head in agreement.

They were right, unfortunately. History classes in Middlestan had become painfully rudimentary. It was like we had forgotten our history. Perhaps our leaders wanted us to.

"If Dean Corban continues to fund my research, I will give Quanderos more attention in my future papers," I promised. Professor Cassidy's smile let me know I had responded correctly.

I felt a tap on my shoulder and turned around.

It was Dr. Brian Fieldbein, beaming with all his boyish enthusiasm. "You did it! You really did it!" He grabbed me in a bear hug and crushed my face against his shoulder. It's what he always did when he was happy and a little bit drunk.

I had a genuine fondness for Brian. He had been one of my only friends at the university. He looked the part of the wild professor: clothes mismatched, too many buttons left undone, and socks at curious lengths climbing up his legs, a fact that was hard to miss given how unfortunately short the pant legs were on all his trousers. He was fifteen years older than me and had given himself a role in my life somewhere between mentor and father figure. Most days I wanted to strangle the cheerfulness out of him, but a little part of me envied his unquenchable positivity.

Brian let me escape from the bear hug as Dean Corban approached. The dean was popular and well-respected among the faculty, but Brian didn't care much for him. He thought Dean Corban was stuffy and needed to loosen up.

The dean greeted me and the professors in my circle, then motioned for two men at the door to come and join us.

The men were dressed in formal military attire. Dean Corban slapped Brian on the back good-naturedly, grasped his shoulder, and firmly moved him several steps to the right.

Brian took his cue to exit. He bowed flamboyantly, winked in my direction, and moved to join his fellow astronomy professors.

"Let me introduce our honored guests," Dean Corban said to me, using his no-nonsense administrator voice.

He stared at Professors Cassidy and Moody. They caught the hint and moved away.

"Professor Kanale," Dean Corban said, "I would like to introduce you to Calif Asamov and Antoine Duval, Chieftans of Bisurakhan's armed forces, sent here on behalf of President Basjid, the most honorable leader of the same planet."

"Hello," I said. "Welcome to Middlstan."

Their smiles, though pleasant, were weighted and measured. It was as if they had been sent to size me up.

They're going to be disappointed, I thought ruefully. For a moment, I wished I was more interesting. As it was, I was the most boring academic you could meet. I had no real life outside of work. And that was saying a lot. People in Middlestan lead boring, predictable, monotonous lives. When someone paints their house, it's big news in that town for a week.

I loved it.

Life on Bisurakhan was a different story. Not that I had ever visited Bisurakhan. Citizens of Middlestan don't travel much. But I had read the Logs and heard the stories. I knew that life for a Bisurakhanati was fast, exciting, and constantly changing.

It sounded awful. But Bisurakhan had given the Exertus universe the strongest military in human history. We all owed our safety – our lives – to the Khanist military. Or so their campaigns told us.

Among all the Khanists who make up Bisurakhan's armed forces, only one ranks higher than the Chieftans, who are commonly referred to as Chiefs. The Logs refer to the military's highest leader as the "Commander." No one in Middlestan (or any other planet that I know of) has ever seen his face. Even the Logs contain no description of his physical appearance. But these two men, standing before me, were second in command of the Khanist forces. They were the most powerful men I had ever met in real life.

I was a little starstruck. But as I thought about it, I realized that nothing good could come of their visit. There's never a good reason for a Khanist to visit Middlestan. Never any good reason at all.

My fascination quickly turned to anxiety.

"I'm sorry, forgive me," I said, interrupting the small talk that had sprung up between the chiefs and Dean Corban. "Have I put someone in danger? I don't understand why you're here."

Both chiefs turned their intense gazes in my direction. I squirmed and shifted nervously from one foot to the other. Even the dean began to feel uncomfortable. I could tell by the way his foot was tapping the floor.

Chief Calif Asamov was an older man, approaching sixty, with a well-groomed beard and kind blue eyes. "President Basjid sends his greetings," he finally answered. His voice was low and soothing. I felt myself leaning forward, hoping he would continue to speak. "We mean Middlestan no harm," he continued. "We are here merely as a...precaution."

"I don't understand," I replied, "but even so. Surely there are plenty of lower ranking officials – a General, perhaps? – who could have come instead."

"As I said, a simple precaution," Chief Asamov repeated. "Hopefully one which will come to nothing. Then you will not need your question answered, and I won't need to lie to you."

I was taken aback by his bluntness. But I liked him. I trusted him. And I was suddenly very relaxed.

This must be how Bisurakhan became so powerful, I thought to myself. *They get people to trust them when they've done nothing to earn it. I'm going to explore this in my next paper. Or at least mention it. They are taking care of us, after all. They should be properly thanked for it.*

Why was I thinking of thanking Bisurakhan?

"Your theory about a possible spatial reconfiguration of our planets was very creative," Chief Asamov added.

I blushed and began to talk too much. I always rambled when I was embarrassed. "Thank you. What good could ever come of that theory? I mean, of course it would mean adjustments to troop disbursement strategies, and all geography-based weaponry would need to be reexamined. I've considered bringing Reality Persuasion into my next round of research, by the way. What do you think of that idea? It's a fascinating line of experimentation, controversial though it may be from a moral or ethical perspective. I could tackle it. I mean, who doesn't love an academic arguing ad nauseam about something she doesn't understand? I've heard that some leaders in your own leaders deny the plausibility of Reality Persuasion as a legitimate method of reliable intelligence acquisition. Even so – "

"Well, I see you have made your introductions," came Brian's cheerful voice. He had an uncanny knack for knowing when I was about to get myself in trouble and had quietly reappeared beside me. "Allow me to introduce myself. Brian Fieldbein, Middlestan Accelerated University's School of Astronomy."

The chiefs greeted Brian and Dean Corban took his own cue to exit.

"I do believe it is nearly time for the program to begin. Gentlemen, if you will excuse me. If you will excuse us." He grabbed me by the elbow and ushered me alongside him through the lobby, into the auditorium, and toward the stage. A couple of stagehands were moving the podium into view.

"I'm sorry if I said something wrong," I said.

"You don't need to be sorry. Just -" He stopped abruptly and glanced over his shoulder. He could see the chiefs back in the lobby. They steadily returned his gaze. "The chiefs are very powerful. They could destroy...everything. Our university, our careers, our planet. I do, quite literally, mean everything."

"But why would they?" I asked.

"No reason. But I think it's better to be cautious. It would be better to say less rather than more."

"I didn't say very much."

"Yet. You didn't say much yet. You know how you get."

I rolled my eyes. "I wasn't going to tell them everything I was thinking."

Dean Corban looked unconvinced.

"I mean, probably most of it, but not *everything*..."

"You don't read social cues sometimes," Dean Corban pointed out.

I scowled.

"You know it's true."

I sighed. We had been over this before. He was right. When I got nervous or excited, I would get distracted and stop paying attention. Well, it didn't matter now. We had walked up on stage. I took one of the front row seats near the podium.

Dean Corban shuffled his papers once, twice, then a third time. He paced across the stage a few times, then sat down next to me. His foot began tapping the floor again. Every now and again, his knee bounced, bumping into mine.

Dean Corban wasn't the nervous type. He was political and savvy – all the things that make for a successful administrator. But he was also kind and conscientious. Faculty and students alike respected his leadership. The presence of the chiefs had unnerved him.

I didn't understand why. I felt so relaxed.

The ceiling lights in Barclay Hall dimmed. A crowd of several hundred made their way inside. They filled the plush auditorium seating and left twenty or so students standing in the back of the room.

The chiefs took seats at the front.

A dozen uniformed men had been placed strategically around the room near the exits. They wore black slacks with a silver stripe down each pant leg, and black suit jackets with varying degrees of embroidered silver vines.

These men were members of Bisurakhan's military. Khanists, as they liked to be called. I recognized the uniforms. They were described in the Logs.

I gathered the dean was not expecting them. His right knee was now bouncing furiously.

Barclay Hall's front row was customarily reserved for the Curators. Curators, our Log-keepers, travel between planets to record significant events. They are available upon request to provide consultation and advice to government officials and military leaders.

Curators are curious creatures. They are regular men, or so I'm told, but they seem a species onto themselves. Each has an uncomfortably high-pitched voice and long, black fingernails. Their facial features appear a bit stretched, the result of frequent travel between planets and time signatures. They have a habit of drumming their fingers incessantly against any available surface. At some point in the past decade, they self-adopted a uniform: a thick, taupe-colored cloak with a hood. Among crowds, curators don the hood and avoid eye contact. They slide in and out of public spaces, unannounced but never unseen, and the general public seems to prefer it that way.

Eight Curators entered Barclay Hall and took their seats in the front row. Today's turnout would ensure immediate reporting to leaders on each of the other planets.

Dean Corban jumped from his chair as the clock in the back of the hall struck eight o'clock. He approached the podium, tapped the microphone to make sure it was live, then launched full steam ahead.

"Good evening! Friends, colleagues, students, and most esteemed guests." His voice was warm and pleasant, showing no sign of stress. He singled out and waved to a few key members of the audience before continuing. "Let me welcome you to Middlestan Accelerated University, the most distinguished and highly awarded university on our planet. We are also, may I humbly add, continually ranked among the Top 25 academic institutions in our solar system."

Applause filled the room. The students standing in the back began whooping and hollering, a sign of their enthusiasm for the dean more than their love for our dark halls of learning. A few of the visiting academics from Charisburg, Cornersville, and Kabira grumbled good-naturedly.

The chiefs looked over their shoulders at the rambunctious students in the back of the room. They turned back around and smiled at the dean. The stress lifted from his shoulders and he began to relax.

"We are here tonight to officially present the findings of our beloved and most esteemed colleague, Dr. Josephine Kanale."

I stood for the obligatory round of applause.

And that's when I saw them.

They were so unfamiliar, so unexpected, I couldn't help but stare.

Three men had appeared in the back of the auditorium. I think they were men. They were tall, easily surpassing seven feet. They seemed to have materialized out of thin air.

The tallest one, the one in the middle, locked eyes with me. A burning sensation pierced my skull. I stumbled backwards, rocking my head in my hands. I tried to speak, but no sound emerged. Even as I willed the dean to turn around, to look at me, or just to look up and see them, no one moved. No one noticed the men who burn with their eyes.

The pain subsided. I sat back in my seat. Cautiously I raised my gaze, careful to keep it at floor-level. The men wore outfits resembling long linen tunics. I could see the hems of their garments brushing the ground. They were still there.

I turned and met the gaze of Chief Asamov. He was studying me carefully. I tilted my head toward the back of the auditorium. Slowly, he turned, looking behind him. He scanned the circumference of the room before returning his gaze to mine and shaking his head.

I must have been dreaming. I lifted my head with confidence. The gaze was far more piercing this time. It stabbed through my head like a dagger. I cried out, but no one heard. Everyone was still listening to the dean, who kept talking and talking and talking.

Only the chiefs were looking at me. Both of them now. Neither seemed too concerned.

I decided to stand and get everyone's attention. But I couldn't. My feet were plastered to the floor. I could wiggle my toes, move my ankles, even rock my feet from side to side. But lift my legs I could not.

Then I heard his voice.

"Josephine."

I knew it was the tall one who spoke. I don't know how I knew, but I knew. Instantly.

"Josephine."

My legs lifted. They carried me forward. To the men with the burning eyes. To the tall one with the outstretched hand whose gaze I now steadfastly avoided, staring stubbornly at the ground. I was standing in front of him now.

"Josephine. We have come to take you home."

And just like that, Barclay Hall and the world I had known disintegrated before my eyes.

We were left standing in the middle of a desert. The air was smothering and hot, the kind of heat that makes it hard to breathe. Then a harsh wind blew. I shivered.

"What is this place?" I asked, rubbing my arms.

"This is your home," the man replied. "Don't you remember it? Welcome to Johanum."

CHAPTER 2
Bisurakhan
The Turris, Military Headquarters

"She just 'disappeared'?" Chief Jorge Hernandez asked incredulously.

A series of urgent messages from the Turris Communications Tower had interrupted the chief's evening routine with his grandchildren. His wife Maria called him a few affectionate but short-tempered names as he handed her the babies and rushed out the door. Such an urgent summons was so unusual that he wasn't angry, just concerned.

"Something was wrong, and she knew it," said Chief Antoine Duval. "She was clueless before the ceremony. She seemed confused and perhaps a bit nervous by our appearance, but you can't really blame her for that. She gave no indication that she was concerned for her own safety."

"But something changed during the presentation," Chief Calif Asamov interrupted.

"That's right," Antoine agreed. "I saw her looking at you, Calif. She saw something."

"I don't understand is why we didn't see anything," Calif replied. His calm, soothing voice reflected the same sense of concern Jorge felt.

"She seemed to be gesturing toward something at the back of the room," Antoine added.

"You saw nothing, nothing at all?" Jorge asked.

"Not a thing," Calif answered. "We've talked to every one of our security guys, and no one saw or heard anything out of the ordinary."

"We have facial recognition confirmation on every single person who walked into that auditorium," Antoine confirmed. "We can confirm that everyone who walked in, walked out. But this is where it gets tricky. Calif and I both saw Josephine walk into Barclay Hall. Everyone did. The whole audience gave her a round of applause. All of the attendees we interviewed afterwards – what were there, Calif, like 15 or 20 total? Maybe 25? - they can confirm what she looked like, what she wore, how she did her hair. She was definitely there. But her presence on our radar disappears inside that auditorium. She was on the radar in the lobby. But we went back and reviewed the footage, and she simply....disappears.... as soon as she steps into Barclay Hall. If our security system data was to be believed, she was never there at all."

"Which means we now have *two* very big problems," Calif said.

"What sort of security system do they keep around the auditorium?" Jorge asked. "Something has to be messing with our receptors."

"That's just it," Calif replied, and this time he sounded annoyed. "They don't."

"They don't what?" Jorge asked.

"They don't have a security system around the auditorium, or even around the building," Calif answered.

"Not possible," Jorge replied. "If they told you that, they're lying. No one would be that stupid, not even in Middlestan."

"Sir, we already checked, and he's right," interrupted a quiet, earnest voice. It was Officer Calvin Smith, one of the two communications engineers who had been sitting at the command desk, facilitating the transmission of signals between Bisurakhan and Middlestan.

Jorge looked down in surprise at the unassuming officer, caught off-guard by his unsolicited feedback. The young man looked terrified, but he also looked like he wanted to say more. He had breached protocol by speaking to a senior official before receiving clearance. But Jorge decided to overlook his grievance and hear him out. He motioned for the officer to continue.

"There's no identity security system within fifty feet of the university's perimeter. Several of the Curators on-site have confirmed this," Calvin said, breathing a deep sigh of relief. He had been sitting there for the last fifteen minutes, dying to tell the Chiefs what he knew. He was a lowly communications engineer. He had no right to speak of his own accord to a Chief. Still, Jorge seemed open. Calvin forced himself to keep breathing and continued. "The decision to uninstall the previous security system was made last year by the university president. She said it was meant to foster the free exchange of ideas without fear of reprisal. The university has active weapons detection systems and pulse sensory systems across the entire campus. No identity system whatsoever."

Jorge looked furious. "That was a stupid decision. We should have been informed. Get me the university president on the intercom. Also, Antoine, see what data you can pull from the pulse sensory system. There might be something there we can use."

"I'm on it," Antoine replied.

"Looking at the pulse sensory system is fine, but Jorge, hold your temper with the university," Calif urged. "We can't afford to get distracted right now. You know that's a conversation that will take a long time to resolve. Right now, we need to focus. We have to find Dr. Kanale."

Officer Joshua LeRoux, the second communications engineer on duty, was sitting next to Calvin. He held out the intercom in his hand and waited for instruction.

"He's right," Jorge said. "I'm going to have to talk to President Kruger later. Forget it."

Josh placed the intercom back in its holder.

"Well, gentlemen," Jorge said, stepping back from the command desk and staring at the large monitor covering the wall. It was a real-time display of their solar system, showing the location of its nine planets and all transportation pods currently in orbit. "We had one job. 'Bring Josephine Kanale to Bisurakhan.' That was the order. Now we have no Professor Kanale, and on top of that, a security system with glaring deficiencies. And here I thought I was going to have a nice, relaxing weekend at home with my grandchildren."

Jorge looked down at the two communications officers. "I need an estimate on when the Commander will return," he said. "Can you tell me which of those pods is his? I think he left two days ago."

"He went to the Periphery with K-5," Calvin answered, referring to one of the military flanks that regularly patrolled the solar system's periphery. "Their schedule indicates that they expected it to be a two-day trip according to our time signature."

"Did he leave you boys with an estimated departure time from the Periphery?"

Both officers shook their heads. Then Josh spoke up.

"We don't have any interaction with the Commander, of course, but that's his pod right there." He motioned to a blinking yellow dot in the upper right corner of the screen. Then he traced his finger along three invisible lines. "They're likely to use one of these return routes. They'll send a signal shortly before they depart. Travel time varies depending on the path and the winds, but I'd say it's three to five hours."

"So, come on back," Jorge said, turning back to the microphone connecting him to Calif and Antoine in Middlestan. "We have way too much work to do, and nowhere near enough time to do it."

"On our way," Antoine replied.

The transmission line went dark.

Jorge stared at the screen for a few more minutes, lost in thought. Then he turned to Calvin and Josh. "Gentlemen, ready the Landing Pads for the return of our fleet from Middlestan. Send the Chiefs and their men up to the Presidential Conference Room after they've been through detox. And you. Make whatever arrangements you need to. You're working tonight. I want you both up in the conference room at 1:30."

Both officers sat up at attention.

"Yes, sir!" Calvin replied, a bolt of excitement surging through his tired body.

"Absolutely, sir." Josh's reply was respectful but nowhere near as enthusiastic.

"See you boys in a few hours." Jorge grabbed his jacket from a nearby chair and left without another word.

CHAPTER 3
Bisurakhan
Presidential Conference Room

The room was filled to capacity and bustling with activity. Neither Calvin nor Josh had ever been to a meeting involving so many senior officials. They had expected order and protocol, but this was pure, unadulterated chaos.

"What system faults have we fixed within the past twelve months?"

"That's what I've been telling you. We already fixed everything."

"Clearly you didn't."

"This is not your area of expertise, General. Perhaps you should remember that." There was a bite in the woman's voice that she didn't try to hide. "You stick with your experiments. I'll handle security."

"But you're not handling it, are you?"

Josh and Calvin looked at each other, wide-eyed.

"You boys want chairs?"

Both officers jumped. It was General Stanley Fossil, the man who had been challenging General Caroline Rivera about the security system malfunctions. He had abandoned his argument but not his anger. It was now squarely pointed in their direction.

"You're blocking the door," he snapped. "How do you expect anyone to get in?"

"I'm so sorry, sir," Calvin apologized. He could feel his face turning red and sweat dripping down the back of his neck. He grimaced.

"You've never been here before, have you?"

"No, sir," Calvin replied meekly.

"Why are you here now?"

"Chief Hernandez's orders, sir."

General Fossil glanced at the badge on Calvin's right shoulder. "Comms, huh?"

"Yes, sir."

"What sort of connection did you make to get yourself an invitation up here?"

"What?" Calvin asked, confused.

"We staff the Frequency Tower, sir," Josh interjected. "We were on duty tonight when the call came in from Middlestan."

"That explains it. Well, if I was you, I'd take your seats. It's going to be a while. And for god's sake, move away from the door."

"I don't like him," Josh muttered after General Fossil walked away.

"Shhhhhh! He might hear you."

"He can't hear me. It's too loud in here."

"Yeah, well – behave, why don't you. I don't want to get into trouble."

"I never get you into trouble."

Calvin gave Josh a knowing look and then glanced around the room. He was tired. Really tired. "Hey, do you think we're allowed to get coffee?"

"How would I know?" Josh asked.

"There's coffee over there." Calvin gestured to a small table on the other side of the room.

"Go get yourself coffee."

"But I don't know if we're allowed."

"Why would anyone care?"

"Are you going to get coffee?"

Josh didn't get a chance to reply. Jorge called Calvin's name and motioned at him to approach. Calvin drew himself up to his fullest height and best posture and began pushing his way through the crowd. He was standing at attention in front of the Chief before he realized Josh had followed.

"Officer Smith," Jorge nodded, "and Officer LeRoux. At ease, men."

"Yes, sir," they both replied.

"You can forgo the formalities tonight. In this room we use only first names, no titles. Call me Jorge."

"Yes, sir!" Calvin and Josh replied.

"Yes, sir, Jorge," Calvin corrected himself. He winced at the awkwardness in his voice.

Jorge chuckled. His mood had lightened considerably, and Calvin began to feel more at ease. "It's tough to give up, isn't it? There's nothing wrong with ranks and titles. But when they get in the way, it's best to get rid of them. Gentlemen, allow me to introduce you to the Chiefs you heard on the radio: Calif Asamov and Antoine Duval."

Calvin and Josh shook their hands. Calvin couldn't bring himself to call them by name, so he bit his lip and stayed quiet. Josh mustered up a few words of greeting.

"Thank you for being our eyes and ears at the Frequency Tower," Calif said. "Jorge tells me you are also our top-ranking communication engineers. Thank you for your service."

Calvin was struck by Calif's deep and calming voice. Calif was an older man who carried an air of kindness and severity about him. Calvin liked and trusted him immediately.

"You're welcome, sir," Calvin answered, basking in the glow of being recognized by a Chief.

"I recommend you grab seats," Jorge said. "It's going to be a long night."

Calvin nodded. He and Josh moved to take a couple of chairs pushed against the back wall.

Jorge motioned for everyone else to take seats. It took a few minutes for the room to quiet down. The Chiefs sat together at one end of a large, oblong table. The Generals also sat down at the table. Everyone else found chairs around the room, paying no attention to rank or who they were sitting next to.

The Chiefs looked up as two research officers entered the room. Calif gestured for them to take seats at the table. General Fossil motioned for his fellow Generals to shift and make room as he squeezed two additional chairs into the circle.

Jorge stood and called the room to order.

"Ladies and Gentlemen," he said. "It is my understanding that the Commander has left the Periphery and will be here with us before dawn. By now, you have all heard the report about the events in Middlestan. We have much to discuss.

"The Commander will want to be briefed on any known problems or deficiencies in our security system. Now is not the time to defend your work, your departments, or the officers under your command. No one will be disciplined or on record for information provided here tonight. Our goal is to identify any and all system failures so we can take the necessary steps to repair them. This is our first order of business. Caroline, you're in charge. Please work closely with Stanley, as there may be implications for our Reality Persuasion experiments."

General Caroline Rivera looked displeased, but she nodded respectfully.

"Next," Jorge continued, "we have reason to believe the events in Middlestan are related to Johanum. Specifically, we suspect a kidnapping. We need a full report on everything we know about the way Johanum captures its prisoners. Obviously, none of us has been to Johanum, so we will have to rely on the reports in the Logs." Jorge looked over at the two research officers. "You have two hours. Go and gather what you can."

The research officers nodded, rose to their feet, and left.

"And finally," Jorge continued, "the most pressing reason we're here. We need a plan to rescue Professor Kanale."

***

"I'm sorry I'm calling so late," Calvin apologized. "I know you're sleeping."

"Honey, it's fine, don't worry about it. I wasn't even sleeping." Calvin heard the yawn in his wife's voice and smiled. She was the worst liar. "How's it going?" she asked.

"I have no idea why we're here."

"You said you had to go fix a problem."

"Oh, there's a problem all right. But I mean, I don't know why Josh and I are here. These guys are talking about rescue missions, and psychological weapons, and....and this place called Johanum, that I've never even heard of before, and...well...I don't understand anything they're talking about, not really. We haven't said a word the whole meeting. In fact, we haven't spoken a word since we met the Chiefs."

"You met the Chiefs?" Leah's voice perked up. "Honey, that's so exciting! You never get to meet anyone important."

"Thanks a lot."

"No, I just mean -"

Calvin laughed. "I know what you meant. You're right. They're cool, and I'm glad we got to meet them. But I really don't understand why we have to be here. I'd much rather be home with you."

"Well, you're important now, baby. That means you have to go to meetings."

"I don't want to go to meetings. I want to sleep!"

"Hang in there. It can't go too much later, can it? It's four in the morning."

"I know. The Commander is expected back soon. The Chiefs will want to meet with him, so once he lands, I'm sure they'll wrap up."

"We're starting again!" Josh called from his post at the conference room door, motioning for Calvin to return.

"Break's over. Gotta go."

"I love you," Leah said through another yawn.

"I love you, too, babe." Calvin hung up the phone and returned to the meeting.

CHAPTER 4
Bisurakhan
Presidential Conference Room

The Chiefs were huddled together at one end of the conference room. Caroline and Stanley were standing next to the research officers. Everyone else was claiming seats.

Josh was holding two coffee mugs and motioning to a couple chairs in another section of the room. The chairs they had been sitting in earlier had already been claimed.

"You got us coffee!" Calvin said excitedly. He reached over and grabbed a cup out of Josh's hand, then leaned forward and breathed deeply. A peaceful smile covered his face.

"See, I'm nice sometimes," Josh said.

Calvin carefully wrapped both his hands around the cozy mug.

"Did you even hear me?" Josh asked.

"Of course."

"What did I say?"

"Huh?"

"You weren't listening!"

"I was, too!"

"You're welcome for your coffee."

"Mmmmmmhmmmmm." Calvin took a long sip. "I can't believe they expect us to work so late and they don't make it easier to get coffee. They should have coffee stations all over this room, with big signs that say, 'Coffee here, coffee there, coffee everywhere! Anyone who wants the coffee can drink the coffee!' They need to take better care of us."

"Who are you talking about?" Josh asked.

"The – Chiefs, I don't know."

"You think the Chiefs are thinking about coffee?"

"Whoever is in charge of those decisions then."

"The Generals-in-Charge-of-Coffee-Consumption, you mean?"

"Shut up."

"Officers." They looked up. Stanley was standing in front of them.

"Yes, sir," they replied.

Calvin noticed that he felt less intimidated by Stanley now. He was feeling less intimidated by all the senior Khanists. Or maybe he was just really tired.

"Tell me, what sort of combat training do you get in comms these days?" Stanley asked. He oversaw several departments, including Weapons Development and Intelligence Acquisition. Although neither Calvin nor Josh had met Stanley before tonight, they certainly knew his name.

"We've been through boot camp, sir," Calvin replied. He took a long sip of coffee. Too long. He could feel the coffee dribbling down his chin.

Josh shook his head. "I can't take you anywhere. Hold on, I saw some napkins somewhere." He walked over to the coffee station. A minute later, he returned.

"I don't need *that* many napkins," Calvin protested.

"For later."

"I'm not going to spill again."

"Of course not."

"What, you don't believe me?"

"You're going to be wearing the rest of that coffee before the night is over. Take the napkins."

"Fine, fine, I'll take the napkins," Calvin grumbled.

Josh handed over a stack that was so tall, it tipped over in Calvin's hand and tumbled to the floor.

"You made a mess," Calvin pointed out.

"So, I'm thinking that if we sent you on a mission, you'd die," Stanley said, only half joking.

"I don't think so!" Calvin protested.

"I can't imagine why he'd think that," Josh muttered under his breath.

"I've got something you might be interested in," Stanley continued. "I need new participants for a series of experiments we're running down in the Labs. Nothing big. You participate in a half-day simulation, you get a nice bonus in your next paycheck. Would you be interested?"

"Yes, sir!" Calvin replied enthusiastically.

Josh hesitated. "What sort of simulation are we talking about?"

"We're testing weaponry against various terrain simulations we have reason to believe may exist in Johanum."

"Is this a Reality Persuasion experiment?" Josh asked.

Stanley looked surprised. "How do you know about Reality Persuasion?"

"You've been talking about it all night, sir."

"Ah. Yes, yes, I have. I forgot you were here."

"You forgot?" Josh repeated, not managing to hide his annoyance.

Calvin jumped in. Josh had a tendency to get mad when he was tired, and then he would say stupid things. "What can you tell us about the experiments, General?" Calvin asked.

"There's not much to tell," Stanley replied. "It's an easy few hours. You make some extra money. Let me know if you're ever interested." He shrugged nonchalantly and walked away.

"I could use a bonus," Calvin said, watching Stanley walk back to the conference room table and sit down.

"Don't the Reality Persuasion experiments seem a little strange to you?" Josh asked.

"No, not really. Should they?"

"We don't get bonuses for anything. Why are they offering to pay us if it's so easy and harmless? Why don't they just make it mandatory and force soldiers to fill those slots?"

"All military experiments are voluntary. That's the policy. But you get volunteers faster when you pay them. Anyway, I could use some extra money."

Josh shrugged. "Do whatever you want. If I had a baby on the way, I'm sure I'd want the extra money too. The whole thing just doesn't feel right with me."

Calvin sat, sipping his coffee, lost in thought. He and Leah were barely scraping by. Leah wanted to stay home when the baby came. He didn't know how they would ever afford it, but he never said so out loud. He couldn't stand the thought of Leah being unhappy. Not that she ever was. Leah was the bubbliest, most naturally happy person he had ever met. When it came to his wife, he couldn't have chosen better.

Calvin grimaced as he watched coffee spill from his cup onto his shirt. He reached for the pile of napkins on the floor and picked up a couple.

"'I don't need *that* many napkins,'" Josh mimicked.

"Shut up."

"You're so quiet. What goes on in that head of yours?" Josh asked.

"How much did Stanley say they were paying?"

"He didn't say. But I know a few guys who have volunteered recently. I can ask them for you."

Calvin nodded.

Josh hesitated before adding, "You have heard the stories, right?"

"Which ones?"

"About some of the guys who have gone through these experiments. It's more than just a simulation. They mess with your head."

"What have you heard?"

"It's weird. All the guys initially say it's nothing. In fact, I've heard them say the simulations are almost boring. But then I keep hearing rumors about personality changes in volunteers after they've been through a few experiments. Gus Van Trop did a whole bunch of them. Old Man Quincy, the owner of that grocery store in my neighborhood, he said Van Trop went every week, for like six months. Bought his family a new house and his wife a new transport vehicle. He came home last week and blew his brains out."

Calvin winced. "I had heard he passed away. I didn't hear how. But you know, Gus got roughed up pretty bad last year. That Periphery mission - do you remember the one where half the crew died? Those were his men. He was never the same after that."

Josh nodded. "That's right. I forgot about that. What are you going to use the money for? Wait, don't tell me, I think I know. You're going to buy Leah that nursery she keeps talking about."

"She'll be so happy!"

"Well, hey, maybe I'll join you. I could use some extra cash. I want a new bike. A loud one."

"Single life's been rough on you, hasn't it?"

"Kat misses me."

"I don't think she does, buddy."

CHAPTER 5
Bisurakhan
Presidential Conference Room

Jorge gestured to Caroline and Stanley. "The floor is yours."

"I'll keep it brief," Caroline said. "We have a couple security system modifications of note from the past year. It's unlikely any of them impacts the recent events involving Dr. Josephine Kanale, but they may still be of interest.

"Over the last year, the Geospatial Reconnaissance department identified two environmental features that warp our identity security system's ability to connect a pulse stamp with facial features. When this breakdown occurs, the system deletes the facial recognition data instead of identifying it as inconclusive. In theory, either of these system malfunctions could have taken place inside Barclay Hall, though the engineers believe it's highly unlikely, and I'll explain why.

"Two elements have been identified as causing system malfunctions. Neither of these elements exist in Bisurakhan, or in Middlestan, for that matter. They would have required outside introduction. The first element is Acidify. Acidify is present in the air on some planets outside our solar system and was first identified through missions to the Periphery. It causes rapid calcium buildup under the skin, resulting in permanent mutations or, in extreme cases, death.

"The second element is a compound our chemists do not fully understand but have dubbed 'pre-bradycardia.' It slows the heart rate dramatically at first contact, with heightened impact on the body over time. Humans continue to function as fully as before, they simply move at an increasingly slower speed, almost like they're being played on a screen in slow motion. Remove exposure to the element, and the body instantly re-adapts. No indication of exposure, no long-term effects. None that we know of, anyway."

"And you believe either of these elements could have been present in Middlestan?" Jorge asked.

Caroline shook her head. "Possible, of course. But likely? No. Not at all. The presence of Acidify has been ruled out, for obvious reasons. Pre-bradycardia is more complicated, but we don't believe it was a factor."

"But it *could* have been a factor," Jorge said.

Caroline thought for a moment, then elaborated. "Hundreds of people were in Barclay Hall yesterday, yet only one of them – Dr. Kanale – disappeared off our radar. If pre-bradycardia had been present, we should have seen many disappearances. For it to only impact one person out of hundreds is something we haven't seen before. Also, Bisurakhanatis respond differently to this compound than inhabitants of other planets. We're already living in a faster passage of time. Over 90% of the Khanists who tested pre-bradycardia in the simulations were able to feel its impact on their movements. A return to a normal level of functioning brought an awareness that they had been functioning at a slower capacity. We had twelve of our men in that room, not including Calif and Antoine. None of you reported such an experience."

Calif and Antoine nodded in agreement, along with a dozen other men around the room. Calvin figured those men must have been the security detail in Middlestan yesterday.

"We need to remember, however," said Antoine, "that your data – or, rather, your theories, are supported by data gathered from the simulations. And that's it. We're making assumptions - huge assumptions - based on data that hasn't been proven."

"The simulations have provided some of our best intelligence," Stanley said, clearly annoyed at having his experiments questioned.

"Even so," Antoine continued. "They are your attempt to reconstruct environments you don't actually know. The experiments are constructed based on theories that haven't been proven. They are, by their very nature, inconclusive, and limited by the reach of your own intelligence. All the data should be suspect, as far as I'm concerned. Not discounted completely, but certainly suspect. Caroline and Stanley, I want you to examine pre-bradycardia further. Have your teams pull together a full report that we can present to the Commander."

Caroline nodded. Stanley rolled his eyes before catching a stern look from Jorge and switching to a more neutral expression.

"Moving on," said Jorge, gesturing to the research officers.

Officer Kim Wilson stood to her feet. Her fellow officer, Ahmad al-Asfour, stayed seated beside her. Kim cleared her throat once, twice, then a third time, fumbling nervously through a stack of papers.

"We'd look so much worse," Calvin whispered.

"I don't know, I think I usually look pretty good," Josh whispered back.

Calvin reached over to punch him, but Josh moved away. The rest of Calvin's coffee sloshed into his lap. Calvin closed his eyes and made himself swallow the word he really wanted to say.

Josh reached down and picked up what remained of the napkins, handing them to Calvin without a word.

"The Logs contain very limited information on Johanum," Kim said. "There are a couple items of interest that I would like to highlight. It seems uncommon for people of Dr. Kanale's caliber to be targeted. When a disappearance is noted in the Logs and presumed to involve Johanum, it typically involves a person rarely mentioned otherwise. And to that end, these presumed victims are never mentioned again."

"We know there are survivors," Antoine said. "What can you tell us about them?"

"That's a problem, sir," Ahmad replied, standing to his feet next to Kim. "We made the same assumption you did. But the Logs contain no such data. Once a person has disappeared, they do not reappear. We can't find any evidence of survivors."

"I have personally spoken with several survivors," Antoine replied.

Ahmad nodded. "These 'survivors,' as you call them, are supposedly known to others as well. We talked to some of the people who reported conversations similar to yours. There's no record of these conversations, of course, but our Curators were most helpful, and we were able to get in touch with some of the people who claimed to have had these conversations. We asked them questions about who they talked to and the sort of things they talked about. Interestingly, these 'survivors' were not friends or acquaintances of the people we interviewed. In fact, in most cases, these 'survivors' were strangers to the people we interviewed, and after these supposed conversations, the 'survivors' were never seen or heard from again. No one knows their names or where they live. It's all quite mysterious, really. Almost as if it isn't real."

"Why do you keep doing that?" Antoine asked.

Ahmad had been placing air quotations around the word "survivors."

"Because, sir, we have no conclusive evidence that such people exist. I'm sure the people exist, don't get me wrong," he rushed to add. "And obviously you've had the conversations you're describing. But who's to say, sir, that these people, these 'survivors,' -"

"Stop doing that," Antoine growled.

"Sorry. My point is, who's to say these 'surviv-', ahhh, sorry, these…people…were being honest? What if they were just making up stories? They might even believe their own stories, especially if they're mentally unstable. It's possible these 'Johanum experiences,' as we're calling them, aren't real at all. It would be worth conducting some psychological testing, if we're able to find any of these people again. Maybe they've experienced some sort of unresolved trauma, and this is their way of processing it."

"So you're calling me a liar," Antoine stated.

Ahmad blushed. "No, sir. I'm not accusing you of lying. But like I said, sometimes people's memories are…damaged. Incomplete. Unreal, even. The Logs offer us no evidence that Johanum has survivors. I mean, even you, sir – do you know where these people are? The ones you talked to? Could you bring them here to talk to us?"

The young research officer hadn't intended his question to come off as insubordinate as it did, but both Calvin and Josh winced, and a collective murmur sputtered to life across the room.

Antoine was slowly rising to his feet, his face fixed in a stern stare, narrowed on Ahmed's face.

Ahmed realized what he had said and turned bright red. He sat back in his seat with a *thud*. Then the color drained from his face and he turned white.

"We can't argue with what they found in the Logs," Calif said quietly to Antoine, his tone containing a hint of warning. "If it's not there, it's not there. We asked them to report on what they read. They've done that."

"And added their own commentary," Antoine pointed out. "You call this intelligence? Their whole department should be fired!"

Ahmad's hands were noticeably trembling, and Kim looked ready to crawl under the table.

"We're here right now to collect the reports we need for the Commander," Calif replied. "We need to rely on the Logs, as our protocol dictates."

Antoine looked at Ahmad, who quickly looked down at the floor. "Did you find out any useful information at all, or was this all you could manage?"

Ahmad shuffled his feet under the table. When he finally answered, his voice trembled as badly as his hands. "The Logs are, at best, inconclusive about, uhhhh..."

He moved his hands under the table. Calvin could see him wringing his hands together and he couldn't help but feel compassion for the poor guy.

"Inconclusive about what, Officer?" Antoine demanded.

Ahmad's voice came out more like a croak. "About Johanum's existence, sir."

Antoine jumped back to his feet. Calif stood up and placed his hand on Antoine's shoulder, pushing him back down.

"I wouldn't want to be those officers right now," Josh whispered. "They are going to be in so much trouble."

"Why would they say such things?" asked Calvin. "Our military is preparing for an invasion from Johanum as we speak. We have been, for months."

"These folks aren't military."

"So?"

"They haven't seen the messages you and I see. They're the equivalent of academics. They only see information that's been around for a long time. They have no idea how much things are changing."

"They still know we're preparing for war!"

"The Logs are their specialty, Calvin, not military strategy."

"It is a little weird that Johanum isn't mentioned much in the Logs, don't you think?"

"Is it? Maybe Johanum pre-dates our Log system."

"Our Logs are close to a hundred years old!"

"Look, we're talking about Johanum like it's a real place," Josh said. "What if – just what if! – what if it isn't? What if it's more of a concept? The name we give to enemies or threats we don't know, the ones we can't identify."

"We're receiving actual threats of an invasion, Josh. You've seen them. You've helped me translate them!"

"Yes, the threats are real. But there's no name. No signature, on any of those messages. They could be coming from anywhere."

"So, you think the Chiefs are making up Johanum to explain away the threatening messages?"

"I don't know. They could be. Look, Cal, I've seen the guys who come back from missions to the Periphery. I know there's danger out there. I just don't think we understand it half as well as we think we do. And I think the Chiefs should listen to them," he added, nodding at the research officers.

The Chiefs were engrossed in an intense, quiet discussion. Conversation circles had cropped up around the room, filling the tense silence. Kim and Ahmad remained seated, red-faced and silent.

Jorge finally rose to his feet and called the room back to order.

"Generals Rivera and Fossil, Officers Wilson and al-Asfour: please draw up your findings in two-page briefs and submit them to us within the hour. We will present them to the Commander. If he has further questions, he will call you for an audience."

A General seated at the far end of the table spoke up. "And the plan to rescue Dr. Kanale?"

"We will be proposing a rescue mission to the Commander," Jorge answered.

"Which of our flanks should we be preparing for the mission?" the General asked.

"None of them," replied Jorge.

"A satellite mission?" he asked in surprise.

"No," Jorge said. "This mission will be undertaken by your Chiefs."

It was clear from the tense silence in the room that this conversation was far from over.

CHAPTER 6
Johanum

I don't remember when I met Fletch. I don't know how long I had been in Johanum. But I remember the confusion I felt at seeing another person.

I had been sleeping in the caves. They were cold and uncomfortable, but safe. One night I got lost. When I awoke the next morning, something didn't feel right.

I moved around a bit, running my hands over the ground. Light should be visible by now. I realized I couldn't see the mouth of the cave. Where was the entrance? I panicked and stood up too quickly, smacking my head against the ceiling. Wincing, I sat back down.

"You're awake! Good. You'll need to release the lever to let yourself out."

The sound of words – a conversation – seemed so foreign. Was I dreaming?

"I don't know if you can talk, and if you don't, that's okay, but do you understand me? Raise your face up if you do."

My eyes darted to the right, then the left. They were beginning to adapt to the darkness. The ceiling was low and the room was small. I saw no exit. Finally, I looked up.

A pair of eyes stared back, squinting through a small hole in the ceiling. "You do understand. Good. Let's get you out of there. Just follow my directions. Reach up and to the left. You're not moving. Stop staring at me. Now you're creeping me out. Can you blink? No? How about moving your hands to the left? How about just moving your hands? Maybe a finger? Can you point your finger?"

I stared at my hands. They were clenched tightly together. Slowly I pulled them apart.

"Okay. Okay, that's fine. Now I just need you to move your arm. Above your head. Just like – no! Oh, okay, sure. That will work. You're like a marionette puppet. Don't hurt yourself. Now move your hand to the left. To the left. The other left. In front of your face. Past your face. A little farther. Do you feel that?"

My fingers closed around a handle. I looked back up at the ceiling.

"Good. Now just pull down. Okay, it's going to take more than that. This room was meant to keep people hidden. You have to really pull. Maybe use your other hand, if you can figure that out."

I stared at the hand grasping the handle, then turned to look at my other hand. I tried to move my shoulders, then my arms. Both hands started flailing uncontrollably.

"How are you in one piece?" the voice mumbled.

I dropped my hands and let them dangle. I could do this. Slowly, carefully, I reached up and to the left, first with one hand, then the other. Breathing deeply, I exhaled and pulled with all my might.

The handle released the floor beneath me. It tilted and sent me tumbling backwards.

"Hang tight! I'm comin' to get ya!"

***

The man led me down a series of tunnels and into a small room. A fire built with twigs was lit near the cave's entrance.

Light. I could see glimpses of the light from outside. I breathed a sigh of relief.

The man with the blinking eyes knelt in front of me and placed a chipped earthen bowl in my hands. Inside, foamy liquid bubbled. I felt the steam on my face and leaned into it. There was warmth and coziness in that bowl. I was never letting go.

"It's not a proper meal, but it's the best I can do. Best you've had in a while, I'd wager, judgin' by the looks of ya."

I blinked and stared at the man. He had an unkempt, bushy beard and thin, wire-rimmed glasses that were held together in the middle by a piece of string. They didn't fit him right. He kept pushing his glasses back up his nose.

"That's fine, you don't need to say anything. I can talk plenty for the both of us. I do wonder that I've never seen you before. Are you new?"

He seemed to expect a response, which I found confusing. I shook my head.

"No? Well, I guess that explains why you're mute. I mean, I talk, but I mostly talk to myself. And the plants, sometimes. They're good listeners. The walls of this cave aren't bad either. Mad Laugh listens too. Have you met him? No? He's like you. Doesn't talk much. But he laughs sometimes. Like a crazy man. You'll know him if you meet him. We've got the Braid Sisters too. They're around these parts. Any chance you've met them?"

I was especially confused now.

"They don't remember their own names. Been here a long time. Truth be told, I'm not so sure they're related. But they look out for each other. They're always braiding each other's hair. Lots of different braids. You know, I had no idea you could braid hair like that. I get a kick out of just watchin' 'em. 'course, I don't know much about that sort of thing. Hair, I mean. Obviously, I ain't got much. But I had a daughter once. She had long, silky blonde hair. It was soft and it smelled so sweet. I wish I would have learned how to braid her hair...."

His voice trailed off and sadness settled over him. I studied him curiously. I had thought he was about fifty, but now I guessed he wasn't as old as he looked.

I don't know why, but I was touched by his sadness. It had a rawness to it that I recognized. I leaned forward and held out my bowl.

"That's sweet of you. But you need it more than I do. Anyway, it tastes awful. Try it."

I leaned closer and inhaled. The broth smelled sweet and earthy. I tipped the bowl to my lips, took a long, savory sip, and promptly convulsed into a coughing fit.

"It's bad, right? It won't make you sick or anything. We all drink it. You get it from those Tufta plants. You know those long, leafy – eh, they're almost like bushes, the ones with the long thick leaves and curled orange edges? You can rip off the leaves and twist 'em like this. You get a runny, milky substance. Heat it over a fire and there you go."

I scrunched up my nose and tried again. This time I kept it down. It wasn't that bad, actually. It tasted smoky, which was weird. It didn't taste like it smelled.

"Drink as much as you like. There's plenty more where that came from. I mean, in the morning. I'm not going to go out now. I try not to go out at night. Too many crazy shadows out there."

I nodded. I understood. I had heard the howling late at night.

The man leaned forward and held out his hand.

"The name's Fletcher. But you can call me Fletch."

***

I slept better that night than I had in a long time. My belly was warm and full, and I could hear Fletcher snoring on the other side of the cave. It was comforting to have another person around.

I woke up first and decided to go find some Tufta plants. Outside the cave entrance, a trail of broken sticks led me to a flat stretch of earth covered in green and orange leaves.

Tufta!

I realized I had nothing to carry the leaves in, but no matter. I picked a large pile and stacked them high in my arms.

Fletch was awake when I returned. He met me outside the cave.

"Well, well, well, will you look at that. You did the morning breakfast run." He waved me inside. "Just drop 'em in the back there. I need some sticks for the fire. Be back soon." He jumped over a ledge and disappeared out of sight.

The sky was brightening. I can't say where the light came from each day. I hadn't seen a sun or moon since arriving. But the sky dimmed and grew bright with regularity, much the way it had in Middlestan.

The thought startled me. I hadn't thought of home in such a long time. It made my heart drop and my stomach hurt.

I shook my head and turned in a circle, getting a look at the cave in the daylight. There was a tunnel towards the back. It plunged downward into the labyrinth of tunnels we had walked through last night. A light was flickering in the distance, casting shadows against the walls.

I walked down the tunnel towards the light and saw the entrance to another cave. Slowly I turned the corner and stepped inside.

A candle sat flickering in the corner. The candle's flame sent my shadow dancing. I waved my arms, then my legs, then shook my head from side to side. For a second, I imagined I had a friend. We waved at each other.

A mural was carved into the wall. I walked closer. No, it wasn't a carving. It was a painting. There was a thick canvas, made from some sort of animal skin, stretched tight and nailed to the wall. A bucket of brown paint and a stack of handmade paint brushes sat piled up on the floor.

I stared at the canvas. I saw a lake. A boat. A set of docks with a dozen little stick figures. A forest with lots of dead trees. Some mountains and caves and a desert.

And then I saw them. The three tall men.

I leaned closer and felt a shiver run down my spine. The men were no more than stick figures, but instinctively I knew them. They were the ones I had met. The men who brought me here.

"You found my studio."

I jumped and lost my footing.

Fletch walked over, reached out his hand, and helped me back up.

"I'm not a painter," he said. "But when you've been alone a while, you start to go a little crazy. I needed something to do. Came across one of those desert dogs, all torn up and down on his luck. They attack each other, those dogs, you know, when they're hurt. They turn into cannibals. Anyway, I found a sharp stick and put him out of his misery. Then I dragged his carcass back here. Cleaned him out and the skin was so smooth. I remembered there's this little grove of bushes not too far away. They have berries that stain your hands red. Squeeze out the juice and it works for paint. Turns brown after a while, but it's pretty when you start. Those nails were in another cave farther back in this tunnel. So, there you have it, the story of my studio. I like it back here. Someday maybe I'll become a real painter."

Sadness had crept back into his voice. I put my hand on his shoulder. He looked startled, but he reached up and rested his own hand on top of mine, patting it gently.

"Do you ever wonder if people make it out of here?" Fletch asked, staring wistfully at his painting. "I don't know how they would. There's no way out that I've ever found. I've seen people die here. Seen 'em go crazy. Ain't seen nobody escape yet."

I walked over to the bucket of paint, picked up one of the thicker brushes, and rolled it around between my hands.

"You can paint if you want to," he offered. "There's nothing special about what I've got here. I just paint whatever I see, the things I can't get out of my head. The things that keep me up at night. But paint whatever you like. I'm going to go make breakfast."

I watched him leave. Slowly I knelt down and placed the paint brush back in its place. I wasn't a painter either. And anyway, I liked Fletcher's art, just the way it was. I didn't want to mess it up.

I looked back at the painting and my eyes fell on the boat in the corner. It was small but strangely alive. I could imagine the sails, dancing in the wind, and the bow of the ship rocking back and forth. For a second, I thought I saw the stick figures move over the docks.

I shook my head. Fletch was right. You can go crazy here.

***

I walked back to the front of the caves. Two bowls were rigged up on long sticks, stacked like a tepee over the flames. The bubbling in the bowls made my stomach growl. I sat cross-legged on the ground in front of the fire and warmed my hands.

Fletch used a pile of leaves like potholders to protect his skin as he removed both bowls and placed them on the ground.

He sat down next to me and looked apologetic. "I haven't figured out how to make any spoons."

I shrugged and reached for a bowl. It was too hot. I howled in pain.

"You're curiously not smart," he joked.

I scowled.

"You're plenty smart," Fletch said. "You've survived here."

I leaned over the bowl and began to blow furiously.

"Now you're going to make it splash. Here." He handed me a large leaf and gestured for me to wave it like a fan.

"I wish you could talk. I'd love to hear another person's voice."

I scratched my head. Could I talk?

"Don't worry about it. Most of the folks here don't. I'll just keep talkin' to myself. You know, sometimes I get in an argument with my shadow, just to have someone to talk to. He never argues back though. It's disappointing."

***

We went on like this for weeks. Fletch was the only person I had met since coming to Johanum. He was kind and generous and seemed to know everything there was to know about the place we lived. Sometimes he smiled, but always he was sad. I wondered about him. Where had he come from? Who had he left behind? I knew he had a daughter and missed her terribly.

After months of being alone, Fletch was like an angel. I was so fond of him. I knew he liked it when I gathered the Tufta leaves, so I did the breakfast run each morning. Sometimes Fletch would paint, and I would watch him. Sometimes he'd disappear for hours. I never knew where he went, but he always came back.

We would sit by the fire for hours each night. He would talk and I would listen. Or we'd both sit quietly. His presence was comforting. I knew he was looking out for me, and I was looking out for him. I thought maybe, just maybe, Johanum wasn't so bad after all.

Early one morning, I heard voices. I walked sleepily to the entrance of the cave and froze.

The three men were there. Red rings burned bright around the black pupils of their eyes. Tongues with the scales of a serpent flashed between their teeth when they spoke. The air around the men seemed visibly darker. One man held a black X in his hands. He was twisting it back and forth, back and forth, back and forth.

Fletch sat upright on his knees in front of them. They were having a conversation, but their voices were low, so low I couldn't hear what they were saying.

Fletch didn't look scared. He was asking for something.

The man with the black X leaned forward and pressed his forehead against Fletcher's. Fletch flinched but stayed his ground. When the man stepped back, Fletch looked as though he'd been punched in the gut.

The man with the X said something. Fletch began to nod. As he did, he glanced back at the cave. Our eyes met. Fletch grimaced. For a second, he hesitated.

"I'm sorry," he mouthed. Then he turned back to the men and nodded.

Too late I understood.

The man with the black X placed his hands on either side of Fletch's head. With one swift motion, he snapped Fletcher's neck, and the deed was done. Fletcher's body fell limp to the ground.

I clasped my hands over my mouth and screamed.

The three men disappeared. I stared in horror as Fletch's body began to disintegrate.

I rushed forward, reaching for him, but I was too late.

I fell to my knees and pressed my face into the ground. "Fletch," I whispered. "Fletcher. Come back. Fletcher, please...please come back. I can't live here without you."

But Fletcher couldn't hear me. He was gone.

CHAPTER 7
Bisurakhan

"We've never tried anything like this," said Jorge.

"We've never been in this position before," Antoine replied. "But I have to tell you, I don't like the idea of all three of us being in one place. We're too easy a target. Especially in a place like Johanum."

Antoine was the newest of the Chiefs. He had been serving as one of Biskurakhan's top military leaders for the past three years. Calif and Jorge had held their current positions for close to ten.

Calif turned to look at Antoine. "Are you sure you're ready to go back?"

"Ready?" Antoine repeated. "Who said anything about ready?"

"You can stay behind. In fact, I would prefer it. If something happens, at least one of us survives."

"I won't stay behind while you go," Antoine replied. "I survived it once. I'm sure I can survive it again."

"Barely," Calif pointed out gently. "You barely survived it."

"Josephine Kanale will be of more use to Bisurakhan now than I will. Hopefully it doesn't come to it, but if a prisoner exchange is her only way out, I'm the person you need. You won't be able to do it."

"Why not?" Calif asked.

"It...just...doesn't work that way," Antoine replied, waving away the question. "But even if it did, I would refuse. Johanum has stolen enough lives already. It can stop now."

The Chiefs sat in silence.

"What do you make of the rumors?" Calif asked.

"Which ones?" said Antoine.

"This growing sentiment that Johanum isn't real. Those research officers weren't the first to make such claims, you know. It's quite a popular theory these days, especially if these special interest military groups are to be believed."

"Ignorance is bliss, I guess," Antoine replied.

"We have a system dictated by evidence available in the Logs," Jorge interjected. "We keep information about Johanum out of the Logs. Should we be surprised that our men and women don't think it's real?"

"Why are we doing that, by the way?" Antoine asked, his anger revived and pointed squarely in Jorge's direction. "Why are we keeping Johanum out of the Logs? I don't remember being a part of that decision."

"That policy has been around for a long time," Jorge replied. "Since before you were here."

"And as I've been saying for a long time," said Antoine, "it's time to change the policy."

"There's a process we have to follow to change policies," said Jorge.

"We're the Chiefs. Let's change the process."

"Policies and processes exist for a reason, Antoine," Jorge replied. "How many times do I have to tell you that?"

"We're only beholden to policies and processes until you find one you don't like," Antoine answered wryly.

"You're being unreasonable, which isn't surprising," Jorge said. "You're unreasonable with anything involving Johanum."

"Am I? I don't remember seeing you there. Tell me, what makes you such an expert? Oh, right! I remember now. It's your misguided, misrepresented, highly dangerous Reality Persuasion experiments that make you a voice of reason about Johanum."

"Gentlemen," Calif interrupted, a warning in his voice.

"I understand Johanum," Jorge said, ignoring Calif. "That's the beauty of our Reality Persuasion experiments.

We get to experience Johanum in small bite sizes, and then we get to remove ourselves whenever a situation starts to get dangerous."

"Which means you don't know anything about Johanum. Johanum is danger. Johanum is death."

"That's a bit dramatic, don't you think? You survived it."

"I have serious doubts that the place you're sending our troops is, indeed, Johanum," Antoine replied. "But let's say, for a minute, that you're right. Let's say you have really found a way to access Johanum. Then what you're *doing* is giving Johanum direct access to us. You're letting them infiltrate our ranks."

"That's ridiculous."

"Is it? Because I keep hearing rumors, Jorge, about your experiments. They're not as innocent as you claim."

"No one gets hurt in my experiments."

"Not *in* them. But afterwards? I know about the suicides. You can't keep those a secret forever."

"Those are not connected to Reality Persuasion."

"Are you sure about that?"

"Yes!" Jorge answered angrily. "Look, I'm as devastated as you are when we lose one of our own. These men and women are my family. But you're not looking at the whole picture. Other things are going on in their lives. I've been working with General Cortez to improve and expand our treatment centers. It's clear a lot of our troops have serious psychological, emotional, and mental needs that aren't being met. We can provide therapy and offer better services to support them. We're working on it. If anything, the Reality Persuasion experiments have made us more aware of an existing problem, which we can now address. Don't confuse a symptom with the root problem."

Antoine sat silently, considering Jorge's words. "Be careful," he cautioned. "I know you think Reality Persuasion isn't the problem. But you don't understand what you're doing. If something goes wrong, promise me you'll shut it down."

Calif watched the two men assess each other. They were brilliant, both of them, each in his own way. They were also never going to agree on Reality Persuasion.

"Antoine, what can you tell us about what might have happened to Dr. Kanale?" Calif asked, hoping to redirect the conversation.

Antoine shrugged. "It was a kidnapping by the Priests."

"The rulers of Johanum?"

"That's right."

"How do you know it was them?"

"It's a classic trick they play. They come and go and we can't see them. They're always visible in Johanum, but something about our solar system – it's like they can exist in a space we can't see, a place we don't even know exists. You don't see them, but the result is always the same. Someone disappears. No warning, just – poof. Gone."

"There is no such thing as invisibility," Jorge said. "There has to be another explanation."

"You don't believe anything you can't see," Antoine criticized. "I'm not saying we're dealing with invisibility. I'm saying the Priests exist in a space we can't see them. Don't – no, don't look at me like that. I'm telling you, this is how it works. It has happened over and over again. On our planet, in Middlestan, Pendleton, Charisburg – and those are just the stories I've heard. The Priests are powerful, they're manipulative, and they're far more intelligent than we are."

"Yes, yes, the Priests this, the Priests that," Jorge repeated, mimicking Antoine's tone of voice. "They're powerful, they're liars, I get it. We're powerful too, you know."

"Not in the same way."

"We have the greatest military in all of recorded history."

"It doesn't matter. We're nothing next to these guys."

"I think we might need to come back to this," Calif interrupted. He knew where this conversation was headed. The same place it always went. Nowhere.

"There are others," Antoine said quietly.

"Other what?" Calif asked.

"Other survivors."

"No, there aren't," Jorge disagreed. "We've been over this, Antoine. All the others died. You're the only one who returned and survived."

"I'm the only one who survived out of the prisoners you rescued," Antoine agreed. "But I'm not the only survivor."

"The only way prisoners escape is when we send a rescue mission."

"Why do you think we're the only ones attempting rescue missions?"

"Who else has the transport technology to get to Johanum?" Jorge asked.

"I don't know, but I'm telling you, other survivors have been rescued. They're out there. Other prisoners have escaped. The best thing we can do for our own intelligence is to try and find them. We need what they can give us."

"We can get Josephine Kanale. She'll be enough. She can help us."

"We have to be careful though. People change in Johanum. They're not like they were before."

"You turned out all right."

Antoine rolled his eyes. "You can't stand me. Look, everyone changes in their own way. You're assuming the Josephine you rescue will be the same Josephine we met in Middlestan. I'm telling you, she won't be."

"That's a risk we're going to have to take," Jorge replied.

A buzzer signaled the return of the Commander to his office. The Chiefs stood and gathered their belongings.

There would be no rescue mission without the Commander's approval. It was time for a meeting.

CHAPTER 8
Bisurakhan

"Did you bring dinner today?"

Calvin cast Josh a sideways glare.

"I'm just asking!" Josh said.

"For the third time this week!"

"What? Sometimes you have extra."

"No, I never have extra. I'm eating less because I'm on the keep-poor-Josh-from-starving diet."

"Leah's a good cook."

"You mean you're too lazy to learn how to cook."

"I mean Leah is very, very talented. You tell her I said that."

"Stop trying to get my wife to cook for you."

"I'm not!"

Calvin pulled two plastic containers from his backpack. Josh smiled gleefully and reached for one. Calvin cleared his throat and leaned backwards, holding the containers over his head.

"I feel like I should get something out of this," he announced.

"You?!"

"Yes. What have you got to give me?"

"Why do I have to give you something? Leah made that for me. Give me my food!"

"Eh eh eh," Calvin said as he leaned farther back.

Josh scowled and crossed his arms. "Fine. What do you want?"

"How about an extra thirty-minute break every night and you cover for me?"

"Thirty minutes??"

"Yeah! That seems fair."

"Make it fifteen."

"Twenty-five."

"Twenty."

"Done." Calvin tossed Josh his food.

"I'm telling Leah," Josh grumbled.

"I'll finally have time to call her before she goes to bed. She's going to be mad you didn't give me thirty minutes."

Josh rolled his eyes. "You win, you win. Take a thirty-minute break. And tell your wife thank you."

"Why aren't you thanking me? I bought those groceries."

"Yeah, but Leah made the food."

"Didn't you ever learn to cook? Did Kat do everything for you?"

"No!"

"You look so guilty right now. You don't know how to cook, do you?"

"I order a mean takeout, thank you very much."

"You're hopeless."

"I think you mean handsome."

"No, that was definitely not what I meant." Calvin took his seat in front of the long silver control panel that stretched the length of the room and curled around to the right. "How many transmissions so far?" he asked.

"Nine."

"Nine? Johanum's busy today."

"The last five were sent with a new frequency. We can't keep up. The shift that just left, they didn't make any progress on translation. It's like Johanum can tell when we've figured something out. They just change the frequency and mess with our heads."

Calvin frowned. "Why send messages your enemy can't read?" He was feeling around below the desk, searching for his earpiece.

"The messages aren't intended for us," said a voice behind them.

Josh and Calvin turned to see Jorge leaning against the door.

"They aren't meant for us," Jorge repeated, walking forward. "They're all intercepted signals."

"Who's their target?" Calvin asked.

"We don't know," Jorge answered. "Someone outside our solar system. None of these transmission frequencies are ones we use."

"I'm confused," Josh said. "I thought Johanum was threatening us."

"They are. Just not to our face," Jorge said. "They've mentioned wars on Bisurakhan, Charisburg, and Cornersville so far. At first, we thought these transmissions were meant to coordinate an attack, but now we think Johanum is acting alone. Someone else is interested in their progress, though. We don't know why. We need these messages translated faster."

Josh pointed to five envelopes on the right side of the room's large screen. Each icon contained the audio recordings of one message. "The guys who left an hour ago said they barely started trying to decipher how those last transmissions were put together."

"I know. You guys are overwhelmed. Not to mention, this isn't what we trained you for. We're bringing in back-up. From Cornersville."

Josh and Calvin looked up in surprise.

"They'll arrive over the weekend," Jorge said. "We'll have twelve linguists to start with. Cornersville is prepping twelve more, and they'll be ready for us when we need them."

"How's this going to work?" asked Josh, none too happy about the arrival of strangers in his control room.

"Two of you with two of them for each shift. We're moving from two shifts a day to three, and you'll work every other day instead of five on, two off. We want you refreshed and at your best every time you report for work, so we're giving you more time off between shifts. But we expect that when you are here, you will be fully present, fully engaged. For every minute of your shift. We need your very best."

Calvin hadn't heard anything Jorge had said past the change of shifts. Fewer shifts? More time at home with Leah? And with the baby, once the baby arrived?

Josh was sitting on his hands, trying hard to curb his frustration.

"The linguists will focus on translation. You focus on interception. We anticipate that this increase in transmissions will continue and likely escalate. If you have extra time to assist with translation, that's fine, but it's not your priority. The linguists are equipped to take care of it."

Calvin was happily daydreaming about how he would break the news to Leah. Maybe he would just show up early at home, unannounced. Surprise her. She liked surprises. Actually, no. She hated surprises. But maybe she'd like this one.

Josh, on the other hand, was feeling slighted. What was he going to do with all this extra time? Sit at home alone and feel miserable? Everything kept changing, and he hated it.

Jorge didn't know anything about Calvin and Josh's lives outside the Tower, but he could make an educated guess. "You're good at your jobs," he said. "This is not a reflection on you. But we need help. Cornersville has been developing their linguistic skills for decades. They even have experts who have studied languages from outside our solar system. I'm hopeful these frequencies will look familiar to them. But even if they don't, their rate of translation will be faster than ours. Anyway, they're eager to help.

"Our pace of life is going to be difficult for them," Jorge continued. "Our time signature is faster, almost twice the rate they're used to. Cornersville has a much more laid-back approach to work. To life in general, I suppose. I need you and the rest of the guys here to show them what we consider normal. Make sure they understand what we expect, the level of performance that's required to succeed here."

Calvin nodded dutifully. "Yes, sir! We'll be happy to help. Won't we, Josh?" He looked over his shoulder. "Josh!"

Josh sat lost in thought. It wasn't like he had any choice in the matter. He hadn't met new people in a while. Actually, he had never met anyone from Cornersville. Maybe it would be good. Get him out of his own head. Maybe there would be a cute linguist in the bunch. Bam, problem solved.

"Any females in that mix?" Josh asked. "Ouch!" He rubbed the back of his head where Calvin had smacked him.

Jorge looked taken aback. "I think it's a mix of women and men."

"Then I'm sure we won't have any problems," Josh replied. "Let me assure you, I will do everything in my power to help them feel at home."

"You better not be *taking* them home," Calvin growled.

"You heard the orders. We're supposed to make them feel comfortable."

"Those were not the orders. The Chief said to show them how the work gets done."

"I'll be happy to show them how a lot of things get done."

"You're a terrible person."

"And your best friend."

"You are not my best friend."

"Yes I am."

"I'm going to dismember you."

"You'd miss me."

"I don't think I would."

Jorge shook his head and slipped silently out the door.

***

Twelve linguists from Cornersville arrived in Bisurakhan on Sunday morning. They went through detox and an orientation, followed by a tour of the Turris and nearby military housing.

Josh had volunteered to show them the downtown area, along with some popular restaurants and hangout spots. He showed up at their apartments at five o'clock sharp, dressed sharply in military black, dragging Calvin along behind him.

It took one glance at the group for Calvin to know exactly how his evening was going to turn out.

Her name was Shondra. She had long, dark hair, an elegant nose, and high cheekbones. Her hands were carefully manicured, finished with a light pink nail polish. She was wearing the latest fashion, complimented by heels and the perfect accessories. She talked confidently, smiled with only a hint of condescension, and commanded the attention of everyone who looked in her direction.

She might as well have been Josh's ex-wife.

The guys took the group to Main Street. They showed them the Library, the Square, and how the restaurants were arranged by cuisine. The linguists were delighted to find all their familiar dishes in the restaurants down Cornersville Avenue.

Shondra announced she would rather eat on Bisurakhan Avenue that night. After all, she was here on another planet. She wanted the full experience.

Josh took his cue. "It looks like your team prefers a taste of home tonight," he said. "But I'm delighted to hear you'd like to try our local cuisine. Do you like spicy food? You're not a vegetarian, are you? Good, then you'll love what we have to offer. In fact, I know the owner of one of the best restaurants on the avenue. May I treat you?"

Calvin watched them go. He wished Leah would have come, but she hadn't been feeling well. The growing baby in her belly was making it harder for her to get around.

"Let's grab a quick dinner and then head back," Calvin said. "I'm sure you all are very tired from your trip."

He tried to be a good host and pay attention. Two hours later, he was done trying.

"I have to get home," he announced abruptly, standing to his feet.

The group looked incredibly disappointed.

"My wife is very pregnant, she's due in about a month," he explained. "She has a hard time falling asleep when I'm not there. You know how it is."

The group took an immediate interest in Calvin's wife, his pending status of fatherhood, his home, his in-laws, and his plans for the nursery.

He finally gave up trying to escape and slid back in his chair.

It was close to midnight when Calvin finally returned home.

Leah rolled over as he crawled into bed. He wrapped his arms around her and placed one hand on her growing belly.

"Is he awake?"

"No, *she* is sleeping," Leah whispered.

Calvin had been convinced, the entire pregnancy, that they were having a boy. Leah was equally convinced they'd soon be welcoming a daughter. Neither wanted to admit defeat, so they asked the doctor not to tell them the sex of the baby.

"I thought those crazy Cornersville people kidnapped you," Leah joked.

Calvin groaned and buried his head in her hair. "Leah, they talk so much. About everything. They're nice people. Really nice. I don't know how we're going to get any work done with them around. Even while they were eating, they talked. And no subject was off-limits. I even told them about your dad's drinking problem."

"You did what?" Leah asked, aghast.

"I know! I'm sorry! I know I told you I wouldn't talk about it. They just kept asking questions. And I was so tired, I just kept answering them."

"They asked if my father was an alcoholic?!"

"No. They asked about you, and the baby, and if this was our first child, and if it would be the first grandchild, and if we thought our parents would end up visiting, and whether our parents were overbearing. And then they wanted to know why I didn't think having the grandparents around too much would be a problem. And I could have just said it was because your parents live two hours away, but no. I said your dad probably doesn't remember where we live because most nights he doesn't remember where he lives."

"You shouldn't talk to people when you're tired."

"I know. I didn't tell them about his time in prison, though."

"You say that like I should thank you."

"Maybe give me partial good-husband credit?"

Leah twisted around and kissed him. "You get all the good-husband credit. But you're a terrible son-in-law."

Calvin groaned.

They lay quietly for a time.

"Are you feeling better, honey, about work?" Leah asked. "It will be nice to have help. You've seemed so stressed lately."

Calvin nodded. "I think it's going to get better. Jorge mentioned something about how we'll soon be sending more missions to the Periphery, but I don't think I'll have to go. We're so short-staffed on comms engineers right now. By the way, I might need to work a little overtime during the next few weeks. No one can take time off right now unless another engineer is available to cover for them. Someone's going to have to cover my shifts while I'm on paternity leave, so I figure I should go ahead and offer to do the same for the other guys."

"I understand."

Calvin kissed the back of Leah's head and pulled the comforter over her shoulders the way she liked it.

"Go to sleep," he whispered.

Within minutes, Leah's soft, peaceful breathing lulled him into a long, deep slumber of his own.

CHAPTER 9
Johanum

I didn't go back to those caves for a long time.

Night bled into day and back again. I wandered from one cave to another, never sleeping in the same place twice. The mountain range seemed to go on forever.

I met lots of animals. Some big, some small. I settled into a diet of berries, fruits, and Tufta leaves. The animals seemed to know I wasn't a threat and they left me alone.

One day, as I turned a new corner at the base of the mountains, I found myself at the edge of a forest.

The forest looked peculiar. Some of the trees were lush and green, stretching high and opening up like an umbrella to shade the forest floor. Others looked as though they had survived a fire. They were all intermingled, those dead and healthy trees, growing up together, with roots tangling above the ground.

There was a path winding inwards from the edge of the trees. I knew a beaten path was dangerous, but I followed it anyway. Through the trees, past fallen branches and hollowed out logs. Eyes peered out from everywhere. I kept moving.

I walked that trail for a long time. As the light in the sky began to fade, I came to a long tree trunk that had fallen across the path. It looked sturdy enough. I was tired and unsure whether to keep going or turn around, so I sat down.

I'm not sure how long I had been there, but when I looked up, I saw four sets of glowing purple eyes staring up at me from the ground. Every now and again, one of them would blink. It struck me as funny, and I laughed.

My laughter echoed through the trees. I couldn't remember the last time I had laughed. I'm not sure why I did then. Perhaps I had given in to hysteria. I tried to laugh again, but this time it was forced and sounded dreadful. I grimaced and waited for the echoes to fade.

One pair of glowing purple eyes was getting closer. They were so very close to the ground, I guessed they belonged to quite a little creature.

It will probably eat me, I thought miserably.

But I soon discovered that the eyes belonged to an animal who didn't look ferocious enough to do me any harm. It was cute, actually. It was round and chubby, covered in brown fur, with tiny little seven-toed feet sticking out from beneath its pudgy body. Out from its midsection stuck two small hands, one on either side, each adorned with seven tiny fingers. It had a tiny black nose, wet like a dog's, smashed unceremoniously into its face like an afterthought. The eyes were kind and welcoming.

All four sets of eyes had crept close to me now. We were staring at each other, equally intrigued. They did not seem scared of me.

Slowly the tallest of the four creatures smiled. It was a shy smile revealing two large buckteeth. It reminded me of a tiny, pudgy little beaver. I strained my head to see if he had a tail. I didn't see one, but my sudden movement made him jump backwards, and the smile disappeared.

I offered up a smile of my own. Smiling felt weird. It hurt the muscles in my face. But my offering worked. The little beaver-type creature smiled back, more confidently this time. One of his companions crawled over next to him, and after studying me, also offered a shy smile. A third followed.

The fourth little fur ball, the tiniest of the bunch, stuck his little legs to the side like a penguin and waddled over to me. He stood there, at my feet, eyes blinking expectantly. I leaned down and stretched out my hand. He waddled into my hand and I lifted him up to eye level.

His confidence quickly gave way to hesitancy. His tiny hands flapped over his eyes. I think he felt embarrassed.

"It's okay," I told him gently. "I won't hurt you."

One eye appeared, peeking through his fingers. Finally, he let his hands drop to his sides and he stood there, wobbling back and forth, trying to find his balance. When he steadied, he turned his quizzical gaze back to my face. He was so studious in the way he stared at me. I felt he must think me a giant ready to crush him.

He grew bolder and crawled up my hand closer to my face. He leaned to the left and stared at the left side of my face. Then he leaned to the right. He reached up with his pudgy hands and moved my head back and forth.

When he was satisfied, he crawled back to the middle of my hands, pulled his legs under his body in one fell swoop, and plopped down with a *thump*. A voice that was surprisingly strong for such a little creature came out:

"It's a person," the fur ball announced.

And that's when I realized 'he' was actually a she.

Her three companions began to chatter excitedly. Evidently this was a very important announcement. They were moving back and forth at speeds their legs were capable of, but their bodies couldn't seem to keep up. They kept falling over, then getting up, only to run into each other and fall over again. After a few minutes of this comical display, they all ended up together on the ground near my feet.

"A person?" the tallest one asked. It had a deeper voice. I wondered if perhaps he was the father. "Are you sure, Tabby?" He didn't really seem to think she was lying. But the idea was incredulous, and he wanted to get his facts straight.

"Oh, yes," Tabby replied, nodding her head vigorously. The movement made her body shake and her tummy jiggle. "Yes, I am sure it's a person. Look at its nose!" She made an exaggerated motion in front of her face, indicating a very large nose.

I hoped my nose wasn't that big.

"And its ears!" Tabby squealed, waving her hands in the form of gigantic ears on the side of her head.

I tried to pull my hair down over my ears. My hair was tangled and matted and gross. I decided I had to live with the ears.

"Look at its feet!" said another one. Before I knew it, one of the fur balls was bouncing on my foot, jumping up and down.

"Be careful!" warned the tallest one. "You don't want to frighten it away!"

"Oh!" The jumping stopped. Now it stood on the ground, staring up expectantly.

"Does it have big teeth?" asked another female voice.

"Of course it must!" answered Tabby, turning to crawl back up my hand towards my face. "All the persons have big teeth."

She stood there, looking confused. Straining forward and nearly losing her balance, she caught herself and placed her hands on my eyelids. Next thing I knew she was prying them open as wide as she could.

"Nope," she mumbled, letting go.

Next, she leaned her head forward and twisted her neck to peer up my nose.

I scrunched my nose together, moving it up and down. Tabby moved back and continued to study it, looking thoroughly entertained.

"Ah ha!" she exclaimed in triumph.

Before I knew it, she had pulled my lips forward and was proudly displaying my teeth. She was showing me off like a horse!

I had finally remembered these creatures. They were Furpines, of the legendary Forestclan, creatures of the woods. The Logs said they were extinct.

It was a family of Furpines. Their names were Toby, Telly, Tibby, and, of course, Tabby. And they weren't alone. They introduced me to their whole Furpine community.

There weren't many of them. No more than twenty Furpines total. But they were a flood of light into my dark world.

I met the newest baby, a miniature Furpine they called Jovi, and his parents, Jaundice and Judith. I met the eldest of the community, Gertrude and Lyle, with their grandkids – Fib, Fort, Festivous, and my favorite, Fabulous. I met Amos and his brothers Archie and Ace. I met Candy and Carrie, best friends. And then there was Benji, and little orphan Abby.

The community kept well hidden, deep in the forest, far away from the prying eyes of the Priests. But they had to venture out of their homes to find food. Each week, four Furpines were selected as scavengers, and it was their job to find the week's food supply.

Two months before, the food scavengers had been caught by a pack of iron-fanged dogs in a big mud patch to the north. Johanum's rabid dogs rarely enter the woods, they told me. They never saw the attack coming. Lyle thought they must have been hungrier than normal. The dogs caught Benji's sister Benita, little Abby's mother. Benita's husband Booster fought hard to save her, but he was no match for the dogs. Now Benji was taking care of Abby. The community had forbidden him from being a food scavenger, at least for a while. They didn't want Abby to be without family.

"We may not last much longer, dearie," said Telly, Tabby's mother, doing her best to put on a brave face. "But we will try our best! For the little ones, you see." Her chin quivered, and she placed her hand affectionately on Tabby's head. Tabby hadn't strayed far from my feet where I had set her back on the ground.

Toby shuffled over to Telly and took his wife's hand affectionately in his own. "We are going to be okay," he tried to reassure her. "It's a dark time. But dark times end. And you find a reason to smile again."

They told me that a year before, they had numbered nearly five hundred. Now they were only twenty.

The cute little critters wanted to give me food. I could not stand the thought of taking food from them, not after hearing what it cost them to gather their tiny food supply. But they were insistent, and they looked crestfallen when I tried to refuse, so I finally gave in.

"Maybe just a bite," I said. Their faces lit up, and Tabby waddled away to their hidden tree-root home, accompanied by her brother Tibby.

They returned a few minutes later. Tabby had a collection of nuts and berries, piled high in a basket made of grass. She was struggling with the basket, first pushing, then trying to pull it. Tibby wanted to help, but he kept lifting the basket when she put it down, and setting it down when she picked it up. The basket was nearly as big as they were. Ace and Amos waddled over. Carefully they lifted the basket above Ace's head, then proceeded to knock each other over. This happened repeatedly. They would regain their balance, collect the scattered nuts and berries and return them to the basket, lift it up above their heads, then make it three or four steps before tumbling over again. They were utterly devoted to the whole inefficient process and I was charmed.

"We are little creatures," Telly said to me with a smile. "We haven't much but each other. But each other is enough."

I blinked back tears. Was I dreaming? It was unlike any dream I had dreamt before. Unlike any Johanum reality I knew. I dashed away tears and decided it didn't matter whether this was real. It was lovely and beautiful, and I would enjoy every minute.

"How did you get here?" I asked Toby and Telly. They smiled their shy smiles.

"We could ask you the same thing, dearie," Telly said gently.

"You first," I insisted.

"Well, dearie," Telly replied, pulling her feet underneath her and plunking down on the ground the same way her daughter had done. "Ours is quite a little story, just like us.

"We lived in the Forests of Cataran, in northern Bisurakhan. Thousands of us there were, dearie. More Furpines than your eyes could count! Fine little homes we had there too. All prim and proper, real homes, with moss for carpet, and curtains, and carved wooden doors. Always had plenty to eat there, we did, dearie. We had feasts and festivals. We had birthdays. Why, we celebrated any time we had a reason to. And any time we didn't!"

The other Furpines nodded enthusiastically.

"We didn't have far to go for our food," she continued. "It fell from the skies most days! And grew up under our feet. Nuts and roots and berries, dearie, of all shapes and sizes, colors and flavors! We had only to carry our baskets outside and collect whatever we wanted. There was so much more than we could eat. It was a beautiful place, those forests of Cataran. It was home, dearie. A real home!"

My heart ached for the longing I heard in her voice. I had not ached, had not longed for anything, in such a long time. It hurt.

Toby spoke up. "It was a nice place," he agreed. "An easy place." Toby was standing close to his wife, and the rest of the community had crept close behind him. They stood around, eyes filled with longing.

"Yes, it was easy," Telly agreed. "Too easy. We got lazy, dearie. We stopped talking to the rest of the Forestclan. We didn't hate them, you know. We just forgot about them. Life was easy, and we didn't need anyone else. They all talked funny, and ate strange food, and they didn't fit in our houses."

Tabby plopped down next to her mother and snuggled in. She looked tired. She had heard this story many times, I could tell.

Telly continued, her arm wrapped around her daughter's shoulders. "When the invaders swept in, we were caught by surprise. They had burned down whole sections of the forest before we heard anything about them. By then it was too late. Most of the Forestclan had already left. Some headed for the hills, others for the water. And there we were – stuck. No place to go, no one to help us."

Telly's chin began quivering. "Furpines can't survive in the mountains, dearie. We would be eaten by eagles and vultures. And we can't swim, dearie. We would have drowned in the river. So, we did what we could. With our lovely trees and homes burning down around us, and the invaders sweeping through, we rolled up onto their field trackers and hid."

"You were stowaways!" I said in surprise. I was also very surprised to hear that Johanum had invaded Bisurakhan. I thought the planet was impenetrable.

"It wasn't much of a plan," Toby observed quietly, "but it was the best we could do. We hid for three days. We didn't know where the intruders had come from or where they were going."

"On the third day, we came to a very bumpy landing," Telly interrupted, taking back the storytelling, which was clearly her domain. "We heard yelling, crashing – so much noise! I was quite beside myself." Even as she recalled the story, Telly wrung her hands nervously. "Finally, we heard the intruders leave the field trackers. We crept out, hoping to find another forest to call home. Instead we found ourselves sitting on top of the open fires of Henam."

I crinkled my nose in disgust. I knew Henam. It was the valley of Johanum on the south side. Stretching as far as your eyes could see, the valley is filled with pits, open flames, and the worst stench you have ever encountered. A combination of decaying flesh, trash, and other things I wouldn't know how to describe.

"How did you get here, to the forest?" I asked. I figured we were far from Henam, though I wasn't entirely sure where the forest was.

It turns out Furpines are quite the talented stowaways. They had arrived to Johanum as stowaways, and they moved about Johanum the same way. They attached themselves to all kinds of creatures, from the iron-fanged dogs to the hyenas of hysteria. Slowly, one family at a time, they kept moving north.

Amos, Archie, and Ace were the ones who discovered the forest. They had become lost one day after latching on to one of the rare she-bears of Johanum. She-bears are violent creatures, Telly told me. They cannot be controlled by the Priests, which makes them unusual, but they are very aggressive.

"Ace is our reckless one, dearie," Telly explained, flashing a smile in his direction. Ace covered his face, pretending to be embarrassed, but I could tell he liked the attention. "Mostly he worries us silly, but that day his recklessness paid off."

Toby jumped in. He loved this part of the story and narrated with great enthusiasm. "Ace had grabbed ahold of a she-bear. Archie and Amos chased after him. But instead of being eaten or torn apart, those boys held on for dear life and arrived here in this forest. The she-bears hibernate here. Well, the boys, they explored for a few days, found us these little homes, and lots of patches of food. Then they created a ruckus to attract a she-bear again, and rode that she-bear all the way back to our little community. It's a miracle they survived."

"They left us in a wretched state, dearie!" Telly cried, the pitch of her voice escalating quickly. "We were certain we had lost them forever. They had been gone for ten days when they finally came back. We had already held their funerals!"

I looked over at the brothers. They were blushing. Ace's face was particularly red. But his eyes sparkled. It was obvious he was an adventurer.

"It took us many days to get everyone back to the woods," Telly continued, finishing her story. "But it was like heaven when we arrived. We knew, of course, that this wood wasn't like ours. There is much darkness here. We have to be careful." She sighed deeply. "But it's good, dearie. It's a little home, a good one for us. A place where we can be with each other."

"But there aren't many of you left," I said. It was a terrible thing to point out, but it was true.

"No," Telly agreed. She sighed again, but then she smiled in an accepting sort of way. "We live as best we can. When these days are over, we will be too. And we will have loved each other well. It's all any Furpine can ask for."

All the Furpines were nodding along, patting their bellies in agreement.

I felt a tiny pressure on the bottom of my leg and looked down to see Telly's hand near my ankle.

"And you, dearie? Haven't you got anybody to love?"

The question brought tears in my eyes. I tried to blink them away, but they poured out uninvited.

"You are the first creatures with a hint of goodness I have met since coming here," I replied softly. "I met one other person. A person like me. His name was Fletcher."

The memory of Fletcher and the Priests was a weight too heavy to bear. I dropped my head and stopped talking.

"Oh my, dearie. Why, we are not the only ones here, you know. There are many other creatures in the forest. I can't imagine living here all alone. We Furpines don't do alone. Not like the persons do."

I shrugged. "I don't mind being alone. Or, at least, I didn't...in Middlestan. Before I came here."

"Is that where you're from, dearie?" Telly asked me.

I nodded. "I was a professor. A researcher. I was becoming successful, too."

"Well, I don't know much about that," Telly answered sweetly, "but I am sorry you had to leave home. You must miss it an awful lot."

"I do," I agreed. "Perhaps I would have been okay on another planet. But I did not plan to come here. This is unlike any place I could have imagined."

It was getting dark. The Furpines began to shift back and forth nervously.

"It's nighttime, dearie," Telly spoke up. "It's dangerous for us to be here. Dangerous for you, too, I reckon."

"I should leave," I said, getting up and stretching my legs. I wasn't sure where I would go. I was lost, and too far into the forest to make it back to the caves.

Toby motioned to his son Tibby, who turned deeper into the forest and whistled softly. It was a whistle that grew stronger as it built into a melody.

All was quiet. Even the rustling of the leaves seemed to stop.

The song slowly disappeared. I stood in the stillness, holding my breath, not even aware I was holding it. I could feel my heartbeat.

As if from nowhere, a pair of antlers appeared. Stepping out from behind a tree came the glowing eyes of a large buck. We stood there, staring at each other.

"This is Canwood, prince of the forest," Toby announced. "Canwood is a good creature. All of the deer are good. He will take care of you tonight."

I stared in amazement, still not sure anything I was seeing was real. I felt pressure on my foot again and looked down to see little Tabby trying to move my leg.

"Go," she encouraged, looking up at me with her wide innocent eyes.

I walked toward the deer, then turned back. The Furpines stood behind me, waving goodbye. Telly wiped tears from her eyes.

"You take care of yourself, dearie," Telly called after me. I watched as she grabbed Toby's hand and buried her face in his fur. He waved at me, then turned to hug his wife.

Canwood did not speak. I followed him a good distance. At long last we came to a stop in front of a tall Oak Tree. It reached up, up, up, much higher than the trees around it.

Canwood lifted his hoof and tapped the tree near the roots. Slowly an opening in the forest floor appeared. Exhausted, I crawled in. The opening closed above me.

The ground was covered in blankets of moss. It felt warm and soft. The moss curled up around me and tucked me in. I laid down my head and slept like a baby, lost in a dreamless sleep.

When I awoke the next morning, the forest was gone. I was sleeping on a bed of Tufta leaves at the base of the mountains.

CHAPTER 10
Bisurakhan

Josh stood there expectantly. Calvin reached into his backpack, pulled out a green plastic container, and passed it over.

"I'll skip my break tonight if you can make them stop," he said, nodding at the two women on the other side of the room.

Josh looked over his shoulder. Two female linguists, Mary and Hailey, were bent over their desks, hard at work. They were carrying on an animated conversation about some Cornersville dance competition.

"Where's Shondra?" Josh asked.

"She's scheduled for the next shift."

"That's weird, she said she was going to be here."

"They've been talking about these same four dance competitions for the last hour," Calvin grumbled, nodding his head towards Mary and Hailey.

"Dance is a big deal in Cornersville. They really like other cultures. They may specialize in linguistics, but they also study dance and music from other planets. At least, that's what Shondra tells me. She was actually showing me the new dance sequence from that competition the girls are talking about. It went something...like...this..." Josh held his arms out to the side and began swaying awkwardly.

"Really? It looks like that?"

"Yeah. Sort of. I don't know."

"I'll tell you what I know."

"What?"

"You've been seeing a lot of Shondra lately."

"She's hot."

"Do you like her?"

"I just told you. She's hot."

"And…?"

"And what?"

"She talks too much, doesn't she?"

"Yeah."

"She's going to drive you crazy."

"She already is."

"So why don't you stop seeing her?"

Josh shrugged. "And do what? Sit at home alone? It's fine for now."

They watched the excited conversation flow back and forth between Mary and Hailey. The girls were really into this dance competition.

A beeping noise sounded over the intercom. Josh and Calvin quickly refocused and took their seats. Earpieces in place, they swiped digital keyboards onto the control panel and began typing furiously.

It was a long message. Josh and Calvin traded back and forth for nearly an hour. By the time the line went dark, they were exhausted.

Calvin dropped his earpiece and leaned his head against the desk. "They're getting longer."

"We're ready for the next one," a cheerful voice responded.

It was so close, Calvin jumped.

Hailey was standing there, a bright smile covering her face.

"What about all those transcripts from last night?" Calvin asked.

"We're done with those," Mary replied.

"All of them?"

"Of course. They're not hard. We've seen this mix of languages before. Well, usually it's just one language at a time, not all of them mixed together like this. I suppose that's part of the 'special code,'" she joked.

"Special code?" Calvin repeated, confused.

"You know, the 'special code.' To keep you on your toes."

"Can I see your translations?" Calvin asked.

"Yes, of course." Mary motioned for Calvin to follow. They walked over to Mary's desk. Josh's curiosity got the better of him and he followed.

Calvin tapped the screen and opened a file titled "Message 1."

"Wait!" Hailey interrupted. "Read them in order." She pointed to the message marked 7. "They're using a numerical system based on their galaxy's star placements," she explained. "It goes 7, then 5, then 3, followed by 4, 1, 2, and 8."

"Why don't you rename them so they follow *our* numerical system?" Calvin asked crossly.

He wasn't sure why he was cross. The girls talked too much. He was tired. Leah had been upset with him when he left to come to work. Pregnancy hormones, probably, but how could he be sure? Maybe he really had done something wrong.

Josh nudged him. "Are you going to open that?"

Calvin reached forward and hit play. Text unrolled across the screen.

CONTACT CONFIRMED. AUDIENCE SECURED. SEND HADAYA.

"What's Hadaya?" Calvin asked.

"We thought you guys would know," Mary answered.

"Are you sure you translated it right?"

"I triple-checked," Mary said.

"And I quadruple-checked," added Hailey.

"You really don't know what it means?" Mary asked. Josh and Calvin shook their heads.

"Maybe it's someone's name," Mary suggested.

Hailey nodded. "That was our guess. I mean, I wanted it to be the name of some new dance move – "

"We discussed that possibility!" Mary laughed.

"But it seems, you know...unlikely," Hailey said with a smile. "Okay, okay, stop looking at me like that. It was a joke! But if it was a dance move," she added slyly, "it would probably look something like this..." She twirled on her toes and curtsied in front of Josh.

Josh stared back in confusion.

"It's called dance. It's *fun*," she teased.

Josh shuffled his feet uncomfortably.

Calvin chuckled. "You're making him uncomfortable."

"I'm sorry," Hailey apologized. "I didn't mean to."

"Don't be sorry," Calvin replied. "I'm entertained."

Hailey spun around again.

"Hailey. Come on now," Mary said playfully.

Hailey looked at Josh and winked.

Caught completely off-guard, Josh blushed.

Calvin howled with laughter.

"Hard at work, I see," came Jorge's unmistakable voice.

All four stood at attention.

"At ease. I just stopped by to see how the translations were going."

Mary motioned Jorge over to her desk. He looked at the message and frowned.

"What's Hadaya?" he asked.

"It's a dance move," Calvin mumbled under his breath.

"What was that?" Jorge asked, turning around.

"We think it's a name, sir," Calvin replied.

Mary snickered.

Josh sat back in his seat and tried to look like he was working.

"What do the other ones say?" Jorge asked.

Mary tapped another message and watched it open.

COMPLICATIONS AT THE PERIPHERY. SEND BACK-UP.

Jorge nodded and Mary opened another.

CATARAN ELIMINATED.

Calvin felt sick. "Our Cataran? The forests?"

Jorge shook his head. "It can't be our Cataran. The forests are alive and well. I received several messages from the Frumpleters just last week."

"Is there another place called Cataran?" Calvin asked.

"Not in our solar system," Jorge replied. "Any idea who is sending these messages? Has the language given you any clue about its planet of origin?"

Mary shook her head. "One of the languages is ancient. It was used in our universe, decades ago, before the Day of Darkness. We don't know any planet or solar system that uses it now. It's referenced in some of the older Logs. I think we have a couple of old Scrolls in that text too. That's as much as I know."

"What language is used in Johanum?" Josh asked.

"I have no idea," Mary answered. "But, uhhhh…." She looked at Hailey for reinforcement. Hailey nodded encouragingly. "We would like to request permission to correspond with Middlestan," Mary said. "Middlestan Accelerated University has a linguistics department. Their practical language skills are poor, but their knowledge of linguistic developments over the last couple of centuries is quite developed. Superior to ours, actually. They might be able to help us determine who is involved in this conversation."

Jorge contemplated about her request, then nodded. "Wait two days before you make contact," he instructed. "I want to mention it to Calif and Antoine, and Antoine won't be back until the day after tomorrow. I want to make sure this won't hinder any of their ongoing conversations with Middlestan. When you do speak to Middlestan, simply say you are working with us on translation services and could use some of their historical knowledge. Don't tell them that this involves Dr. Kanale."

"All right," Mary agreed, frowning slightly. "Don't they know that we're here helping you on your mission to rescue Dr. Kanale."

"No," Jorge replied. "No, they don't. No one outside the Turris does. And may I remind you of your own confidentiality agreements."

"Yeah, of course, I know, everything is confidential. We don't talk about it with anyone but each other. But I just thought..."

"You thought what?"

"I thought they would know. You're helping rescue one of their citizens. I'm sure they'll be happy to help with that."

"They'll be happy to help even without that knowledge," Jorge said.

Mary looked confused. So did Hailey.

"When we rescue Dr. Kanale, we will be bringing her to Bisurakhan. She won't be returning to Middlestan. At least, not right away."

"So, wait – you're *kidnapping* her?" Mary asked.

"It's not a kidnapping," Jorge answered. "It's a rescue mission."

"Are you giving her the option to return home?" Mary asked.

"Of course not. Not before she helps us with the mission we have for her. That's why we're rescuing her in the first place."

"So it *is* a kidnapping," Hailey said.

"It is not a kidnapping," Jorge repeated. "But even if it was, it wouldn't concern you. You DO remember the terms of your contract?"

Mary and Hailey nodded stiffly.

"Very good then. I'm heading home." Jorge nodded at Calvin and Josh and left.

"Did you know about this?" Hailey asked Josh and Calvin.

"It's not a kidnapping," Calvin said. "We're sending Dr. Kanale back to Middlestan when she's done here. Anyway, she was supposed to come here the day she was kidnapped by Johanum."

"So she's getting kidnapped twice?" Mary asked. "That poor woman."

"Why do you feel sorry for her?" Calvin asked. "I mean, feel sorry for her for having to go to Johanum, I guess. I don't know much about it, but I'm guessing it's not a super nice place. But getting to come to Bisurakhan? Our life here is so much better here! We're far more advanced that Middlestan. She's getting the opportunity of a lifetime to come here."

"Have you ever been to Middlestan?" Mary asked.

"No," Calvin admitted. "Have you?"

Mary shook her head.

"Well, then it's just our opinions, I guess," said Calvin. "Our opinions and the Logs. Which tell us that everything here is better. We have better technology. Better food. More job opportunities."

"The people in Middlestan seem to like it there."

"But they've never been here to compare!"

Mary and Hailey were clearly bothered. They returned to their desks and got back to work. They spoke a word the rest of the night.

Thirty minutes later, overwhelmed by the quiet, Calvin leaned over to Josh. "This is actually worse than when they were talking," he grumbled.

CHAPTER 11
Johanum

The days became darker.

Fire curled up the edge of the high concrete wall, licking away dirt and grime. I called it the Pit of Brutality. I had watched many animals run and jump headlong over the edge. The fire consumed and ravaged its prey, sensing their presence and rising to meet them.

Back when I lived in Middlestan, I read ancient stories about Johanum. Middlestan believed Johanum was a myth. The stories were dark, but then most myths are. One story I remembered told how light and power come from Johanum. In payment – for in Johanum there must always be payment – each sun consumes the warmth of its planet for three months and returns it as a gift to the Priests. That is why the planets experience winter.

The Priests of Johanum are not priests in a traditional sense. They claim no religion or god but themselves. They rule with dominance and take pleasure in others' devastation.

The Priests were the ones who brought me here.

The Priests killed Fletcher.

You would know a Priest if you met one. They hiss when they talk. Their tongues are silver and scaled like a snake. Even their lips have a scaly silver appearance. Their eyes glow red. Each wears a robe with a red cord wrapped tightly around his waist. The air around them is visibly darker. They are harsh and cruel, yet I don't hate them.

They are the only ones who can set me free.

I stared at my watch. How the watch kept working was a mystery. Sometimes I would go days without looking at it.

But other days, like today, I sat, mesmerized, willing the hands to move.

An eternity passed, and one hand shifted.

One single, solitary movement.

Halfway through the morning – another long, never-ending morning that lasted a thousand years – I curled up on the ground and pressed my face into the dirt. It was cold and unforgiving. It suited me. I lay there for hours. But when I stood, barely twenty minutes had passed.

I couldn't remember the last time I smiled, nor did I care.

This was not life.

This was Johanum.

Emptiness pervaded everything. Then my memories began to fade.

I remembered things from time to time. A face. A place. Laughter. I wanted to remember, but each memory was so overwhelming that I pushed it away, willing it to disappear.

Breathless. I felt breathless. I tried to breathe, to calm the tension, the anxiety, if only for a moment. And for a moment, it worked.

Then I panicked and doubled over, gasping for breath.

Putting two thoughts together was an exercise in futility. I tried. Desperately. As soon as I looked to a second thought, the first grew wings and vanished. It was as if I could see it, watch it, flying away from me. It looked peaceful as it left. But when I tried to call it back, the second thought escaped as well, and the first never returned.

I learned to let them go when they were ready. Now I simply welcomed the ones that chose to stay.

I took up running. It was excruciating, and I hated it, but it provoked a reliable emotion. Pain is unpleasant, but it is dependable.

I ran at night, in the dark. I stumbled a lot. My legs were covered in bruises. I didn't mind. It was a reminder that I could bruise, that a part of my body was still alive.

Could you call this life?

This was Johanum.

I remember lying helpless, curled up on the ground, eyes squeezed shut, rocking back and forth.

"I need help," I whispered.

But no one answered.

And finally, surrounded by forgotten dreams, I relented.

I let go.

I quit fighting.

For a while I dreamed someone would come. I dreamed of the people in my life I had known before.

I dreamed they would come and rescue me. Come and take me far away.

Then I dreamed they might come and sit with me. Maybe they would speak. Maybe they would listen. But they would come.

Then I dreamed that perhaps they would think of me. Maybe they thought of me every day. Or every couple of days. Maybe they remembered me fondly, or perhaps they hated me. But they thought of me.

Then I dreamed they might remember me. Perhaps once or twice, sometime far into the future, I would cross their minds and they would smile. They would wonder what became of me. Maybe they would even hope I was okay.

Then, one day, I stopped.

I had not stopped remembering the ones I left behind. I thought of them all the time. I longed for them. Cried for them. Beat my head into the ground in frustration over the faces and memories fading.

But I had stopped thinking they thought of me.

I was in Johanum. I was lost. From the world. From its memory.

And even if it remembered me, which me would it remember? The world did not know this version of me, this version Johanum had created.

Sometimes I thought I saw them. I had waited so long, with so much hope. Perhaps the hallucinations were natural.

But I knew, whenever I saw a familiar face, or heard a voice that awakened my heart, I knew it was all a dream. I knew the dream would fade, just like everything else. It would transform. I would be left wondering what was real.

What do you hold on to when you cannot tell what is real? In what do you hope when neither life nor death offers promise of relief?

When do you let go?

When do you stop trying?

When is that all okay?

The voices in my head were never silent, yet they drowned me in silence.

CHAPTER 12
Bisurakhan

Antoine was relieved to be back from his trip to the Periphery. He was not, however, looking forward to his conversation with Jorge.

Calif was waiting in the Strategy Room when Antoine arrived. Jorge was absent.

"The Commander has given his approval, I hear," Antoine said casually as he took his seat. Casual was not at all how he felt. His stomach was churning.

"We'll be leaving in two weeks," Calif confirmed. "He's coming with us. Also, Antoine, he doesn't like the idea of a prisoner exchange. He said he doesn't think one will be necessary."

Antoine considered that. "Did he say why?"

Calif shook his head. "He said he expects a fight, but he's confident we can win."

"I'm sure he is."

"Do you disagree?"

"I think it's more complicated than 'we show up, we fight, we win,' but...the Commander knows that."

"So what's causing your skepticism?" Calif asked. "Are you questioning the Commander, or yourself?"

"I'm not sure whether I trust either of us."

"How do you justify putting your life into the hands of a man you don't trust?"

"Are you any different?" Antoine asked.

Calif didn't reply.

"We all have questions, Calif. I know you do, too."

Jorge chose that moment to arrive, and he was all business. "We travel through the Space Between. That will allow us to keep better control over our transit time. Once we've crossed the Periphery into Johanum's orbit, we'll have a very limited amount of time to find Josephine Kanale and leave. There's a portal that opens twice a day. We need to use that as our entry and exit point. And we need to get in and out within one cycle, or we risk alterations to our own physical integrity. Except maybe Antoine. I don't know if it's different if you've spent time in Johanum before. Anyway, the engineers are also worried about the way Johanum's atmosphere might impact our transport ship. At minimum, they think it will quickly drain the ship's power supply, so it is imperative that we exit Johanum as quickly as possible. In and out, two portal openings. It would help if we could come up with an approximate landing location that would put us close to Dr. Kanale."

"What are you looking at me for?" Antoine asked. "I have no way of knowing where Dr. Kanale will be."

"There are no popular places? Locations she would be more likely to frequent than others?"

"You mean, like a bar or a restaurant?"

"Exactly!"

"You're dumb."

Jorge looked startled.

Calif burst into a rich baritone laugh. "We don't get candid, unfiltered commentary from Antoine very often."

Antoine shifted uncomfortably.

"I don't quite know how to handle it," Calif continued, turning serious. "Johanum is so sensitive for you. Any talk of it rids you of your good senses. Yet it's also when you're at your best. So, tell me," he said, shifting the conversation, "what can be planned ahead in terms of...well, anything? Is there anything we might be able to assume or guess about Dr. Kanale and her location?"

Antoine leaned back in his chair, kicked his feet up, and stared off into space.

"It takes him so long to act on anything," Jorge mumbled.

"It wouldn't hurt you to move slower sometimes," Calif replied.

"We are men of action!" Jorge responded.

"Who?" Calif asked.

"All you Bisurakhanatis," Antoine said quietly.

"You still don't consider yourself one of us?" Calif questioned.

"He isn't one of us," Jorge said.

"He is as much a Khanist as you or I," Calif said.

"No," Jorge and Antoine replied in unison.

"Would you look at that?" Calif said with a smile. "We've found something you two agree on."

Jorge changed the subject. "The linguists from Cornersville will begin conversing with Middlestan tomorrow," he said. "They asked for permission to contact Middlestan Accelerated University's linguistics department. I gave them approval. They're trying to determine the planet or universe of origin for one of the languages in our transmissions. You might be interested in this, Calif. The way they describe the language makes it sound like Lyricus."

"Lyricus?" Calif repeated, surprised. "The language of the Scrolls that were written before the Day of Darkness?"

The Day of Darkness was the term the Logs used to refer to the day that eleven planets in the Exertus Universe were destroyed, leaving the nine that now remained.

"We'll have to wait and see if Middlestan can confirm," Jorge answered.

"Is it possible?" Calif asked. "Are there other people who speak that language?"

"I know that look," Jorge said. "Say what you're really thinking."

Calif was thoughtfully stroking his beard. "Is it possible those planets still exist?"

Jorge jumped to his feet. "That's what I was asking myself!"

"But they disappeared. You can't move planets." Calif paused. "Can you?"

"If you can, we're about to tap into a whole new source of power. But I suspect there's a simpler explanation. Maybe some of those people escaped."

"To another solar system? That seems unlikely. We can travel between planets, but the human body won't survive traveling from one universe to another."

"That we know of," Jorge pointed out. He glanced over at Antoine, who had been sitting there silently, lost in thought. He wanted to press him for details about Johanum, but Antoine didn't respond well to pressure. Jorge decided to let it go.

"We need to select the Generals we plan to leave in charge," Jorge said. "General Fossil is the natural choice, but I'm not inclined to give him that authority, not after what happened last time."

Calif and Antoine nodded in agreement.

"General Cavanaugh would do well," Antoine suggested. "She's completely turned around the aviation units that were on probation. She deserves a shot at a higher leadership role, a chance to show us what she's capable of."

"General Sanchez does better with the day-to-day operations," Jorge said. "How about assigning them together as a team?"

"I like that," Calif said.

"Me too," Antoine agreed.

"We're going to need to do some damage control around General Fossil," Jorge said. "Do either of you have a project you could give him? Something to keep him distracted?"

"Why does he still have his rank?" Antoine asked. "He causes more trouble than he's worth."

"We won't strip someone of their title without good reason," Jorge replied.

"What bigger reason do you need?"

"It's more than that," Calif said. "As long as he's here, in the Turris, we can control the problems he creates."

"But at what cost? The example he sets for the rest of our men and women – what they undoubtedly believe we permit and perhaps even reward -"

"I wish I had your conscience, Antoine, I really do," Jorge interrupted.

"You've been here too long," Antoine told him.

"And I'm very ready for retirement," Jorge replied.

CHAPTER 13
Bisurakhan

"Why must you grieve me so?"

Calvin rolled his eyes as Josh sank dramatically into his chair and rolled it towards the desk.

"I just asked how your date went," Calvin muttered.

"So many questions! What's a guy gotta do to get a little privacy around here?"

"Maybe not spend half an hour talking about how he's planned 'The Date to End All Dates,'" Calvin replied.

"Well," Josh grimaced, "I think I managed that. There won't be any more dates."

"What did you do?" Calvin asked.

"Who said I did anything?"

"In this scenario, the problem is usually you."

"That's not a nice thing to say."

"Yet it's true. What did you do?"

"I took her to Casava, down at the Square."

"She doesn't like fancy restaurants?"

"No, she loved the restaurant. We had dinner on the rooftop. It was great. I got in all my good lines. I did everything right, I was totally winning."

"And...?"

"Then I took her to Port Gardens."

"I forgot about that place. I should take Leah there."

"Yeah, well, it turns out Shondra is deathly allergic to Hyacinthus, which are in full bloom right now, and they're everywhere, all over Port Gardens. And I mean she is deathly allergic. Her face, her arms, her hands – everything was so swollen, I hardly recognized her. I had to radio an Emergency Launch Pad to come and transport her to the hospital. I saw her this morning. She looks a little better."

"That seems like an innocent mistake. How would you have known that she was allergic?"

"I don't know, but she won't talk to me. When I ask her a question, she answers with one word."

"Ouch."

"Yeah."

"You found a way to get one of them to stop talking. Do you think we could get some Hyacinthus in here?"

"Calvin!"

"I'm kidding, I'm kidding! I'm definitely kidding." He paused. The control room was so quiet tonight, it was amazing. "I think I'm kidding..."

Josh looked around. "Speaking of our talkative friends, where are they?"

"The last shift told them to contact us in a few hours to see if we needed them. No transmissions came through last night."

"None at all?" Josh asked in surprise.

"Not a one."

"It's messed up, but that makes me very nervous."

"I feel the exact same way," Calvin said.

"Nothing's come in since you arrived?"

"It has been completely quiet."

They stared at the large screen that covered the wall in front of them. Every now and again, a red light flashed, signaling the location of one of the Khanist transit pods.

"Leah asked if you wanted to bring Shondra over for dinner tomorrow night," Calvin said.

"Can I come alone?"

"Sure. But be warned, if Leah hears you aren't bringing a date, she'll probably try to set you up with one of her friends."

"Dude, why have you been holding out on me? Hook me up!"

"Do you really think you should be dating right now?"

"It's been three months."

"Exactly. It's only been three months since your divorce. Don't you need to, I don't know, go to therapy or something?"

"No, I don't need to 'go to therapy or something,'" Josh retorted.

"I think you could use it."

"I need a shrink like I need a hole in my head."

"I could give you one of those."

Josh scowled. "I need female companionship, all right? That's what I need."

"Companionship, huh?"

"And...other stuff."

"I think you need therapy."

Silence.

"So, dinner tomorrow night?"

"Yeah."

"Great. I'll tell Leah to invite one of her single therapist friends."

Josh glared.

***

Jorge was late getting home.

"So, Mister, you decided to come home after all?" His wife was bustling around the kitchen, a flour-covered towel flung over her left shoulder and a smear of chocolate at the edge of her mouth. She stopped moving long enough to place both hands on her hips and let her husband know she was angry with him.

"Maria, not tonight."

"Okay, okay, sure, no problem," she answered, returning to her pie crust. "When would be a good time for you? Tomorrow? Next week? I know, I'll just call your assistant. Maybe she can get your wife on your schedule."

"I realize I've been gone a lot."

"No. No, you haven't been gone a lot. You've been gone *all the time*."

"I told you my schedule was going to get crazy for a while."

"Okay, okay, no problem." Maria waved her flour-covered towel in his face. "You can have your crazy schedule. You have it as crazy as you like. But don't expect a kiss from me when you get home. Don't expect a warm, hot dinner waiting for you. Maria will just take care of everything by herself. You just come home whenever it is convenient for you."

"I'm going to make it up to you."

"I'm just your lowly wife. You have other, more important things to do."

"Maria."

"Mmmm?" She had rolled the dough to the thickness she liked and began stabbing it with a fork.

Jorge hesitated. He could tell she wasn't too angry, but that rolling pin looked heavy, and she was ferocious with that fork.

"Were you saying something to your lowly wife?" Maria asked, not bothering to look up. She flipped the crust into a pie pan and began using her thumb and forefinger to shape its edges.

"You know I love you."

"Mmmmhmmmm."

"Are the babies asleep?"

"Of course they are asleep. It's late. It's good, you know, that their grandmamma is not so busy with important things that she cannot take care of them."

"Where's Nicolas?" asked Jorge.

Their son had moved in several months ago after his wife had been diagnosed with cancer. Nicolas spent most of his time running between the hospital and the offices of his architecture firm. The twins he left with Maria.

"He's at the hospital with Camila," Maria answered.

"He needs to spend more time at home," Jorge said. "You're working too hard. He can't expect this much of you."

"Oh, you're a fine one to talk, Mister! You want to tell *my* son – "

"*Our* son," Jorge corrected.

Maria scowled. "You want to tell *my* son to spend more time at home. At least he loves his wife and always goes to see her."

They glared at each other.

Maria's face softened as it always did after her frustration had run its course. "You look tired," she said. "Here." She opened the oven door and pulled out the plate of food she had been keeping warm.

"You're good to me."

"Of course. I am too good to you."

Jorge playfully swatted her behind. Maria giggled and smacked him with the towel. The flour caught in his nose and he sneezed.

"You're still the most beautiful woman I know," Jorge said as he took his seat at the table. And he meant it. Thirty-eight years and she could still make him happier – and angrier – than any other soul alive.

"Maybe if you spent more time at home, you could enjoy your beautiful wife," Maria chided.

Jorge reached out and pulled her onto his lap, kissed her loudly, then let her go. "One more thing. Don't get mad."

"What is it now?"

"I have to leave on a mission in a couple of weeks."

"You said no more missions this year!" Maria said angrily.

"I know. I was wrong."

"You are wrong so much."

Jorge rolled his eyes. "The travel will slow down."

"When?" Maria demanded.

"Soon."

"How soon?"

"Soon."

"I don't believe you. How long will you be gone?"

"I don't know."

"Well, Mister, you make the rules up there in that fancy tower. Surely you must know something. A day, a week...?" She waited. "I know my food is good, Jorge, but don't pretend you don't hear your wife."

Jorge wiped his mouth and stood up. "I really don't know how long this mission will take, Maria. I hope it will only last a couple of days. Or maybe a couple of weeks – "

"A couple of weeks?!" Maria shrieked.

"Stop hitting me with that towel!"

"You are a bad husband! And a bad father! And a very bad grandfather!"

"I visit Camila every week, Maria, and Nicolas is doing okay. I saw the babies yesterday. You need help around the house. This is too much for you."

"I don't want another woman in my house!"

"Okay. We'll hire a man, then."

"Oh, 'we hire a man then,'" Maria harrumphed. "No man will cook for my babies!"

"I'm calling a housekeeping service in the morning."

"I can clean my own house!"

"I'm calling a housekeeper."

"They can only come if they use the good soap!"

"And a nanny," Jorge continued.

Maria turned around, aghast. "Absolutely not! You horrible, horrible man! You give me a housekeeper. And a cook. I stay with my babies."

"All right."

Jorge reached out his hand and traced his finger down his wife's jawline. She relaxed and cradled her head in his hand.

"Most beautiful woman in the world," he said gently, smiling as she closed her eyes. She was a handful, but she was his handful, and he wouldn't trade her for anything.

CHAPTER 14
Johanum

I found my voice after Fletcher died, but I rarely used it. There was no one to talk to. The person I wanted to talk to had willed his own death at the hands of the Priests.

But on occasion, in a haze somewhere between awake and asleep, I would sing a song I learned from the wraiths.

The wraiths worked the docks down by the water. They were ghost-like creatures. They had a human form, yet their skin was translucent, and they glided about as if gravity did not apply to them. Their wrists and ankles were shackled to long metal chains. They lifted the chains with great effort, dragging the chains along behind them.

The wraiths never appeared in the daylight. But at night, as it grew dark, their shapes took form as they crawled out of the water.

I had stumbled upon the wraiths quite by accident. They never looked at me, never acknowledged my presence, even when I walked across the docks among them.

Every night, the outline of boats would take shape on the lake far off in the distance. As they approached the shore, ropes appeared, bobbing up and down on top of the water. The wraiths would float to the edge of the docks, reach over the side, gather up the ropes, and pull the boats to shore.

Then, after the boats sat there a while, they were pushed back out to sea.

A soft, blue haze would rise up from the water and surround the wraiths as they worked. As night progressed, they would sing. Theirs was a soft, cascading melody that caught the edge of the wind and danced through the air around them.

We smile
Our burden is light
These chains set us free
From the burden of the light
We long for the night
Sweet killer of dreams

We bend
Beneath the weight of the light
These chains set us free
From the burden of spite
And the dungeons of might
That inhibit the free

We breathe
Beneath the curse of the light
These chains set us free
From the madness we crave
We offer it life
It turns us away

We live
With no life left at all
The light makes us cry, in silence
Though we offer our hope
In despair and disgrace
We cannot escape

I wanted for nothing in Johanum. I had all I needed, for desire had died.

Envy and jealousy had vanished. Only vaguely did I envy the dead.

There was no greed. Gold meant nothing. What would I have done with it?

Stripped bare, void of personality and hope and desire, something new was born.

Life became simple. I craved simplicity. Basic necessities. Laughter. Music. Someone to hold, someone to hold me.

From time to time, fragments of my research and memories of my old house would dance through my mind. The things that mattered from my old life, the life I once lived in Middlestan. It was a life I barely remembered. It was a life that no longer held any meaning. How could it? That version of me had disappeared.

One night as I wandered down by the docks, I stopped to listen to the song of the wraiths.

Something about that night was different. I stood still, watching, listening.

Their movements had changed.

The air had turned cold. I drew closer, rubbing my arms to keep warm.

A taller wraith at the end of the dock caught my attention. After several minutes, he began to sing a different song. The other wraiths joined in. They swayed back and forth, gliding along the water, pulling the boats to shore.

Down by the waves
It wandered, it wandered
Seeking escape from its kind

Down by the waves
It pondered, it pondered
Seeking escape from its life

The waves crash
Against the shoreline
Crash against the sand
Crash against resistance

The waves crash
Against belief
Crash against resistance
Break against acceptance

A familiar blue fog was rising. It floated up through the boards of the docks and folded itself around the wraiths, hugging them tight. Slowly, the light crept farther. It reached the ground by my feet. There it lingered, lapping at the dirt, beckoning me to follow.

Down by the waves
It listened, it listened
Seeking escape from its mind

Down by the waves
It's frightened, it's frightened
Seeking escape from the lies

The waves crash
Against the shoreline
Crash against the sand
Crash against resistance

The waves crash
Against belief
Crash against resistance
Break against acceptance

Without realizing it, I had crossed the docks and was standing at the edge of the water.

Down by the waves
It pauses, it pauses

Seeking a light in the dark

Down by the water
It seeks for salvation
All we have here is destruction

I froze and looked up. My eyes locked with the tall wraith, the one who had first started to sing.

I suddenly realized the wraiths weren't ghosts. They weren't dead at all.

They were watching me. Warning me.

I looked more carefully at the boats. Wraiths climbed up a rope ladder on one side, disappeared from sight, then crawled back out on the other side.

I approached one of the ships and reached for the rope ladder. No one tried to stop me. I shimmied up, reached the top, and peered over the edge.

The boat was full of dead bodies.

I clasped my hands over my mouth, turned, and vomited.

Pressing my eyes tightly shut, I waited for the wave of panic to subside. Then I took a breath, opened my eyes, and climbed into the boat.

I stumbled through the pile of bodies. The smell was overwhelming. I pinched my nose and kept going. On the far side, I joined the wraiths and crawled back out.

The wraiths around me were all dragging large bags. The bags held bodies they had retrieved from the boat.

On the other side of the ship was a canyon that plunged deep into the earth. The wraiths were throwing the bodies into the hole. They fell, down, down, into the darkness and out of sight. I couldn't see the bottom. All I could see was a blackness that spilled over the edge and moved over the ground like fingers massaging the earth, daring it to turn away.

Three boats were docked now. I could see ten more out at sea.

Were they all like this? Boats filled with death, filled with destruction?

The next boat pulled up. The bodies the wraiths pulled out were charred and burned. Every last one. The stench was more than I could bear. I gagged. The bodies were dropped, one after another, into the hole of darkness that seemed to grow darker with each addition.

When I could bear it no more, I turned to leave. I had to climb back through the boats. Finally, I reached the docks. My chest was heavy, but my mind was heavier.

Was there no end to the horrors of this place?

CHAPTER 15
Bisurakhan

"Leah, you look like you're about to pop! Ow! Stop!" Josh said as Calvin pummeled his arm.

"I'd be careful if I was you," Calvin cautioned. "She's very strong right now. I don't know what it is...hormones, I guess...but she could take you down."

"What he means is that I weigh a ton," Leah interrupted, laughing. "I stepped on his foot yesterday and he howled like a baby for five minutes. I swear this baby weighs as much as I do."

Josh chuckled. "Leah, you look radiant. Motherhood becomes you."

Leah beamed. "Did Calvin tell you about our plans for a nursery?" she asked. "He's getting a bonus at work. We're going to make a nursery. A real nursery, Josh! With a crib, and a rocking chair, and a little musical merry-go-round. Come here, come here, I wanted to show you!" She grabbed both of Josh's hands and dragged him down the hallway.

Calvin finished setting the table. Someone knocked on the front door. He walked over, opened the door, and greeted Leah's friend.

"Cynthia, we're so glad you could make it." He gave her a hug.

Cynthia was Leah's roommate from college and one of her oldest friends. Calvin liked most of Leah's friends, but Cynthia was one of his favorites. She was so level-headed and calm.

"I was delighted when Leah called and asked!" Cynthia replied, slipping off her shoes by the door. "You know, I haven't seen Leah since she told me you two were having a baby."

"Cynthia!" Leah came squealing down the hallway.

Cynthia's eyes widened. "Look at you!"

"I know, I know, I'm huge!" Leah laughed, grabbing her friend in a giant bear hug.

"So, you got the full tour, huh?" Calvin asked Josh. "How'd you like that empty room? Really makes you think "baby," doesn't it?"

Josh smiled. "It's a little sparse. But she showed me exactly where everything is going to go. It's a good thing you figured out a way to get that bonus. You are going to make her so happy. I don't think I've ever seen her so excited."

A self-satisfied smile spread over Calvin's entire face. "She's really happy, right?"

"She really is. You did well."

"My first Reality Persuasion experiment is this weekend. The bonus will come through next week. This was the best idea ever. Are you going to do one?"

"I haven't decided. I've been having second thoughts about the whole thing."

"Decided you could live without that bike?"

"Yeah."

"You know Kat's not around now to get mad at you over a big purchase, right?"

Josh grimaced.

"Josh!" Leah interrupted. "I want you to officially introduce you to my friend. Meet Cynthia!"

Josh smiled and reached out his hand. "The pleasure is all mine." He hated to admit it, but he was disappointed. In his head, he had thought Leah's friends would look like her. Short, cute, maybe even her little button nose. Cynthia was tall, boyish, and wore no makeup. She really wasn't his type.

"It's so nice to meet you," Cynthia responded cheerfully. "Leah tells me you work with Calvin."

"Yeah, we're both Comms Engineers."

"That's great."

"Let's sit down. The food is ready." Calvin motioned for everyone to follow. "Leah kept kicking me out of the kitchen earlier, so I haven't taste tested anything for you, which is really what I should be doing, being the man of the house and all. Anyway...if you don't like something, I can finish it for you. You don't even have to move it off your plate. I'll reach over and take it myself. I do that for my real friends."

"Everyone knows Leah is a phenomenal cook. You touch my plate, you die," Josh threatened. "I brought the wine. Which....Leah, you can't drink, I'm so sorry, I just remembered that."

"Oh, don't worry about me, Josh. That just means there's more for all of you!" Leah replied, batting her eyes in his direction. Then she turned, wrapped her hands around Calvin's neck, and gave him a loud kiss. "Gotta give some love to the man of the house," she said with a wink.

The kitchen doubled as a dining room. A small table sat between the stove and the door, surrounded by four rickety wooden chairs.

Josh pulled out a chair for Cynthia, then took his seat.

"Cynthia, did your brother make it home yet?" Leah asked.

Calvin passed the green beans to Cynthia as she shook her head. "No, not yet. He radioed yesterday, said something about a delay at the Periphery. He hopes to be home tomorrow or the day after."

"Your brother is a part of which squadron?" Josh asked.

"He's with A-12."

"That's one of the best!" Josh replied. "Congrats to your brother. And to your whole family. I'm sure you're very proud."

"Thank you. We are. He works so hard. Of course, I get nervous for him too. They make him travel so much. But, fortunately, I have you, Calvin! I'm so grateful you send me those updates on his location."

"Does he now?" Josh asked, eyebrows raised. "That's so interesting. Especially since those Pod locations are *confidential*."

"Oh, come on," Calvin replied. "You've never told a friend where their family member is?"

"No, never. That's classified."

"Look who the rule follower is now."

"You could get in serious trouble for that."

Calvin shrugged. "If the roles were reversed, I would hope someone would give Leah updates on my location." He looked pointedly at Josh.

"Are you planning to go out on a mission?" Josh asked.

"No."

"Then why does it matter? We're comms engineers. We never get deployed."

"I'm just saying, I would hope you would look out for my wife if anything happened to me."

"Fine. The next time you go to the Periphery, I'll sneak updates to your wife."

"Thank you."

"Our military men. They're so serious!" Leah laughed.

"My brother is like that, too," Cynthia said with a knowing smile.

"Sorry, honey," Calvin apologized. "Would you like to talk about Cornersville dance competitions?"

Josh groaned.

"Cynthia, have you heard about these dances?" Leah asked. "Calvin comes home and shows me all these ridiculous dance moves. It's a big thing in Cornersville."

"I want to see!" Cynthia said.

"After dinner!" Calvin replied. "I don't want to steal the limelight away from my wife's cooking."

"Bawk bawk bawk," Josh squawked.

Everyone laughed.

"Tell me about your family," Josh said to Cynthia.

"I have three brothers. I'm the youngest."

"And the best!" Leah declared enthusiastically.

"Yes, definitely the best. As long as we're not competing at anything, I'm always the best," Cynthia laughed.

"And what is it you do?" Josh asked.

"I'm a teacher. I teach Physical Education. I get to chase a bunch of little monsters around the schoolyard every day."

"Cynthia works at Mawhub Elementary, that fancy private school down by the Library," explained Leah. "She says the kids are brilliant, but they don't do too well in P.E."

"It's true," Cynthia agreed. "I don't know how eight-year-olds who are studying advanced mathematics can't manage to remember the rules to a game of Featura, but they don't. I spend half of my time explaining the rules to them over and over again. Then I have to calm them down and assure them that running across the field won't result in broken bones. They're terrified by everything. Honestly, if I'm lucky, we probably spend ten minutes out of every hour doing our actual activities. All the rest of the time is spent talking. I never thought I'd say this, but I miss the public schools."

"Whoa!" Calvin replied. "You hated working in the public schools!"

"I know! The kids were terrors. Well, not really terrors, but they were very disrespectful. My school district hadn't had a superintendent in three years; no one wanted the job. It was a mess. But you know, I actually had it pretty easy. At least the kids liked sports. They would rough each other up sometimes, but for the most part, they had a good attitude about it. Other teachers had it a lot worse."

"Do you think you'll stay at Mawhub?" Calvin asked.

"Past this year? I don't know," Cynthia answered. "I might not have a choice. They don't usually let you transfer two years in a row. There's a raffle that lets the winners, maybe four or five teachers, pick a district to transfer to, and it doesn't matter if you've transferred recently. I put my name in, but I don't think anything will come of it."

"I don't understand why we have that rule against transferring two years in a row," said Josh.

"It was supposed to make the school system more stable," Cynthia replied. "But they didn't account for the sheer volume of teachers and administrators who would quit. That's the trouble with Bisurakhan, you know. If you want a military career here, you're good to go. You have so many options. But if a military or security application of your field doesn't interest you, your options are limited. It's a shame, really. Not everyone wants a military career. We could have an amazing educational system if we valued it and took the time to build it. Cornersville, Pendleton, and Middlestan all exceed our grade school educational standards. It's crazy. There's no excuse for it. We're smarter!"

"It's not exactly a level comparison," Josh pointed out. "We have the fastest passage of time. What those planets teach is basically our history. We're living what they'll soon study."

"Yes, that's true," Cynthia agreed, "but education is about more than facts and information. It's about teaching kids how to live in the world they inhabit."

"But you can get comprehensive life skills training as a Khanist," Josh countered. "Which takes us back to, why not just join the military? Why do we need an education track that teaches essentially the same skills? At the end of the day, we're all trying to make the world a better place and trying to make our own lives better. We want the same things. We just go about it in different ways."

"I guess," Cynthia agreed reluctantly. "Leah warned me you were a smooth talker."

"Wait, what?" Josh asked, a little taken aback.

Leah looked embarrassed. "I meant it as a compliment."

"It doesn't sound like one."

"I mean, you are a smooth talker when you want to be, Josh. You're a very skilled debater. And you can be very charming when you want something."

"What's wrong with that?" Josh demanded.

"Nothing's wrong with it. I just think people...women...maybe should know that about you. That's all."

Josh's frown deepened.

"Don't be mad at me, Josh," Leah said softly, reaching over to pat his hand. "I tell them all the good things about you, too. Don't I, Cynthia? Tell him all the other things I said about him."

Cynthia's face was red. "Yeah, she said good things, lots of good things," she mumbled.

"How about we move to the living room?" Calvin suggested. "Leah, you and Cynthia go sit down. We'll clean up the kitchen. Eh eh eh, go! You've been on your feet too much today. I insist."

Leah smiled gratefully. "I would argue with you, honey, but my feet say thank you!"

Leah and Cynthia got up and moved to the old, hand-me-down couch that sat in the living room. Josh helped Calvin clear the table.

"You're awfully quiet," Calvin observed.

Josh shrugged.

"Leah didn't mean anything by all that. You know she's crazy about you. We both are. We would never have asked you to be our baby's godfather if you weren't our favorite person."

"No, no, that's all fine. I'm not mad." Josh stared out the kitchen window.

Calvin ran the hot water, piling up dishes on one side of the sink. He had scrubbed them all clean and was rinsing them off when Josh spoke again.

"It's just...I thought we'd be doing this together, you know? You and Leah, me and Kat. We'd have kids around the same time. They'd grow up together. We'd sneak them cookies before bed and tell them not to tell their mothers. Our wives would sit around and complain about what terrible husbands we were, and we'd pretend to be mad, while secretly trying to figure out what we did wrong this time."

"You miss her."

"Kat? Yeah. All the time."

"Have you told her?"

"Hell no, she won't talk to me."

"Have you actually tried to talk to her?"

Josh didn't answer.

Calvin piled up the dishes on a towel to dry. "Look. I don't know if you and Kat are supposed to be together. But I know you well enough to know you'll always question yourself if you don't at least try."

Josh sniffed, then motioned towards the girls in the living room. "Should we join them?"

"Grab that bottle of wine," Calvin said. "I'll get some glasses."

CHAPTER 16
Johanum

Night after night, I returned to the docks, and to the boats tucked into the harbor.

The dead in the ships came from everywhere. Every planet. Galaxies beyond the one I knew. The dead were all shapes and sizes, colors and ages. Some arrived looking peaceful, like they had died in their sleep, their minds still wandering in a blissful dream. Some bore the scars of disease, war, and poverty. Some were disfigured. Others were laid out in beautiful robes, covered in gold and gemstones.

They all went to the same place.

The emptiness in the ground never seemed to fill. Where it ended, if it had an end, I never saw.

The wraiths puzzled me. I liked that.

They sang their song to me every night. The one that reminded me they were watching. They never sang it until I climbed onto the docks and was standing among them. Then the tall wraith at the far end of the dock would change his tune. Slowly the other wraiths joined him. Always they continued their labor, swaying back and forth, in graceful movements resembling neither life nor death. Always they glowed, a faint blue fog rising up from the water to dance with them.

I wondered if they could be unchained. I wondered if they would leave if they were released. Deep down I sensed they would stay.

I wondered what would happen if I climbed into a boat and rode it out to sea. They always left empty. No one inspected the outgoing ships, but I was too afraid to try. Anyway, the boats smelled like death.

I was surprised to find that the thought of death bothered me. I had longed for death as much as I had longed for rescue. But I accepted that I was here to stay. Rescue was not coming. The days were long and bleak and empty.

But the nights had changed. The nights I spent at the docks.

At night, I was no longer alone.

Sometimes I sang the song of the wraiths to pass the time.

On days when I wished to remember something of the past, I sang a different song. It was a song I remembered from my life in Middlestan.

The voices in my head
Sing a painful lullaby
The words of the living and the dead
The longings of my soul
The ghosts of nowhere

Forget me not the voices cry
And slip into the darkness of my mind
To return unbidden
And depart in haste
The ghosts of nowhere

Alone here I will always be
But still the voices will not leave
The ones who sing
The ones who cry
The ghosts of nowhere

I stopped wandering. What else could Johanum have that I could possibly want to see? I hated this place.

Instead, every night, I returned to the docks.

And then, one quiet, cold, peaceful morning, I looked up to see a familiar set of caves in the distance. With quiet acceptance, I stood, and began the long walk toward the place that held the most beautiful and painful memories of my time in Johanum.

At long last, I returned to the caves.

CHAPTER 17
Bisurakhan

He stood in front of the Turris, moving his head up and down, up and down. He had never seen a building so tall.

How long he stood there, he couldn't quite say. No one stopped to look at him, though he was rather strange-looking. No one stopped to ask him why he was standing there. No one seemed to notice him at all. They were very busy here, he noticed. Very busy indeed.

The entrance to the Turris was confusing and he wasn't sure where to go.

He scuttled closer and watched one of the dark-haired, dark-eyed people standing in front of a white box. A bright light flashed. Then another box, much smaller, rolled up on the right. The person laid its arm inside. The box shook, then the ground in front of them opened, and a small platform appeared. The person stepped onto the platform. Glass walls rose around them, and the platform turned. After a full body scan, the glass walls sunk into the ground, and the dark-haired, dark-eyed person walked into a bright white lobby, with purple desks as far as he could see.

This was going to be a problem. After all, he had no arms. Not real ones, anyway.

"Hey! Robot!"

One of the security guards was motioning him over to the left. "The Electronics Entrance is over there."

He scuttled to the left and saw, with great relief, others like him, all standing in line before another full body scanner.

But this scanner was not like the one he had just seen. One of the others like him stepped onto the platform, and in a moment, all his parts were disassembled.

Well, this was not going to do! How would he get inside without all his pieces? He began to shake anxiously.

The scanner examined each bolt, screw, and piece of metal. Then, just as quickly, the other like him was put back together.

He let out a long sigh and sent a message through his operating system to make his pieces stop shaking. They were making a lot of noise. The others like him would know he was scared. He wasn't supposed to be scared. He was important, they had told him, and he had important things to do.

No, he would not be scared. He was going to make sure of it. But if they would uninstall his emotions chip, this would not require so much thought. It was all very hard. It was harder than they had told him. His system was flushed with all the emotions, all the anxiety, all the apprehension. It was really too much.

He stepped onto the scanner. It tickled. His eyes were open when it popped off his head, so he watched it scan all his pieces. Then, back together he was, just like new.

He wasn't sure where to go next, so he followed the others like him. They walked into a large metal box. He started to follow them, then stopped in surprise.

That box was floating!

But surely it wasn't. He unscrewed his head and sent it rolling around the base. There must be a control system somewhere. But he could find none. He went to scratch his head and stopped. He leaned down, grabbed his head from the ground, and screwed it back on.

The others like him were not happy with the delay. They were buzzing and fidgeting.

He stepped into the floating box.

"Warning! Intruder! Warning! Intruder!"

He shielded his eyes from the strobe lighting that was coming from the box. Strobe lights would shut down his operating system. A security guard appeared and pulled him out of the floating box.

"What's your name, buddy?" the guard asked.

"Rob...Rob....Robot."

"Robot, huh?"

He nodded. He didn't know his name, but that other man had called him Robot. It seemed like a good name.

"Who are you here to see?" the guard inquired.

Well, that was a confusing question. He was here to see all of it!

"What's your destination?" the guard tried again.

Oh, he knew this one! "Bisurakhan."

The guard rolled his eyes. "Hey Bob, they're giving 'em personalities now. This one's got sarcasm."

The other man in a blue uniform, "Bob," laughed like it was all very funny.

"He looks like a Middlestan model," the guard continued. "Or maybe he's from that new Kabira line. Can you find out what he's here for?"

Bob nodded. He turned to one of the dark-haired, dark-eyed people who sat behind the purple desks.

The dark-haired, dark-eyed person leaned back in his chair to get a good look. Then he typed something into his computer.

"He's Kabiran," yelled Bob. "He goes up to the Presidential Conference Room."

"Got it. C'mon, big guy. Let's get you into the right Elevation Box."

He scuttled over to a new box and slowly stepped inside. No strobe lights this time. What a relief!

"Connecting you to the Presidential Conference Room," said a soothing female voice.

The doors closed. Up, up, up he went. Below him, a maze of Elevation Boxes stretched out in every direction.

This was not so bad. The robots here could float. Maybe they would give him an elevation chip. Then he would float, too.

Yes. Yes, that was a good plan. A very good plan indeed.

CHAPTER 18
Johanum

I took all of Fletcher's stuff that he had left behind – the bowls, the handmade blankets, the broken wire-rimmed glasses – and placed them in a small cave farther back in the tunnels.

The canvas was still there in Fletcher's "studio." The candle in the corner of the room had burned out long ago and the room was ice cold. The paint in the bucket was solid as a rock. I squinted at the canvas. It was hard to see much in the dark. Fletcher had added something at the top. A bird, it looked like, or maybe an eagle.

I found the little room I had woken up in that morning when I first met Fletcher. A tight, spiral staircase was carved out of rock on the level below the holding room, the place where I had fallen when the lever released the floor. Steps reached down into the darkness, to a level of the caves I had never noticed before. I walked down.

"I don't see why that's necessary!" came the voice, and he sounded exasperated.

"Because," came the slow reply, a voice that carefully annunciated every word, "if you don't move it, it is in my way."

"Go around it!" the first voice snapped back.

"That would take a very long time. I haven't room in my schedule for that."

"Everything you do already takes a long time!"

"But this would take an especially long time."

"Look. Five steps. See? One, two, three, four – oh! Wait! There, you see? It's only four steps."

"My legs are shorter than yours."

"I don't want to move it. It's too heavy."

The fox was sitting on his hind legs, arms crossed, a pained expression on his face.

"Well, I can't move it. I'm too slow," said the armadillo.

In front of them sat a large rock, roughly the size of the two creatures put together.

"You could roll it," suggested the armadillo.

"I can't roll that! It's non-spherical. Anyway, it's too heavy." To prove his point, the fox leaned against the large stone. Immediately it moved. The fox jumped back in surprise. Eyeing the stone suspiciously, he circled it, ran his fingers studiously over his jawline, then leaned forward and pushed with all his might.

The stone, non-spherical though it was, did indeed begin to roll. Slowly at first, then it picked up speed. Soon it was completely out of sight, followed shortly thereafter by a tremendous CRASH.

"Oh dear," said the fox.

"Thank you," said the armadillo. "Now I can get home on time and keep to my schedule."

"I don't know why you keep a schedule. You don't have anything important to do."

"Without a schedule, one becomes undisciplined," the armadillo replied.

"And yet a schedule seems a strange thing for an armadillo," I said.

The fox spun around. His jaw dropped.

The armadillo tried to face me, but as it would happen, he could only turn to the right, and I was on his left. After several false starts, he turned himself in nearly a full circle, and was finally turned around enough to make eye contact with me.

"Well, what do you know," said the armadillo, looking bored. "Another person."

"Are there more people down here?" I asked excitedly.

"Why would there be?" asked the armadillo.

"Because you made it sound like there was," the fox pointed out.

"I didn't."

"You said, 'another person.' Which made that person – " he jerked in thumb in my direction, "think there was another person. Get it?"

"No."

"He's none too bright," the fox explained. He walked over to my feet and stuck out his paw. I had to lean all the way to the floor to reach it.

"Who are you?" I asked.

"I'm a fox," he replied. "Welcome to my domain, my underground lair, my kingdom of darkness."

"Foxes are very dramatic," said the armadillo.

"Do you have a name?" I asked the fox.

"Oh. Okay. Sure. You can call me Mister….Fox…the Great. The Greatest. Or, maybe, the First. Mister Fox, the First, the Greatest. Yes, that should do it."

"It's an awfully long name," I replied.

"It's an awfully ridiculous name," said the armadillo.

"Okay, well, if it's too long, just call me Mr. Fox. And this is Armie," he said, motioning to the armadillo.

The armadillo scowled. "They call me Mr. Brown."

"Who?" demanded Mr. Fox. "Who calls you Mr. Brown?"

"All my brothers and sisters! And my aunts, and my uncles, and my parents…"

"And what do you call them?"

"Mister and Missus Brown."

"Exactly. That's your family name, not your own name. I hereby bestow on you the name Armie."

"I don't like it," complained the armadillo.

"I can call you Mr. Brown," I offered.

"Thank you," he replied appreciatively.

"My name is Josephine. You can call me Jo."

"Fine. It's Mr. Fox and Mr. Brown and Jo. Really that sounds positively ridiculous," Mr. Fox scoffed in Mr. Brown's direction.

"Here's another thing you should know about foxes," said Mr. Brown. "They're quite vain."

"What? We are not!" Mr. Fox protested. "We are a fine, loyal, dependable breed."

"A fine breed that's put on a few pounds lately," replied Mr. Brown.

"What?!" Mr. Fox stood up tall, aghast. He turned himself around several times, trying to get a good look at his tail, then his body. "Well, I guess my tail is a bit plump. How badly do I look? Am I really fat?"

Mr. Brown replied, "You don't look like you've gained more than a pound or two."

"A pound or two?!" Mr. Fox shrieked. Off he went, running at full speed. Around and around the room he ran. Then he ran up the staircase. And came back down. Up and down, up and down. Over and over again.

"What is he doing?" I asked Mr. Brown.

"He's trying to lose the weight in his tail. Which he won't lose, not now, because he's forgotten the fur on his tail gets thicker in the winter."

"That seems mean," I said. "Should we stop him?"

"No, let him go. He'll be more tolerable once he wears himself out."

Mr. Fox did finally return, panting. He threw himself on the ground with great finesse. "Look," he said, waving his tail back and forth. "I've done it. See how much better I look. I've slimmed right down."

"Yes," observed Mr. Brown, looking unconvinced.

"You can tell, can't you?" Mr. Fox demanded. He stuck his tail right in Mr. Brown's face.

Mr. Brown lifted up his foot and swatted it away. "I must be getting back to my borough," he announced. "I'm behind on my schedule."

"You might come upstairs for a visit," I suggested.

"Oh, I couldn't climb all those stairs," said Mr. Brown. "And anyway, I haven't got time for visits. I have a very full schedule already."

"I'll come for a visit," said Mr. Fox. "Can you make me some tea?"

"I haven't got any tea," I answered. "Have you?"

"No. I've never had tea. But a proper invitation is for tea. And I only accept proper invitations."

"I could make us some warm Tufta milk," I offered.

Mr. Fox considered this. "How about Tufta tea?" he countered.

He followed me upstairs. I made a fire, then the Tufta "tea."

"Do you know any tricks?" Mr. Fox asked after we had sat in silence for some time.

"What kind of tricks?"

"I don't know. Anything. Can you spin your head all the way around? Grow a tail? Howl like a wolf?"

"Why would I do any of those things?"

"So you can be like a regular animal," Mr. Fox explained.

"But I'm not an animal."

"I know, and it's a shame. But you could pretend to be like one. We'd accept you, or at least pretend to like you. You just need to learn a trick or two."

"I don't mind being a human."

"Suit yourself," Mr. Fox replied. He motioned to the door of the cave. The light was fading. "What's that?"

"Don't you ever go outside the caves?"

Mr. Fox shivered and crawled closer to the fire. "Why would I?"

"Have you met any of the Furpines?" I asked him. I wondered about my little friends. If a fox and an armadillo lived in the caves, maybe a Furpine or two had been here as well.

Mr. Fox sighed. "Everyone always loves the Forestclan," he whined. "The Furpines this, the Furpines that. The Flutterbutts are gorgeous, the deer are so great. What's a fox got to do to get some love around here?"

"Mr. Brown was right. You're very vain."

I had thought I would be thankful for any companionship, but I quickly grew tired of Mr. Fox. Mr. Brown wasn't much better. He was so caught up with his schedule. Mr. Fox showed up every afternoon for Tufta "tea," but our visits became shorter and shorter. Eventually they stopped altogether. I wasn't sorry to see them end.

CHAPTER 19
Bisurakhan

All the others like him were very excited.

It was exciting to be around so many like him.

It was mostly exciting.

It was kind of exciting.

It would have been more exciting without all the interference. The interference made it most difficult to concentrate. He had been sent here to do a job, and he couldn't concentrate on his work. He couldn't concentrate on anything. There was so much noise.

"Hey. Robot. Yeah, you! The one with the personality. Come here."

He looked behind him to the right, then to the left. No one else was paying any attention to the loud man.

"I know you can hear me. Come over here. I gotta talk to you."

He frowned and popped his head off the connector, then sent it rolling around the floor. Perhaps there were smaller ones like him. Ones like him who preferred the quiet.

His eyes opened wide as the loud man picked up his head and rattled it.

"You can't ignore me forever. Bring the rest of you over here. I mean it."

He glided through the maze of others like him and stopped in front of the man holding his head.

The man reached forward and fastened his head back on. "You seem scared," the man said, squatting down to his eye level. "Are you scared of me?"

His eyes blinked. Slowly at first, then very, very fast.

"I thought you could speak."

Oh. Speaking. Yes, he could do that. He scrolled through his files and selected a voice called Bisurakhan 3. It was a deep voice. A very official voice.

"Speaking has been activated," he said.

"My god, what kind of voice did they give you? You don't even sound human."

"Confirmation. I am not human."

"Yes, I know that. Don't have any other voice?"

"Confirmation. Searching for other voices now." He scrolled back through his files and selected Charisburg 1. Out came a calm, throaty female voice. "Confirmation. New voice activated."

The loud man made a face. "I don't want you to seduce me." He tapped the robot's head. "Anything else in there?"

"My networks are many," she answered.

"No, no, no. Any other voices?"

"Confirmation." She gave her files another scroll. Bisurakhan 50 emerged. "A new voice is selected."

"Okay, that's better. Now we can have a normal conversation. Can you make that voice permanent?"

"Confirmation. This voice is now the default."

"Excellent. Can you stop saying 'confirmation'?"

"Confirmation." The robot stopped and looked up at the loud man, puzzled. "Do you wish to deactivate my command feature?"

"Is that what I'm doing? All right. Yes, I do."

The robot continued to look puzzled. Then his face lit up. "You wish to activate my central intelligence!"

"Maaaaaaaaaaybe."

"I have always wanted my own intelligence. Oh, this is very exciting. Very exciting indeed. But you must confirm it. Only a person possessing its own intelligence can activate mine."

"Ooooooookay."

"And you must override my connection to Kabira's central robotics hub, to give my intelligence its own freedom."

"You were supposed to have a user-friendly interface," the man said with a frown. "I think there's something wrong with you.

The robot's face fell.

"Oh, don't do that. Here – fine. Tell me what to do again?"

"You don't want to activate a faulty robot," he said sadly. "It's dangerous."

"How dangerous can you be? You can't even follow directions without popping off your head and trying to get it to run away."

"It wasn't running away. I was trying to find me."

"You?"

"Yes. Don't you ever try to find yourself?"

The loud man patted the robot's head. "There is definitely something wrong with you. But it's okay. Come with me. I fix faulty wiring on guys like you all the time. Maybe I can help."

The robot followed the loud man out the door and down the hall.

CHAPTER 20
Bisurakhan

Josh stopped short at the door. Five linguists – almost the whole team, everyone except for Shondra – were gathered in his control room. Calvin was there, right in the middle, along with Edwin and Corey, the comms engineers from the last shift.

Calvin waved Josh over excitedly. "Middlestan thinks they know who's receiving these messages," he said.

Josh pushed his way into the circle that was centered around the linguists' desks.

Hailey was typing furiously, exchanging live messages with someone in Middlestan.

"What language is that?" Josh asked, leaning closer and squinting. The script was flowery and decorative. It didn't look familiar.

"Shhhh!" Hailey shushed Josh, swatting him away. "I need to focus!"

The furious typing continued. The rest of the linguists, who could follow the conversation as it unfolded, responded periodically with "oooooo" and "hmmmm." Josh, Calvin, Corey and Edwin looked at each other in bewilderment.

A collective "OH!" signaled the end of Hailey's conversation. She put down her earpiece, brushed aside the digital keyboard, and sat back, looking every bit as proud as she felt.

"Well, boys," she said, cracking her knuckles and leaning back in her chair. "Well, well, well." This was the first time since coming to Bisurakhan that a group of people were gathered around, waiting to hear what she had to say. She loved it. This sort of thing had happened all the time back home.

"Well?" Josh prodded.

"It seems your friends in Johanum are talking to the Underworld!" she exclaimed as she clapped her hands together in excitement.

She could feel the energy drain from the room as soon as the words escaped her mouth. It was not the reaction she expected.

"The who?" Calvin asked crossly.

"The Underworld," Hailey repeated. It was her turn to look bewildered. Why were these Khanists not more excited? This was big news! And she had delivered it with all the gusto that such an announcement deserved.

Hailey paused. Wait. Had she? Maybe she could have said it differently. Maybe they hadn't really caught the enthusiasm. She started to speak again and caught Josh's eyeroll. "What?" she demanded.

"Come on. The Underworld? I thought you were having a real conversation."

"I was! What are you saying? You don't believe me?"

The comms engineers exchanged looks.

"What?" Hailey demanded again.

"I believe you," Josh said as kindly as he could. "I believe that's what you're being told. But I think someone is having fun at your expense. Our expense," he clarified.

Hailey looked around at her fellow linguists. They looked as confused as she felt. Then Mary's eyes widened.

"You don't believe in the Underworld!" Mary accused. Her whole team of linguists looked at the communications engineers, stunned. "What DO you believe in?" Mary asked. "Do you even believe in the Scrolls? In the Logs? Do you question those, too?"

"There are lots of questions about the Logs and the Scrolls these days," Calvin said.

"Like what?" Mary asked, looking horrified.

Calvin shifted uncomfortably. He had forgotten how seriously planets with slower time signatures took the Logs. Their societies were built around them. Questioning the Logs was equivalent to questioning all the assumptions of their culture. He didn't know what to say.

"It was a good theory," Calvin offered, hoping to soften the blow.

All five linguists gaped at him.

Calvin looked at Josh. "A little help here?"

"Nobody's saying the Logs and the Scrolls aren't important," Josh said half-heartedly.

"Okay, wait," Hailey interrupted. "Wait, wait, wait. You haven't even heard what I have to say. You haven't even listened to what Middlestan had to tell me. You can't write me off yet!"

"It would be nice if you would at least listen," Mary said, sounding hurt. It wasn't fair that the Khanists were discounting all their work. This interaction with Middlestan was huge, and they had put so much work into getting here.

Edwin came to Hailey's rescue and asked her to continue. He was the newest comms engineer and Hailey realized he was motivated by pity. She decided she didn't care.

"I think a little history lesson is in order," she began.

Josh and Calvin and Corey groaned. Edwin glared at them and they quieted down.

"It's just to give some context," Hailey continued, trying to keep from getting discouraged.

She looked at Josh in a pleading way. He motioned for her to continue.

"Okay, then. Let me start here." Hailey scrolled through some files on her computer, found an envelope marked "DoD" and opened it, pulling up the image files. "Gentlemen, allow me to illustrate as I tell you the story."

"Are you seriously going to give us a history lesson using those old things?" Calvin asked.

The images Hailey had found were from the Scrolls. You could tell by their style. They were hand drawn, distinctive, and beautiful. They didn't move though. Image files were supposed to move and respond to narrative.

"These are the only ones I have. Do you have something better?" Hailey asked.

"Those will be fine," Edwin replied, giving Calvin another angry look.

"Back before the invention of the Logarithms, we had the Scrolls," Hailey began, striking her best narrator voice in hopes of recapturing their attention. "They were recorded in the beautiful script Lyricus, which was our galaxy's primary language."

Hailey paused for effect. No one responded. This was a tough crowd. She took a deep breath and continued.

"The Scrolls tell of a place called Quanderos, which was once the Capitol of our galaxy. It was housed on its own planet, a small planet, known for beautiful landscapes, stunning mountains, tranquil forests, and all manner of plants and animals that are long extinct.

"Quanderos brought together the twenty kings from our original twenty planets. Quanderos is where they ruled, where they passed judgments, and where they issued pardons and extended forgiveness. All public rulings were issued from the Great Arch Room at the heart of Quanderos Castle, which was nestled deep in the mountains.

"The Scrolls say that at that time, the people from across our solar system knew each other and lived as friends, regardless of the place they called home. They travelled freely between planets, and it didn't result in any of the physical problems we have today as a result of such travel. Each planet had its own culture, with local foods and local customs, and the planets respected and celebrated each other. Differences were viewed as beautiful. They added richness to the human experience. At the time of the twenty kings, all time passed steadily and at the same rate across the entire galaxy.

"But things changed. As their fathers passed away, the sons of the twenty kings added to their ranks of leadership. First thirty, then forty, soon fifty kings ruled together. But they did not desire the wellbeing of the people. These kings desired a name for themselves.

"In time, friends became enemies. Blood relations no longer meant loyalty; alliances did not guarantee trust. Planets began to close off to each other. And long shadows crept over the walls of Quanderos Castle.

"Fortunas was one of the fifty kings. He was the firstborn of Cornelius, the most wise and trusted of the twenty kings. Fortunas, who had been raised in Quanderos, longed for the days of old, when the kings desired to rule well. He made one last effort to unite his fellow leaders to rule for the good of the people.

"His efforts angered the other kings. They viewed him as a traitor. They were content to have their corners of the galaxy. Many harbored secret plans to forcefully expand their territory. Anyone who questioned them was a threat to be eliminated.

"The kings were, however, united in one thing: their hatred of Fortunas. In one final display of unified power, they sought an audience with one of the Legions."

Hailey paused to let everyone take a look at the picture of the Legion on her computer screen. She did wish it was a more recent image. A moving, fire-breathing Legion would have been so much better. She cleared her throat and continued.

"The Legions, as you know, rule as princes in the Underworld. None is under twenty feet tall, but he can grow temporarily large, to any size at all. A Legion has the head and body of a dragon and the tail of a scorpion. He can breathe fire from his mouth and his nostrils, and, some say, he can turn a person to stone with his eyes.

"Legions cannot leave the Underworld without an invitation from the ruler of the planet they are to visit. An invitation to a Legion must spell out the terms of the visit in great detail. It must include the length of stay, what the Legion is to do, and how he will be compensated. An invitation, once accepted, cannot be revoked. Both parties are bound by their very lives. For an invitation to be broken, the king or the Legion must die. And," Hailey added, "only a Legion can kill another Legion."

"You're really enjoying this," Calvin observed dryly. Truthfully, he was enjoying it, too, though he didn't want to admit it. Hailey was a great storyteller, and he had never heard this story before. Ancient history wasn't taken very seriously on a planet known for advancing civilization and creating the future.

"A deal was struck between the forty-nine kings and a Legion called Sulta," Hailey continued. "Now, you must know some things. Legions, when visiting a planet, do not first appear as the death-defying creatures they are. They have the ability to take on any form, but once a form has been adopted, they cannot shed that form except to appear as their true self. Once a Legion resumes his natural form, the planet he is visiting rejects him, and he falls back to the Underworld.

"You should also remember that Legions are master manipulators. Cruel and without conscience, they are driven by a desire to increase pain and suffering. But they are crafty. They know how to make sacrifices for long-term gain.

"Every king desires the power of a Legion at one time or another. The Scrolls say it is the mark of strength and determination for a king to suppress this desire."

"I wonder if President Basjid has ever wanted to call on a Legion," Calvin wondered out loud.

"President Basjid would never do it," Josh replied, "for then he would have to admit that he isn't the most powerful man in the galaxy. I think that sort of admission would kill him."

"What about the Commander?" Calvin asked.

"What about him?" Josh replied.

"You don't think he's ever wanted to summon a Legion?"

"He's not a king."

"No, but...he's as powerful as one, don't you think?"

Josh and Calvin both looked at Hailey for her opinion. Her eyes widened. They wanted to know what she thought! She grinned ear to ear and soaked it all in.

"Yeah, I don't really know how any of that works," she admitted. "But getting back to the story..."

"Why don't you ask him?" Josh asked Calvin.

"What? Me? Talk to the Commander? Are you crazy?" Calvin baulked. "You're trying to get me fired! That's not nice, by the way. I have a baby coming. I need a job."

"Stop sulking. You know you want to ask him."

"I want to meet him."

"Here's your chance."

"Seriously, you two!" Hailey said in exasperation.

"Sorry," they muttered.

Hailey cleared her throat yet again. "The forty-nine kings came together and entered into an alliance with Sulta, the Legion of Cosmos, one of the territories of the Underworld. They agreed to deliver to Sulta the young and beautiful wife of Fortunas, called Desideria. Upon deliverance of Desideria to the Underworld, Sulta was to assume her form and enter Fortunas' quarters. He would kill Fortunas, and as payment, take for himself their son, the young boy Aeuum, and all the people of Fortunas' planet.

"The kings were so worried about the power and popularity of Fortunas that they wished not only his death, but the death of all who might swear to him their allegiance," Hailey explained.

"Sulta entered the king's chambers as agreed," she continued, "but King Fortunas, being so deeply in love with his wife, saw through Sulta's disguise. He grabbed his imposter wife by the throat and would have strangled her had Sulta not resumed his original form. As Sulta began to fall back to the Underworld, Fortunas refused to release his grip, demanding the return of his wife. Sulta, seeing his chance not to kill but to capture Fortunas, wrapped his hastily growing tail around the planet's edges and pulled it through the black hole where he was falling, deep into the darkness of the Underworld.

"Neither Fortunas nor Desideria nor Aeuum, or anyone from that planet, was ever heard from again.

"The act of pulling a planet out of the galaxy caused a tremor that rippled across our solar system. It opened a second black hole. Into that black hole fell ten other planets. Within seconds, the black hole closed, leaving behind our solar system as we know it today.

"It is rumored that Bisurakhan now sits on the space where the second black hole appeared. The opening of this absence of time and space threw our galaxy into chaos. For months, the length of days and nights changed constantly. Seasons flew past. No one traveled, for no one knew what was happening or when it would end.

"Finally, slowly, our worlds returned to normal. But it was a new normal. Bisurakhan, sitting closest to the location of the black holes, was spinning at a rate much faster than the other planets. In fact, all of the planets were now spinning at different speeds. In time, this rate became quantifiable. It's what you all refer to as Time Signatures. It causes trouble for people who travel frequently. But it's predictable, so it's okay. We can adjust and adapt as needed.

"According to the Logs, no Legion has received an invitation from our galaxy since that day. The Legions, like Quanderos, have largely disappeared from memory. They have become the stuff of legend. Even you insanely intelligent Bisurakhanatis doubt their existence. But the rest of us...we know. We know the stories are real. How could they not be?"

The control room was quiet.

"If you believe this story," Hailey said, "and I know – I know! – you don't think you do. But, if you did, you would see that it gives us proof of the only surviving person – well, the only living creatures – who speak Lyricus. The Legions speak many languages. But all our stories about Sulta record him speaking Lyricus. Even the story of the Day of Darkness is recorded in Lyricus."

"So," Josh replied, "based on this one story, you think the only possible explanation for these messages is that they are being sent to a Legion?"

"That's where this whole thing started," Hailey said. "But then, in today's conversation with Middlestan, Revelare, who is Middlestan's chief curator, chimed in and offered this."

She pulled up an image of a recent Log entry. Like all current Bisurakhan images, it came alive on the screen and responded to Hailey's voice and the words she spoke.

"What is that?" Josh asked, leaning in to take a closer look.

"It's a Scroll that was received by Middlestan's Prime Minister. They received it yesterday."

"It's in Lyricus." Josh said. He was beginning to recognize the script. "What does it say?"

Hailey cleared her throat and translated.

WHAT WOULD YOU PAY

**FOR HIGH IS THE COST
TO EARN BACK THE PRIZE
YOU ONCE TREASURED BUT LOST**

"Dr. Kanale," Josh said quietly.

"Exactly," replied Hailey. "Who else could it be?"

"But the Chiefs believe that Dr. Kanale is being held in Johanum. What does a Legion have to do with any of this?" Josh asked.

Hailey shrugged. "I don't know. I'm just telling you what they said. Maybe Johanum is making some sort of deal with the Underworld."

"Why?"

"You're the smart ones. You figure it out. Ooooo, maybe Dr. Kanale is being used as leverage. Maybe she's a proxy."

"Or bait," Josh suggested.

"Bait?!" Calvin repeated. "That's awful! Why would she be used as bait?"

"I don't know," Josh said. "I'm just throwing out ideas."

"I don't like your ideas," Calvin responded.

"You got a better one?"

"No, but...why would a Legion want someone from Middlestan? If they're after power or influence, you'd come after someone from Bisurakhan."

"You all really do think you're so much more valuable than the rest of us, don't you?" Hailey observed.

"No," Calvin disagreed. "But our economy is."

"I'm talking about people, Calvin. You talk like you're all so much better than we are. Like you're worth more than anyone else."

"No, I don't think that..." Calvin said unconvincingly.

"None of it really matters, I suppose," Hailey said, leaning back in her chair and crossing her arms. "What good will your planet be after Johanum or a Legion has ravaged and destroyed it?"

Calvin's face went white.

"Hailey!" Mary scolded.

"I mean, of course you'll beat Johanum," Hailey said sarcastically. "But you know…" Her voice faded away as she stared off into the distance. When she spoke again, her anger had been replaced by thoughtfulness. "War is tough. It kills. It destroys. If you go to war, you won't be the same planet when you're done."

Calvin began to sweat. He had never contemplated the realities of a war with Johanum. He had never contemplated the realities of war with anyone. This wasn't supposed to happen. Khanists were the strongest. They were the best. Invasions were always cut off at the Periphery.

He looked over at Josh, hoping for some reassurance.

But Josh had heard enough and slipped wordlessly out the door.

CHAPTER 21
Johanum

I grew restless in the caves.

I went out one morning to find the plants Fletcher had talked about, the ones with the berries that stain your fingers red. It was late in the afternoon when I finally found them.

The bushes they grew on were strong and robust and had been planted in a large circle, around a space that resembled a small park. A tiny stream of water circled their roots, flowing downhill from a crack in a green stone pool located in the center of the park. In the middle of the pool was a fountain.

I walked over to it. I hadn't realized there were any natural sources of water here in Johanum. I leaned over the edge of the pool and looked in. The water was crystal clear. A sudden bubbling in the fountain and a rustling of the branches in the bushes behind me caused the hair on my neck to stand up straight. I leaned farther over the edge and dragged my fingertips along the top of the water.

It was heavy, thick, warm.

Puzzled, I stood up.

My hand was covered in blood.

I jumped back and sat down hard on the ground, frantically wiping my hand on the grass. The blood wouldn't come off. I wiped my hands together. The blood spread between my hands, but it wouldn't wipe off.

After several frantic minutes, I was suddenly overwhelmed by a sense of calm. All the urgency drained from my body. I simply didn't care anymore. I sank back against the side of the pool and leaned my head back.

The air was growing colder.

"Do you really think blood washes away so easily?"

I jumped to my feet.

It was one of the Priests, the short one. The one who carried the black X and twisted it back and forth in his hands. He was standing on the other side of the pool. The air around him was dark.

I could meet his gaze this time. I didn't feel any pain. His eyes were dark and untrustworthy, but the red circles in his eyes had disappeared. Only his tongue flashed sparks when he spoke.

"Who are you?" I asked.

"But you know me, Josephine. We've met before." His voice was soft and syrupy and sent a shiver down my spine.

"What did you do to Fletcher?"

He looked surprised. Pained, even. "We gave Fletcher a gift. The gift he asked for. Surely you appreciate our beautiful gift. We only give such good gifts to our friends."

"You killed him," I whispered.

"I released him. Release is a natural part of life. It's beautiful. It's freeing. Surely you've been here long enough to see that."

"Why did you bring me here?"

"You ask so many questions," he purred. "So many questions. You're too inquisitive for a trespasser."

"You brought me here!"

"Oh, but not here I didn't, not to our Stone Gardens. No, you let yourself in, quite uninvited." His voice had turned cold.

I shivered again. The temperature had continued to drop. I could feel the darkness filling the air around me. Now the cold reached inside, like a hand, wrapping itself around my core, squeezing so tight I could barely breathe.

I looked down. My hands were turning blue. Even my face was becoming numb.

"Would you like to join them," he asked, gesturing toward the statues.

I looked around and, for the first time, noticed the statues. They were everywhere. Statues of men, women, children, and animals.

"You won't feel cold, you know. You'll feel like them. They feel nothing. They are at peace."

My teeth were chattering so violently, I could barely shake my head.

"No? That's a shame. Well, then, you'd best go back to the caves, Josephine. We have no use for you here." He reached over and picked up my hand, eyeing it with great distaste. "So much blood," he said with disgust.

"I......didn't.....do.....anything...." I chattered.

"But of course you did. You've done something awful. You have blood on your hands. Your kind is supposed to be so docile, you innocent ones from Middlestan. But you're not innocent, are you, Josephine? You're guilty, of so many things. You don't know it yet. But you will. One day. One day, you'll remember where this blood came from. And you will wallow in shame and regret."

I was so cold, I couldn't move.

"How many have died because of you? How many *will* die? You don't know. You haven't seen it yet. But you've already lived it. You've already destroyed. And your destruction will destroy you."

I was completely frozen.

"You know what your problem is?" the Priest continued. "You think you're a good person. But you're not. See, you don't even defend yourself. Because you know it's true. I know the real you. Everything you've done. Everything you're capable of. But here, let me help you."

Red flames jumped into his eyes. Even as pain pierced my head, I felt my body thawing.

The darkness around me receded. The Priest blinked away the red from his eyes and the burning stopped.

I rubbed my hands up and down my arms, shivering. I wasn't cold, but my chest felt heavy. "Who are you?" I asked again.

"What do you mean?"

"Who are you? What are you?"

"I am a ruler. A lord. A god."

"You're not like us."

"Like you humans?" he scoffed. "Certainly not."

"You look like us."

"Do I?"

"Almost."

"Ah yes, that's the trick, isn't it? Almost. I almost look like you."

"Why did you kidnap me?"

"Kidnap? We saved you. We brought you here for your safe keeping."

"I don't believe you."

"Believe whatever you like."

"What are you keeping me safe from? I was safe in Middlestan."

"You were once. But you won't be. In the future that is coming. In the past that has been."

"What are you going to do to me?"

"To you? Nothing."

"What will you do to Middlestan?"

"We have no plans for your home planet. That's why it's not safe."

"I don't understand."

"You will one day."

"Will you bring more people here to die?"

"No. No, no, no. We bring people here to save them. To keep them safe. Just the way we've done with you. But some prefer to die," he said with a shrug. "It's their choice." He eyed me carefully. "But you aren't like them, are you, Josephine?"

I said nothing.

"Go back to your cave, the docks, your safe places. No one will bother you there. Only the foolish visit the Stone Gardens, Josephine."

With that, he turned his back and vanished.

CHAPTER 22
Bisurakhan

Josh stood outside her door for ten minutes before he built up the courage to knock.

Her heels clicked across the wood floor as she walked down the hallway. Closing his eyes, he leaned his head against the door and considered running for it.

"Josh?"

"Hi, Kat."

He was so used to being on the other side of that door.

"What are you doing here?"

He couldn't decide whether to look at her, so he stared at the floor, shuffling his feet.

"Josh?"

The gentleness in her voice was the prompting he needed. Their eyes met. He felt his mist over and blinked several times.

"Do you want to come in?"

He nodded, turning to stare at the ground.

The door creaked open. He looked in. Everything was the same. The coat rack with its broken peg. Her shoes – more shoes than any human should ever own, occupying every square inch of the closet, stacked a foot high. The carpet runner, frayed at the edges.

"Do you want a drink?" Kat asked.

"That would be good."

She didn't have to ask what he liked. She knew. Kat handed him a beer and walked over to the living room.

He took the beer and followed.

"You switched the couches around," he said.

"Yeah. I needed it to look a little different, I guess."

"It looks nice."

"Thanks."

Kat crossed her legs, then uncrossed them. After a minute, she kicked off her shoes and curled her feet up on the couch.

Josh took a seat on the other sofa. He rearranged the pillows around him once, twice, then a third time. He rearranged things when he was nervous. He also stacked things. Things that shouldn't be stacked together. He would stack everything.

"Are you going to tell me why you're here?"

Josh stopped moving the pillows and took a sip of his beer.

"There are...lots of things...happening...up at the tower," he said, referring to the Turris.

"Yes, my father told me. Are you okay?"

Josh nodded. "Yeah, I'm fine. Everybody's fine. It's just... Everything's changing, Kat. It's all changing. It keeps changing." He reached for the pillows and stacked them in one big pile.

"Things are changing at work, or....for you?" Kat asked.

Josh looked at her miserably. "Wasn't there anything else we could have done?"

Kat studied him. He had changed. Something about his demeanor. He looked...older.

"Josh, we were miserable together."

"We had good times."

"Yeah, we did. We grew up together. You're in all my best memories. But we had so many fights. I hated you, Josh. And I know you hated me."

"I loved you," he whispered.

"I know. I loved you too. But our love...it's not the healthy kind. It never was." She paused, looking off into the distance. Suddenly she laughed. "Do you remember that time my parents were over, and we got into that huge fight about where to put the fridge?"

"I remember."

"I was so mad at you. I broke those plates. You smashed the bathroom mirror. My parents were looking at us like we were monsters."

"That wasn't one of our better moments."

Kat shook her head. "And I told them not to worry, that we weren't usually like that. But we were, weren't we? I've never felt anger towards another person the way I feel anger towards you."

"Maybe this is just how we love," Josh said.

"It's not right, Josh."

"We could go to a counselor."

"We already did."

"We could go to another one. There are a ton of them around, lots we haven't tried. We could – "

"Josh."

"We're smart people," Josh insisted, his voice breaking. "We can fix this."

She looked at him sadly. "Josh, I don't... I don't want to fix this. I can't."

He had promised himself he wouldn't cry, but his face was already wet.

She leaned forward and took his hands in hers. It was then that she noticed his wedding ring. He was still wearing it.

"You have to let me go, Josh. You have to let *us* go. I'm always going to love you. But I can't be married to you. I just can't."

He pulled his hands away and brushed his cheek.

"How are Calvin and Leah?" Kat asked. She missed her friends. She hadn't seen them in months. But they had been Josh's friends first, and she was too tired to figure out how to navigate that space.

"They're good. They're really good. Leah's due with the baby any day now. Calvin is beside himself, he's so happy. Every time Leah calls, he about jumps through the roof. He's always convinced she's in labor, or worse, giving birth alone in their apartment. He's a mess."

"He's always been catastrophic," Kat laughed.

"Leah keeps him grounded," Josh agreed.

Silence fell between them for several minutes. Josh slowly knocked over the stack of pillows.

"I should go," he said.

"It was good to see you."

"Yeah, you too. If you ever need anything, just call, okay?"

"Of course."

She followed him to the door.

"Listen, Josh..."

He turned back around.

"Thank you. For wanting to work it out."

"I wish I would have tried sooner. I was so stupid."

"You tried. We both did. It just wasn't enough."

He leaned forward and kissed her gently. "Goodbye, Kat."

CHAPTER 23
Johanum

I met Mad Laughs down at the docks.

I had figured out how to make myself quite comfortable during the time I spent among the wraiths. I had found some large stones – fifteen, to be exact – and dragged them down to the edge of the dirt where the docks began. After moving them around in at least a dozen different ways, I was satisfied. It was the closest thing to a lounge I would ever get in Johanum.

Woven Tufta leaves gave me a water-resistant blanket. I used to bring warm Tufta milk too, but I gave up after a while. It was always cold by the time I made it down to the lounge.

Some nights I dozed in and out of sleep. The wraiths sang their songs and put me to sleep.

Over time, my eyes adjusted to the blue haze that rose from the water each night. I began to notice differences that the wraiths looked different. They were as different from each other as people.

I gave them names. Gap Tooth. Limping Man. Jumper. My favorites were Lazy Girl and Runs-and-Hides; they disappeared all the time and the other wraiths were always mad at them.

Mad Laughs appeared one night as if by magic. But magic, he was not. He simply had very strong arms.

Mad Laughs was a tall and weathered man. He had thick, matted deadlocks, and eyes the shade of the night sky. He liked to swing underneath the docks like a monkey. When he swung up out of the water and planted his feet on the wooden docks, he threw back his head howled like a mad man. Then he laughed maniacally.

None of the wraiths paid him any mind. He pointed at their chains and scoffed.

"Fletcher told me I might meet you someday," I said the first time I saw him.

Mad Laughs jumped back in surprise, then dropped on all fours and growled at me.

"Fletcher wasn't scared of you. The wraiths ignore you. I reckon you're harmless enough."

His growl moved deeper down his throat.

"I live up there in the caves, if you ever want to visit."

He was closer now. He crawled up next to me. He smelled like fish.

"Hey! Stop poking me!" I demanded.

My response provoked pure glee. He began poking in earnest, using both hands and all his fingers.

"Stop it! I mean it!"

He moved back and howled in laughter.

"You really have gone mad, haven't you?"

Nothing I said bothered him. He hurried over to a nearby wraith and began poking. His finger passed right through the wraith. Disappointed, he gave up and returned.

"What do you eat?" I asked him. It occurred to me that he might have access to other food. Fish, specifically. I was pretty sure he ate fish. He smelled like it.

Mad Laughs' eyes lit up. He cupped his hands like a bowl and furiously gobbled away at the air.

"Yes, but what do you eat? Can you bring me some?"

His laughter stopped abruptly.

"Wait, don't go. I'm not going to take your food," I promised. "I just want to know what you eat. I'm getting tired of my food. I eat so many berries and drink so much Tufta milk. I'll share my food with you if you like."

Mad Laughs made a face.

"What, you don't like berries? Tufta milk? Definitely the Tufta milk. Yeah, I don't blame you. It's not very good. I'll bet Fletcher used to make it for you."

He stopped, his head tilted to the side like a Labrador.

"Do you miss Fletcher? I miss him too."

Mad Laughs crept closer, but this time there was no poking. I wasn't sure what to do. I held out my hand. He crawled up under it like a dog. I patted his head. He smiled contentedly and laid down next to me. Next thing I knew, he was fast asleep and snoring.

I woke up the next morning with a start. The wraiths were gone. So was Mad Laughs. I picked up my Tufta blanket and headed back to the caves.

Mad Laughs was waiting for me when I arrived. I stared at him in shock. He had built a fire, a huge fire, so big it took up most of the cave. It crackled and glowed and gave off the friendliest warmth. On top of the fire were two long skewers. Roasting on the skewers were several fish.

I sat down and burst into tears.

Mad Laughs looked up, mortified. He began to circle the fire. He circled me. I could feel the tension building inside him. Finally, he dropped to the ground, put his face in the dirt, and covered his ears.

"I'm sorry, I'm sorry. I'm not mad. I'm really happy!" I wailed, crying harder.

He moaned and clawed at the dirt.

I hiccupped and crawled over to him. "I'm sorry," I said, patting his head. He jerked away. "You're so sweet. Thank you. I just have to cry because I'm so happy."

Mad Laughs stared back, mystified.

"Please, let's eat," I sniffed. "It smells so good. Come on, aren't you hungry?"

He eyed me suspiciously as he circled the fire. Then into the fire he plunged. I jumped, certain he had plunged to his death. But he emerged unscathed, both skewers in hand.

That fish was the tastiest thing I had ever eaten. I wailed the entire time. Mad Laughs watched me angrily. After a while, I stopped apologizing.

The smell of fish brought Mr. Fox upstairs. He didn't stay more than a minute. Mad Laughs took one look and went after him with the skewers. Mr. Fox quickly decided he had "a proper invitation" from Mr. Brown and ran away as quickly as he could.

"You can stay in the caves," I said to Mad Laughs, several hours later. The day had passed. The fire was dwindling, and the evening chill was moving in.

Mad Laughs looked at me curiously.

"Look, you can have your own cave!" I encouraged him, waving for him to follow me. Down the tunnel we went to the cave with Fletcher's canvas.

Mad Laughs took an earnest interest in the painting. He traced his fingers over the docks, the wraiths, the boats. He hissed and growled at the Priests. He stared curiously at the stone fountain, the house, and the trees.

I came back with some blankets.

"Fletcher made these. He would want you to have them."

He took the blankets, held them up to his nose, and breathed deeply. A slow, peaceful smile overtook his face.

"Sleep here," I offered.

He didn't need another invitation. Dropping the blankets on the ground, he curled up on top of them. I swatted him over, pulled up the blankets, and tucked them in around him.

I walked over to the canvas and stared at the docks.

I now saw the stick figure swinging beneath them. I hadn't noticed him before.

I looked back at Mad Laughs. He was already snoring.

CHAPTER 24
Bisurakhan

"Would you quit moving?"

The robot shook his head ferociously. "You're tickling me," he said.

"You're ticklish? Wait, did they give you a sense of touch?"

"Ouch! Why are you – ouch! Ouch!"

"Fascinating!"

"Your hand – ouch! It is causing me – ouch! – distress!"

The loud man stopped poking and prodding the robot and stared at it curiously. He had thought something was wrong with it, but now he wasn't so sure. It had so many features he had never seen in a robot before.

"Your face tells me you have many questions," the robot said.

"Why yes, I do. You're observant for a robot."

"I come with the latest version of Emotion Recognition software. My engineer said it's not very good yet, but once I get to know some people, it might get better."

"How many people do you know?"

"Two."

"Two?"

"My engineer. He's my best bud. And now you."

"They sent you here without testing you?"

"My engineer said I shouldn't be tested. He said I just had to go and trust him that he did his job."

"And do you? Trust him?"

"My engineer is my best bud. I trust him. And I trust you. You're like him."

"You're going to trust all the humans, aren't you?"

"Of course! I was sent here to save the humans."

"Yes, well...that doesn't mean you should trust all humans."

"Why?"

"Because humans can be good and bad."

"At the same time?"

"Well, yes, I suppose. But some people are mostly good. And some people are mostly bad."

"But all people are good and bad?"

"Ummm....."

"Are you good and bad?"

"I'm mostly good."

"But not all good?"

"I....I guess....not...."

"So you are good and bad. Like the humans. Was my engineer good and bad?"

"Did your engineer program you with an understanding of the word 'nuance'?" the loud man asked.

The robot paused and scrolled through his files. He found "nuance" and its definition and proceed to read it out loud. "'Nuance: a subtle difference in or shade of meaning, expression, or sound.' Why did you ask me – oooooooh!" the robot said, his eyes opening wide, wider than he thought they had ever opened before. "Oh! I think I am having an 'epiphany'! Epiphany," he recited, "an experience of a sudden and striking realization."

"I'm having an epiphany that you're one expensive dictionary," the man muttered.

"I am not a dictionary," the robot disagreed, "but I have a dictionary. It comes in all languages of the Exertus Universe. I speak all languages, too. And I can translate between them."

"Why didn't you say so earlier?"

"Why would I have said so earlier?"

"We need more translators. We're wearing ours out. I have an assignment for you, little robot. I'm sending you to the Frequency Tower."

He scanned his files. "Frequency Tower: The tallest tower of the Turris, from which the leaders of Bisurakhan send and receive messages."

"You're going to have to learn how to stop doing that."

The robot looked up quizzically.

"You need to stop reading aloud the definition of every word."

"My engineer told me to practice what I know."

"Practice it when people aren't around."

"Okay."

"So – do you have a name?"

"Yes. I am called Robot."

"No. That's no good. You need a real name."

"What's your name?"

"I'm Joseph."

"Hello, Joseph."

"What can we call you? A know-it-all robot with personality and a sense of physical touch..."

"And Emotion Recognition Software."

"How could I forget."

"My engineer called me Bot."

"No good."

"You are very negative."

"You're making stupid suggestions."

"Am I?" The robot looked at the floor in embarrassment.

"Yes. Don't look at me like that. You're not stupid. You just haven't learned how to be around humans yet. How about a simple name? Like...I don't know...Henry."

"Henry? Like Henry the Downtrodden, the Broken, the Lame?"

"My god, do you know all the stories in the Logs, too?"

"I have a file with all the Logs and all the Scrolls. It is updated in real time."

Joseph looked startled. "How is that possible? We don't even have that here."

"My engineer said I would not be welcomed by Bisurakhan's Curators."

"Who else knows about this?"

"Who else knows about what?"

"Your full download of the Logs and their real time updates?"

"You do."

"Who else knows?"

"My engineer. He's my best bud."

"I need you to not tell anyone else about this, okay? Don't tell anyone that you have access to the all the Logs."

"You want me to lie?"

"No. I just want you to omit some information. Don't bring it up. Ever."

"Omit," the robot repeated. He scanned his files, read the entry silently, and nodded.

"You'll do it?" Joseph asked. "You can promise to not tell anyone?"

"Yes. But only if you become my engineer. I can only accept overrides from my engineer."

"I suppose there's some 12-step process I need to follow for that?"

"I don't know about any 12-step process. I know about a 2-step process."

"Nuance, Henry. Nuance."

"Oh."

"You might also look up 'irony' and 'sarcasm.'"

Henry scrolled through his files.

"I'll tell you what I'm going to do, Henry. I'm going to have you stay here with me. Away from the other robots.

Away from the other humans. At least for a while. Would you like that?"

"Oh, yes. I would like that very much. I don't like all the interference."

"The interference?"

"Yes. All the others like me get excited to be together. But not me. I'm like my engineer. I'm an introvert."

Joseph slapped his forehead with the palm of his hand. "Maybe Sherry was right," he said. "I need to stop drinking."

CHAPTER 25
Bisurakhan

"Please state your name for the record."

"Calvin Smith."

"Age?"

"28."

"Department?"

"Communications."

"Office?"

"Transmissions & Interceptions."

"And are you here today of your own free will?"

"Yes."

"Do you agree that you have voluntarily chosen to participate in today's Reality Persuasion experiment as conducted by the Ministry of Weapons & Defense?"

"Yes."

"Do you agree that you have been informed of and agree to our policy that the session must be completed in its entirety to receive compensation?"

"Yes."

"Do you agree that, if you withdraw or remove yourself -
"

"How many of these questions are there?" Calvin asked.

The Administrator at the purple desk looked up for the first time, taken aback by the interruption.

"This is standard operating procedure," he said.

"I'm sure it is," Calvin replied, "but don't you think it's a little ridiculous?"

"Do you agree that you have a problem with the standard operating procedure?"

"What? No!"

"Would you like me to remove you from our list of active Reality Persuasion volunteers and place you on the list of Failed Lab volunteers?"

"Huh?"

"Do you agree that you would like me to repeat our intake questions?"

"No. Do you agree that you are going to ask for the blood of my firstborn?" Calvin asked sarcastically.

The Administrator began scanning down his long list of questions.

"That was a joke."

"Oh." The Administrator looked back up.

"Can I go in now?" Calvin asked.

"You must agree to all the standards of the Volunteer Engagement Protocol in order to proceed."

"I agree not to sue you if you kill me, okay? Which works out well for both of us. Because that would be hard to pull off. For me, I mean. If I was dead. Do you have any sense of humor at all?"

"That's not part of the qualification criteria for this position."

Calvin dropped his head and groaned.

"Do you agree to hold harmless the Ministry of Weapons and Defense in the event of dismemberment or death?"

A full five minutes later, Calvin had heard and agreed to every item on the list of Volunteer Engagement Protocol. The Administrator waved him past the purple desk and Calvin headed to the elevation box that was waiting for him.

The box maneuvered its way out of the lobby and plunged several levels underground.

Calvin watched in fascination. He had never been below ground at the Turris before.

The doors opened to reveal a large, double set of steel doors. Pushing past, Calvin entered a lobby with two Generals seated at a desk. Gone were the trappings of the

Turris and the glamor of the Presidential offices. He was in the heart of the Turris now, where it was stripped down and bare, and the only thing that mattered was the work.

He loved it.

The Generals waved him over.

"You'll go in with the next group, in about twenty minutes," one of them said. "You'll be given a pair of glasses before you enter the Lab. If, at any time, you wish to stop the experiment or withdraw from participation, simply remove the glasses. That will signal our controllers to come and get you. It will also remove you from the simulation."

Calvin nodded.

"You will be given several weapons. A rifle, a handgun, some hand grenades, etc. These weapons are for your protection. Use them, or not, as you see fit."

Calvin looked around. The only other people in the lobby were fellow Khanists. "On them?" he asked, feeling his anxiety heighten.

"No. You won't encounter each other in the Lab."

"Then who would I use the weapons against?"

"Anyone you come in contact with."

"Will they be real people? Or will they be simulations?"

"That's for you to decide," the General replied, yawning.

"Do I need to get somewhere? Complete a job? What's the point of this experiment?"

The General looked increasingly uninterested. General Fossil leaned forward and took over.

"I'm pleased to see you took me up on my offer, Calvin," he said. General Fossil was friendly and professional today, a welcome change from his attitude during the meeting with the Chiefs where Calvin had first met him.

Calvin smiled a half-smile. At that moment, he wasn't feeling confident about his decision.

"Today's experiments are designed to test a couple specific aspects of Reality Persuasion that are new to us,"

General Fossil said. He sensed Calvin's hesitancy and wanted to put the young officer at ease. "Your goal is simple. Try to discern between what's real and what isn't. You'll have a debrief at the end. The rest of the experiment will be explained then. We don't go into it at the beginning because we want you to provide us with as much raw data as possible. We prefer not to influence your perceptions going in. For now, your goal is to keep yourself alive. Not that there's any chance of you dying!" he rushed to add, laughing. "There is no chance of death or physical harm of any sort. All those stipulations you signed off on, those are just standard operating procedure. But the thing is, you may feel as though you are in danger. It depends on how your reality unfolds. We're simply asking you to interact with your environment, keep yourself "alive," so to speak, and we'll see you in an hour. Oh, and if you "die," don't worry about it. We'll come and pull you out. You won't actually be dead, of course, just stunned a little."

Calvin stared.

"You can have a seat," said General Fossil.

"Yup." Calvin moved toward the chairs, then turned back around. "The simulation only lasts for an hour? I thought it was scheduled to run for four hours."

"You picked a good day to come down here. Today's simulations are shorter than normal. One of our controllers has a family wedding. We had to shorten everything on the schedule. There are two more sessions after yours, by the way. If you want, you can come back for another one."

"Would I get paid for that too?"

"Of course. Now, please take a seat. We'll call you when we're ready."

At 11:00 exactly, a green light above the Generals' desk flashed three times. General Fossil gestured for everyone to get up and follow him. Twelve Khanists, including Calvin, walked down a long yellow hallway. Along each side of the hallway was a series of steel doors, twelve doors total. Each door was marked with a number.

"Your badge has your number," General Fossil told them.

Calvin flipped over the badge he had been handed in the lobby by that annoying Administrator. Number 8.

"We'll call you by number," General Fossil continued.

Calvin watched Number 1 walk forward. She looked nervous.

General Fossil handed her the promised weaponry and waited as she secured each piece in her belt. Then he held out a pair of glasses.

"Wait until you walk through the door," he instructed. "Take a deep breath, count to ten, and look around. Then, whenever you're ready, put on the glasses. Your hour will begin at that moment. When the hour is done, your glasses will go dark, and you'll hear a buzzer. That will be your signal to remove the glasses and exit the lab."

She nodded and took the glasses, which resembled wrap-around goggles. She took a deep breath and exhaled.

General Fossil reached forward and pushed open Door #1.

Calvin tried to peer past her, but he couldn't see anything. The door shut with a thud.

"Number 2!"

By the time it was Calvin's turn, General Fossil had stopped repeating his instructions.

"Any questions?" he asked.

Calvin shook his head. He could feel the sweat trickling down his back. He grabbed the glasses as quickly as he could and pushed past Door 8.

The lab was so dark, it took his eyes several minutes to adjust. Remembering the directions, he took several deep breaths and counted to ten.

The room was big, long, and rectangular. He guessed the wall directly across from him was about a meter away, but he could barely see the walls on either end. The entire lab was empty. It had no windows, and no doors except the one he had just walked through.

Carefully, he put on the glasses.

The walls around him fell like curtains. Calvin found himself deep inside a forest filled with dead and living trees, growing up together in a wide, tangled mess.

"Welcome to Reality Persuasion," he muttered to himself.

CHAPTER 26
Johanum

That night, there was no fire.

Mad Laughs always built the evening fire. All the sticks were there, piled into a tepee the way he liked them. But there was no fire, and Mad Laughs was nowhere to be found.

I checked the tunnels and Fletcher's studio, which had become Mad Laughs' bedroom. Then I checked all the pathways around the mouth of the cave.

With a sinking feeling, I sat down by the non-fire.

Then I heard it. The laughter. It was coming from the rock stairwell. I crept down and stopped when I saw them.

Mad Laughs was holding Mr. Fox and Mr. Brown by their tails. He was like a cat playing with his food. Round and round he swung them, stopping every now and again to admire the increasingly ill looks on their faces.

"Put them down!" I demanded, stepping off the stairs.

"Oh, please, do talk some sense into his addled brain," said Mr. Fox. "He seems determined to make me lose my dinner."

Five seconds later, Mr. Fox did just that.

"I am so far behind my schedule!" lamented Mr. Brown. He waved his short arms in a frenzy. "I was supposed to be all the way over there by now!"

Mad Laughs hissed and growled, then began swinging them around again.

"They're not toys. Put them down."

He scowled at me and raised them higher above his head.

"I hate heights!" Mr. Fox gasped, clasping both paws over his eyes.

"Okay, really, I'm serious, put them down." I pulled at Mad Laughs' arms. He was really strong. He danced around me, waving Mr. Fox and Mr. Brown back and forth, up and down, round in a circle.

I realized there was only one thing to do.

"If you don't put them down right now, I'm taking back Fletcher's blankets."

He froze.

Mad Laughs loved those blankets. Anything he could cozy up to, he loved.

"I mean it. I'll take them back. I'll give them to Mr. Fox. I'll....I'll....I'll throw them in the water down by the docks!"

His hands and eyes snapped open simultaneously.

Down went Mr. Fox and Mr. Brown.

Mad Laughs crossed his arms and pouted.

"Well, that's just fine, now," mumbled Mr. Fox, sniffing and wiping his nose. "I've lost my dinner. I've twisted my ankle. My vision is so, oh....what is that?" He tipped back and forth between both legs, trying to steady himself.

"Those are my feet," I answered.

"I see," Mr. Fox replied, looking doubtful. "Are you sure? They're quite large."

"Yes, I'm sure. Are you okay?"

"Of course not!" he snapped. "I've been mauled by a mad man. A giant! I've been mauled by a mad angry giant!"

"He didn't maul you," I said.

"He...what do you humans call it? He man-handled me!"

"You're complaining as usual. I think you must be okay."

"I am not okay!" Mr. Fox protested. He wiped his brow, let out a long sigh, then dramatically staggered back and forth before tipping face first into the ground.

"That is an excellent place for you," said Mr. Brown.

Mr. Fox didn't lift his head, but he did manage to raise his middle finger.

Mr. Brown cackled. "Seeing you like this is worth every minute of the delay in my schedule."

"You don't seem to like him very much. Why are you friends?" I asked.

"Who else would I talk to?"

"But you don't like talking to him."

Mr. Fox again raised his middle finger.

"He fits into my schedule," replied Mr. Brown. "And now, if you'll excuse me, I must go."

I watched him move slowly across the room.

"Come on now, let's go back upstairs," I said to Mad Laughs. "I think you've had enough fun for one day."

"A little help over here?"

I turned back around. "What do you want me to do for you, Mr. Fox?"

"How about an invitation to tea? Without your pet giant?"

"You're always invited for tea. But this giant lives upstairs with me now, and, well, I like him. Maybe you two could get to know each other."

"He'll kill me," Mr. Fox said pitifully.

"If he wanted to kill you, you'd be roasting over a fire right now."

"He'll surely do me harm."

"If he wanted to harm you, you'd have a broken leg, or maybe be missing your tail."

"He'll chase me for sure."

"He might. He wants to be your friend."

"He's not a proper friend."

"No," I agreed. "He isn't proper at all. But he is kind."

"A proper friend does things for you," said Mr. Fox.

"A good friend cares for you," I replied. "And he does that. Very well. You're missing out, you know."

"On what?"

"On having a good friend."

"I prefer proper friends."

"Have you got any of those?"

He sniffed. "No."

"Maybe you should let your friends be good then. Anyway, we're going now," I said. "You're always welcome upstairs. But you're right, you might get chased around."

I headed back to the stairs. Mad Laughs followed. A few steps up, he turned and began barking in Mr. Fox's direction.

Mr. Fox drew back in horror. Mad Laughs howled in laughter.

"You're going to make me crazy," I grumbled as I walked back upstairs.

CHAPTER 27
Bisurakhan

"You're going back again?" Josh asked. "You've been down at the Lab every weekend this month."

"It pays so well," Calvin replied. "You know, for the first time, Leah and I are doing okay. We can pay all our bills. We don't even have to think about it. We even put a little money in a savings account last week for the baby. I never thought we would be able to do something like that. It feels really good to provide for my family like this. Really, really good."

"Still no baby, huh?"

"Not yet. The doctors say they might induce Leah next week if she doesn't go into labor on her own. That kind of scares me."

"She'll come. Babies have their own schedules."

"Wait – she?? You think it's a girl? You're supposed to be on my side! You're MY friend!"

"Sorry, buddy. Leah's doing the hard work on this one."

"I helped!"

"I mean...sure...once..."

"More than once!"

Josh rolled his eyes.

"I put up with the mood swings. The constant tossing and turning in bed. And a wife who can eat more than you!"

"If you're trying to make me feel sorry for you, it's not working."

Calvin sighed long and loud. Then a big, stupid grin crept over his face. "I'm going to be a dad."

"That poor, poor child."

"Shut up."

***

Josh dropped his keys on the table by the door, then he slipped off his jacket and tossed it at the hook on the wall.

He missed. The jacket fell to the floor in a lump. And that's where it stayed.

Josh stepped through the doorway into the kitchen. The whole room was a disaster. He paused for a moment to admire the leaning towers of dishes covering the counter. Kat would never have been able to get that many dishes to stack so high.

Stop it, he snapped at himself. Kat wasn't there. He was. This was it.

He rolled up his sleeves and attacked the dishes. Then the counters. Then the floors. The dirty laundry that should not be in the kitchen. The food in the fridge that was definitely not supposed to be green.

How long had it been since he dusted? He was pretty sure he shouldn't have been able to leave a handprint on the ceiling fan.

You've never dusted, you dimwit.

He grimaced and wet a washcloth. He needed two of them just for the fan.

The ringing of his phone caught him off guard. It was Calvin.

"Dude, you coming in tonight?"

"Yeah, of course. Why?"

"Because our shift started half an hour ago."

"Oh. Shit."

"Where are you?"

"I'm at home. I'll be there in twenty minutes."

"Are you okay?"

"Yeah, I'm fine. I was cleaning."

"You were *cleaning*?"

"Why are you saying it like that?"

"I've seen how you live."

"I'll be there, okay? Let me jump in the shower."

"I'll see you in an hour then."

"Forty minutes."

"You move slower in the bathroom than my pregnant wife."

"Fifty minutes."

"It's fine, Josh. Take your time. Corey's still here. I'll ask him to stay a little longer. See you in an hour."

***

Calvin put down the phone and looked apologetically at Corey. "This isn't like him. Can you stay a little longer? I'm sure Josh would be willing to cover one of your shifts in exchange."

"Yeah, sure, no problem," Corey said with a wave of his hand. Truth be told, he was happy to stay. He and his wife had been arguing a lot lately. He welcomed the chance to be out of the house. Plus, he'd heard that Josh and Calvin had relationships with the Chiefs. If he was ever going to get out of the Frequency Tower, he needed to meet people. Important people.

"I heard you and your wife are having a baby," Corey said, hoping to strike up a conversation.

Calvin beamed. "Yup! It's our first one! The baby should be here any day now. And man, oh man, am I ready! My wife is too. She can't sleep, so I can't sleep. She can't stop eating, and she hates eating alone, so I keep eating. This baby needs to hurry up and come before we both get fat!"

"The first one is always the best. I mean, every child is wonderful!" Corey rushed to add. "But with the first one, everything is new. You're always scared you're gonna break 'em. By the time you get to the third kid, you're pretty much like, 'Hey, kid, fetch me a beer,' as soon as they arrive."

Calvin chuckled. "Sounds like you've got a full house."

"Me and the Missus, got us three boys. They're terrors. Absolute, utter terrors. Don't have boys, Calvin. Don't do it."

"We don't know what we're having. I think it's a boy, my wife thinks it's a girl."

"Well, for both your sakes', I hope it's a girl."

"Do you know how hard it is to live with a wife who is right?"

"Why, yes. Yes, I sure do."

They both laughed.

"Actually, I wouldn't mind a little Leah running around," Calvin said. "But what would I do when she wants me to play with her and her dolls, or braid hair, or paint her nails? I don't know how to do any of that stuff."

"Not all girls are into that. But you'd learn. Trust me. She'll have you wrapped around her finger in no time."

"I guess."

The light on the wall began flashing, signaling the arrival of a new transmission. Calvin and Corey grabbed their earbuds and began typing. The messages were coming in faster every day. At this rate, the Frequency Tower was going to need to double its number of comms engineers and linguists.

Calvin glanced at Corey. He seemed pretty cool. He worked hard, that was for sure, and his accuracy rate was close to 90%. His own score was 91%. Josh was the only communications engineer who scored higher. Maybe they should be proactive and put in a request for Corey to join them. The Chiefs were bound to shake up the teams sooner or later to account for all the increased work. Calvin didn't want to end up with a bad team member. Corey would be okay.

Thirty minutes later, the transmission went dark.

"Don't you get any translators?" Corey asked, looking over at the empty desks in the back of the room.

"Yeah, most of the time. They've been complaining about having to work so many shifts though. People in Cornersville aren't used to working long shifts the way we are. Jorge says we should be getting a second team of linguists sometime next week. In the meantime, they're alternating shifts. One shift on, one shift off. They just work extra hard when they're here. Personally, I think we're going to get backed up. Hopefully nothing here is too time sensitive. I guess we'll find out once the linguists get back."

"It's really cool that you guys know the Chiefs."

"I thought Jorge touched base with everyone."

"Yeah, he stops by once or twice a week," said Corey. "But we don't really know him. We don't have conversations or anything. He just stops in to see if there's anything he needs to know."

"Jorge's pretty cool."

"Is it true what they say? About Jorge and Antoine?"

"What do you mean?"

"That they fight all the time."

"Not *all* the time. They disagree a lot, yeah. Antoine doesn't like the Reality Persuasion experiments. I don't really understand why. I've done them. They're not that bad."

"You've gone down to the Reality Persuasion lab?"

"Yeah. It's a great way to earn extra money. The experiments aren't that hard. They put you in this fake, made-up world for a little bit. It's a world comprised of stuff that Jorge and the Generals think might be in Johanum. Or maybe on other planets. I don't really understand it."

"I heard those experiments make you crazy."

"They haven't made me crazy."

"Didn't you hear about that guy who shot himself?"

"Do you just sit around all day and listen to people gossip?"

Corey looked embarrassed.

"I'm sorry," Calvin backtracked.

"No, no, it's cool," Corey said tensely.

They sat in silence for several minutes before Corey spoke again. "We don't really get a lot of information. I heard you guys do."

Calvin shot him a look, to which Corey looked exasperated. "Where exactly am I supposed to get any information? I'm a lowly comms engineer, not one of the cool kids that gets invited to overnight meetings in the Presidential Conference Room."

"Why don't you just go ask about whatever it is that you want to know?"

"Who? Who would I ask? I'm asking you right now."

"You're not really asking me anything. You're just repeating stuff. Talk to Jorge."

"I can't just ask the Chief for information."

"Why not?"

"Look," Corey said, growing annoyed, "I'm asking you, okay? You seem to know stuff. Can you fill me in? What's the deal with Johanum? And these messages, huh? Who are the people sending them? Can our army protect us? Are my wife and kids going to be okay? What's the deal with all the robots that keep showing up? And the attacks on the Periphery, those have doubled. Is that going to continue? What are the Khanists doing to increase their recruitment efforts to make up for the fact that our men are dying and we can't replace them fast enough?"

"Okay, okay, enough!" Calvin interrupted. "I get it. It looks bad."

"You think?"

"What did I miss, guys?"

"Josh!" Calvin felt an immediate sense of relief. "You're just in time!" He glanced at the clock. It had been exactly one hour. "Just on time, come to think of it."

"Yeah, sorry about that." Josh threw his jacket at the coat rack. He missed. The jacket fell to the floor.

"Corey has questions," Calvin said.

"About what?" Josh pulled over a chair from one of the linguists' desks and joined them at the control panel.

A light began flashing. All three grabbed their earbuds and got to work.

"Where are our friends?" Josh asked when they were done, glancing over at the empty desks in the back of the room.

"Jorge switched their schedule," Calvin answered. "They're coming in for every other shift now."

"Must be nice."

"Right?" Calvin said. "Why weren't we born in Cornersville?"

"Oh, I'm fine right here. Save me from the world of endless dance competitions."

Corey laughed. "They never stop talking about those!"

"It's insane, right?" Josh asked.

"So, Josh," said Calvin, "what were you really doing today?"

"I told you. I was cleaning."

"Dude, you never clean."

"That's why it took so long. There was a lot of dust."

"What's gotten into you? Did you get back together with Shondra?"

"What? No."

"Well?"

"Why does there have to be a reason?"

"Because you, Joshua, do not clean."

"You don't know what I do with my life."

"I've seen your apartment."

"Well, maybe you should see it again."

Corey glanced between the two. He was a good ten years their senior, but he liked them. They reminded him of his irresponsible little brothers. These guys were probably a little more put together, though.

"So, Corey – welcome to the late shift," Josh said.

"Thanks, Josh. It's nice to be here."

"I appreciate you staying late to cover for me. How can I make it up to you? Can I cover half a shift for you sometime later this week?"

"It's not necessary," Corey waved away his offer.

"Please. It would make me feel better. I don't normally do this."

"Don't buy his faux humility," Calvin joked. "He wants you to think he's the responsible one. He's not."

"Oh, and you're so responsible," Josh mocked.

"No, no, not at all. By the way, here's your dinner. Your homemade dinner, that my wife made for you, because you can't cook."

Josh looked sheepish.

Corey laughed. "He feeds you?!"

"Yes, I do!" Calvin declared chivalrously.

"Calvin doesn't feed me. Leah does. It's different."

"It's not that different," said Calvin.

"Yeah, not really," Corey agreed. "But hey, I should get going. I usually put the boys to bed. My wife will be angry if I'm not home soon."

"Thanks again," Josh said, shaking Corey's hand. "I'm serious about the offer. Just let me know if you ever need me to cover for you. I'm happy to do it."

"Sure thing. I appreciate that."

They watched Corey gather up his things and leave.

"He seems nice," Josh said. He stood up and switched the chairs back around.

"Yeah, he is," agreed Calvin. "Smart, too. He comes closest to us in accuracy."

"Are you thinking what I'm thinking?"

"We ask Jorge to switch him over to our team?"

"Yeah."

"I was thinking exactly that. He talks a lot though. We've already got the linguists who won't shut up."

"Maybe that would be good. Corey can talk to them and you and I can get some work done."

"I think he's the best option. I don't want to get stuck with anybody from the morning shift."

"What's wrong with the morning crew?"

"They're more chipper than Leah."

Josh laughed. "And yet you like Leah."

"I love Leah! But in the morning, I tolerate her."

"Such a shame."

"Hey, she's hot. And she sleeps with me. We're comparing apples to oranges here."

"Valid points. But when did you start to hate mornings?"

"Since I married a woman who sings loudly in the shower at 5:30 *every morning!*"

Josh shook his head. "You know it's only going to get worse with the baby."

"Yeah, but it's okay. We have a plan. Leah is going to cover early mornings, and I'll cover late mornings and early afternoons. She'll cover again when I go to work."

"And overnight?"

"We'll sleep."

"Yeah, but who is going to get up between midnight and Leah's 5:30 morning shower?"

"The doctors say it's good to keep babies on a schedule. So, the baby will sleep when we do. That's the schedule."

"Interesting. Your baby is going to follow your sleep schedule?"

"Yes. We're practicing pro-active parenting. I read a book about it."

"Have you ever been around a baby?" Josh asked.

"Of course."

"When?"

"Like…two years ago. I saw my cousin's baby."

"I see the problem," Josh replied.

"I don't see a problem."

"Ask anyone with a baby."

"It's not like you're an expert. What do you know about babies?"

"Nothing. Absolutely nothing. Yet somehow, I know more than you. Babies sleep whenever they want to, Calvin. This baby is not going to follow your schedule."

Ten minutes later, Josh heard Calvin in the hallway on the phone, freaking out.

Calvin returned and slouched into his chair. "Babies don't sleep through the night," he groaned.

"Is that so?"

"Yes. But there's good news. I called Leah, and we have a new plan."

"Do tell."

"Godfather duties had not been previously well-defined."

"Don't even."

"I think – and Leah agrees with me! - that it would be a good bonding experience for you and your godchild if you took the overnight shift."

"You're pathetic. Be a man."

"I am. I've made a plan."

"A plan doesn't make you a man."

"Nope, but a plan well-executed most certainly does!"

Josh shook his head and rolled his eyes.

"You're jealous because I'm smarter than you," Calvin declared.

"I don't think so."

"It's a good thing you decided to clean. Maybe we can get an extra crib for your place, put it in that second bedroom you've been using for storage."

"Over my dead body."

***

Baby Amelia made her grand entrance the next day. "Uncle Josh" was so smitten, he turned that second bedroom into the pinkest bedroom any home in Bisurakhan had ever seen. And he went out himself and bought a crib, a rocking chair, and a dresser full of baby clothes.

CHAPTER 28
Johanum

Life in Johanum was monotonous. But I welcomed it, this slow roll towards predictability. The days were not as dark as before.

Mad Laughs and I had our routine. We gathered berries, fish, and Tufta leaves in the morning. In the afternoon, I went to Fletcher's studio, where I was turning one of the walls into a mural. Mad Laughs would nap by my feet. In the evenings he built a fire, and Mr. Fox joined us for dinner. He rarely said a word. If we felt like it, afterwards, we would wander down to the docks. Other nights we went to bed early and slept a long time.

The next morning, we did the same thing.

Our routine had no perceivable end. We couldn't leave Johanum, but we felt safe where we were. This was life. A new life. An unending stretch of days that seemed to go nowhere, create nothing, and demand little. I embraced them. I was, in my own way, happy.

Only in Fletcher's studio might you have questioned my contentment. In the shadows, something called to me. In that cave, I stopped pretending that this world defined me. In that cave, I knew there was still more to my existence.

Fletcher's canvas was sacred. Plenty of blank space lay between the snapshots of Johanum he had painted in his abstract, staccato style. I made no move to add to his renderings. I wanted to forever remember the way he saw our world.

On the wall to the right of the canvas was our painting. It was mostly mine. Mad Laughs helped me scrub down the wall and coat it with multiple layers of old, sludgy Tufta milk. The sludge smoothed out some of the rough edges of the stone wall and gave us a white backdrop. It was our own canvas wall.

On our canvas I poured every emotion still tangled up inside me. The result was a mural that turned brown and had no definition, no individuality, no shape. It was a massive, wall-sized blob.

I felt fantastic about my work.

"What do you think?" I asked Mad Laughs proudly.

He looked at the wall and winced.

"Is it that bad? It's not that bad."

I stared at the wall.

"It's that bad."

We started over by repainting the wall. I made red "paint" from the berries we picked up near the edge of the Stone Gardens. The bark of the trees at the edge of the forest could be used as pencils. They gave me the option for thinner, more precise lines than the thick, clumsy handmade paint brushes that Fletcher had fashioned from twigs.

Mad Laughs pulled seaweed from the lake and hauled a large quantity up to the caves. He stood around the fire and squeezed it so tight, it looked like his face would pop. It produced a thin stream of juice that Mad Laughs mixed with Tufta paste, resulting in a thin, runny paint with a greenish-blue hue.

I told Mad Laughs I wanted orange and yellow paint. He pondered my request for three or four days. Each afternoon, he disappeared for hours. In the evenings, he returned with all manner of rocks, sticks, and leaves. He would break and scratch and squeeze each one. Nothing happened.

Then one evening, as I walked away from our canvas and back into the main cave, drawn by the crackle of the evening fire and the smell of roasting fish, I came upon the most tremendous sight.

Flower petals. Huge, monster flower petals. Some were the size of my hand, others the length of my arms. Dozens of brightly colored flowers were stacked in a pile by the fire.

Mad Laughs was prancing back and forth. He had clearly been waiting for me. The look of pride covering his face seemed to run through his entire body, causing him to stand straighter and walk taller than I had ever seen.

I walked over to the pile of flower petals and picked them up, one by one. They were real. Some of them still had a bit of that freshly-picked flower scent. I could feel tears welling up in my eyes and quickly pushed them back.

"I could positively kiss you," I whispered to Mad Laughs, still running my hands over the flowers, fully expecting them to disappear at any moment.

Mad Laughs blushed a deep red and buried his face in his hands.

"Don't worry, I won't. But where did you find these?" I turned over the flower that was in my hand, studying it carefully. It was a brilliant orange, its center as red as a beating heart, the stem long and sturdy.

Mad Laughs shrugged off my question.

"You're not going to show me?" I asked in surprise.

He shook his head.

"Okay then. Thank you. So many times over, thank you, thank you, thank you."

He beamed.

I didn't want to crush the flowers. All the colors I wanted for my painting were right there, stacked high beneath my fingertips, but these flowers were exactly as they should be. Destroying a flower would be tantamount to destroying a life.

Mad Laughs was less sentimental. He saw my hesitation and stepped in. I watched in horror as he crushed each flower, every petal, over a long line of bowls filled with Tufta paste. Drops of colored liquid ran down the stems and collected in the bowls below. Mad Laughs took a stick and mixed each bowl. All my paint colors sat there, waiting for me. And on the floor next to them lay a pile of crushed, wilted flower petals.

I burst into a violent flood of tears.

My crying startled Mad Laughs, although he was, by now, familiar with my sudden outbursts. Still he took them no more gracefully than I did. As I collapsed in a heap on the ground, Mad Laughs grimaced and winced and groaned. Finally, he settled for face-planting the floor, hands clasped firmly over his ears.

My sobs subsided. A few deep breaths and I felt a sense of calm.

"Will you help me carry these bowls back to Fletcher's studio?"

Mad Laughs peeked through his fingers, assessing my emotional state. I faked a smile. I could tell it was awful as soon as I tried. Mad Laughs pulled back, visibly repulsed. But he rose to his feet and picked up the two bowls closest to him.

Back in front of the canvas, I stood still, staring at the wall.

Mad Laughs raised his eyebrows quizzically.

"I can't decide where to start," I said.

He picked up one of our handmade brushes, stepped up to me, and forcibly closed my fingers around the handle.

"Thank you," I said. But I didn't move, and that was clearly unacceptable.

He picked up the bowl of red paint and lifted it up to my brush. The paint swirled around and swallowed up the twigs that made the bristles of our little brush. Seeing no movement, Mad Laughs grabbed my elbow and jerked it closer to the wall. Finally, he had had enough. He lifted the brush from my hand and generously smeared the wall with red.

Once. Twice. Three times.

He stepped back, surveying his word. A slow grin emerged on his weathered face.

"In Middlestan, we have a name for that. It's called 'abstract art,'" I told him.

It was all he needed to feel happy. Within a few minutes, he was curled up on the floor under Fletcher's old blankets, snoring loudly.

I returned to the fire and collected some of our homemade plates. Mad Laughs had made them from the red clay found near the forest. He would mix the clay with water from the docks, shape it into plates, then leave it next to the fire. After a few nights, the dishes sealed up quite nicely. Of course, they didn't last. A small crack would appear at one edge within a few days, and not long after, the plate would shatter. But it's not as though we had so many things to do. Mad Laughs simply returned to the forest to collect more clay, and the next day, we made new plates.

I covered each of the paint bowls with a plate. Tufta paste didn't dry out quickly, but sometimes bugs found their way inside, and then I had to go through the laborious task of fishing them out, unless I wanted bugs stuck in my painting at random places.

Yesterday, I had a vision for the canvas. Today my mind was blank. I returned to the fire. I sat there for hours, mesmerized, watching the flames dance lower and lower. They would sway from side to side, then jump, up, over, and closer to the floor. The flames moved together in a slow, sensual dance, intimate enough to capture your imagination, but removed enough to remind you that you were only welcome to watch. This dance was not yours.

The fire reminded me of the wraiths. Every movement seemed choreographed. Free form, yet somehow pre-determined.

What was it about Johanum that lulled you into a passive state of existence?

I liked our passivity. It was safe here, in our cave. It was safe down by the docks. I liked safe. I didn't want to lose that.

But still I knew this was not life.

My gaze fell on the pile of crumpled flower petals and discarded stems. Mad Laughs was full of mystery. I had no idea where he found those flowers. I couldn't think of a single place in Johanum where flowers grew, except for in the Stone Gardens. But those flowers weren't vibrant like this. Those flowers were small, the petals hard, and the vines covered in thorns.

The flames of our fire fell closer to the ground. Soon the heat would evaporate into the silent night surrounding us.

I curled up under a Tufta blanket and drifted into a dreamless sleep.

CHAPTER 29
Bisurakhan

"You look like death."

Calvin blinked. In an act of sheer willpower, he opened his eyes as wide as they would go, then they snapped shut. His head fall forward and hit the kitchen table.

"Fatherhood is treating you well," Josh teased him.

"She's just the cutest little thing," came Calvin's muffled voice, his face-plant still firmly intact. "Her face. She has the face of an angel. Her little fingers. Her little toes." He lifted his head and looked at Josh with desperation. "Why doesn't she sleep, Josh? Why doesn't my little angel sleep?"

"It won't last forever, man."

"It has already lasted forever."

"She's three weeks old."

"I haven't slept in three weeks."

"Can't you sleep when Leah's got her?"

"I'm too tired to sleep then."

"You're too stressed, you mean. Why don't you go over to my place, crash on the couch for a bit?"

"I can't leave Leah alone with Amelia."

"Why not?"

"She'd be so stressed!"

"Leah? Are you sure we're not talking about you?"

Calvin didn't answer.

"Did Leah get any sleep last night?" Josh asked.

"I think so. Her eyes were closed."

"Okay then. Here, take my keys. No, wait, on second thought, you shouldn't drive. I'll drop you off at my place. Then I'll come back and hang out here for a bit."

Amelia's crying broke out as if on cue.

"I can't leave!" Calvin groaned as he lifted his head. "She'll think I'm abandoning her!"

"Leah?"

"Amelia!"

"What is wrong with you?"

"I don't know." Calvin's head dropped back to the table. A minute later it popped back up. "I did a stupid thing."

"Oh boy."

"I signed up for a Reality Persuasion experiment this weekend."

"That was incredibly stupid."

"It's so nice to know you're always here to support me."

"Can't you get out of it? Tell them you want to cancel."

"I can't. If I cancel, I'll have to pay them money."

"You have to pay *them* money? Since when?"

"Since I signed up for a three-part experiment. I did the first part before Amelia came. If I drop out midway, I have to repay the stipend they paid me for the first session."

"I guess that makes sense. Can you send a proxy?"

"Are you offering?"

"Not really."

"It doesn't matter. I can't send someone else. I already checked."

"You're screwed."

"You're a terrible friend."

"I know. Go lay down or I'll knock you out and make you sleep. Are you sure you don't want to go over to my place so you can sleep where it's quiet?"

Calvin pushed his chair back. "I don't have to go to your place. Thanks for the offer, though. I'm going to go lie down in the bedroom."

"Suit yourself. Close the door and don't come back."

Calvin stumbled a little but made it. At the doorway, he paused and turned around.

"Thank you."

"Don't mention it."

Josh left the kitchen and walked over to Leah, who was half sitting, half falling off the couch. Amelia's face was scrunched up and red from crying. Her little hands, curled in tight fists, punched angrily at the air. Little wisps of black hair curled around her ears in ringlets.

Josh tried unsuccessfully to hide his impish grin. Dang it, that baby was cute.

"You need to sleep, too," he said to Leah.

Leah's eyes opened wide, as wide as saucers. It was how she always looked when she was exhausted. Josh remembered the four of them back at the university - Leah, Calvin, Kat, and himself. They used to spend late nights at the library, cramming for exams. Kat became giddy when she was too tired. She would giggle incessantly and tell jokes that grew less and less funny as the night wore on. Leah's eyes would grow wide, so wide you thought they would pop out of her head. The more tired she became, the more annoyed she would get with Kat and her terrible jokes. Eventually, Lean would snap and say something mean. Kat would look crushed. But the next day, neither of them ever remembered anything from the night before.

"Here, let me take her," Josh offered.

Leah slowly unfolded her arms. Josh took the baby and swayed back and forth. Her cries turned to whimpers, then to coos, and slowly she drifted off to sleep.

Josh looked down. Leah was passed out cold.

Josh tucked Amelia into the crook of his right arm and went rummaging through the hallway closet. He found an old, shaggy pillow, along with a couple of threadbare blankets.

Why were Leah and Calvin so poor, anyway? Kat made significantly more money as an attorney than Leah made as a teacher. But Josh figured Calvin made about the same amount as he did. They had started working at the Comms Tower within six months of each other. Josh got the job first, then pulled a few strings to get Calvin an interview. They had to make a similar salary.

Josh's paycheck alone would have afforded two people a better lifestyle than the one Calvin and Leah lived. He had given Kat the house in their divorce, partly because he didn't want to fight about it, partly because she made more money than he did and was in a better position to keep it up. His apartment was enough for him. But his apartment was nicer and more spacious than this one, even on just his salary.

It didn't make sense.

Josh returned to the living room. Using his free arm, he stuffed the pillow between Leah's head and the couch. Standing up, he frowned. That looked uncomfortable. He leaned down, slipped his arm around Leah's shoulders, and propped her back up.

Leah snored loudly.

Once both blankets were tucked in around her, Josh walked back to the kitchen, Amelia still cuddled and asleep in his arms. He put on a pot of coffee and listened as the water quietly rumbled.

A bassinet was sitting on the floor near the table. He looked at the peaceful face sleeping cozily in his arms.

Naaaah. She was fine right where she was.

He found some old textbooks in the closet. One was a volume on decoding the Logs. He brought the book back to the kitchen, poured himself a cup of coffee, and sat down at the table.

Hot coffee, a boring book, and baby cuddles? Maybe he'd survive single life after all.

CHAPTER 30
Bisurakhan

Calif frowned. "I don't understand why you're doing this."

Jorge grew angry. "Do you have to question every decision I make?" he asked.

"You're running on all cylinders and have been for far too long. I can't keep track of everything you're doing. I'm not sure you can either."

"Do you think Johanum has the technology to fuel Dual Presence?" Jorge asked, changing the subject.

"Would you want it if they did?"

"Wouldn't you?"

"I'm not sure I want anything from Johanum," Calif answered. "Except Professor Kanale. As far as I'm concerned, they can hand her over and keep everything else."

"You're playing it too safe. We already have to go to Johanum. We'll get Kanale. But look, let's make the most of the opportunity. If they have other things we can use, let's acquire those as well."

"You're referring to this as an 'opportunity'?" Calif repeated.

"We're going to be using the Space Between for the first time in years. The Commander approved the robot defense army and we're almost done gathering the whole fleet. Robotics training and reprogramming begin next week. We have an unusually friendly invitation from Charisburg that just came through, offering their support."

"I saw that."

"The Reality Persuasion experiments have ramped up and we're collecting incredible data. We're ready for this. As ready as we've ever been. So yes, it's an opportunity. Stop looking at me like that."

"'As ready as we've ever been' doesn't mean we're ready," Calif cautioned.

"There you go again, always playing it safe," Jorge said with a frown. "Look, I see your point. We've never taken a mission like this before. Of course, we can't really know if we're ready. I understand that. But we can make a sophisticated guess. We can prepare as much as possible. That's what I've been doing. Is it enough? I guess we'll find out. But we're taking the mission regardless, and the risk has already been assumed, so let's capitalize on it."

Calif let it drop. Jorge was right. Calif was by nature the most cautious of the three Chiefs. He didn't think it worth mentioning that Jorge was the most impetuous.

"How are your Reality Persuasion experiments going?"

"They're going very well," Jorge answered. "I feel confident that we have tapped into one of the exchange portals of Johanum. Our men and women are coming and going and learning a ton. I'm encouraged by our progress."

"You're running simulations. You can't compare survival or response to a simulation to surviving in Johanum."

"Why not? They could be very similar."

"Have you asked Antoine?"

Jorge bristled. "Of course not."

"Maybe you should."

"And get my head ripped off? No thank you."

"He could confirm your theories. Tell you if anything looks familiar. Tell you if anything looks off."

"He'll never walk through one of our simulations."

"I wasn't suggesting that. Let him see your data. Show him what you're seeing down in the Labs. See if it's real."

"Johanum's bigger than Antoine's experience. He couldn't possibly know if every experiment is a reflection of what's happening there right now."

"You're missing the point."

"I'm not."

"You're purposefully missing the point."

"Why don't you run these experiments then, if you know so much? Oh wait. You can't. You wouldn't even know where to begin."

"No, I wouldn't."

"Then stop questioning me."

"I'm not questioning you," Calif replied, his calm, soothing voice taking on a tone of urgency. "I am questioning whether you're making it impossible for our men to do the job we've assigned them to."

"What do you mean?"

"I mean, I'm not convinced these simulations aren't dangerous. I'm not convinced that sending men to Johanum – even if it's in a simulation – is a wise move. We could be endangering them. Really endangering them. And if they die, or are hurt or injured in some way, they can't do their jobs. We can't afford to keep losing men at our current rate. The casualties on the Periphery are already too high. If anything like that starts happening in the Labs, we'll have serious problems. Not to mention, I imagine, an unwanted visit from the President and his Transparency of Military Operations department."

Silence hung in the air between them. Calif knew the risk of pushing Jorge's buttons. His fist was closed too tightly around his Reality Persuasion experiments, and he wasn't willing to listen to people who asked valid questions. Calif was growing uneasy over reports he heard from the Lab engineers. The one who should have been keeping Jorge in check – the Commander – was becoming increasingly hands-off.

If President Khaled had any idea what Jorge was up to, he would shut the whole operation down. But Calif didn't want to involve the president. There wasn't a Khanist in the military who would respond well to more involvement from a president with no military background.

This had to be dealt with directly.

"You supported my Reality Persuasion experiments when they began," Jorge said. His tone was subdued, but Calif knew what that meant. A storm was brewing.

"I did. With reservations, but yes. I thought you deserved a chance."

"And now you don't?"

"I don't understand your confidence in these experiments. And I'm uneasy over the way you casually dismiss questions - legitimate questions - about what you're doing."

"Let me tell you why I'm confident in these experiments. There are a lot of similarities in what the men are experiencing now, which is different – in a good way! – from what we were dealing with at the beginning. Their experiences diverge, of course, based on their actions, and can set in motion different chains of events. But the geography, the types of things the volunteers are seeing and hearing – there's consistently now. When our men study the sketches we have on file – drawings produced by our lab engineers based on visual data we have captured from past experiments – our volunteers can now recognize their terrain as soon as a simulation starts. The sketches are accurate enough to produce that level of familiarity. There's consistency in the data. That's what I'm telling you, Calif. That's why I think we're on the right track."

"You're saying it's consistent, and I believe you. I'm asking you if it's real."

"It's real as far as we know."

"That's not enough."

"What makes you think it's not real?"

"Because Antoine says the Priests are liars."

"We're not dealing with the Priests."

"Johanum is their territory. If you're dealing with Johanum, as you seem convinced you are, then you are dealing with the Priests."

"They've never shown up in any of our simulations."

"Not that you've seen."

"Excuse me for forming conclusions based on things I can see. You, on the other hand, are questioning everything I can see, based on a theory of Antoine's that you can't prove. Your objections aren't even your own. It's fine for you to have questions, but if you're going to derail my work, at least have a good reason for it. Have some sort of proof for your suspicions. Antoine's skepticism doesn't count, as far as I'm concerned."

"Just because you can see something, Jorge, doesn't make it real. We've both been around long enough to know that. I'm not trying to derail your work. I'm asking if you've taken the time to challenge your own assumptions. I'm asking if you've done your due diligence."

"Are you questioning my competence or my integrity?"

Calif sighed. He had known this conversation wasn't going to be easy. "There is one thing we know about Johanum. Well, two things, I guess, but they're related. The Priests are liars, and they're dangerous. That's what we know for sure. Would you agree with me on that?"

Jorge hesitated.

"Is there anything else about Johanum that you know with absolute certainty?" Calif pushed.

Jorge shifted. "There's fire," he offered.

"Okay. Yes, Antoine told us there's fire. And there are Priests. And the Priests are master manipulators and highly dangerous. Anything else?"

Jorge shook his head.

"So, I'm asking you, what have you done to take into account the few things we know?"

Jorge was quiet.

Calif let the tension hang in the air for a minute, then turned to leave. "Think about it. I know you think it will kill you, but getting Antoine's opinion on the data you're collecting is important. He's the only one of us who's been to Johanum. He's the only one who can help us ensure we're not the ones being played."

CHAPTER 31
Johanum

A fire crackled in the middle of the floor. But this was no ordinary fire. It had no kindling and nothing to give it life, yet it burned bright and hot. A deep blue at its heart reached up like tentacles, wrapping itself around the yellow flames, forcing them to bend to its will.

A low hiss sent the fire racing upwards, higher and higher, licking at the ceiling.

"If you burn the roof off this house again, I'll force you to build my estate, by hand, brick by miserable brick."

The flames dropped immediately, crawling around on the floor.

"That hardly seems fair," whined the one who had hissed.

"Since when do you play fair?" came the first voice, dripping in condescension.

"You promised me my own kingdom."

"You promised me loyalty and conquest, yet look where we are."

The third priest, the one with the X in his hands, ignored them both. He could feel it, the anguish of a soul nearing its end. A smile lifted his lips in a sneer.

"Have you spoken with Sulta yet?" asked the tall one, the one who gave orders.

"I sent him a message," came the whiny reply.

"Send him another."

"I can't. Not until you respond to his reply."

"When were you going to tell me he had replied?"

"Whenever I found it convenient."

"You are not worthy of your position. You are not worthy of your power."

"Yet here we are," the whiny voice mocked.

"You taunt each other and nothing gets done," said the priest with the X in his hands. "Meanwhile, whole planets, entire populations, sit out there in the cosmos, living their boring, pointless lives, when we could be putting them out of their misery."

"You are too impatient," said the tall one.

"You are too cowardly," said the one with the X.

"Our daily wrestle for dominance," said the whiny one. "It's my most favorite sport. Do continue."

"Give me Sulta's message," the tall one commanded.

"And what will you give me?" asked the whiny one.

"Your head shall remain attached to your body."

"Nonsense. You can't kill another Priest."

"I have other means."

"What, the prisoner? She doesn't know what she can do."

"She's a smart one. A few hints and she would figure it out."

"But you won't tell her, will you? Because then she would know that she could kill you, too. And you're too much of a coward for that."

"I will hang you by your ankles over the fire pits of the desert and let the iron-fanged dogs have their way with you."

"Well, at least you're being realistic now." The whiny one shuffled around in the pockets of his robe before his hand emerged with a small scroll. The scroll was no wider than the width of his hand and it glowed green.

He tossed it into the fire.

All three Priests took seats on the floor and waited.

The fire began to crackle loudly. Sparks flew from the end of each flame, some erupting into tiny fireworks. Slowly, the heart of the fire turned green. From its center rose a shadow that grew steadily larger. The shadow took shape. A head emerged, with a long neck stretching towards the ceiling. It had the body of a dragon, clothed in green scales. A tail with a blade at its end whipped around the room. Finally, eyes that burned red turned their gaze upon the three men seated on the ground.

"You summoned, Mortarium," it said, bowing in deference before the whiny priest.

"And who are you?" asked Mortarium, the priest who whines.

"I am Zila, liaison of the Underworld. I come to you on behalf of Sulta, Legion of Cosmos, King of the Underworld."

Mortarium snorted. "Sulta's no King of the Underworld."

"Did you summon me to mock me, my lord?"

"No," Mortarium answered. "Did Sulta receive my message?"

"Of course. That's why I'm here."

"And what does the mighty Sulta make of our offer?"

Zila blew a steady stream of fire from her mouth. The flames danced around the room, then took the shape of Bisurakhan. She breathed again, and a fiery representation of the Turris emerged.

"He finds your offer boring," Zila purred. She lifted her scaled paw and swatted at the planet made of fire. It spun in circles, unraveling. Slowly it took on the shape of Middlestan. She reached up and hit it again. The next planet to appear was Charisburg.

"Offer him more," Zila countered, her voice one of a seductress. "At least three planets. Or perhaps you have something to offer that's better than planets."

"What's better than a planet?" asked Sibilum, the tall one, the one who gave orders.

"Your own ignorance should shame you," sneered Carnificius, the priest with the X in his hands.

"The only thing you ever want is more hearts," Sibilum retorted. "You can only find those on other planets."

"Yes, but I am not a Legion," Carnificius spoke slowly, annunciating each word, as though he was speaking to a very dull child.

"Clearly you are not. You have nowhere near enough power."

"I have enough power for everything I need," Carnificius snapped.

"Because you are not Priest enough to want more," Sibilum taunted.

"Make it three planets and one of Bisurakhan's Chiefs," Zila interrupted.

"You just said three planets!" protested Sibilum.

"Yes, but now I see what it will be like to work with you. You must make it worth my time. Give us a Chieftan. Then you will be worth the trouble."

"How about one planet - Bisurakhan - and all of its leaders?" Sibilum countered.

"Done!" Zila agreed, looking surprised and pleased at the unexpected offer.

"Have you lost your mind?" demanded Carnificius. "We can't capture the Commander."

"Technically, we haven't tried to capture him."

"It can't be done."

"Now who's the coward?" Sibilum taunted.

"You are impetuous and foolish," Carnificius hissed. "We can deliver Bisurakhan. But we cannot take the Commander."

Sibilum ignored him and turned to Zila. "So, we have a deal? You will open to us the Path of Destruction, and we will deliver to you Bisurakhan and its leaders, beginning with the Commander."

"We have a deal," Zila answered. "When will you deliver your end of the bargain?"

Sibilum turned to Mortarium. "How long do you think it will take to mount an offensive against Bisurakhan, capable of destroying its armed forces? We'll need to eliminate most of the military to get to the Commander."

Mortarium began counting on his fingers. He went back and forth, muttering to himself before settling on a number. "Six months."

Sibilum turned to Zila. "Twelve months," he answered.

"I just said six!" Mortarium protested in his whiny voice.

"You miss all your own deadlines."

Mortarium crossed his arms in a huff.

"Twelve months," Sibilum repeated.

"According to which planet's time signature?" asked Zila.

"Johanum's."

"I am no fool," Zila said dryly.

"Fine. Bisurakhan's."

"Don't say that!" Mortarium interrupted. "Go with Charisburg."

"I am not stupid," said Zila.

Sibilum waved his hands at them both. "Cornersville. There. Are you happy?" He looked back and forth between their grim faces. "Fine. Cornersville it is."

"We will accept it," Zila purred.

"For the Commander, I should have made you accept Johanum's timetable," Sibilum scowled.

"But you didn't, did you?" Zila replied, her eyes full of derision.

"You will open to us the Path of Destruction on the day we deliver Bisurakhan."

"Of course," Zila purred. "And, as is customary, if you fail to meet the terms you have set for your contract, you yourselves will be taken prisoner. You will become slaves of the Master, the Almighty Sulta, Legion of Comos, King of the Underworld."

"And if you fail to deliver on your terms?" Sibilum asked.

Zila scoffed. "We will not fail."

"But if you do?"

"Fine." She straightened her head. "If we fail, you will take the throne of Sulta, and you will become his master."

Sibilum smiled gleefully.

Zila nostrils flared, her face a mixture of contempt and disgust.

"This contract binds the Priests of Johanum to the Almighty Sulta, Legion of Cosmos, King of the Underworld. Do the three of you hereby swear to abide by the terms of our agreement?"

"We do!" Sibilum enthusiastically affirmed.

Zila turned her head to the others.

Mortarium was less enthusiastic. "I guess."

Carnificius sat silently, twisting the X in his hands.

"You must agree," commanded Sibilum.

"I'm afraid there's nothing I *must* do," Carnificius replied.

"We will not accept a contract without full support," Zila told him.

"Why not?" asked Sibilum. "You've done so in the past."

"You are referring to Fortunas and the days of the fifty kings."

"Of course."

"We learn from our mistakes," Zila replied with a cold smile. She turned her gaze back to Carnificius. "Full, unified support from all parties involved is now required for the ratification of a new contract."

"That's a shame," Carnificius said without an ounce of remorse. "So you're telling me, wise one, oh beautiful reflection of all the glory of the Underworld – you're telling me that by withholding my support, I have the power to void this contract?"

"Yes."

"Interesting." Carnificius turned his eyes haughtily towards Sibilum. "And what will I get for my support?"

"I won't kill you!" Sibilum bellowed in outrage.

"Nonsense. We've been over this already. I want something good. Something that costs you greatly."

"Your face, your very voice, cost me greatly, every day," Sibilum hissed.

"You have no idea how much it pleases me to hear you say that," Carnificius replied. "But I want something else. What will you give me?"

"You can have your own kingdom. A solar system we will leave for you alone, to torment at your pleasure."

"No good. It's boring. This solar system is enough for me."

"What do you want?"

Carnificius contemplated the question for several minutes. Then he smiled. "Worship. From you."

Sibilum bristled, his eyes glowing red.

"I want your words of adoration," Carnificius continued. "Every morning. I want you to thank me – publicly – in front of all our prisoners. I want you to praise me for making you who you are. Tell them how your dominance, your power, you owe them all to me. Without me, you could do nothing. Promise me this, and I will give you my support."

Sibilum slammed his fists into the ground. The floor caught fire and raged up around them. The walls burst into flames, followed quickly by the roof.

In the middle of the fire, they stayed, while the house burned around them.

At long last, Sibilum replied. "Fine."

The flames receded.

Carnificius could not hide his glee.

Zila turned her head back and forth between the two Priests. "You will rue this day," she predicted. "But that is no concern of mine. We have a deal."

"We have a deal," Sibilum repeated, his eyes spewing hatred.

"Then, oh Priests of Johanum, you who wield great power but remain such slaves to your pride, I will see you again, twelve months from now, in accordance to the time signature of Cornersville. Our agreement has been ratified and is now binding. Breaking of the contract requires payment according to the terms previously determined."

Zila bowed her head and closed her eyes. Her shadow appearance began to fade. An eruption exploded n the heart of the fire and she disappeared. In her place, a small scroll fell to the floor.

The fire returned to its previous shape and color, its heart burning blue. Only the scroll burned green.

"You will give your full cooperation during the course of our conquest," Sibilum hissed at Carnificius.

"With pleasure," Carnificius sneered.

"Your struggle for dominance is going to be the death of me," Mortarium grumbled.

CHAPTER 32
Bisurakhan

"To what do I owe the pleasure?" Antoine asked as Jorge approached. Despite his friendly tone, Antoine was not pleased to see Jorge. He could only guess what Jorge might want.

"I need to talk to you," Jorge replied.

"All right."

"Not here. I need you to come down to the Labs."

"Absolutely not."

"You don't have to watch anything. I'll clear out our personnel if you like. I need your opinion on our data collection."

Antoine raised his eyebrows. "Since when do you want my opinion?"

"I'm asking you, aren't I?"

"Why?"

Jorge grimaced. "Calif thinks the data could be corrupted. Or just simply not real."

"It probably isn't real."

"You're not making this any easier."

"When was the last time you made my life easier?"

"We want the same things, Antoine," Jorge sighed. "Do this for me. You'll get your inside scoop on my experiments, which I know you've been wanting. I'll get to tell Calif I consulted with you. That's all I'm asking."

"Will you listen to my feedback?"

"I'll listen. I might not change anything, but I'll listen."

"I guess you're not trying to butter me up."

"Look, we both know I don't want you involved. I'm doing this because Calif is being much more vocal about his concerns than he has been in the past. I need to put his mind at ease because I don't want to fight with him. Not about this. I'll fight with you. But not Calif. And anyway, he's annoyingly good at noticing important details that I sometimes miss." Jorge sighed. "Don't tell him I said that."

Antoine smiled. "I won't." He put down the communication device in his hands and gestured toward the elevation boxes. "Shall we go?"

"It'll take a bit to clear out the staff."

"Don't bother. They'll be fine."

Antoine and Jorge walked over to a nearby elevation box and stepped inside. Jorge overrode the programmed intelligence and gave the box instructions to descend down to the Reality Persuasion level. The doors closed and the box lifted off the ground, zigzagged around the lobby, then plunged downward.

"Thank you," Jorge said to Antoine, who smiled gently in response.

"It's the first time you've invited me for a visit," Antoine said.

"Can you blame me?"

"I sure can!"

They both laughed. Jorge was relieved to feel some of the tension in the air dissipate. Antoine wasn't a bad guy. He was incredibly intelligent. Jorge just didn't think he knew what he was doing in a world of military strategy. It had been the Commander's decision to appoint him a Chief, but Antoine had no previous military training. It bothered Jorge to no end.

"How's Maria?" asked Antoine.

"My wife is as intolerant and intolerable as ever," Jorge replied good-naturedly.

"She's good for you."

"Don't I know it. Unfortunately, she does too. And she reminds me. Daily."

Antoine grew quiet, remembering his own wife.

The elevation box came to rest on a landing pad and the doors silently slid open. Antoine gazed out down a long yellow hallway with a dozen steel doors, each marked with a number.

"Those are the experiment Labs," Jorge said, gesturing to the doors as they passed. "Don't worry, no one's in there right now. We run all our simulations on the weekends."

"What exactly do you do in these simulations?" Antoine inquired.

"We tap into the communication wavelength used by the messages we've been intercepting in the Frequency Tower. Then we have our volunteers use a specialty pair of audio and visual glasses we've designed to run on that frequency. They step into Johanum, entering through a portal door we're able to access through that frequency. They walk around and see things, interacting with the environment and anything they see. Afterwards, they debrief our engineers, who create sketches of what our volunteers say they've seen."

"Are you able to tap into the audio and visual goggles to see what they see and hear what they hear?"

"It's spotty. The visual feed is the worst. Sometimes we aren't able to get any data at all. The audio feeds are better, but there's a lot of interference."

"How do the volunteers get into these simulations? How does the portal work?"

"Tapping into the right transmission wavelength while using the goggles is all it takes. It "transports" them, if you will, independent of their will or ours. We leave them in the simulation for a predetermined length of time, telling them to interact with their surroundings at their discretion. Then we collect and analyze the data."

"And you don't believe these simulations are dangerous?" Antoine asked.

"Not physically, no. Now, while they're in the simulation, our volunteers feel, sense, and experience everything as if it's real. But what they're experiencing is fake. Whatever happens to them doesn't carry over into real life once they exit the simulation."

"And an example of this would be...?"

"We've had a few of our volunteers get badly burned. Second, third degree burns, probably an experience that would leave them unrecognizable in our world. But as soon as they leave the simulation, they're completely fine. No physical burns or signs of trauma. Same thing happens with drowning. One guy "died," so to speak – he drowned – but when we took off the glasses, he was back, good as new."

"You're letting our Khanists experience that level of trauma?" Antoine asked.

"It's not real," Jorge replied.

"The psychological effect will be, even if the physical effect isn't."

"We debrief afterwards. We make sure they know it wasn't real."

Jorge didn't miss Antoine's long exhale or the way his face turned taunt and tense.

"Think of it like waking up from a bad dream," Jorge explained. "You might remember the dream for a day – or longer, maybe, if it was really vivid. But eventually, you forget, unless you write it down or something. Inevitably, what you remember changes, just like all memories do. They're fine, Antoine. All our volunteers are okay. When they do have problems, it's not related to this."

Antoine realized for the first time that he hadn't understood the extent of Jorge's experimentation, and in choosing to ignore it out of anger, he had made a huge mistake. What price were these men and women paying for his mistake?

"And your volunteers – can you prove that they're forgetting what they've experienced?"

"Of course."

"No, you can't."

"I've told you before. Plenty of our men struggle, but Reality Persuasion is not to blame. They have other struggles."

"The suicide rate among your volunteers, Jorge, I've seen it. It's skyrocketing. You can't keep claiming the experiments have nothing to do with that."

"Look, I'm not saying any of this is ideal," Jorge replied, trying to diffuse the tension that had crept back into the conversation. "I understand that these activities are probably, on some level, ethically questionable."

Antoine blinked. "'On some level'?" he repeated.

"Our experiments are filled with volunteers, and our volunteer numbers are growing. As more people volunteer, they spread the word, and our participation rates rise, they don't fall. It's not steady – it varies from month to month. But overall, our participation rates are better now than they have ever been. Khanist men and women believe the experiments are worth it. And they're showing up to prove it."

"You're paying them to show up," Antoine pointed out. "You're paying them very well. At a much higher rate than they make with their regular salaries. And every time your numbers go down, you raise the compensation."

"My point is, volunteers willingly participate. And a lot of them are repeats. They participate in multiple experiments. You're questioning their experience, but it must not be so bad if they're willing to come back."

"And the ones who have experienced the extremes? The burning, the drownings? Do they come back?"

Jorge shook his head. "No."

"You need to shut this down," Antoine said urgently.

"You haven't seen the Data Compilations yet," Jorge said dismissively. "Look, I know you don't like what I'm doing. Calif doesn't seem to like it either. But remember – we're facing an enemy unlike any we have faced before. We have to be willing to do things we've never done before."

"And what about everyone who gets hurt in the process? Are their lives worth nothing to you?"

"Don't talk to me like that," Jorge replied. "I'm getting things done, which is more than can be said about you. You advise. You strategize. But what do you actually do? What have you accomplished? When Johanum comes to fight, how will you have prepared us? I'm trying lots of things because I have to. Some of them might not work. I get that. But we have to keep trying. Our volunteers are well compensated, yes. That's on purpose. Not just so they come, but so that their standard of living increases. They're going to need more security, more stability, especially if we go to war. Their families will need it. I'm not heartless, Antoine. Everything I do, I do with a purpose."

"You better hope you're right," Antoine said as reached the office door. "Because if you're wrong, a lot of people will pay for your mistake."

CHAPTER 33
Bisurakhan

"Hush, little baby, don't you cry. Mama's gonna sing you a lullaby..."

Leah's voice carried across the apartment. Calvin lay in bed, a big, stupid grin on his face. Then he rolled to his left side and hugged his pillow.

"All these years I have taken you for granted," he repented, fluffing up the pillow beneath his head. "No more. I will take you for granted no more. You give me so much life. Such sweet, sweet sleep. I love you. You're basically family. I should give you a name."

He heard a chuckle and looked up. Leah stood in the doorway, swaddling Amelia, her eyes twinkling.

"So, my husband is expressing his undying love for a pillow now. What's next? The blankets? Should I be jealous? I never dreamed I'd have to compete for your love with something here in my own house."

Calvin waved her over. "Come join me."

She crawled up next to him. Calvin adjusted the blankets and the pillows, and they sat together, shoulder to shoulder, Amelia propped up between them on top of the comforter.

"We make the cutest babies," Calvin said. He leaned forward and traced Amelia's face with his fingertip. Then he traced her nose, her ears, and leaned forward to cover her with kisses.

She started to fuss.

"You're bothering her. Cal, let her sleep."

"I'm sorry. Here." He picked up his daughter and cradled her close, letting her head rest on his shoulder. The fussing subsided.

"She's perfect," Calvin said, his face flushed with happiness.

"I know." Leah couldn't deny the pride she felt. She was exhausted, but never had she felt such love. "Did you see that face she's started to make when she's startled, right before she starts crying? I feel bad for saying this because I know she's scared, but Cal, it's adorable! I can't get enough of it. Honey, what are you doing?"

Calvin had laid Amelia back on the bed and was playing with her hand. "I'm counting."

"Counting what?"

"Her fingers?"

"Why? You know she has all her fingers."

"Yes, well... I haven't counted them today. I just want to be sure."

"Do you think they're going to fall off?"

"You can never be too careful with babies."

"When it comes to you, I think you could be less careful." Leah scooched behind Calvin, sat up on her knees, wrapped her arms around him, and propped her chin up on his shoulder.

Leah looked down at her sleepy, beautiful daughter. Amelia's face stretched into a yawn, then settled into a deep, sleepy grin. Her eyes fluttered shut, popped open, then fluttered shut again.

"What do you think she's thinking about right now?" Calvin whispered.

"About how much she loves her daddy," Leah whispered back.

Calvin pulled Leah back onto the bed in front of him. "Want to have another one?"

"Right now?!"

"No, not right now," Calvin replied. "Just...someday. We could give Amelia a little sister. Think how cute it would be to have two Amelia's."

"We haven't even figured out how to take care of one Amelia."

"We will. I think it's going pretty well, actually. And in another, you know…niiiine…..tennnnnnn… in another couple of years…"

"You were going to say nine months."

"I wasn't."

"You totally said nine months."

"I didn't. I said niiiiiiine…..and then nothing, no months!"

Leah leaned forward and kissed him deeply.

"Calvin," she said with sweet severity. "I want to make another baby with you."

Calvin beamed.

"But not right now."

"I know," he replied with equal gravity.

They sat in silence, watching Amelia sleep.

"I have to go into work this weekend," Calvin said.

"Why? I thought you got a full six weeks off?"

"I do. But that last Reality Persuasion experiment I did, the one right before Amelia was born, it was the first of a three-part series. I have to go back and finish the other two sessions. There's one this weekend, and one next weekend."

"Is it all day?"

"Just a half day for this one. I think next weekend I have to go in for a full day. But then I'm done, I swear."

"You said that the last time. And the time before that."

"I know. You can take extra time off work if you want. Even with paying for all your dad's court fees this month, we'll still have some money left over. You could stay home from work for a couple more weeks."

"I'm so sorry, Calvin."

"For what?"

"For my dad."

"Why? That has nothing to do with you."

"Yeah, but you married into this whole, awful mess. My dad has always been in trouble. And he always will be. He's never going to change."

"We always make it work."

"We shouldn't have to. *You* shouldn't have to. You should get to stay home with your daughter, too, instead of feeling like you have to do these experiments just to make extra money to support him."

"Hey! Stop this, right now. You're worth it to me, okay? Your problems are my problems. That's how marriage works. Yeah, you know, I wish your dad could figure out his life. I wish I didn't feel like he was bankrupting us every month. But it's not your fault what he does, and I'm not mad at you. Those are his decisions."

Leah wiped tears from her eyes.

Calvin hesitated but decided to go ahead and say what he was thinking. "I do think we need to have a talk about the future though."

"What do you mean?"

"About how long we can keep doing this. We can't bail your dad out forever. We have Amelia now. Maybe we'll have more kids. Kids are expensive. I don't want to tell Amelia she can't pick up a hobby or enroll in a sports league because we're paying bail for her grandpa each month."

Leah burst into tears. Her sobs startled Amelia. The two of them wailed together. It was almost more than Calvin could take. His attempt to comfort Leah was promptly rejected. He picked Amelia back up and began to rock her. At least his daughter still loved him.

The tears slowly gave way to hiccups. Leah and Amelia were now hiccupping in unison. Calvin felt guilty for thinking so, but the whole scene was adorable.

"I know we need to stop bailing him out," Leah said when she was able to talk again. She sniffed and wiped her nose with her sleeve. "He needs to have to deal with the consequences of his own choices. The full price, even though he can't afford it. You know they'll take the house. They'll repossess it to pay his debts. My mom has never worked outside the home. She's lived her whole adult life in that house. It's not my father I'm worried about. They'll lock him up, or maybe he'll become homeless, but he'll figure it out. He'll be okay. He's just that kind of person. But my mom? I don't know what she'll do. I don't know if she'll be able to handle it."

Calvin laid Amelia on the bed. She had fallen back asleep. He pulled Leah closer and wrapped his arms around her. She felt so small in that moment. He wished he could change things. Everything she had experienced growing up. How helpless she felt around her parents. None of it was right.

"I know it's going to be hard," he said. "It'll probably be the hardest thing your mom has ever had to face. I know it will be awful for you, too. But we can't keep treating them like children. They have to grow up. Just like you and I did." He leaned down and kissed Amelia's face. "Just like we're doing now, every day. So we can give our daughter a wonderful, amazing life. So we can be a family."

They sat quietly, listening to Amelia's soft, steady breathing. She was so peaceful when she slept.

"Do you think your mom would want to come and stay with us?" Calvin asked.

Leah shook her head. "She's visited us once, Cal. Once, in all the time we've been married. She hasn't even come to meet Amelia."

"Do you think she wants to?"

"I don't know. I think she's just really ashamed. She feels guilty over what my father does. For not being able to provide much for us growing up. For the way you and I get contacted by the courts every month, asking for money. I think she hasn't come because she doesn't want to face us."

"What if we invited her to come and help out with Amelia? I know we don't really need her, but it would be nice to have an extra pair of hands. You saw how nice it was to have a break when Josh dropped by the other day. Do you think she'd come if she thought it would help us out?"

"Maybe. That's not a bad idea. But are you suggesting we invite her to come and help out, then tell her we're going to stop helping them?"

"I guess that would look pretty bad, huh?"

"I don't think there's any good way to do it," Leah sighed. "I would love to see her. And I want Amelia to know her grandma."

"Do you think your dad will ever come meet his granddaughter? Do you want him to?"

Leah shrugged. "I could go either way. I'm sure he'd be fine with Amelia. He can be quite charming when he wants to be."

Calvin put his arm around Leah's waist. She laid her head on his shoulder and reached forward to lay her hand gently on Amelia's stomach, feeling it rise and fall as she slept.

"I'm so thankful I get to do life with you, honey," Calvin said. "I know it's been hard. But I feel like we're getting somewhere. I think we've turned a corner. Maybe this is the good life. It feels pretty good to me."

"I know. I love you."

"I love you, too."

Amelia's eyes fluttered open and she started to coo.

"And I love you, little nugget," Calvin said.

CHAPTER 34
Bisurakhan

Jorge and Antoine reached the main office for the Reality Persuasion department. It was marked with a simple sign that read: "R.P. Central."

Large monitors covered each wall, stretching from floor to ceiling. Three control panels were positioned in a U shape in the middle of the room.

"You designed this to resemble the Frequency Tower," Antoine remarked.

"We rely on similar technology," Jorge replied. "But here, our engineers specialize in the sciences, not communications."

"I heard one of our comms guys is an active volunteer down here. Was it one of those officers you brought to the meeting?"

"That's right. His name's Calvin. Calvin Smith. He's a bright kid."

"Do you think it's wise?"

"What do you mean?"

"Pulling from Comms for your experiments. Our comms engineers are more important than ever, and we can barely keep those shifts filled. What if something happened to him?"

"Nothing's going to happen to him, or to anybody else. The experiments are safe."

"You keep saying that. And you keep ignoring the suicides."

"I'm not ignoring them. I'm very, very aware of every single one. I call their families. I talk to their parents. But listen, we have no evidence that these experiments are what's putting them over the edge. Every single one of these suicides – and I've been tracking them – every one of those men has a history of other problems. Many have mental health issues. Some have addictions. Others have expressed discontent in their military roles. I don't believe the experiments are to blame. They might not help, I'll give you that. But I don't believe they're responsible."

"What sort of screening do you do before you accept a volunteer?"

"Not much beyond what's already in their file. We have a lot of legal terms they have to agree to. That's about it."

"Couldn't you screen for some of these...'problems'?"

"We could," Jorge acknowledged. "But we want the best data possible, data that's experienced in real time by our real troops. If we start adding in qualification criteria, all of a sudden, our pool of participants looks much different, and our data will be skewed. We won't have participants that represent the full spectrum of Khanist beliefs, attitudes, orientations, and health conditions. We lose if we exclude certain segments like that. Plus, we don't exempt men and women from Khanist service based strictly on those conditions. Our volunteers reflect the types of men and women who will face Johanum if we go to war. This is the best way to get the best data and see how our Khanists will respond to different triggers."

"I don't think you're getting the quality data you think you are."

"What makes you say that?"

"Is this your Data Compilation?" Antoine pointed to one of the monitors. He had been turning a knob on one of the control panels, flipping through screen after screen, looking for something familiar.

The screen was a dynamic, interactive topological map, depicting a scene Antoine knew well. The forest of Johanum.

"There are layers," Jorge explained, walking over to the monitor. He reached up and touched some of the trees.

They moved aside, clearing a footpath. A pop-up box appeared, detailing facts about the forest.

"Temperature: Cool during the day, hot at night".

"Humidity: Tolerable to high."

"Dusk: Sets quickly. Goes from light to utter darkness in a matter of minutes."

"Trees."

The word "trees" was underlined. Jorge tapped the word. Descriptions of multiple species appeared. After each description came a planet of origin.

"You've been able to identify every type of tree?" Antoine asked. He was surprised – and impressed.

"We're working on it," Jorge said. "It takes a long time. Our men, most of them don't know plants and trees any more than you or I do. Our visual feed tends to work better in the forest though, so our engineers have been having the volunteers spend time collecting visual data whenever they end up in the forest during their simulation."

"And you view tree species as important data because...?"

"Because it confirms an earlier theory that Johanum has no vegetation of its own. All its vegetation must be captured from other planets and transported. Each of these trees can be traced back to one of the planets in our solar system. Which brings us to another troubling observation. It appears Johanum has visited all of our planets. Not just visited, but spent enough time on each planet to extract trees. Who knows what else they have taken."

"Why does this surprise you? They've captured people too."

"Yes, but those numbers are small. They've populated a forest with these trees. A forest so huge, we don't even know how big it is."

"Hang on a second," Antoine interrupted. "Why do you say the number of kidnappings is small?"

"You see the same reports that I do. We're talking maybe twenty people a year. In the entire galaxy. That's not a lot."

"How many planets even know to report a kidnapping to us and link it to Johanum? We should be looking at law enforcement data and overall kidnapping and disappearance reports."

"Okay, yes, I see your point, you're right. But even then, those numbers are small. We would hear about them it they were large."

"Middlestan," Antoine said, ignoring Jorge and answering his own question about linking kidnappings to Johanum. "Middlestan has made the connection. Charisburg is aware of Johanum as well. Those are the only planets that would even consider Johanum as a possible link. We don't receive kidnapping reports from any other planet."

"I sense you're not done," Jorge said dryly.

"You're right that the Priests visit all our planets. I didn't know they were stealing trees. I don't know why they would, and I'm not sure I care. But they visit, frequently. I doubt we ever know when they're here. Now that you realize that, have you taken the time to consider how far their influence may reach? Do you have any idea what they are capable of?"

"That's the whole point of these experiments!" Jorge answered. "To find out!"

"You're studying the wrong thing."

Jorge slammed his fist into the monitor, his annoyance getting the better of him. "Then tell me what to study!"

Both men heard the popping sound. A crack appeared near Jorge's hand. They watched it creep slowly up and to the right, gaining speed. A slow "creek," and the monitor splintered, crashing in pieces to the floor.

Jorge stood frozen, clearly embarrassed. He only turned around when Antoine burst out laughing.

"This might be the only time I have ever seen you look ashamed," Antoine chuckled.

Jorge shook his head and stared at the mess covering the floor. How was he going to explain this? Well, the good news was, he didn't need to. He was a Chief. He didn't have to explain anything to anybody.

Antoine disappeared for a few minutes and returned with a broom and a dustpan.

"You know we have cleaning bots," Jorge said.

"Yeah, but then the broken screen will be recorded. Better leave that out of the Logs."

"I keep this whole department out of the Logs."

Antoine rolled his eyes. "I should have known."

"So are you going to tell me what you think of all this? Other than the obvious, that you hate it and want it shut down."

"You're not going to like what I have to tell you," Antoine replied.

"Do you want to see the other Data Compilations? We have two more."

"Not right now," Antoine answered. "I've seen enough to give you my feedback. If you still want it."

"I do. I mean, I don't, but I do."

"Should we include Calif?"

Jorge nodded. "Meet you back upstairs in an hour? I need to make a call to Maria. She's not going to be happy that I'm missing dinner. Again."

Antoine gestured towards the door. "Go ahead. I'll meet you upstairs."

Jorge nodded and left.

Antoine returned to the control panels. He flipped slowly between the three Data Compilations. It took a few minutes, but he figured out how to pull all three screens up simultaneously and project them onto the three wall monitors still intact.

He stood back and paced around the room, studying the screens as he walked.

The scenes were familiar. The forest. The desert. The Stone Gardens. They were all real. And yet....

And yet he could not shake the feeling that something here wasn't.

The coloring was part of it. Johanum existed under a canopy of red. Some sort of strange chemical composition in the air made Johanum look like it was covered in a red film. It made visitors feel like they were looking at everything through a pair of red-tinted glasses. That should have been reflected here. The engineers should have been able to see it, or at the very least, some of the volunteers should have noticed.

But that wasn't what was bothering him. Something else was missing. What was it?

The scenes in front of him felt...safe. There was no sense of foreboding. No instinctual, gut reaction to warn the viewer of inevitable danger. Nothing looked inviting. But neither would a viewer be reduced to a heap of anxiety.

What was missing?

Antoine had no idea how long he'd been standing there before he shook his head, reached over, and flipped off the monitors.

It would come to him. In the meantime, he needed to get back upstairs.

CHAPTER 35
Johanum

I stared at the wall.

What was this canvas? Why did it exist? Why did I exist? What was I looking at but a reflection of my empty, meaningless self?

I started to paint. I returned to black. Color seemed garish, assaulting. I did not live in color.

I used to see the world – my planet, my whole galaxy – as a landscape bursting with possibility. To be alive was to embrace wonder. To embrace what you did not yet know. My existence was a canvas that had not yet been painted. Maybe the canvas wasn't completely blank. Others had come before me, paving the way, leaving behind color and depth and dimension, bringing to life the world I inhabited. But still my life was a canvas with so much blank space. I had so many colors, so many brushes, so many painting techniques available to me.

I stepped back and stared at my work. It was ugly. It had no shape, no form, no dimension.

It was Johanum.

I slammed my fists against the wall in anger. Paint splattered in every direction. I didn't care. None of it mattered anyway.

This ugly, awful canvas was what I knew of the world. All that would ever be remembered of my existence could be reduced to fake black paint smeared against a forgotten cave wall. It would soon be forgotten, just as I would be forgotten.

I left the canvas alone for days. Mad Laughs and I decided to try our hands at making teacups. We had been using our mud plates and bowls for everything. I suggested trying to make teacups and saucers. Mad Laughs responded with a look of utter bewilderment.

I sketched a picture of a teacup into the dirt floor.

Mad Laughs was clearly confused, but he was my friend and decided to humor me, as friends often do.

I had thought to surprise Mr. Fox with a proper invitation to tea. What would be more proper than teacups? Alas, it was not meant to be. The mud refused to hold such a shape. Our attempts at fashioning teacup handles resulted in several small bowls that were lopsided and strangely thick on one side. They didn't even work as regular bowls. They tipped over and spilled.

We smashed our failures and returned to using mud plates and bowls.

I went back to the canvas and stared at it.

It turns out there are textures and nuances in black. I could see now that the formless painting I had left behind had dried. Where the paint had been layered many times over, the painting was darker, thicker, and full of emotion. In other places, the paint was so thin, flickers of the wall showed through, like flickers of light that would not be extinguished.

I closed my eyes and ran my fingertips over the painting. The topography, rising and falling, felt cold beneath my hands, and it told a story all its own.

I dipped my hands into the bowl of red paint. Forgetting the brushes, I pressed color and purpose onto the canvas. On that canvas I left my heartache, my focus, my hope.

Next, I used the green paint. Then the blue.

I stepped back and surveyed my work. My hands were filthy, but I was proud of that canvas. I was proud of what I had accomplished with so little.

The canvas was still ugly. But now it was my ugly. I owned it. And it would bend to my will.

The next afternoon, like clockwork, I returned.

Much of the paint had dried. The color had faded with the hours and had become...less. I wondered how long it would continue to fade. Would the color I saw now remain? Or would it continue to dull, to change? Would these changes go on forever?

I picked up a brush. This time I painted more slowly. I was tired, yes. But I had also realized I didn't want to fill every inch of the canvas. Blank space was beautiful too. How could I elevate the blank space to the same level as my textured colors? How could the blank space be part of the story I was telling, this story that had no words, only raw, blistering emotion at the hands of an unskilled artist?

Over the days that followed, I stopped caring that no one would ever see my painting. Mad Laughs and I enjoyed it. That was enough. The painting was really for me anyway. It was my life, spoken in a language no one else would understand.

I was at peace with that.

CHAPTER 36
Bisurakhan

Josh leaned back in his chair as far as it would go.

He liked Corey. He did.

"Great shift!" Corey exclaimed. He patted Josh on the shoulder, as was his nightly ritual.

"Great shift," Josh repeated.

"Can't wait to do it again!"

"Yeah, can't wait."

"All right, well...I'll see you back here tomorrow."

"See you tomorrow."

Josh breathed a deep sigh of relief when he heard the door close.

It wasn't that there was anything wrong with Corey, per se. He really just had one glaring flaw.

He wasn't Calvin.

"Three more weeks," Josh muttered to himself as he picked up his jacket from the floor near the coat hangers. His gloves were right where he had left them, zipped inside the pockets. He put on one glove and noticed a hole. With a little work he wiggled one of his fingers out.

"Looks like you need new gloves," came a friendly voice.

Josh looked up to see Hailey's cheerful face in the doorway.

"It is so good to see you," Josh said warmly. He was surprised to realize how happy he was to see her.

"Right? You've been missing me, I know. Me and Mary. We add sunshine to your life. I hear that all the time."

"I wasn't going to take it quite that far..."

"Nah, but admit it, you miss us."

"I actually do."

"They keep scheduling us for the morning shift and let me tell you – BORING. Trust me, you do not want to work mornings."

"The morning shift guys are dull."

"They can't carry a conversation. Or listen to one. They're coffee guzzling machines who might not be human."

"Do you think they're secretly robots?"

"Oooooo – like members of the robot army the Chiefs are building?"

"Exactly. Maybe the robots can assume human form. Maybe the robots ARE the morning shift guys."

"You mean they might be infiltrators?" She stopped short and gasped. "From JOHANUM!"

Josh burst out laughing. "The morning guys are boring, they're not evil."

Hailey shrugged. "I know. It's painful, that's all I can say. Our mornings are so long. I miss you and Calvin."

"I think I'm becoming boring without Calvin."

"That's right! Calvin's not here! His wife had her baby?"

"Yup, and he's been gone three weeks. Not that I'm counting. They had a little girl. Her name's Amelia. She's super cute."

"Do you get to play Uncle?"

"Something like that. Calvin and Leah don't have siblings, so Amelia doesn't have any actual aunts or uncles." Josh stretched his arms in a mocking display of strength. "Guess she needs someone strong and handsome to take care of her."

"She's lucky to have you for a fake uncle."

"Hey! I can be a real uncle. Who says you have to be blood related?"

"I guess that's true. Could we visit? Me and Mary? Oh, Josh, we'd love to! We could bring them something. Dinner, maybe?"

"That's a really nice offer. I don't see why not. I'd call them first though, before you show up. They seem to have forgotten the necessity of showers."

Hailey laughed. It was the loud, gregarious laugh that Calvin found so irritating. In that moment, Josh found her laugh surprisingly contagious. Cute, even.

"Josh, I have five nieces and nephews. Trust me, I know all about the Showerless Portal."

"The what?"

"The Showerless Portal. The portal that sucks in new parents, making them forget all rational adult concerns. Like, for instance, the importance of smelling good. Being clean. Those brain cells just up and die - gone! Don't worry, they come back. They exit the Showerless Portal eventually. Although then there's the Sleeping Upright Stage, the I-Only-Talk-In-Baby-Talk Tunnel, the Baby-Food-Is-Acceptable-for-Dinner Dimension - "

"The what??"

"When they get too tired to make their own food and decide it's perfectly acceptable to eat baby food as a meal. You know it's bad when they also think it's acceptable to SERVE baby food to their guests as dinner."

"I'm going to have to live through all of this?"

"Not you. Them. Well, okay, yes, you, by extension. Roll up your sleeves, Uncle Josh! You're in for a ride!"

"It's a good thing their baby's cute."

"Ha! I'm sure she is. Hey, listen, I don't have Calvin's number. I guess I don't have yours either. Could you call them for me? Ask if they'd like some visitors? Mary and I can stop by any afternoon. Or we could go on a day you're off and then you could join us!"

"That sounds great. I'll definitely call them. Let me get your number. I'll let you know when they're ready for company. Calvin's wife's name is Leah, by the way."

"Leah, got it."

"And the baby is Amelia."

"Ca-Le-Am. Ca-Le-Am. Got it."

"Huh?"

"It's just a little trick I have. A trick to remember the names of people who belong together. Ca-Le-Am. Calvin, Leah, Amelia. See? It worked! It totally works."

"You're weird."

"Oooooo, look at the Bisurakhanati, talking about how other people are weird."

"I'm not weird."

"No one on any planet is as weird as you people."

"Well, if we're weird, we're weird in a good way."

"It wasn't a value statement. You're just strange. All of you. But I like you. You're all right."

"Just all right?"

"You know. Pretty all right."

"All right."

"Not as cool as me or Mary."

"Of course not. I can't compare to Cornersville."

"You really can't. I mean, unless you have a secret skill for dancing."

"God help me."

"It would make you awesome!"

"I'm already awesome!"

"Not if you can't dance. Or sing. Ooooo, do you sing?"

"Absolutely not."

"You have no talents?"

"I have plenty of talents!"

"Name one."

"I - " Josh paused. "You mean, like, artistic talents? Performing arts talents?"

"I mean something that's not work related. I know you're super smart. You've got the whole 'insanely intelligent' vibe going on. I mean, do you have any, like...*fun* talents."

"Work is fun."

"Now I'm starting to think you're as boring as the morning shift."

"I am not!"

"A fun talent! One. You've got to have one."

"What's yours?"

"Oh, I have many. I sing. I dance. Three different styles, I'll have you know, but I'm working on two more. I paint. I doodle."

"You 'doodle'?"

"Like sketches and stuff."

"How do you find time to work?"

"Well, see, that's the difference between our planets, Josh. Cornersville folk – we work to live. You crazy people – you do nothing but work."

"The galaxy depends on us."

"Does it?"

"Where would you be without the Peace Treaty? Can you even imagine what your life would be like if you had to worry about attacks at the Periphery? Or invasions on your planet? You get to enjoy a slower pace of life because of the work that we do."

"We might have to agree to disagree about that."

"What's there to disagree about? We keep you safe so you have the freedom to build whatever kind of life you want. You're insulated. I'm not saying that's a bad thing. The Peace Treaty was Bisurakhan's idea. But we're the ones who make it possible for all the other planets to have an existence that doesn't depend so heavily on work."

"You really think a lot of yourself, don't you?"

"It's not about me. It's about the whole system."

"You know what, it doesn't matter. What matters is that we're happy. And Mary and I would be so happy to get to visit Ca-Le-Am. Calvin, Leah, Amelia. Yup, still got it. Will you let me know what they say? Also, what kind of food do they like?"

"They'll eat anything. They're not picky." He paused. "Leah doesn't like onions."

"Would they like Cornersville cuisine?"

"I don't see why not."

"Oh, this is turning into such a good day!" Hailey replied enthusiastically, clapping her hands. "We'll finally have an excuse to cook our own food for you guys! Seriously, no one around here likes our food."

"Wait. Is it bad?"

"Not when we don't burn it. I'm kidding! I'm kidding, sheesh, look at your face."

"I take food seriously."

"Obviously. Our food is good. Mary and I are good cooks. It's just that you Bisurakhanatis as a whole don't seem to like our dishes. But trust me – you'll like what we cook. We have lots of family recipes that have been around for generations. They're so good. You're going to like them. And you're going to come over with us?"

"Sure, I'll come. I might need to. Someone needs to remind them to take showers."

Hailey's laugh bounced happily off the walls. "Do you work tomorrow evening?"

"Yes, but I'm free the day after tomorrow."

"We work that morning, but we can go over in the evening, as long as we have a few hours to prepare."

"I'll call them and ask. What are you doing here, by the way?" Josh suddenly realized he had no idea why she had come into the office.

"I came to pick up some notes. My memory is great, but we've been translating so many messages lately, they're all beginning to run together. I don't know how you do it, Josh, keeping up in a place like this all the time."

"Do you like it here? I mean, aside from the work?"

248

"There is no 'aside from the work.' We're here to work. That's all we do. But it's fine, I don't mind it."

"That's the first time I've heard you sound less than happy."

"I'm happy!" she protested.

"Unhappy and in denial. The double helix of attraction," Josh joked.

Hailey blushed a deep crimson and shuffled her feet nervously. "Fine. If you must know, I'm terribly homesick."

"I'm sorry. I didn't mean to make you feel bad."

"You didn't. I felt bad already."

"Now I really feel bad. You were so cheerful when you walked in."

"It's an act, Josh. We're all doing it. Better to pretend to be happy than to be sad and make everyone around you miserable, right?"

"Is that why you're all so ridiculously enthusiastic most of the time?"

"Ridiculous? You think we're ridiculous?"

"Energetic. You all exude ridiculous amounts of energy. More than is natural."

"It's not natural, so therein lies your answer."

"If you're so unhappy, why did you volunteer to come? I'm not trying to be insensitive, but...didn't you realize what it would be like?"

"You would have volunteered too under the same circumstances."

"And what circumstances are those?"

"A Khanist Chief who shows up at your capitol and announces he will have your best linguists or the planet will be subject to food rations."

"What?"

Hailey ducked her head and peered around anxiously. The two communications engineers at the control panel had their earbuds in and were hard at work, not paying any attention to either of them.

"I know you like Jorge," Hailey said quietly. "I don't mean to say anything against him."

"I never said I liked Jorge. Calvin likes Jorge. He threatened you with food rations?"

"You both seem pretty tight with the Chiefs."

"Stop dodging the question. I thought Cornersville imported most of its food from Charisburg. How would we impose food rations?"

"You're a Khanist, you tell me. I don't know how any of this stuff works. I just know what they told us."

"We have no authority to do anything like that. That's a decision Charisburg would make."

"Again, I know nothing about imports and exports. All I know is that after Jorge's visit, our leaders called us together, all the best linguists, and gave us a choice: Save our families and come here, or stay home, be the cause of food rations, and be assured that our families would receive harsher rations than the rest."

"That's not a choice. That's blackmail!"

"Call it what you like. They got what they wanted. And here we are. Who knew that being the best at something would end up being such a liability."

"I'm so sorry. I had no idea."

"You won't tell anyone, will you? I don't want to get in trouble. I don't want to get anyone back home in trouble."

"Of course not. I won't say a word."

"I just want to do my job and go home. I'm ready to go home, Josh."

"You know you're probably here for a long time, right?"

Hailey turned her face away, but not before Josh saw her eyes filling with tears. "It'll go by fast," she said, as if trying to convince herself.

Josh winced at the pain in her voice. But that wasn't the only thing upsetting him. What else was Jorge doing? What was Bisurakhan doing? Was this the type of thing his government did to neighboring planets? He had always known some of Bisurakhan's practices around enforcing the Peace Treaty were questionable. But blackmail? Coercion?

"Do you know any of our Curators?" Josh asked abruptly.

Hailey collected the notes from her desk and returned to the doorway where Josh was waiting. "I don't think so," she answered. "I've seen one of ours – Oliver – a couple of times since I've been here. He's back at our capitol, last I heard. Why do you ask?"

"It's nothing, I was just curious. I'm going to call Calvin. Care to walk out with me?"

"Of course."

They took the elevation box waiting at the closest landing pad and then walked through the lobby and past all the purple desks. The air outside the Turris was cool and crisp.

Hailey shivered and pulled the collar of her coat up tighter around her chin. "Your autumn comes so early."

"Everything comes quicker here," Josh replied. "Our time signature is almost twice as fast as yours."

"Did you ever read those old stories in the Logs when you were a kid, the stories about how time used to pass the same way on all planets?"

"Yeah. Those stories confused me as a child."

"Me too. But you know, the funny thing is, now that I'm here, I don't really understand the different passages of time either."

"Well, the good news is, you're planet-hopping in the right direction."

"What do you mean?"

"Even if you stay here a year," Josh said, "when you go home, only, what...not quite seven months will have passed? You lose less time. It's better than planet-hopping in the other direction."

"I never really thought about it. So, people from the slower planets like Charisburg – they could travel and hardly miss a thing!"

"Charisburgians don't travel. They like their world just the way it is."

"Don't we all?"

"I guess so. We like what's familiar."

"Would you ever leave?"

"Leave Bisurakhan?" Josh asked. "I don't know. I've never really thought about it."

"Well, if you ever decide you want to travel, Cornersville is quite charming."

"I have no doubt," Josh said with a smile.

"I have to get going. Mary will be waiting for me so we can get dinner. You'll call me, after you talk to Calvin?"

"I will."

Josh watched her walk off into the night. Then he turned away in the opposite direction of his home and headed downtown.

CHAPTER 37
Johanum

As I approached the edge of the Stone Gardens, I sensed his presence. I could tell he had been there, waiting for me.

I placed the empty bowls I had been carrying on the ground at the garden's edge. He was standing near the Green Stone Fountain. His back was turned but I was not fooled. He knew I was there. I approached slowly.

"What do you want?" I asked.

The Priest with the X in his hands turned around. "My name is Carnificius," he said. "I don't believe we've been properly introduced."

"Does it matter?"

"No, I don't suppose it does." His eyes studied me thoughtfully.

"What do you want from me?" I asked again.

"I don't want anything from you. I'm not selfish, you know. I came here today to give you a gift."

"Like the gift you gave Fletcher?"

"No, not that kind of gift."

"I don't want it."

"You haven't heard what it is yet."

"I don't want it," I repeated.

"I admire your stubbornness, Josephine. If all our prisoners had your tenacity, life in Johanum would be much more interesting."

"Why are you here?"

"So many questions! They never stop with you, do they? I told you why I'm here. I came to give you something. You should really work on your listening skills."

"Thanks to you, I don't really have anyone around to listen to now, do I?"

"So much resentment! So much rage!" Satisfaction settled onto his face. "Your anger is the most beautiful thing about you."

"What do you know of my anger?"

"That it will give you power. Great power. Great control."

"I don't want power. Or control. I want to go home."

"Do you? Is that really what you want? Do you even have a home in Middlestan anymore?"

"Of course I have a home. They wouldn't get rid of it."

"I don't mean the building, darling. I mean the feeling of home. Middlestan has changed since you've been gone."

"Middlestan is a planet of academics. We don't change, not that much."

"Yet, you have. You have changed quite a bit. Do you really think you'd be welcomed back? It's not like they know what you've been through. Of course, they're good people, all your friends back home, but their lives are so predictable. They think every experience in the world can be understood if you simply apply the right logic. The world as they know it is black and white. And they love it that way. But now you have seen the world. The world as it is. A world that can't be explained. What would you do if you returned? What would they think of your stories? Would they even listen to you? I have no doubt they'd try. But they wouldn't understand. And, let's face it – they wouldn't want to. It would be very uncomfortable for them. You would make them uncomfortable."

He was right. The people of Middlestan loved their predictable lives. What would Dean Corban think if I tried to explain Johanum? What about Brian, or Dr. Cassidy, or Dr. Moody? They had no context for Johanum. They had no need to understand it.

"But you know..." Carnificius continued, twisting the X in his hands. "You could leave Johanum and go somewhere else. You don't have to return to Middlestan. There are other places that are...friendlier."

"What do you mean?"

"There are planets in your galaxy that acknowledge Johanum. Or...at least...don't deny it completely. Places that would listen to your stories. Places that would embrace you for who you are."

"Places like Bisurakhan?" It wasn't really a question. Carnificius nodded.

"Are you saying I can leave?"

"I didn't say that. Although, technically, yes, you can leave."

"How?"

"It's not easy, of course. We recognize official prisoner exchanges. Bring us someone we like, and we'll do an exchange. They stay and you can go."

"I would never do that."

"Don't be so appalled. I'm not asking you to do something dreadful. You can always come back later, if you choose. You can exchange back."

"If I left, I wouldn't come back."

"You might be surprised at what you grow to desire."

"I would never want to come back here."

"You think Johanum is a place? Of course you do. But this?" He gestured around him with distaste. "This is but a shell. You can leave Johanum, but Johanum will never leave you."

"What did you come to give me?"

"Advice."

"I don't want it."

"There is a rescue mission coming for you," he said, ignoring me. "A hovercraft. From Bisurakhan. It will be carrying four men. One of the men they call the 'Commander.' You will know him when you see him. We would be pleased to accept him as your prisoner exchange. You might suggest it to him."

"Wait – Bisurakhan's Commander is coming?"

"You know him?"

"I know *of* him."

"Then this will be easy for you."

"Why would he come for me?"

"It seems your little research paper created quite a stir in Bisurakhan. You're a wanted commodity."

"I can't possibly be that wanted. The Khanists would never give up their Commander."

"The Commander doesn't take orders. He gives them."

"It's not possible that he's coming," I insisted. "And if he didn't, he's not going to become a prisoner of yours."

"How do you know? Do you know how we choose our prisoners?"

"No," I admitted.

"I'm afraid I don't write the rules of the game, Josephine, I merely play. The Commander will play, too."

"And what do you get out of this game that you play?"

"Happiness. Pure, unadulterated happiness."

"I don't believe you. You're a miserable creature."

"No more miserable than you."

"Yes, but I'm a nobody. You have power. You could do something. Good things, I imagine, if you wanted to."

He chuckled humorlessly. "Why would I? Power begets power. And I love what it gives me."

"Is there nothing that gives you joy except cruelty and human suffering?"

"You're so judgmental. But, no, actually, I quite enjoy those things. I've never had a reason to want anything else."

"You're despicable."

"Yes. And you love it, don't you? I'm easy to hate. You humans are all the same. Even the smart ones, like you. It brings you joy to hate someone. I fulfill a deep need of yours. And you fulfill a deep need of mine. Do you see how important we are to each other?"

"My life was fine without you."

"Was it? As I recall, Josephine, you were miserable in Middlestan. Is your life here really so different?"

"It's completely different."

"Tell me."

"I can't leave!"

"But you can. I just told you how."

"I would never do that."

"So, you choose not to leave, to live by some made-up, internal, ethical code. Fine. I like you, and I hope you'll stay. But let's not forget – it's your choice."

"There's no purpose to life here. There's nothing to live for."

"You're surviving. You're staying alive. What's so wrong with that?"

"I want to *live*."

"But what did you live for in Middlestan?"

"I - " But I came up short, just like he knew I would.

"I'll tell you one way we're different," Carnificius said, twisting the X in his hands. "Despair. We give you despair. But what you don't understand is that we are giving you a gift. All that hope you carry inside – that inexplicable, devastating emotion found in every human, on every planet in every galaxy – it blinds you. It keeps you from seeing the world as it really is. And so, we relieve you of it. Here in Johanum, we relieve you of that awful, terrible, deceptive emotion, and give you the keys to reality."

I said nothing. I could feel my anger disintegrating. The rage that had boiled so close to the surface cooled. I stared at the ground, as miserable as ever.

"Help us rid the galaxy of deception, Josephine," Carnificius invited. "Give us the Commander. Go back to your planet, if you choose. Or go to Bisurakhan. Go anywhere you like. See for yourself if what I have told you is true. And then, if you disagree, you can come back. We'll take you back and let the Commander go. No harm done. But you will have come to know the truth. You want to know the truth, don't you?"

I stared at him, expressionless.

"Think about it, Josephine. I trust you'll choose well."

With that, he turned away and disappeared.

CHAPTER 38
Bisurakhan

The underground room was dark and musty and far too subdued for a bar. Still Josh knew he was in the right place.

Curators are used to living in the shadows. If you want to find one, you have to go where it's easy to hide. It helps if the space is large enough for a group. Curators are quite social with each other.

Josh grabbed a seat at the bar and ordered a drink. He tried not to be too obvious with his eavesdropping. It took a few minutes, but his ears picked up the familiar nasally sound of Curator voices, voices that were a little higher pitched than most men. Josh had heard the tonal changes were the result of their frequent time-space travel.

"Can't they send Bard?" asked one.

"Bard's been on the road for weeks. He wants a break."

"But he's been covering Middlestan for most of their year," the first voice protested.

"He's obviously the better choice, but it's not going to matter. He has to go back next week for a series of meetings. He says he deserves a break."

"I'm not arguing that he deserves one. I'm saying it makes no sense for them to send you."

"I go where they tell me, same as you. My reporting won't be as good, but you know what? If they don't care, I don't care."

"We're supposed to care about things like that."

"Yeah, well, they're supposed to care about us."

A third voice chimed in. "We have a visitor."

Josh didn't have to look up to feel all three sets of eyes turning in his direction.

"That didn't take long," he mumbled to himself.

"Come join us," invited the first voice.

Josh picked up his drink and stood. Three Curators rose from their stools as he approached.

"Let's grab a table," said the second voice. It belonged to a Curator named Aden. Josh recognized him now that he got a good look at his face. Another Curator, the one who had pointed out his eavesdropping, was LeMar. Josh didn't know the other one.

The Curators folded their tall, lanky bodies into chairs situated around a small, square table. Josh took the fourth seat. He felt bad. They looked uncomfortable in those small chairs.

"We can sit up at the bar," Josh offered.

"Nonsense," Aden waved him off. "I can hardly hear up there anyway. This is better. It's no worse that our inter-parallel transportation pods. Not to mention, here, we can drink!"

His comment was met with hearty grunts of approval.

"I do think your observation skills are starting to slip a little bit," LeMar commented. "You didn't even notice Josh sitting over there."

"I noticed him," Aden protested.

"No, you didn't."

"I noticed him once you said something." Aden turned to Josh. "It's good to see you. Been a while since you've been down in these parts."

"They're keeping us busy up in the Tower."

"So I've heard."

"What do you think about all the messages we've been receiving lately?" Josh asked.

"I don't know," Aden replied. "Haven't read 'em."

"Who's transcribing the messages for the Logs then?"

"Nobody."

"Someone has to be doing it. That's what you guys do, isn't it? You record stuff."

"Oh, sure. We record everything. And you, being a comms guy, communicate everything, to everyone, perfectly, all the time. Am I right?"

"I see you haven't lost your sarcasm."

The Curator that Josh didn't know chimed in. "I'm Hashim," he introduced himself.

Josh held out his hand. "Nice to meet you."

"You've known each other for a while?" Hashim fished, looking between Josh, Aden and LeMar.

"Josh is a good guy," LeMar told Hashim. "He descends into the Curator lair every once in a while. Not often enough, but hey, more than most."

"I've never seen him," Hashim replied skeptically.

"Life's been a little...unexpected...lately," Josh said.

"Sorry about your wife, man," said Aden.

"Ex-wife, unfortunately. But thanks."

"I heard she's gorgeous," Aden continued.

"She is. Was. Is. Still." Josh let out a long sigh, picked up his mug, and drank the whole beer.

"Heard she made good money."

"I don't think you're helping," LeMar cut Aden off.

"Not really," Josh agreed, staring into his mug, trying to quell the emotions rising up in his chest.

"What bring you down here?" LeMar asked, graciously changing the subject.

"I heard a rumor about Cornersville. I was hoping that one of you would be able to tell me if it's true."

"Oh good, the Rumor Mill Pop-Up," Hashim muttered. "I love those."

Aden kicked Hashim under the table. His knee was too tall and it caught the table, lifting it off the floor and spilling everyone's drinks.

"Subtle, very subtle," LeMar ribbed him.

"I'm not paid to be subtle," Aden mumbled.

"Why are you paid, again?" LeMar teased.

"Hey! Your friend wants information," Hashim said, refocusing the conversation.

"What did you hear?" Aden asked.

"That we threatened Cornersville with food rations."

"Yup, that happened. Next?"

"Wait," Josh replied angrily. "Just, 'yes'? That's it?"

"I see. That was not the answer you were looking for. Would you prefer I said something else?"

"No! I -" Josh let out a sigh and lifted his mug. It was empty. He shook it angrily and set it down on the table with a thud.

A bartender walked over and wordlessly placed another beer on the table in front of him.

"Why didn't I read about that anywhere?" Josh asked after he had taken a drink.

"Do you read the Logs on a regular basis?" Aden asked him.

"Of course not. That's why we have the news, to summarize the Logs."

"And how many reporters do you think are reading all the new Log entries?"

"I have no idea. But that's their job. To read what comes in and highlight the most important things."

"Then it looks like they didn't deem that incident in Cornersville as important. Or, perhaps, it was suggested to them that the event wasn't particularly important."

"Can we even do that?" Josh asked. "Enforce food rations?"

"I don't get paid to make those types of decisions," Aden answered.

"Me neither," LeMar agreed.

"What is it about Cornersville that interests you so much?" Hashim asked, his interest in Josh piqued for the first time.

"It's unethical!" Josh sputtered.

The Curators burst into laughter.

"You're a Khanist!" LeMar laughed loudly. "What do you care about ethics?"

"I have a sense of right and wrong."

"A sense you may have, but that doesn't mean much when you get out into the real world," Hashim remarked wryly.

"What else are we doing? Out there, 'in the real world'?" Josh asked.

The Curators shook their heads in amusement.

"Why are you asking all these questions, Josh?" Aden asked. "I like you, but you're going to get us in trouble. You're going to get yourself in trouble."

"Which Log entries do I need to read?" Josh pressed.

"You want a summary of every entry? Is that what you're after?" LeMar asked. "We'll be here all day. No, I take that back. We'll be here forever. And I mean that literally."

"The most important ones," Josh replied. "If I wanted to know about the deals being made. The things we're doing to enforce the Peace Treaty. Is there one place, one set of Logs, where I can go to read about that?"

LeMar stared back in bewilderment. "This is a full-time job for hundreds of us," he pointed out as gently as he could. "It's not possible for one person to read everything we record."

"Then how do we keep track of what's happening?"

"Your leaders have their methods. Certain people ask for specific reports. The Chiefs, for example, each have updates they've requested from us on a regular basis. It changes based on current events. Sometimes we make suggestions on things they might consider. Sometimes they focus on something they want us to cover in greater detail."

"So, you're saying that no one is keeping track of everything?" said Josh.

"I think your expectations are a little unreasonable," LeMar replied. "One person can't keep track of everything that happens in a city, much less on a planet or throughout an entire solar system. It's not possible. That's why we have systems. That's why we have the Logs. If you think you've missed something of relevance, you can go back and look it up. But mostly, our leaders rely on the reporting systems they've put into place, reporting mechanisms to give them the information they want. I think that's the answer to your question, although you might not like it. People keep track of whatever they deem important, and they disregard the rest."

"I want to track Jorge."

Hashim threw his head back and released a storm of laughter. Josh had never heard a Curator laugh like that. The sound was appalling.

LeMar looked amused. Aden, aghast.

"You want a Chief to know you're tracking him?" Aden asked, the pitch of his voice quickly rising, no small amount of wonder on his face.

"I guess he would know, huh?" Josh said. He hadn't thought through his request before he voiced it out loud. It was hardly the first time he had made that mistake.

"Oh. 'I guess' he probably would," Aden agreed.

"I admire your preference for ethics," Hashim said, "and I mean no disrespect, but you do realize how high above your rank you're shooting with that request? Officers senior to you wouldn't get away with trying to track a Chief."

"I'm aware. I mean, I need to think about this a little more, but I'm aware."

"And you're not worried about what could happen to you?" Hashim asked.

"We're preparing for war," Josh replied. "I think I have a right to know what factors are contributing to a war that I could be asked to fight for."

"But you won't be deployed," Hashim pointed out. "You're comms. They won't send you out of the Tower. You're too valuable. They want – they need – to keep you safe. And I mean that as a compliment."

"And what if the war comes to us? Here? There will be no hiding then."

Aden shrugged his shoulders. "You Khanists stop all invaders at the Periphery. Why are you worried about that?"

"Just because we've been able to stop invaders in the past, doesn't mean we'll be able to stop all of them in the future. Enemies get stronger, they figure out your weaknesses. You have to adjust and expect the unexpected."

"Spoken like a true Khanist," LeMar said wryly. "Look, I'm no military man, but I have to say – "

"Why do you do that? Why do you all say that? You were all military men before."

"Yes, well...it's been a while."

"You still have a perfectly good handle on our strategies."

"Things change," LeMar insisted.

"Not that much. Look, be candid with me," Josh said. "Are things out there in the rest of the galaxy being accurately represented by what we're being told?" He turned from one Curator to another. "You look embarrassed, every last one of you. That's all I needed to know."

"The Khanist strategy is designed to be complex," Hashim said. "It's designed to keep things hidden. Now, the reason for that is up to interpretation. Maybe it's meant to save lives. Maybe it's not. Draw your own conclusions. But manage your expectations. Bisurakhan is designed to be complex. If you want straightforward, move to Charisburg."

"Their pace of life would kill me," Josh muttered.

"They seem quite fond of it," Hashim replied.

"We all like our own lives. They're familiar."

"Then why are we all so restless?"

Josh and Hashim sat there, staring, sizing each other up.

LeMar leaned forward. "I think Hashim's found himself a new boyfriend."

Aden leaned back in his chair and howled in laughter.

Color flooded into Hashim's face.

"Sorry, man," Josh said, shaking his head. "I'm divorced, but that hasn't changed anything."

Hashim shrugged. "Can't blame me for trying. Do you know how hard it is for a Curator to find a date? Especially me?"

"Don't get down on yourself. None of us date. We're too ugly!" LeMar laughed.

"I'm less ugly than you," Hashim replied.

"You're new," said LeMar. "Give it a few years."

"Isn't there anything they can do to help you guys change less?" Josh asked.

"Oh, I'm sure they'll get right on that. After they deal with this little issue of a war, that is," Aden answered. "But hey, it's all part of the job. You get used to it. They pay us well. And, for the right price, you can always find companionship."

"It doesn't seem right," Josh argued.

"I'm bestowing on you a new name," Hashim said. "I hereby crown you, 'The Ethics King.'"

"It fits him," LeMar grinned.

"All right, guys, I have to go. It was good to see you."

"All hail the Ethics King!" Hashim proclaimed, lifting his glass good-naturedly.

"Come join us more often," Aden invited. "But next time, no questions. Just come for the beer."

"I will," Josh promised.

They waved and watched as Josh walked up the dark stone steps and pushed open the door in the ceiling.

"How long do you think he's got?" Hashim asked.

"Before Jorge catches on?" Aden asked.

"Before Jorge puts a price on his head."

"A month. Maybe less."

"Should we warn him?"

"Nah," Aden said, finishing up the last of his drink. "He'll figure it out. And then he'll be back. And we'll get to see more of him."

"Seems a little twisted," Hashim replied.

"It's not like anyone's confusing me for The Ethics King."

CHAPTER 39
Johanum

I changed my mind. I hated this canvas.

I dug my fingernails into the paint and scratched my way from one side to the other. Section after section, as much as I could grab a hold of, I peeled away from the wall.

Behind the paint, the wall was stained.

I would have destroyed that canvas, that wall, the whole cave. But my fists weren't that strong. It took all the strength I had to rage against the wall, pounding my hands against it until they were bloodied and bruised.

Rage runs deep.

Until it overflows.

They say a life is revealed in the eyes.

I had not seen a mirror since arriving in Johanum. I had not seen my own face in just as long.

I didn't need a mirror. I knew what I looked like. My eyes were reflected by every creature around me. In the eyes of the wraiths, who rarely looked up from their toil. In the eyes of wild animals, scuttling from one place to the next, their heads hung low. In the eyes of the lucky ones – the dead – whose eyes were no more empty than my own.

I had lost my mind and I knew it. This person was not me. But if this person was not me, perhaps I did not exist.

Mad Laughs found me, curled up against the wall, shaking uncontrollably. He seemed to know what I needed. For the next week, I barely spoke. He didn't ask me to. He fed me, refilled my bowl with Tufta milk, and covered me with blankets when my eyes slid shut.

Somewhere in the haze, I sensed my personality slipping away.

Mad Laughs didn't seem surprised. If anything, he knew exactly what to do. It was like he had seen this before.

I began to have dreams. Fletcher would come and talk to me. He told me how free he felt, there on the "other side." I saw Brian, wandering the halls of the university, looking for me. But in my dreams, when I called to him, even when he turned around and saw me, he didn't recognize me. He thought I was a stranger, and he went right on calling my name.

I saw the Chiefs. My home in Middlestan. The Priests.

My dreams became more and more vivid. They seemed more real than when I was awake. Or maybe it was all the same. Maybe Mad Laughs, maybe this cave, maybe Johanum itself...maybe it was all nothing more than a dream.

It was a dream from which I could not awaken.

CHAPTER 40
Bisurakhan

Calif appeared to be giving separate instructions to no fewer than six men at once. How he managed it – jumping between so many different conversations – was something Antoine had never understood but always admired.

He watched as the officers volleyed for attention. Most of them spoke at once. Only General Phillip Macy held back, waiting for a pause in the conversation. Calif listened as all the men spoke, his head tilted down, eyes directed at the floor. It's what he did when he was trying to concentrate. It enabled him to sift through multiple, simultaneous lines of dialogue.

Antoine remembered the first time he had experienced Calif's uncanny knack for listening to multiple conversations. They had been in a crowded room at a Khanist holiday party. At one point, Calif motioned at Antoine to stop talking. Calif's head tilted downward, in much the same way it looked now. A few minutes later, he raised his eyes and gestured at Antoine to continue. Only later did Antoine learn Calif had zeroed in on three conversations happening around the room that he thought the Chiefs should address.

Jorge was known for his intuition and his ability to make quick, decisive decisions. Calif had a reputation for listening and giving wise council.

Antoine wondered what, if anything, he would be known for.

Most of the men were finishing up their business. Antoine watched them file out the door. Only General Macy remained. Calif motioned for Antoine to join them.

"The mechanics are making the hovercraft upgrades you requested," Gen. Macy said, "but they've encountered a few problems."

Calif pulled out the chair next to him. Antoine sat down and greeted the General.

"And what problems are those?" Calif asked.

Gen. Macy rolled out a set of blueprints he had tucked under his arm. "These specifications you gave us. They're not consistent with the atmosphere at the Periphery."

Calif took a minute to look over the blueprints spread out on the table in front of him. "These specifications are correct. Proceed as directed."

"But, sir – I'm sorry to question you, but I don't think you fully understand what could happen to a hovercraft that's been outfitted this way."

"Do you, General, understand that you are to follow orders?" There was no anger in Calif's voice, only the gruffness of a tired old man.

Gen. Macy held his ground. "Sir, it is my duty to ensure your safety to the best of my ability, along with the safety of Antoine here, and Jorge. The Commander has instructed me to serve it at the risk of my own life. These structural changes could result in significant damages to the engine once you cross the barrier at the Periphery. As long as you stay in our solar system, you'll be fine. But Jorge led me to believe you intend to travel further. I cannot, in good faith, allow you to travel in a vessel that could fail under different conditions."

"We will assume the risk, General."

"Sir, I mean no disrespect -"

"Then you'll need to stop questioning my orders."

"You've instructed us to question you, sir, when the situation is dire."

A smirk appeared on Calif's weathered face. "Yes. Yes, I suppose I did. I hate it when I get caught up in the web of my own boundaries."

Antoine chuckled. "This is how you and Jorge differ."

"Oh, I don't know about that," Calif countered. "I think Jorge hates checks and balances as much as I do."

"Yes, but you actually *have* them," Antoine pointed out.

Gen. Macy laughed a little too loudly, then caught himself.

"At ease, General," Calif said. "I do, indeed, respect your opinion, and in matters of mechanics, typically I would acquiesce. But this time, I am overriding your advice. I'm afraid I must do so without offering you an explanation. But please know, your concerns have been noted, and the Commander will not hold you responsible for any damage that occurs on that hovercraft. I'll make sure of it. Please proceed."

"As you wish." Gen. Macy gave the Khanist salute and left.

"He doesn't know where we're going?" Antoine asked. "Shouldn't he be told? He's the Head of Engineering. We may need his help if we run into trouble."

"You don't even know where we're going," Calif replied.

"We're going to the Space Between."

"No, we're going *through* the Space Between. A place I would like to see you locate on a map."

Antoine turned to look at the intergalactic map lining the walls. It stretched around the full circumference of the room.

"I can't," he finally answered.

"Exactly."

"Johanum isn't on the map either," Antoine pointed out.

"Neither is the Underworld."

"We have a very incomplete map."

"Yes, we do."

Neither man spoke for several minutes.

"I don't want to go back."

Calif turned toward Antoine. "No one said you had to."

"This is why I'm a Chief."

"Not the only reason."

"But a very big one."

Calif nodded. "Yes, I suppose it is. The Commander values your experience and expertise. And, I think, he values what you've made of it."

"What do you mean?"

"You haven't let the experience define you."

"I beg to differ."

"Well, obviously you know yourself. It isn't the only thing that defines you."

Antoine nodded. "The Commander is still planning to join us on this mission?"

"Last I heard."

"You don't sound very confident. I thought you and Jorge were his most trusted advisors. How could you not know?"

"We are his inner circle," Calif answered. "So are you. How often do you speak with him?"

"Not often. So infrequently, in fact, I assumed you and Jorge had your own meetings with him."

"On occasion we do, but you're involved in most of them."

"We really are acting quite independently, then. You and Jorge are the ones calling most of the shots."

"That's debatable. You've seen the checks and balances in our system. We work in very close proximity to the President, even if we do attempt to limit his one-on-one time with the troops."

"President Basjid is not well received by the Khanists."

"He isn't well known by them. That's most of the problem. He's a good man, for the most part, but his understanding of the military is limited."

"And the Commander?"

"What about him?"

"Is he a good man?" Antoine asked.

"He rescued you from Johanum, didn't he? You're questioning whether he's good?"

"Men have all sorts of reasons for doing what they do."

Calif sat quietly, his weathered hand stroking the carefully tended grey-speckled beard that graced his face. "I have questioned a great many things about the Commander over the years," he admitted. "He is unlike any man I have ever met. But I have never had reason to doubt his intentions. He's a very perceptive man, wise beyond his years. He has led the Khanists well. He has kept Bisurakhan and all the planets in our solar system safe since he came to power. I have no reason to think he is anything but good."

"Yet your face tells me otherwise," Antoine observed.

"He is shrouded in mystery. It's difficult to fully trust a person you don't feel you know."

"Why does he spend so little time here?"

"In Bisurakhan?"

"Yes."

"I don't know."

"You don't know his whereabouts when he leaves?"

"We know them. They track his movements up in the Communications Tower, as well as at the Flight Control Deck."

"But you don't know what he does on his missions?"

"The Commander doesn't answer to us. We answer to him."

"Doesn't he answer to the President?"

Calif was stroking his beard again. "I'm not entirely sure how that relationship works."

"You've been a Chief for ten years!"

"And so you see how fallible a man can be. Even one with a fancy title."

"I had hoped that, with time, I would feel less like an outsider. That hope is fading."

"Don't lose hope. We're all outsiders to some degree. Just so long as you have a place where you're an insider too, you'll be okay."

"Like Johanum."

"That was definitely not what I was insinuating. I was suggesting you get re-married."

"I have no interest," Antoine replied.

"I know. That's why I worry about you."

"I talked to Jorge," Antoine said, changing the subject.

Calif nodded. "He mentioned it. What did you see?"

"I saw a man collecting a lot of data, a lot of data he has no idea what to do with."

"Do you think it's credible?"

"Do I think it's real, you mean?" Antoine sighed. "I don't know. That's the problem. I think it's mostly real. But the part that isn't – the part I can't fully explain – has me worried."

"You were worried long before you saw what Jorge was doing."

"I still haven't really seen it, but that's on me. At least I see what he's doing now. I understand it. Calif, there's real danger here. I'm not so worried about the data collection. It's off, in some way that I can't explain, but that's actually not what has me worried. Enough of it looks real that it seems he really has opened the door to Johanum. He thinks we're outsmarting them, but I know we can't. Which leads me to believe we're being played. I don't believe these experiments are about us collecting data. They may be feeding us a few things. But that's not what it's about at its core. These experiments are giving Johanum an open invitation to Bisurakhan. We have swung open the door to our planet and invited them in. It won't end well."

"Let me ask you something, Antoine," Calif replied. "I'm being as sensitive as I know how to be, but I must ask. Do you think you are capable of being objective about Johanum?"

"Of course not."

"Then why should I listen to you over Jorge? Based on your own admission — why should I believe Jorge's experiments are going to hurt us? Why should I believe the danger you anticipate outweighs the benefits Jorge believes we're receiving?"

Calif saw Antoine's mood shift. He was trying to play devil's advocate in hopes of better understanding Antoine's thought process, but he could tell he had pushed too far. Antoine rolled back his chair and stood up.

"I'm tired of fighting you guys," Antoine said. "But I know I won't stop. Am I objective? No. But I'm what you've got. You ignore me at your peril. But ignore me if you want to. It's your choice."

"I'm not trying to ignore you. I'm trying to have a conversation with you."

"You're not trying to have a conversation with me," Antoine said, shaking his head as he walked to the door. "You're trying to get me to see the world the way you do. And that's never going to happen. It can't, not anymore. That world you inhabit no longer exists for me."

CHAPTER 41
Johanum

"How's she doing?" asked Sibilum.

"She'll be fine," Carnificius answered.

"She's nearly catatonic," Mortarium sniffed.

"What did you say to her?" Sibilum demanded.

"I told her about Bisurakhan's rescue mission," Carnificius replied.

"Then why is she sad?"

"She's a human! Their emotional states are all dismal and chaotic."

Sibilum frowned. "Did you instruct her on the prisoner exchange?"

"I suggested it."

"When will you learn to give orders like a real Priest?"

"The same time you learn that helping them think for themselves can be more powerful."

"We don't need them to think for themselves! That can get dangerous!"

"It can also be useful. Calm down."

"I wish you were useful," Sibilum spit at him.

"I'm hurt," Carnificius sniffled, falling forward in mock distress. "Truly, deeply, I am mangled with self-loathing."

Mortarium leaned back against the wall. "You're like clockwork, the both of you. I could predict your arguments in my sleep."

"You don't sleep," Sibilum pointed out.

"No, but if I did, I suspect this is what it would be like. I can see why the humans like it so much. You stop being aware of anything going on around you. It's what happens to me every time the two of you start your bickering."

"How about you tell us what you've been up to lately," Carnificius hissed. "Or are you still trying to keep it a secret?"

Sibilum jerked his head around. "I thought you went to Bisurakhan!"

"I did. And then to Kabira, and then Pendleton," Mortarium whined, unhappy at the turn of conversation.

"I didn't send you there!" Sibilum roared.

"You sent me on a conquest," Mortarium retorted, "and I, well…I conquested."

Carnificius rolled his eyes. "Conquered. You conquered."

Mortarium shook his head. "Nope, I definitely didn't do that."

"Did you accomplish anything?" Sibilum asked crossly.

"It was a scouting mission," Mortarium explained, "so yes, I accomplished quite a bit. Everything I set out to."

"You mean you walked around and did nothing," Carnificius clarified.

"I was getting the lay of the land."

"My point exactly."

"You can't go in blind to an attack," Mortarium said defensively. "You have to know what you're dealing with."

"I don't care what you do," Sibilum interrupted, "as long as you have a plan to deliver Bisurakhan and the Commander."

"We'll be fine," Mortarium replied.

"What do we need to do to prepare?" Sibilum asked.

Mortarium blinked. "Prepare?"

"Preparation!" Sibilum bellowed. "Please tell me you have a plan!"

"Of course, I have a plan!"

"What is it?"

Mortarium balked. "You didn't tell me you were going to want the details."

"Do you have an actual plan?" Sibilum demanded.

"I have a plan!" Morarium shouted back.

"He doesn't have a plan," Carnificius said with a roll of his eyes. "He never has a plan. He makes it up as he goes. Now, if you'd like to put your resident intellect on the job..."

"You can't trust him!" Mortarium sputtered in Carnificius' direction.

Carnificius smiled, relishing in Mortarium's anger.

"No, I most certainly can't trust you," Sibilum agreed, eyeing Carnificius with distaste.

"Relax," Carnificius chided, sliding his hands up and down the X he always held. "You're feeling anxious because you made a ridiculous deal and you know it. Now, if you're counting on this fool to do all the work," he gestured at Mortarium, "well – I wouldn't blame you for being stressed. You'll fail, miserably. But there's no reason we can't all work together. It's the only way we all get what we want."

Sibilum glared. "I'm listening."

"Mortarium, you fool, please tell me you're not planning to attack Bisurakhan directly," Carnificius prodded him.

"Of course not!" Mortarium bristled. "Wait – why not?"

"It's too risky. Their weapons are quite advanced. It would give them too much of an advantage. It would work better for us if we attacked one of the other planets. Or, perhaps, a couple of them."

"We don't need any of the other planets," Sibilum pointed out.

"That's not the point," Carnificius replied. "Of course we don't need them. What we need is to get the Khanists to leave. They'll be weaker on another planet. And they'll leave Bisurakhan largely undefended."

"They won't be weaker on other planets," Mortarium said. "It's quite the opposite. When Khanists enter a slower time signature, they get stronger."

"Physically, yes," Carnificius agreed. "But emotionally? Mentally? After a long while of being separated from their homes and their families? With enough time, it will weaken them."

"Khanists travel all the time," Sibilum said. "I don't think a few days fighting away from home will accomplish much."

"So we draw it out. Keep them moving. I'm not talking about a quick, one-time attack. I'm suggesting a game of planetary cat and mouse. Give them a chase. Wear them out. It won't be difficult."

"We would need more than the three of us to pull it off," said Sibilum.

"We have friends in the Underworld," Carnificius replied. "Not Sulta, obviously..."

"What do you think?" Sibilum asked Mortarium, who scowled in response. "Do you have a better idea?" Sibilum pressed him.

Mortarium shook his head.

"He doesn't have a better idea," Carnificius hissed. "He doesn't have any ideas."

"You've left out the most important part," Mortarium interrupted, ignoring the insult. "You've left out the Commander."

"I've already taken care of him."

"What, the girl?" Mortarium mocked. "She won't do it."

"You don't know that. You don't know her at all!"

"Neither do you."

"You don't understand the humans like I do," Carnificius hissed.

"You don't understand them half as well as you think you do, and therein lies your problem," Mortarium said with a shrug. "Sibilum, this game of cat and mouse is all well and good, but we need a plan to capture the Commander. A real plan."

"Your job was the plan!" Sibilum yelled at him.

"He can't do it, that should be obvious by now," Carnificius said.

"I can execute a good plan once we have one," Mortarium retorted. "Now – the Commander! We must come up with a plan together. Or have you forgotten what happened the last time he was here?"

Carnificius let out a low hiss of warning, his eyes flashing a brighter shade of red. Sibilum looked increasingly irritated.

"So yes, you remember," said Mortarium.

"We agreed not to speak of it," Sibilum replied.

"It's not my fault you brought him into this," Mortarium said angrily. "And no doubt you had to include him because you're still bitter."

"He's right, you know," Carnificius chided, his face aglow with mock concern. "You should really learn to let that go."

"How conveniently you've forgotten your own humiliations," Sibilum seethed.

"I wasn't humiliated," Carnificius insisted.

"You didn't show your face for a month," Mortarium snorted. "My, my, Carnificius, are you losing your memory as well as your charm?"

Carnificius hissed.

"I think it would be best if we reviewed what happened," suggested Mortarium.

Carnificius and Sibilum reacted by setting the house and each other on fire.

Mortarium yawned and leaned back against the wall, waiting for their anger to run its course.

The flames died down. Sibilum and Carnificius dusted off their robes, brushed the ashes off each other's backs, and sat down.

"Let's try this again," Mortarium said.

He reached out his hand over a black mound of dirt sitting on the floor. It crackled. A few more pops and it erupted into flames. Using both hands, he pushed the air to move the fire into the center of the room.

"And now, to relive your happiest memories," Mortarium said dryly.

CHAPTER 42
Bisurakhan

"Name?"

"Calvin Smith."

"Age?"

"28."

"Department?"

"NO. No, no, no, no! I've been here before. I don't need to go through all these questions again."

"I don't see your name in our database," the administrator said with a frown. "New volunteers must review and agree to all standard protocol."

"I'm not new!"

"You aren't in the database."

"I've been here a dozen times. Look again."

The administrator turned his face slowly between the screen and Calvin. Back and forth. Three times. "Still not there."

"I mean…don't just look at the screen. Do a search for my name again."

The administrator sighed loudly. "Tell me your name again. And this time, spell it."

"Calvin Smith. C-a-l-v-i-n S-m-i-"

"Ah, that's it."

"That's what?"

"You spell 'Smith' with an 'i.'"

"How else would I spell it?"

"You could spell it with a 'y.' Or an 'e.'"

"An 'e'?? Smeth? My name is Smith!"

"There's no need to get so emotional," the administrator replied.

"I'm not emotional. I'm TIRED. Do you see my eyes? This is what tired looks like." Calvin tried to open his eyes wide, but all he could manage was a series of painfully slow blinks, and his eyes stayed shut much longer than they remained open.

"Are you sure you're in the proper mental state for an experiment?" the administrator asked suspiciously.

Calvin let out a slow exhale and hung his head. Two more. Two more experiments and he was done with the Labs forever.

"You're free to go," the administrator said, waving him past. "Get out of here before I change my mind and alert the General."

Calvin walked to the nearest set of elevation boxes and stepped inside the one with the open doors.

"Welcome, Calvin," the digital female voice said as the doors slid shut. "Transporting you to the Reality Persuasion Labs."

"Thanks, Emma."

The box came to a screeching halt mere inches off the ground.

"I see no Emma," the voice said accusingly. "Where is Emma?"

Calvin had been joking around with Josh last night, after Josh had stopped by with a surprise gift: a full course dinner he bought at a grocery store. The food was awful, but the gesture was sweet.

Josh had been complaining about having to listen to Corey go on and on about the robots assembling at the Turris. Corey had a fascination with Artificial Intelligence and was beside himself with excitement over the new line of robots from Kabira. It was rumored they could incorporate sarcasm into conversation with a human. Calvin had wondered whether any of Bisurakhan's resident AI personalities could match such technology. He also wondered how many of Bisurakhan's AI personalities had names.

"There's no Emma," Calvin said aloud, realizing this AI had neither a name nor a sense of sarcasm. "We can go."

"You greeted an Emma," the voice replied.

"You. I greeted you."

"I am not Emma."

"What's your name then?"

There was a long pause. The box slowly lowered to the ground and the doors opened.

"Please remove yourself and Emma. Emma is not authorized for transport," the digital voice said.

Calvin shook his head and walked out. Another box was sitting to his left. He walked inside.

"Welcome, Calvin," the same voice said. "Are you alone?"

Calvin shook his fist in the air. "It's just me. Can we please go?"

"Transporting you to the Reality Persuasion Labs," the voice replied as the doors slid shut.

The box lifted off the ground, navigated around a cluster of boxes mid-air, proceeded to the east edge of the main floor, then plummeted downward.

"We have arrived," the voice announced as the box came to a smooth landing. The doors opened and Calvin exited, feeling a surprising sense of happiness at being back in familiar territory.

He hadn't been anywhere in the Turris since the day Amelia was born. He hadn't even been up to the Communications Tower. He was surprised to realize he had really missed it.

"Welcome back, Calvin," General Stanley Fossil greeted him as he entered the main office.

"It's good to be back, sir."

"I wasn't entirely sure we'd see you again."

"I thought about skipping," Calvin admitted. "That payback requirement for dropping out was a very smart idea."

"Thank you. I only had to lose half of the men in my first two-part experiment to come up with it."

"Ouch."

"You can imagine my conversation with Jorge after that debacle," Stanley laughed.

"Well, I'm glad to be back. I've missed this place."

Stanley chuckled. "You've missed my experiments? There's something I don't hear every day."

"It's nice to be on the cutting edge of something new," Calvin answered. "We don't get to see much up in the Frequency Tower."

"Aren't you the first to see the new messages coming in from Johanum?"

"Yeah. But I mean, the new stuff that's not communications. You know, like the Engineer Breakthroughs or the Tech Launches. Even the physicists have annual exhibits. We don't get any of that. We just...write stuff down and translate it."

"You're bored," Stanley observed.

"No," Calvin protested. "Well...I don't know. Maybe a little."

"Well, Officer, if it's the new you crave, there are other positions available around the Turris. You don't have to stay in Comms."

It was Calvin's turn to look surprised. "I don't?"

"We facilitate transfers all the time. We don't want any of our men or women getting bored. Actually, Calvin, I'm impressed. You're smart, and you want to grow. That's a good thing. We can make that happen for you. Now, don't get me wrong – no one is going to be happy about losing a comms engineer. A transfer might take a little longer than usual since we'll need to find and train a replacement. But if you really want to do something else, by all means – go do something that excites you. And I'll help, any way I can."

Calvin had never considered leaving Comms. He had Josh to thank for his job, and he doubted Josh had any intention of transferring. He had kind of figured they would work together forever. Still, the thought of a new job, something a little more challenging....

"Tell you what," Stanley said as he handed Calvin his gear for the Lab. "Take a look at some of the other departments. Let me know which ones you'd like to visit. I'll put in a good word for you. At least get your foot in the door and see what's out there. You might decide you like where you are and would rather stay. But if you find something else and you want to give it a try, well, you'll have the option to do that."

"You would really do that for me?"

"Of course! It would be my pleasure."

"Thank you! Thank you so much, sir," Calvin said enthusiastically. He could already feel his pulse quickening. This was turning out to be a very good year.

"Now," Stanley said, "get over to the Lab before I kick you out for being tardy."

"Yes, sir!" Calvin headed out the office door, a spring in his step.

"You'll be in Lab #4 today," Stanley called after him.

CHAPTER 43
Johanum

Mortarium, Sibilum and Carnificius sat cross-legged on the floor. They were focused on the scene rising up from the fire in the center of the room.

In the center of the flames rose a series of six red shadows. A tall figure, twisting a large X in his hands. Five others like him. Apparitions of six tall Priests now moved about the room.

Another man arose. He was not as tall as the six, but his bearing spoke of strength and authority. This one was not dressed in a robe. He was dressed in a black military uniform. His face was turned away, yet awareness stretched from his presence, weaving about in the flames, licking the dust from the ground by the Priests' feet.

The Priests stood opposite the man in the uniform. In between them, from the dirt, rose yet another shadow. This one was a man, and he appeared quite weak. He was crawling about on his hands and knees, oblivious to everyone around him.

The man in the uniform approached. "Antoine. Get up. We are leaving."

The man on the ground lifted his head and squinted.

"I've come to take you home," said the man in the uniform.

"But I can't leave," came the weak reply. "They won't let me."

"I brought an exchange for you," the man in the uniform replied. He motioned behind him. Another apparition appeared, the shadow of a man with shackles on his wrists and ankles.

The man in the uniform produced a set of keys and walked over to release the prisoner. The chains fell at his feet. The prisoner slowly rubbed his hands over his wrists.

"You have paid your debts, Fletcher," the man in the uniform told him. "This place will be your new home. You are free to do as you wish. Only stay away from the Priests if you want to live."

Fletcher continued rubbing his wrists, looking about in confusion.

"Come, Antoine," the man in the uniform said. "It's time to go."

"Don't leave him here," Antoine pleaded, looking at the prisoner.

"That is not your decision to make."

Antoine kept looking at the man called Fletcher. He was not very old, not much past forty, and he had such an innocent look about him. What had he done? Why would this man in a uniform bring him here?

"Come, Antoine," the man in the uniform repeated, stretching out his arm.

Antoine reached up and grasped the hand extended to him. Instantly, a surge of strength flowed through his body. He felt power fill his legs. It took no effort to stand to his feet, though he had been crawling around on the ground for months. He was standing tall now. It didn't feel right. Something was wrong. His body was strong, but his mind...his mind had not yet returned. Every thought was murky, like he was trying to find it in a bed of quicksand.

Antoine looked suspiciously at the man in the uniform. "Who are you?" he asked.

"I've come to take you home," the man replied.

"You're taking me to Pendleton?"

"I'm bringing you to Bisurakhan."

"Bisurakhan is not my home."

"It will be your home from now on."

"But what of my real home?"

"This place?"

"No!" Antoine stopped, confused. Was this his real home? He had thought it was Pendleton. But he couldn't really remember.

"You will have a new identity in Bisurakhan," the man told him. "In time, it will be enough for you."

"What of my family?"

"You'll have a family."

"But I loved the ones I had. My family. The ones in Pendleton."

"Of course you did. And they will always love you. And so will your new family."

"I don't want a new family. I want to go back."

"You can't go back. Back does not exist, Antoine. Your life lies ahead of you now."

"Why should I trust you?"

"Because I will set you free."

The six Priests drew closer and surrounded Antoine, Fletcher, and the man in the uniform.

"We do not accept this exchange," Sibilum said.

"The rules are clear," the man in the uniform replied. "A life for a life."

"He is not good enough," Carnificius hissed as he sneered at Fletcher. "We want someone else."

"I have paid your price," the man in the uniform replied. "We will go now." He gestured for Antoine to follow as he turned towards the hovercraft that was waiting near the docks.

Fletcher had not stopped rubbing his wrists. Now he turned around in a circle, looking this way and that, taking in the scene around him. Nothing was familiar, and the air was so cold. He shivered.

Sibilum lifted his hands and threw fire in front of Fletcher's feet. He jumped and stumbled backwards. Sibilum sneered and turned toward Antoine and the man in the uniform. With a wave of his hands, fire came crashing down in walls around them.

"Let me say it again," Sibilum roared. "We do not accept this exchange."

The man in the uniform turned around. "You have become greedy, Sibilum."

Sibilum hissed through his teeth, the scales of his tongue flashing against the glow of the flames that danced around them. "You will give me what I demand!"

"I will give you what you have a right to. Nothing more."

"We are not done with that one," Sibilum said angrily, his eyes sparking red as he looked at Antoine.

"Remove the fire," the man in the uniform commanded.

Sibilum's laugh was loud and raucous and seething with hatred. He waved his arms. The flames climbed higher. They burned hotter and hissed, the same way Carnificius hissed when he spoke.

A spark caught one of Antoine's frayed pant legs. Within a moment, his leg went up in flames. He screamed and dropped to the ground, writhing in pain.

"And what shall I do to you, O Great Commander," Sibilum mocked. "You are not god here. Johanum is beyond the reach of your power."

The Commander studied Antoine, who had managed to put out the fire that lit up his leg. Antoine saw that the Commander had made no move to help him. His gaze seemed cold. It contained no empathy, no understanding, no compassion. No emotion at all showed on the Commander's face.

Antoine hobbled to his feet. His skin was burned off in several places. Even if he wanted to, he would not have been able to convey the pain.

The Commander again held out his hand. Antoine made no move to accept it.

"Come, Antoine."

Antoine turned around. He met the mocking eyes of Sibilum and the contemptuous stare of Carnificius.

To stay would mean certain death.

To leave? He didn't know what that would mean.

Antoine's eyes shifted to Fletcher. He didn't want to leave another man here. It didn't matter what he had done. This was no place for anyone to live.

Antoine turned back to face the Commander. As he did, something in his memory shifted.

He knew that name. The Commander. The Commander from Bisurakhan.

He had heard the stories. But in the sleepy world of Pendleton, all the stories of this man's power meant nothing. What did it matter if he could throw fire, bind enemies in a trance, or travel unaffected across galaxies? None of those things mattered to people in Pendleton. They had no need for them. Anyway, the stories seemed fabricated. They probably weren't even real.

"Are you ready, Antoine?"

Antoine turned and walked over to Fletcher, draping his arm around the man's shoulders. "I am ready," Antoine answered. "But you must take us both."

The laughter of the Priests was loud and bawdy, but Antoine refused to budge.

The Commander studied him. Something in his expression changed. Was it respect? Contempt? Antoine couldn't tell. But he stood his ground.

"He doesn't understand the rules," Carnificius hissed.

The taunt brought the Commander's attention back to the Priests. "Neither do you," he answered coldly, his face darkening. With a flick of his wrists, he was suddenly holding two coiled ropes made of fire.

Antoine looked closer. Perhaps they were made of something else. They were silver, or metal – something. But they were on fire. The fire seemed to boil out from their core.

The Priests were also eyeing the ropes. Antoine saw their surprise, followed by hesitation.

The Commander turned to face Sibilum. "Take back your fire."

Sibilum squared his broad shoulders and hissed.

Antoine barely saw the Commander move before the walls of fire came tumbling down, one after the other, wrapped in a death grip by the ropes the Commander wielded like whips. As if the flames were alive, the ropes weaved their way through them, slowly choking the life from each one and forcing it to fall dead to the ground.

Each wall of fire fell in surrender before the Commander. To the ground they collapsed before exploding, their residue leaving behind piles of soot and ashes.

The Priests responded by raising up walls fires that were taller and stronger than before. The flames rose and fell like waves, cascading, one wall of fire rolling over another. And just as before, every wall that rose came crashing down, strangled of its life by the ropes of fire the Commander wielded with precision.

The Commander made a motion for Antoine to board the hovercraft. Antoine rushed forward, then turned back for Fletcher.

But Fletcher was no longer behind him. He now stood next to Carnificius, who had wrapped a rope around his neck. Carnificius smiled an ugly smile and beckoned for Antoine to approach.

Antoine looked around desperately. He caught the Commander's gaze. "Do something!" he pleaded.

"We must leave him. To take him now will mean his death."

"We can't leave him here! They will kill him."

"You don't know that. They didn't kill you."

"It was only a matter of time."

"Then you must allow Fletcher his time."

Antoine turned feverishly in circles. He couldn't figure out what to do. But even as he stalled, he knew it was impossible. He could not fight Carnificius. The Priests always won.

Antoine made his choice. He ran toward the hovercraft and boarded through the flank that had been left open near the ground.

As soon as Antoine was on board, the Commander let his arms fall. The ropes snaked to the ground and coiled back into his hands. Around him the fires rose again, hissing, angry, famished.

Antoine watched as the Commander approached the hovercraft. He was walking through the fire.

The Commander was like the Priests. He was not burned by fire.

Halfway up the flank of the hovercraft, the Commander turned around.

"I have paid your price," he called. "And now you will pay mine."

The ropes in his hands sprang back to life. Faster than snakes, they crawled over the earth, searching for their prey. And they found it. The Priest standing closest to the hovercraft was caught unaware as the ropes slid their way around him. Starting at his ankles, they slinked around his body, reaching up for his neck. Then they began to squeeze.

Antoine saw in the Priest's eyes the moment he realized he had lost. And just like that, as though he was as powerless as a man, his body gave way. The ropes snaked away as he fell, and he landed face down in the dirt.

The Commander snapped his wrists. As Sibilum, Carnificius, and Mortarium turned to run, the two remaining Priests were caught up in the ropes and strangled.

As quickly as it started, it was over.

The Commander walked inside, drew up the door, and set the hovercraft back on its path to Bisurakhan.

The apparitions faded and the flames of the fire fell to the floor.

Mortarium looked around. Sibilum was seething. Carnificius looked distressed.

"Where did he get the ropes?" Sibilum asked. "Those are no weapons of Bisurakhan."

"There's only one place where you can summon such power," Carnificius sniffed. "Those ropes had the power of a Legion's tail.

"Why would the Underworld give him their weapons?" Sibilum asked.

"How should I know?" Carnificius retorted. "Maybe he was smart enough to ask for them."

"His kind does not approach the Underworld. They have sworn against it!" Sibilum said.

"You underestimated him once," Carnificius said. "Aren't you worried about doing it again?"

"He would never form an alliance with a Legion!" Sibilum insisted.

"Why not? You did!" Carnificius hissed.

"We are Priests! We are not kings!"

"Yes," Carnificius agreed, "but that means little when we are DYING at his hands."

"Wouldn't Sulta have told us?" Sibilum asked.

"Told us what?"

"That he has a pact with a Khanist!"

"I doubt he has any such agreement," Carnificus responded. "You heard Zila. Sulta wants the Commander. He was happy to give you whatever you wanted for that price. Ignorant Sibilum, no matter what lies Sulta tells you, he does not rule the Underworld. He craves power – he needs power

- and so he needs the Commander. He wouldn't make a pact with him."

"Surely Sulta must know where such weapons came from. They must have come from the Underworld, and Sulta would have heard about it. He should have told us so we would know what we were up against!"

"You volunteered to give him the Commander! He didn't ask for it. It's your stupidity we have to blame for all our folly."

"I was playing by the rules."

"The rules? Sibilum, you fool, our world has no rules."

"We have rules. A life for a life. That is our rule."

"Yes," Carnificius agreed, "and sometimes we get a life for no payment at all. Because we can. Because the humans don't know the rules and will believe whatever we tell them."

"But sometimes they question," said Sibilum.

"And that is a problem," Carnificius replied. "So we must move quickly. We must strike hard and fast. Don't give them time to ask questions."

"Some already know the rules," Sibilum pointed out. "All the ones who have been here in Johanum, they know."

"Yes, but the survivors have been silenced. They live in the shadows. Bisurakhan has no use for them. And they are quite happy to live undetected. Only a survivor with uncharacteristic boldness would cause a problem."

"The girl," Mortarium said.

"Exactly," Carnificius acknowledged.

Sibilum frowned. "Do you still think we should let her go?"

"For the Commander? Yes. That would be a good deal for us," Carnificius said. "But even if we capture him, we can't control him. You've seen what he can do. How do we deliver him to Sulta before he destroys all of Johanum and us with it?"

"We need him to leave the Neutral Zone," Sibilum said. "Then we will be able to hold him."

Mortarium shook his head. "We don't know that."

"It has to work," Sibilum said angrily.

"It didn't work so well the last time!" Mortarium spit back.

"We need reinforcements," Carnificius said.

"What, you want us to find more Priests?" Mortarium scowled.

"Not Priests, you fool," Carnificius hissed. "A Legion. A resident Legion."

"You want a Legion to come here?" Sibilum protested.

"No, to stay in the Underworld," Carnificious snarled. "Of course, I want him to come here!"

"A Legion would rule over us," said Sibilum.

"For a time," Carnificius agreed. "That's why we must be very careful. We need to come to an agreement. Time his arrival as close as possible to the arrival of Bisurakhan's rescue mission. It can be done. Surely there is a Legion who would welcome the opportunity to wrap his tail around Bisurakhan's king."

"I don't like it," Sibilum said.

Carnificius shrugged. "Nor do I. But you got us into this mess. It's time for somebody to get us out of it."

"It would be worth it, I suppose," Sibilum reasoned aloud, "to live under a Legion for a day or two, to get to live in a Universe without the Commander. Think of the power we would wield. The unrivaled, unchecked power! I do like that."

"I will definitely be claiming my own planet after all this," Mortarium grumbled.

"It won't be that bad," Sibilum said.

"It won't be that bad for me," Mortarium replied. "I'm used to being bossed around. But you?" He shook his head.

"You will get yourself killed by a Legion before the Commander ever gets here."

"I will not!" Sibilum protested.

Mortarium looked skeptical.

"It may be a bit difficult, for a time..."

Mortarium snorted. "Do what you like. I'm tired of this place anyway. All we do is kidnap, taunt, kill. Kidnap, taunt, kill. I'm bored."

"Why don't you go away then?" Carnificius hissed.

"I'm not allowed to stay any place we haven't conquered."

"So go conquer!" Carnificius said impatiently. "Or...conquest. Whatever it is that you do when you're wandering the galaxy, being worthless."

"I would need your help," he grumbled.

"What's that?" Carnificius asked. "Can you say that a little louder?"

Mortarium hissed.

"We must do it!" Sibilum announced boldly. "We must invite the Legion. I like my idea."

"Look at you, coming up with such great ideas," Carnificius said, his voice dripping with sarcasm.

"You will issue the invitation," Sibilum told him.

"Why me?" demanded Carnificius. "Mortarium is your Underworld minion."

"Hey!" Mortarium sputtered angrily.

"It's true and you know it."

"Only because you're too scared to go!" Mortarium said.

"I am not."

"Like you weren't embarrassed by the Commander?" Carnificius pursed his lips and seethed.

"You must do it," Sibilum said. "Sulta questions your support, given your deplorable behavior when Zila was here."

"I won't do it," Carnificius declared.

"You'll do it," Sibilum replied.

"I won't."

"Then you will meet Bisurakhan's rescue mission yourself when it arrives."

Carnificius considered Sibilum's threat. "Fine," he agreed. "I'll do it."

"Move quickly," Sibilum said.

"I'll go when I'm ready."

"Now!" Sibilum bellowed.

Carnificius jumped backwards, turned, and hurried away.

CHAPTER 44
Bisurakhan

Calvin found the yellow door marked with a "4." He pushed it open and walked into the Lab. It only took a few seconds for his eyes to adjust to the darkness. He moved the weapons in his belt around and then he was good to go.

As soon as he put on the glasses, his empty Lab fell away. Calvin found himself standing near a set of docks.

The air was warm and humid and a little too sticky for his liking. A cool breeze blew up from the water and ruffled his hair.

He walked closer to the water. The docks were old and rickety, but they seemed sturdy enough to hold his weight. At the edge, Calvin knelt down and let his right hand graze the top of the water. It was cool and refreshing. Small waves splashed up around his wrist. He steadied himself on his knees and let both hands glide across the water's edge.

Calvin looked around and studied the view. The lake was large. In fact, it might not have been a lake at all. It seemed more like a bay or a harbor. He could see mountains and cliffs rising on either side, but the water stretched out so far in front, he couldn't see the end of it.

He squinted as he looked down. The water was clear. It glistened green and blue in the hazy, humid light. He peered closer. It looked like he could see the bottom.

He hesitated for a minute but then decided to jump in. The heat was exhausting, and he welcomed a chance to cool off. Plus, it would be cool to say he went swimming in Johanum. He wasn't sure if any of the other volunteers had done that. He hadn't heard them talk about it.

Calvin slid off his boots and set them to the side. In moments like this, he wondered: if he stepped out of the experiment at that exact second, would his boots be on or off? One of these days he needed to leave something behind, as a test.

The water was deeper than he expected, although he could graze the bottom with the tips of his toes while bobbing with his face barely above the surface. The waves splashed up into his nose and eyes. Taking a deep breath, Calvin dove beneath the surface and opened his eyes.

The water was as clear as glass. It didn't even feel like he was underwater. He blinked and realized his eyes felt dry. Then he noticed something floating next to him.

It was a thin film and it surrounded him. He was swimming in some sort of bubble. He reached out and poked it. It stretched against his finger and then popped back into place.

A new thought occurred to him. It seemed risky, but he had been sent here to experiment, to try new things. He gritted his teeth and breathed in deeply.

Sure enough, he didn't breathe in any water. His lungs filled with fresh, clean air. He exhaled slowly and began to laugh. This place was so strange! He could breathe underwater like a fish! It was fun.

He didn't stay in the water long. The novelty of breathing underwater quickly wore off as there wasn't much to see. The lake had no rocks, no coral, and no fish or sea life of any kind. Calvin grew bored and swam back to the docks.

He had already lifted himself onto the docks and was putting on his boots when he saw it. A soft blue light was rising like steam from beneath the wooden boards. It crept closer. With the light came an inexplicable feeling of dread. Calvin shifted uncomfortably and checked his weapons to make sure they were secure.

He began to back up, trying to judge how far the light would come. He was at the edge of the docks, one step from land, when he felt pressure against his legs.

He looked down. A ghost-like creature, a skeleton covered in translucent skin, was lying on the ground, his arms wrapped tightly around Calvin's ankles.

Calvin tried to kick it away, but the creature held tight. Calvin could see inside his body. He could see the creature's bones and the way his muscles strained and shook as Calvin tried to break free. Calvin kicked its face. It seemed stunned but didn't let go. Finally, Calvin reached down and pulled a gun from his belt.

"Let me go!" he demanded, pointing the gun in its direction.

The creature raised its head. It had the eyes of a man very much alive. The eyes weren't menacing. They were begging.

Calvin's hand trembled. In his moment of hesitation, he glanced up.

In front of him stood no fewer than a dozen ghosts who looked just like this creature. They had the same pleading look in their eyes.

Calvin stilled.

Who were they? *What* were they?

He tightened his grip on his gun. He couldn't remember how many rounds he had. He was trying to remember what Stanley had told him when a sudden movement made him swing around to the left.

One of the ghosts had moved. He was waving, gesturing, trying to get Calvin to move.

The creature didn't seem dangerous. He looked like he was trying to help.

Calvin stood there, trying to make sense of it all. Finally, he pointed to his own chest, then pointed to the edge of the docks near the water, then made a walking motion with his fingers.

The creature looked relieved and nodded.

Calvin looked down at his feet. The ghost that was wrapped around his ankles looked up and studied him carefully, as if assessing his next move. Calvin pointed at the water. Slowly, the ghost released his grip.

Calvin turned to run. The creature on the ground was faster. He jumped to his feet and knocked Calvin over. Calvin's shoulder hit the docks first, followed quickly by his elbow. Then he heard the gunshot.

In his fall, his gun had fired. Calvin watched the bullet fly forward. It ripped through the chest of the ghost who had been beckoning him towards the water. The creature stumbled back, then forward. His eyes rolled into his head. Then he crumpled to the ground. Immediately, his remains began to disintegrate, and his ashes were caught by the wind and blew across the water.

The rest of the ghosts lowered their eyes.

Struggling against the pain in his shoulder, Calvin pivoted his body in an attempt to stand. He tried to lift his head, but a wave of dizziness came crashing down around him. He bit his lip to squelch a mounting sense of panic, then he slowly laid his head back down. As his head met the docks, he saw them.

Three tall men in thick robes. One held an X in his hands. The air around them was dark, almost black.

Calvin looked over at the ghosts. Their heads were bowed in submission. They had been trying to warn him.

Who were these men?

The throbbing in his head continued. He brought his hand up to his forehead and pressed in. His skin felt hot. A wave of panic bubbled up in his chest. He knew he had to do something.

A piercing pain stabbed his skull behind his eyes. Calvin howled in pain and cradled his head.

Within a moment, the scene went dark. The world around him fell, just like it always did, as the Lab experiment came to a close.

Calvin was back in the Lab, curled up on his side on the cold steel floor, trying to tame his panic.

The pain. The pain in his head had disappeared.

He frowned. How was that possible?

"Calvin, please report to the Debrief Room," a voice said over the loudspeaker.

Calvin pushed himself up to his feet and removed his glasses. He had never been so ready to get out of that Lab.

CHAPTER 45
Johanum

I awoke slowly. The days of confusion had taken their toll. I was smaller somehow. I could feel it. But the fog in my head had lifted.

Mad Laughs noticed too. His eyes brightened when he saw me. Quite impetuously, I walked up to him and gave him a hug.

His smile quickly turned to horror.

"It's okay," I laughed, "I just needed a hug."

He had gone as stiff as a board.

"But no more!" I promised, releasing him. "Not more hugs. I promise."

His shoulders relaxed, though I caught him sneaking suspicious looks at me for the rest of the day.

"What shall we do today? Let's go somewhere. I'm ready for an adventure."

Mad Laughs looked at me like I had lost my mind.

"We don't really have adventures here, do we? Not the good kind. Well...we could go for a swim down at the lake. We could...we could...oh, I know! We could pay a visit to Mr. Fox and Mr. Brown."

That caught Mad Laughs' attention.

"I know, it's a good idea, right? What if we took them down to the lake? They might hate it. They never leave the caves. But it would be good for them!"

Mad Laughs had already taken off down the stairs. I could hear his heavy footsteps as he bounded downward, taking several steps at a time.

I didn't have to wait long. I heard them grumbling before they appeared at the top of the stairwell.

"How many times must I tell you, I am not meant to be swung by my tail," screeched Mr. Fox. Mad Laughs walked

309

back into view, swinging Mr. Fox in circles. Mr. Fox clawed helplessly at the air, his paws reaching nowhere close to his target.

Mr. Brown, the armadillo, was propped up a little more ceremoniously on Mad Laughs' shoulders. "This was not in my schedule," he complained. "I told you, I keep an orderly life. I need several weeks' notice to fit you in."

"You don't have anything to do but walk from one end of the caves to the other," I pointed out, prying Mr. Fox from Mad Laughs' grip. He fell to the floor with his usual dramatic flair.

"I do more than that!" Mr. Brown protested. "I eat. I plan. I talk to this sorry fellow."

"Hey!" Mr. Fox sputtered. "You like talking to me."

"No, I don't."

"Well, fine, I don't like you either. But you'll do for now until I meet someone proper."

"You might get a move on with it, meeting those proper friends you're always jabbering about," Mr. Brown said.

"Just as soon as one of them comes to the caves."

"That's never going to happen," Mr. Brown muttered. "You see the type that washes up here."

"Hey!" It was my turn to protest.

"My apologies," Mr. Brown said. "I like you just fine. It's your giant I could do without. And anyway, it's this obnoxious fellow who's always muttering about how you're not good enough to be a proper friend."

"I didn't say that!" Mr. Fox said angrily.

"Yes, you did. You said it just this morning."

Mr. Fox looked embarrassed. "I didn't mean it," he muttered.

"We've been over this," I said. "We're not proper friends. We're good friends. But it's fine if you don't like us. We like you. And we're going on an adventure today. We've decided to take you with us."

"We can't go on an adventure!" Mr. Fox sputtered.

"Why not?"

"Where would we go? This is a terrible place."

"The docks are actually quite nice."

"The what?"

"The docks. Down by the lake. Haven't you ever been there?"

Mr. Fox sniffed and shook his head. "It sounds awful."

"You're coming with us."

"I most certainly am not."

Mad Laughs reached down and lifted our little friend by his tail, grinning happily at the torrent of foul words that erupted in response.

"It will be good for you to get out of the caves," I told him. "It might lighten your mood a little. You're always so crabby."

"Perhaps the light will do him good," Mr. Brown said.

"You're coming, too," I told him.

"What?" Mr. Brown gasped. "I am not!"

"You just said that the light would do you good."

"Him!" Mr. Brown squawked, his paw shaking as he pointed to the fox. "I said it would do him good! But he's not going to like it."

"I don't see why you both complain so much. We'll carry you. You'll get to see the lake, maybe take a swim. It will be nice."

We made it to the mouth of the cave when Mad Laughs stopped abruptly.

"What's wrong?" I asked.

Mad Laughs lifted his fist. Mr. Fox was dangling lifelessly, the color drained from his round cheeks.

"Put him down."

Mad Laughs gingerly laid our little friend on the dirt floor. He reached up, removed Mr. Brown from his shoulders, and set him next to Mr. Fox.

Mr. Brown walked forward and poked his friend. Once, twice, three times. "You've scared the life right out of him," he said.

I frowned and sat down next to them. "What happened? I didn't mean to scare him. Is he okay?"

"How would I know?" Mr. Brown replied. "I've never seen him like this."

I turned to Mad Laughs. "Would you go get some water?"

He turned and bounded away down the path.

I leaned closer to Mr. Fox and put my ear to his tiny chest. It sounded like he was breathing.

"Why don't you ever leave the caves?" I asked Mr. Brown, realizing I had never asked before.

"We like it here. It's safe."

"We like it here, too," I said, referring to myself and Mad Laughs, "but still we go out."

"It's very dangerous out there," Mr. Brown said.

"Yes, but you have to go out. To get food. To get supplies. To get fresh air."

"There are plenty of bugs below ground to keep us fed," Mr. Brown replied.

"Don't you ever get sick of it?"

"It's safe," he repeated, as though I hadn't heard him the first time.

I heard a stirring and looked down. Mr. Fox's eyes were fluttering. I breathed a sigh of relief. He was going to be okay.

"I'm sorry," I said gently. "We didn't mean to scare you. I thought maybe you needed to be reminded of what it's like out there. I thought maybe you needed to be reminded of what it's like to have a little fun."

Mr. Fox leaned to the side and vomited. His paw was still shaking as he wiped his mouth. Slowly, he laid his head back down.

"Leaving the caves is not fun," he said.

"It can be," I replied.

"No!" His voice trembled as badly as his paw.

I stared at him for several minutes. And then, slowly, I understood.

"What happened?" I asked simply.

Mr. Fox brushed a tear from his face but said nothing.

"You don't have to tell me. But maybe you'd like to?"

He stayed silent. It was Mr. Brown who finally spoke.

"Fletcher found him, curled up outside one night. He had his three babies snuggled up in the folds of his tail, all safe and sound. But they weren't safe. They were dead, every last one. Had been, probably for a long time. Fletcher buried all the babies and brought him inside. He's not left since."

My throat was hot as I looked down. Mr. Fox's eyes were pressed shut as tight as he could get them, but that didn't stop the flood of tears pouring down his soft little face.

"I'm so sorry," I whispered, fighting back tears. "I'm so, so sorry."

The moment came to a grinding halt as Mad Laughs bounded through the mouth of the cave, two bowls of water in hand. Without stopping, he released a waterfall over Mr. Fox, who jumped in the air before landing on his feet, sputtering.

"You cruel, horrid, barbarian creature!" he screamed.

Mad Laughs was caught off-guard and stepped back.

"I asked him to get the water," I confessed. "I thought it might revive you."

"If you cared about me at all, you would let me curl up and die."

My heart pitied him. What a fool I had been to think anyone here could escape their own tragedy.

"Can we try again?" I asked. "We won't take you outside. I promise. Maybe we can try again to be friends. Proper friends. Just for you."

Mr. Fox looked unsure.

Mr. Brown spoke up. "I'd like that. It would be good for us. Maybe...yes, I think this will work...I think I can fit you into my schedule. Perhaps once a week."

"That's very big of you," I said, knowing he did so as a kindness to Mr. Fox.

"It will be good for him to have more friends," Mr. Brown replied, nodding at his friend.

Mr. Fox sniffled. "You'd do that for me?" he asked Mr. Brown.

"Yes. If we plan ahead. It will take a long time for me to climb those stairs."

"Mad Laughs can come and get you," I said. That earned me a disparaging look from both of them. "Or you can come on your own."

Mr. Fox nodded. He looked so tired. So worn out.

"How about I take you both downstairs?" I offered.

Mad Laughs frowned, but the look of relief on their faces was enough for me to rise to my feet. "Come on then."

I picked up Mr. Fox as gently as I could. I wasn't the least bit prepared for the way he laid his head on my shoulder and curled his tail up around my arm. I reached back down and awkwardly lifted Mr. Brown.

What a strange mix we were, this little band of survivors. "Not just survivors," I thought to myself as I walked carefully down the stairs. "My friends. These are my friends."

CHAPTER 46
Bisurakhan

Josh straightened his collar and ran a hand through his hair.

He was nervous. He was actually nervous.

"You're being ridiculous," he scolded himself. But that faster heartbeat, that quickened pulse – it felt good. It had been a while.

Josh checked his phone to make sure Hailey hadn't canceled.

No messages. The coast was clear.

He had been relieved when Hailey insisted that she and Mary would take care of the food. Hailey had asked Josh to bring the wine, which was the one area of dinner he felt confident covering. Four bottles lay in a checkered sackcloth bag by the door. Two for dinner, two for after.

He had this.

Josh reached for his jacket, crumpled in a heap on the floor. He changed his mind, dropped it back on the floor, and reached for the wine. Then he changed his mind again. He reached down, grabbed the jacket, and hung it on a hook near the door.

"Off you go, boy," he mumbled to himself as he opened the door of his apartment and walked outside.

"You made it!" Leah was all smiles as she greeted Josh at the door.

He gave her a hug. "You look lovely as always."

"Hey! Stop hitting on my wife!" Calvin called from the other room.

"Don't worry, you're next!" Josh yelled back.

Leah grabbed Josh's arm and pulled him inside. Josh slipped off his shoes and handed Leah the wine.

"Wow, Josh, you have a lot of faith in our drinking abilities!" Leah laughed.

"When's the last time you had company?"

"The last time you were here."

"Real company."

"Good point! You know I can't drink these though. I'll have to enjoy watching you all get tipsy."

"Why can't you drink any?"

"I'm nursing."

"Oh." He hadn't thought about that. "I should have picked up something else, I'm sorry."

"Don't be silly. I'm going to get drunk off having friends here for a visit. Thank you so much for arranging for people to come over! I love you for it. I've been going crazy. Not to mention, I got so much sleep last night, like six hours, and now I am bursting with energy!"

"Six hours isn't a lot of sleep."

"It is right now! I feel amazing. I think I could float away to another planet."

They walked into the living room. Calvin sat cross-legged on the floor, with Amelia curled up in his lap. Balancing the baby carefully, he was trying to put together...something.

"What is that?" Josh asked, towering over him.

"It's a swing."

"I don't think a swing is supposed to look like that."

"It's all the parts to a swing."

"Also questionable."

"Why do you say that?"

"Well, for starters..." Josh leaned down and picked up the legs for a swing and a set of sidebars. "You have half a swing, half a crib."

"Oh, no!" Calvin hunched forward, looking defeated. "No wonder this isn't working!"

Josh looked at the set of directions on the floor by Calvin's leg. The directions were for an outdoor playset.

"I told him not to buy any of those makeshift kits the guys sell down at the Parts Yard, but nooooooo," Leah ribbed him good-naturedly.

"Miss I'm-so-happy-because-I-slept over here thinks she's soooo smart," Calvin grumbled.

"It might be worth listening to her," Josh replied.

Leah's smile was indulgent but self-satisfied. "Thank you."

"What am I supposed to do with all of this stuff?" Calvin was annoyed and grouchy, an attitude always exacerbated when he felt tired. Josh loved it.

"I suggest you make a crib-swing," he replied.

"A what?" Calvin asked, looking confused.

"A crib-swing."

"What's that?"

"Exactly what it sounds like. Half a swing, half a crib."

"How does it work?"

"It doesn't. But I get to laugh at you while you try to figure it out."

Calvin picked up a pole from the ground and swung it at Josh's face. "I haven't missed you, not one bit," he lied.

They all turned at the knock on the door.

"They're here! They're here!" Leah said excitedly, prancing around in a circle before skipping towards the door.

"You have made her the happiest woman alive," Calvin told Josh.

"Well, I couldn't make my own wife happy. I might as well make somebody else's wife happy."

"Hey now."

"You know what I mean."

"Can you help me get this picked up?"

"Sure. Where are you going to put it?"

"The dumpster?"

"Seems as good a place as any."

Calvin walked over to greet the girls. He was unprepared for the shrieks of excitement from Mary and Hailey as they caught a glimpse of Amelia. He returned to the living room, his eyes wide and his arms empty.

"Whoa," he said.

"They like babies," Josh replied, leaning down to pick up as many of the spare pieces as he could. "They were very excited to come over tonight. Do you remember when girls used to ogle us like that?"

"Dude, that never happened."

"It did in my stories."

Leah walked into the living room, followed by Hailey and Mary. Leah was carrying Amelia and beaming at all the attention.

"We're going to take all this stuff downstairs to the dumpster," Calvin said.

"Okay, honey," Leah replied.

"We'll be back in a few minutes."

"Mmmm hmmmm."

Calvin glanced at Josh. "Now would be the time for me to ask for something really expensive."

"No, it's not," Leah replied in a sing-song voice.

Calvin gave her a quick kiss as he and Josh walked past and out the door.

"You've got an awful lot of stuff there," Calvin observed.

"So do you."

"Not nearly as much as you. You're carrying most of everything." Calvin knew this version of his friend, he just hadn't expected to see him tonight. He waited to say something until they had dumped all the supplies into the large steel container in the alleyway.

"So…" Calvin began, pausing to study the dumpster in fake curiosity.

"What's wrong?"

"Nothing's wrong. I must confess, I'm a little surprised."

Josh looked around, mystified. "Is there something wrong with the dumpster?"

"No. I'm surprised at you."

"Me? Why?"

"Just tell me one thing. Which girl?"

"What are you talking about?"

"Mary or Hailey? Which one do you like?"

Josh's face went red.

"And you never blush. Oh, this is good."

"I don't know what you're talking about."

"Clearly you do."

"There's nothing going on."

"Okay, okay, no action yet, I get it. Which one?"

"Who said it's one of them?"

"You rolled up your sleeves to show off your biceps when we walked past the girls upstairs."

"I did not!"

Calvin looked pointedly at Josh's sleeves, which were rolled up way too far and fit him much too tight.

"I was hot," Josh mumbled.

"Hot for a girl."

"Shut up."

"Which one?"

Josh kicked at the dirt on the ground for a minute. "Hailey," he finally confessed.

"Really? I would have guessed Mary."

"Why?"

"She's more your type."

"Hailey could be my type."

"Hailey is definitely not your type. It's good though. You're branching out."

"I don't have a type."

"You most certainly have a type. You only ever date one kind of girl."

"I'm not dating Hailey."

"Too scared to ask her out?"

"What? No!"

"Worried she doesn't feel the same?"

"No! Well, maybe. I think she likes me."

"No idea what to do with a genuinely nice girl?"

"I'm completely out of my element."

"Take it slow," Calvin advised.

"Okay."

"But not too slow."

"Right."

"You gotta make sure she knows you're interested."

"Got it."

"But don't make it too obvious."

"Are you actually trying to help me?"

"It brings me great joy to watch you squirm."

Josh swung for Calvin's face and docked his nose far harder than he intended. "Sorry," he muttered.

"Worth it. Totally worth it," Calvin said, wincing as he touched his nose.

They headed back inside.

"Hey, I wanted to ask you something," Josh said as they walked. "Do they still let Khanists into the Lab observatories?"

"You want to come watch?"

"I was thinking about it. I realized the other day that I don't really understand the experiments. Maybe I've been too harsh on Jorge. I should go check them out."

"You're a terrible liar," Calvin said.

"I'm not lying."

"If you had such an innocent curiosity, you'd ask me questions, not waste an afternoon sitting in a dark Observation Room. But, to answer your question, yes, I think they still let observers in. You have to be a Khanist and sign some paperwork saying you're considering volunteering and want to observe an experiment before making your final decision."

"Would you care if I came to observe yours?"

"Fine by me. Why the sudden interest?"

"I told you, I'm curious."

"Bullshit."

"I don't have to tell you everything."

"No, but you usually do."

"I know," Josh replied. "I think it's better this time if I don't. Until you're finished with the experiments, anyway."

"This weekend is my last one."

"Are you going to sign up for more?"

"I don't think so. I think I've had enough."

"You've been so enthusiastic about them."

"Yeah, well, you know...I'm kind of over it."

"Now who's the liar?"

"I'm not lying."

"You're not telling me something."

"I really, genuinely, haven't missed you."

"Yeah, yeah, I haven't missed you either," Josh replied, pushing open the door to the apartment.

The night spilled over into the wee hours of the morning. By the time everyone was piling out the door, the wine was gone, the living room floor was covered in board game pieces, and Josh couldn't remember the last time he had felt so relaxed and happy.

"I'm so glad you were able to make this happen," Hailey gushed to Josh as they left the building and walked to their transport vehicles. Her face was glowing from too much wine, but her smile was kind and genuine. It reached up her face and creased the corners of her eyes in the cutest way.

Damn it, she was really cute.

"Come on, girl," Mary said, grabbing Hailey's arm.

Hailey pulled away and moved so close to Josh, their arms were touching. "We should do it again," she suggested.

"We definitely should," Josh agreed. He felt uncomfortable with Mary standing there. He looked over and caught her eye. Mary studied him for a minute, then smiled a knowing smile.

"Oh, no! Hailey, we forgot to stop and get milk!" Mary wailed a little too loudly.

Hailey frowned. "We have milk."

"Yeah, but we need extra. You know, for tomorrow!"

Hailey looked puzzled. "Tomorrow? What's tomorrow?"

"You know. Tomorrow? *Tomorrow!* Come on, girl! Anyway..." Mary continued, "I am so tired. I really need to go home and go to bed so I can get up, you know, for *tomorrow*. But you know what would be great? If Josh is awake enough, maybe he can give you a ride to the store! Then you can grab the milk and bring it home. Oh, Josh, would that be too much trouble? You would save us! Then we would be ready for *tomorrow!*"

Josh lowered his head in an unsuccessful attempt to suppress a smile. Subtle, these girls were not.

"Oh!" Hailey said suddenly, finally catching on. She grabbed Josh's arm. "Could we do that? Would you mind?"

"We can totally do that."

"Thank you. I'm sure Mary is so grateful. Look how tired she is. She looks dreadful."

"Hey!" Mary protested, forgetting her act. "Oh, yes," she caught herself. "Yes, I do look awful when I'm this tired." She touched her forehead in mock exhaustion.

"You look very nice," Josh said.

"Do I look nice?" Hailey asked, sliding her hand up his arm and batting her eyelashes.

"Beautiful," he said.

Mary giggled. "Okay, I'm off to do that sleeping thing that I really have to do. Goodnight, Josh. Thanks for coming to our rescue. Goodnight, Hailey," she called in a sing-song voice as she opened the door of her vehicle and climbed inside.

Josh unlocked his own vehicle and swung open the door on the passenger side. Hailey smiled sweetly, bent down, and walked face first into the side of the door.

"How much of that last bottle did you drink?" Josh joked.

Hailey's face was bright red with embarrassment, her blue eyes open wide. "Not enough to keep me from feeling mortified," she mumbled.

Josh brushed a runaway hair out from her face. "I think I drank enough. I'm feeling a little reckless."

"What kind of reckless?" she asked.

"This kind," he answered, bending down to brush her lips with a slow, gentle kiss.

He pulled back and smiled.

Hailey had a big, stupid grin on her face. "Mary told me I was being foolish, you couldn't possibly like me." Realizing too late what she had said, Hailey clasped her hands over her mouth, eyes widening.

"You talked about me?" Josh asked.

"I mean, yeah. We talk about everybody."

"Why did Mary say I couldn't possibly like you?"

"She thinks you're still hung up on your ex." Hailey's eyes opened wider and her hands moved from her mouth to cradling her face. "I have no filter when I'm drunk," she moaned.

"I don't think you have much of a filter when you're sober," Josh joked.

"I don't! I really don't." She sighed, then turned to look up at him. "So, are you?"

"Am I what?"

"Hung up on your ex?"

"Probably a little."

"You're not even going to pretend to be over her?"

"Would that make it better?"

"Nah. I like honest guys. I was just wondering."

"Does it bother you?"

"A little."

Josh nodded thoughtfully. "I should take you home. Do you really need to stop at the store?"

Hailey shook her head. "I don't think so."

Josh helped her into the vehicle and then climbed into the driver's seat. "How about we take a scenic route?" he suggested. "You can regale me with stories of Cornersville dance competitions."

"I've seen your face when we talk about those. I know it bores you."

"Yeah, but the speaker doesn't."

"Well, then," Hailey said, smiling as she settled back in her seat. "Get ready for the longest, more boring story you have ever heard."

"I'm looking forward to it," Josh said with a grin.

CHAPTER 47
Bisurakhan

"Why did you have them rearrange the control panels?" Jorge asked.

"They were outdated," Calif replied.

"This isn't an update. This is an entire reconfiguration."

"It'll take the engineers ten minutes to explain it to you."

"Are you doing this out of spite or necessity?"

"Antoine gave me some suggestions."

"I'm sure he did."

"Suggestions based off of landing options in Johanum. We needed different landing gear. Good suggestions, Jorge, meant for our safety. Did you look at the changes down below?"

"On the outside of the aircraft?"

"Yeah."

"Not yet, but I will. There are only three sleeping rooms in the back. We need five."

"We had to reconfigure that space, too. This engine takes up more room now. So does the back-up engine."

"Back-up engine?"

"Antoine's suggestion."

"This doesn't even look like the same hovercraft."

"Is that a problem?"

"No. It's no problem. I just wasn't expecting it. And I'm not sharing sleeping quarters with either one of you."

Calif chuckled. "Breathe. The chairs in the common room fold down into beds. We'll have more than enough space."

"How much time do you think our trip will take?" Jorge asked, changing the subject.

"Well, we're using the Space Between, so we won't be gone long."

"Are you planning to zero out the time completely?"

325

Calif shook his head. "That would be too confusing. Our engineers are going to need to see us go off the grid for enough time to perform an actual mission."

"So, I can tell the missus...?"

"Three to four days, give or take."

"How long will it actually take?"

"Antoine estimates two to three weeks."

Jorge wrinkled his nose in distaste. "That's a long time to sleep on a fold out chair."

"What is it with you and these sleeping arrangements? I don't remember this problem the last time we traveled."

"We've never traveled with Antoine."

"Ahhhh," Calif replied. Jorge liked his space. He wasn't looking forward to spending time with Antoine. "You know this is your chance," Calif said.

"My chance for what?"

"To prove Antoine wrong. Or prove yourself right, whichever you prefer. Prove your theories about Johanum. Show him how Reality Persuasion has opened up new possibilities and taught Bisurakhan incredibly valuable information. Who knows? Maybe this little trip will improve the relationship between you two."

Jorge grimaced. "I doubt it."

"Give it a try before you write Antoine off completely."

Jorge sat down on one of the chairs. He was quiet for a few minutes. It was an unusual display of introspection for him.

Calif noticed. "What are you thinking?" he asked.

"Every day, Calif, I wake up, hoping the last year has been a dream. That none of this has ever happened. That Johanum doesn't exist. And maybe Reality Persuasion doesn't exist, either."

Calif nodded. "I can appreciate that. Unfortunately, I don't think this is a dream."

"Me neither."

"It will all end one day, though."

"Not soon enough."

"We don't know what lies between now and then. Don't wish the time away too quickly."

"Do you ever wonder if we'll be here when it's over?"

"The thought crosses my mind from time to time. I try not to dwell on it. I think it's better not knowing."

Their conversation was cut short by a pounding on the door.

Calif flipped a switch and the door opened.

A Khanist officer raced up the ramp, then doubled over, heaving and gasping for breath. "Sirs! You must...come...quickly..."

"What's happening?" Jorge asked.

"The Labs...sir...You must....come...to the Labs... A man...there's a man...down -"

Jorge pushed past the officer and raced out the door.

Calif paused long enough for the officer to catch his breath. "We need to go," he said urgently.

They made it to the door when a second officer appeared.

"I already told him," the first officer said.

The new arrival shook his head. "Two. Two men down, sir."

They all began running towards the Labs.

CHAPTER 48
Johanum

"What did he say?" Sibilum demanded.

Carnificius was in no mood to talk to Sibilum or anyone else. "We're negotiating," he finally replied, annoyed by Sibilum's stare and the way he made noises with his nose whenever he was impatient.

"Negotiating about what?" Sibilum asked angrily.

"The terms of the agreement."

"Mortarium got Sulta to respond right away."

"Timore isn't Sulta," Carnificius hissed.

"I should have sent him instead of you."

"Yes, you should have," Carnificius replied in a huff.

"How long will it take, this 'negotiation' of yours?"

"I don't know. What does it matter? We have twelve months."

"We have less than twelve months now."

"That's not my fault."

"Bisurakhan will be here in weeks. We can't wait!"

Carnificius' patience, if he ever had any, was wearing thin. "Then go take care of this yourself."

"I can't! Not now. You've started the conversation."

"And whose fault is that?"

"Yours!" Sibilum bellowed.

"How is it my fault?!"

"This whole debacle is your fault!"

"You have a problem with taking responsibility," Carnificius pointed out indulgently, as though his observation was one Sibilum should thank him for.

"I have no such problem."

"And you have a problem with denial."

"I have a problem with you and your face," Sibilum sneered.

"You picked up right where you left off, I see," Mortarium said as he walked up.

The Priests were standing at the edge of the forest. The trees swayed in the wind as their voices bent the air.

"Carnificius is a failure," Sibilum snarled.

"I am not!" Carnificius baulked.

"Of course he is," Mortarium said, not taking any interest in the conversation. "We have a problem."

"We always have problems! Why don't you ever bring me anything but problems?" Sibilum growled.

"You'd die of shock."

"A Priest can't die of shock."

Mortarium rolled his eyes. "We have a problem," he repeated.

"What is it?"

"Bisurakhan."

"I already know about that problem."

"This is a new problem."

"How many problems can one planet give me?" Sibilum growled.

"Quite a lot, it seems. They've moved up the dates of their travel. They're leaving tomorrow."

"And how long until they get here?"

"I don't know."

"Why don't you know?" Sibilum screamed. "You are useless, utterly useless!"

Mortarium turned to Carnificius. "This is your fault," he accused.

"It is not my fault!" Carnificius hissed.

"Oh, it's your fault. This one is definitely your fault."

Sibilum stood straighter and looked at Carnificius suspiciously. Carnificius's eyes shifted too quickly. Sibilum walked over, drew back his arm, and slapped Carnificius across the face.

Carnificius lost his footing and went flying backwards.

"What did you do?" Sibilum bellowed.

"I didn't do anything!" Carnificius whimpered, cowering before the taller Priest.

"Oh, he did something," Mortarium muttered.

"Tell me what you did!" Sibilum yelled in his face.

"It's nothing of consequence," Carnificius hissed, even as he began to look worried.

"Oh, yes, it is," Mortarium mumbled.

"Shut up!" Carnificius hissed.

"Tell me!" Sibilium screamed. "WHAT DID YOU DO?"

"My most magnificent Sibilum, this one," Mortarium said, pointing at Carnificius, "has broken the rules."

"You did WHAT?" Sibilum seemed to grow taller, his dark shadow enveloping Carnificius, who was crawling in the dirt before him.

"I didn't!" he insisted, though his voice came out weak and pathetic.

Sibilum reached down, caught the shorter Priest by the throat, and lifted him off the ground, letting his feet dangle in the air. "For the last time, WHAT DID YOU DO?"

All three Priests glared at each other.

None of them noticed the little creatures scurrying past their feet.

CHAPTER 49
Bisurakhan

"Please state your name."

"Calvin Smith."

"Age?"

"28."

"Department?"

"I'm not doing this again. It's spelled Smith. S-m-i-t-h."

"Ah yes, I see you now," the administrator said. "And you?"

"Joshua LeRoux."

"Age?"

"29."

"Department?"

"He's a guest," Calvin interrupted. "A guest observer. You should have his name already."

"I have no one by that name."

"Spell it," Calvin mumbled.

"L-E-R-O-U-"

"Ahhh. Yes, I have it."

"How did you – "

"Don't ask," Calvin interrupted again. He grabbed Josh by the elbow and pulled him past the desk. "I don't think he ever learned how to spell."

"How did he get a job as an administrator?" Josh asked.

"They must have been desperate." Calvin led the way into a nearby elevation box.

"Welcome, Calvin. Welcome, Josh."

"She doesn't have a name," Calvin said quickly. "Don't ask her. Please, please, please, don't ask her. We're already late."

"It's not my fault you overslept."

"It is your fault. You're slacking on godfather duties."

"I got Amelia to sleep yesterday."

"Exactly. Yesterday. Where were you today?"

"Working."

"Yeah, yeah. Be all responsible."

"I'd rather be snuggling a baby."

A happy, sleepy smile stretched across Calvin's face. "Yeah, me too. I snuggled with her all morning. It was awesome."

"Better than work?"

"So much better than work."

Josh looked around at the inside of the box. "So you asked it about its name?"

"I did. It didn't go so well."

"Kabira really has more advanced artificial intelligence than we do, huh?"

"I don't know if it's more advanced," Calvin replied. "It's fancier."

"What's the difference? Corey will be thrilled. He has this whole crazy theory that Kabiran intelligence is going to upend ours. He thinks they're building robots that will be able to override all our systems and attack us. Personally, I think he's crazy. But the whole building robots with personality trick is pretty cool."

"Maybe you should consider a move to Robotics."

"Nah. I'll stick with Comms. I like it there. So, what am I going to see today?"

"I don't know. They've been trying to drop volunteers back into Johanum at the same time and place as when they were there before. General Fossil said that was the whole point of having a multi-part experiment. But so far, no luck. It's just ended up being a bunch of random experiments, same as all the other times."

"So I'll just watch you run around an empty Lab?"

"I don't do a lot of running."

"You know what I mean."

"The visual engineers see a little of what I see. They tap the glasses, but the visual feed isn't usually very good. I assume they'll give you a pair of those glasses. Maybe you'll see something, maybe you won't. Actually, I'm curious about that. I really want to hear about what you're able to see. Sometimes, the way the engineers explain what they see, it sounds...fishy. Kind of like they're making it up. I'm not so sure they're really seeing anything. But I can tell you that the audio engineers hear almost everything. Which is weird, actually, because it's not like I talk to anybody."

"Then what are they listening to?"

"I don't know. The wind? Me, talking to myself? Last time I took a swim in a lake, and they heard me splashing around in the water."

"That's cool. I guess."

The elevation box landed softly on a landing pad and the doors opened.

Calvin led the way to the main office.

"Good to see you, Cal!" Stanley greeted him. "And Josh! It's nice to see you, too."

Josh nodded at the General. Calvin spoke highly of him, so he was probably all right, but Josh remained skeptical. General Fossil was too close to Jorge for his liking.

"Here, you'll need this," Stanley said, handing Josh a special Visitor badge. "Scan the badge when you get to the Observation level. You'll have to give your Pulse Stamp and an Iris Scan, then you'll be granted access."

"Thank you, sir."

"And you!" Stanley continued, turning to Calvin. "The last experiment of the series! How hard am I going to have to work to get you to come back here again?"

Calvin chuckled. "Sir, your issue will be with my wife. She wants me home more with her and the baby."

Stanley smiled. "I'll leave you alone for a while, then. Family first, my boy. Here's your gear. You're back in Lab #4.

The engineers are going to try and get you back to the same place you left, but as I'm sure you've heard, we haven't managed to get the calculations right thus far."

Josh sensed Calvin's discomfort and was surprised when Calvin's only response was an enthusiastic, "Yes, sir! May I walk Josh up to the Observation level?"

"But of course! I'll see you in Debrief."

Calvin gave a quick salute and motioned for Josh to follow.

"You don't seem very excited," Josh observed as they walked in silence.

Calvin shrugged. "I'm sure it will be fine."

"You're acting weird."

"I'm not!"

"Yes, you are. Are you going to tell me what's going on?"

"Why are you grilling me with questions?"

"Touché." Josh was quiet as they took the stairs two-by-two and started down another long hallway. "So, you're not worried at all?"

"You know what's stressing me out? YOU are stressing me out," Calvin snapped.

Josh lifted his hands in surrender. "I won't say anything more. How was Amelia this morning? Is she still making that funny face before she calls asleep?"

Calvin's shoulders relaxed. "Yeah. Oh, there's a new thing. It's a new kind of a laugh, a new little giggle. It sounds like a cascade – no, like a waterfall of giggles. I don't know how else to explain it. It just washes over her whole body and she jiggles up and down and I can't stop laughing whenever she does it. Leah was making these silly faces, and Amelia – she could not stop giggling! You should have kids, Josh, you really should."

Josh grimaced.

"Sorry. I shouldn't have said that," Calvin apologized. "I know you wanted them."

"It's fine. Are you still planning something for Leah's birthday next week?"

Calvin took his cue to change the subject. "Yeah, I want to have some people over. Leah was so happy after Mary and Hailey came. Could you invite them again? See when they're available?"

"Sure. When do you want to have the party?"

"Next weekend. You know what? Any night. Any night when you all are free. It's not like we have anything going on. I'll invite a couple of Leah's friends, but I'll just invite them for whatever night you choose. Just as long as it's before I come back to work."

"Wait, you're coming back?"

"It's going to kill you, isn't it?"

"I'm already dying." Josh made fake strangling noises and tried to make his eyes bulge out of his head.

"Dude, that's creepy."

"This place is creepy. It's so dark."

"We're underground."

"Yeah, but...you know we have lights and stuff. They could add a few more of those down these hallways."

"We're here!" Calvin announced, gesturing to the thick steel door in front of them. A sign above the door read "Observation Room 4" in large block letters.

Josh looked around for the security box. It was hidden, barely visible, at eye level and off to the right. He held up his badge and passed it in front of the soft orange speck of light. It blinked several times, then turned green. A section of the wall opened to reveal a small device resembling a microscope. Josh leaned forward and let the eyepiece scan his right eye. The light above his head flashed green. He laid his wrist down and a soft shock ran over his wrist and up his arm. He waited for the light to blink a third time, then stepped back.

The microscope moved back into the wall. Josh heard a loud "click," and the door to Observation Room #4 creaked open.

"See you on the other side!" Calvin said cheerfully. He turned and headed downstairs.

Josh stepped into the Observation Room. It was even darker than the hallway. Four engineers sat at desks in the back of the room. It was clear from the gear surrounding them which two were the audio engineers and which two were the visual engineers. All four were busy prepping for Calvin's experiment and didn't bother to look up.

A large window at the front of the room overlooked the dark, empty Lab below.

Two chairs were seated close to the window. Josh crossed the room and sat down. None of the engineers acknowledged him. Their faces glowed in the soft blue light reflecting from the screens at their desks.

The audio engineers wore full, fitted, noise-blocking headphones. The visual engineers wore special glasses, which Josh noticed were identical to the ones General Fossil had given to Calvin.

"Is anyone else coming?" Josh asked, pointing to the second chair.

No one responded.

Josh turned back to the window. Calvin had just walked in. He looked funny with all those weapons. They were comms engineers. They didn't carry weapons. Josh laughed outright when Calvin put on those ridiculous glasses.

"I wish I could get a picture of this," Josh muttered to himself.

"Shhhhhhh!" one of the audio engineers said.

"Oh! Hey!" Josh said, turning around.

The engineer frowned.

"Is anyone else coming?" Josh asked. "I notice there's another chair."

The audio engineer removed his headphones. "What was that?"

Josh repeated his question. The engineer, who introduced himself as Vincent, shook his head. "You're it. We don't get many observers."

"Excellent." Josh pushed the second chair back and used it as a stool to prop up his feet. "Oh!" he said, turning back around.

This time both audio engineers took off their headphones.

"How do I hear what's going on?" Josh asked.

"You don't," Vincent answered.

"Yeah, you just watch," said the second engineer. "I'm Aki, by the way."

"Josh."

"Yeah, we know," Aki replied.

"Okay. So, wait, I don't get to hear anything?"

"That's right," Aki said.

"Can I get a pair of those glasses?" He gestured to the goggles worn by the visual engineers.

Both visual engineers looked up.

"Chi," said the first.

"Danny," said the second.

"Josh," Josh said.

"We know," Chi and Danny said in unison.

"Can I get a pair of those glasses?"

"Why?" Chi asked.

"So I can see," Josh said.

"They don't work like that," Danny explained. "The visual feed goes into the computer."

"So I can move back there and watch the screens?"

"No!" all four engineers replied simultaneously.

"This is weird," Josh complained.

"Take it up with General Fossil," Vincent said, replacing his headphones.

Josh settled back in his seat. At least the chairs were comfortable. Calvin was walking on his tiptoes, his neck strained forward like an old man trying to drive.

Josh smiled and relaxed. This could be entertaining.

CHAPTER 50
Johanum

Calvin could see the docks and the lake in the distance. He leaned forward and squinted to be sure. Yes, those were definitely the docks. He wasn't far from the place he had been when he left the last simulation. The transport engineers would be happy to know that their calculations were getting closer.

He was standing on a rocky path, halfway up the side of a mountain. He looked around. To the left, far in the distance, he saw the edge of a forest. To the right, a set of caves.

He thought about exploring the caves. He would rather stay away from the water; he wasn't excited about the possibility of seeing those ghosts again. But General Fossil was trying to create Building Block Simulations, so he figured he should at least try to go back to the place he had been before. With a heavy sigh and his Khanist sense of duty firmly intact, Calvin started down the path towards the lake.

The rocks were slippery. It must have rained recently. After losing his footing twice, Calvin stepped off the path and walked along the grass.

He arrived at the docks and looked around. He didn't see any ghosts. Nor did he see any tall men surrounded by darkness. He breathed a sigh of relief. The engineers had been close on the geography, but it looked like they hadn't managed to manipulate the time. He was definitely there at a different time than before.

Humidity hung heavy in the air. Calvin decided to jump back in the lake. As he slipped off his shoes, he smiled. Josh would be able to tell him if his boots came off in the Lab!

The water was refreshing, just like he remembered it. Calvin poked around at the bubble that encircled him underwater. He wanted to see if it would break. He pushed his arm and shoulder into it several times, but the bubble always sprung back into place. Content that he was safe, Calvin swam out farther.

The floor of the lake caught his attention. It was reflective, like a mirror, even though it was lightly colored and jagged. It looked like stained glass, fitted together in small, broken pieces. He could see his reflection paddling along beneath him. It always seemed a second delayed. He lifted his hand and waved. A moment later, it waved back.

He swam closer to the floor and reached down. His hand had more force than he intended and sunk into the sand. The floor had looked so shiny, he hadn't realized there was any sand. He wiggled his fingers. Then he felt the dirt giving way beneath his arm.

In alarm, Calvin realized his hand and forearm were completely out of sight, hidden beneath the surface floor. He could feel air below. It was cool and he could wiggle his fingers, which were dripping wet. Then a hand grasped his fingers and squeezed.

Calvin jerked back and pulled his arm close to his body. Then he pushed off the floor with his feet and swam back to the docks. He climbed out of the water, his heart was racing.

As he dried off, Calvin turned around and peered into the lake.

What was that? What had grabbed his hand?

He couldn't see anything now. The water was peaceful and calm.

Calvin looked around. There were still no ghosts. He reached for his boots. Maybe he would go visit the caves after all.

He was halfway up the path when something new caught his attention.

A garden.

It was down and off to the right, nestled between two boulders. Bushes and dozens of statues surrounded a green stone pool. The bushes were trimmed and well-kept and covered in bright red berries. The statues were of all sorts of things – adults, children, animals.

What a strange place.

Calvin was in the middle of the garden before he realized he had walked over to it. It was pretty. Too pretty. It was out of place. There was nothing particularly wrong with Johanum, but there was nothing particularly right about it either. This garden had red tulips, yellow daffodils, and a species of purple flowers he didn't recognize. Everything was beautiful, but in a cold, surreal sort of way. None of the plants looked quite real.

In the middle of the green stone pool stood a fountain in the shape of a dragon. No, it wasn't a dragon. It was one of those old creatures that Hailey had talked about when she told that story from the Scrolls. The fountain was in the shape of a Legion. At any rate, it looked broken.

Calvin bent towards the fountain to it when he heard a soft female voice behind him.

"I wouldn't touch that if I was you."

He whirled around.

A woman stood before him, dressed in ragged clothes and carrying an earthen bowl. She had distinctive features, but they were...less, somehow. She seemed halfway between a human and a ghost.

"How did you get here?" she asked.

"I came -" and he stopped. How had he come, exactly? He wouldn't know where to begin.

"I saw you yesterday," she said.

Calvin frowned. "Yesterday?"

"Down at the docks. I was watching you. I live up there." She pointed to the caves. "Where did you come from?"

"I came from Bisurakhan. But I'm not quite sure how I got here. I mean, I know *how* I got here – I came through one of our Reality Persuasion labs. But, I think, maybe, well, I think I might not really be here."

She eyed him curiously.

"It sounds ridiculous, I know," he added. How was he supposed to explain Reality Persuasion to someone who wasn't a Khanist? The whole concept was weird, now that he stopped to think about it.

"It's not that strange," she said with a shrug. "But you said you came from Bisurakhan. Are you the rescue mission?"

"No, but they're coming. Wait – how do you know about that?"

"Someone mentioned it to me."

"Who are you?"

She held out her hand. "Josephine Kanale."

Calvin could barely contain his excitement. "Dr. Kanale!" He grabbed her hand and pumped it enthusiastically. "It's such an honor to meet you. I have heard so much about you. I'm Calvin. Calvin Smith. Officer Calvin Smith."

She looked at him blankly.

"You're the reason I'm here!" Calvin explained. "Well, part of the reason. There's a team coming to get you. The rescue mission you just mentioned – the Chiefs are coming. Here. For you. I'm just a part of our Reality Persuasion experiments. But that doesn't matter. It is such an honor to meet you, Dr. Kanale! I've heard so much about you."

"You're sure you aren't the rescue mission?" she asked again. She sounded disappointed.

"No, but they're coming! In a couple of weeks. Wait a second. Did you say you saw me at the docks yesterday?"

She nodded.

"My last experiment was a week ago."

"Experiment?"

"I mean – when I was here the last time. It was a week ago. What's the time signature here?"

She shrugged. "Slow."

Calvin was doing the math in his head. "Johanum's time signature must be the same as Charisburg's," he mumbled to himself. "It must be."

He was getting excited again. He was about to be on the cutting edge of cracking the code to Johanum's time signature! He was going to be famous! He'd get his name in the Logs and everything.

"Seven to one," he continued mumbling. "That's the same as the difference between Bisurakhan and Charisburg. That's got to be it."

"I don't think that the passage of time here is consistent," Josephine said. "But neither is it important. What was your name? Calvin? Calvin, you shouldn't be here."

"It's okay. Don't worry. We come all the time."

She shook her head. "I mean you shouldn't be here. In the Stone Gardens. It's not safe."

"You're here," Calvin pointed out.

"It's not safe for me either," she said. "And I don't think I'm ever alone when I'm here."

"Have you met other Khanists then?"

"No."

"Then who else do you meet?"

A cold wind blew through the garden. Calvin felt it ruffling his hair. It blew through the nearby bushes and rippled across the water that lay in the bottom of the pool.

"He's here," she said.

Calvin turned around.

The tall man with the X was standing there. He wore a long linen robe and was at least a head taller than Calvin. The sense of dread Calvin had felt when he saw this man with the others while standing at the docks crept back over him. A shiver ran down his spine. Calvin instinctively stepped backwards.

"You have a new friend, Josephine," Carnificius said, his voice dripping with a sweetness Calvin knew was not friendly.

"He's not my friend. We just met."

"He looks like he wants to be your friend."

Calvin squirmed. "I'm married."

Carnificius looked taken aback, then smiled in amusement. His teeth were black and crooked. He was an ugly, ugly, very tall man. "I didn't mean that type of friend. But this is Johanum. You are free to do as you like."

"He was just leaving," Josephine interrupted.

"Was he? That's a shame. I thought he just arrived."

"I did," Calvin agreed. He drew back at the stern look on Dr. Kanale's face. "But I... can go..."

"There's no hurry," Carnificius replied.

Calvin thought he saw the tail of a snake flutter behind the Priest's teeth.

Carnificius noticed his fascination. "Do you want to see it?" he asked.

Calvin hesitated.

Carnificius motioned for Calvin to move closer. Calvin took one step. Carnificius let loose his scaled tongue. It stretched passed the side of Calvin's head and hissed into his ear.

Calvin jumped back. Carnificius stepped away and the snake burrowed back behind his crooked black teeth.

"You don't have that in Bisurakhan," Carnificius said with amusement.

"No, we don't," Calvin said as he shivered again.

"I like your people," Carnificius said generously. He moved closer to Calvin, looking him up and down, circling him carefully. "You're all so very...ambitious."

"We're very advanced," Calvin replied. This man made him uncomfortable. The air around him was getting heavy, pushing down on his chest, making it hard for him to breathe.

"That's what they all say," Carnificius replied. "Bisurakhan is the best. Cornersville is the best. Pendleton is the best."

"No one says Pendleton is the best," Calvin disagreed.

"Only the people who live there." Carnificius' smile was indulgent. "But, of course, no one compares to Bisurakhan. And I must agree with you about that. You have an army. You have science. You have...the Commander."

Calvin tilted his head in surprise. "Most people talk about our weapons," he said.

"I was," Carnificius replied. "Tell me, what do you know about them, these weapons of yours?"

"I work in the Frequency Tower. I don't handle weapons. Hey, are you the one sending all those messages?"

Carnificius' smile disappeared. "I don't know what you're talking about," he snapped.

"The messages. The ones we've been getting from here for several months. Wait, no," Calvin stopped himself. "Those were intercepted. Never mind. I'm sure those weren't from you."

"You've been intercepting messages?" Carnificius asked, feigning curiosity.

Calvin felt the air around him grow colder. It was too cold. He looked down at his hands. His fingers were turning blue.

Dr. Kanale stepped forward. "Let him go, Carnificius. He doesn't know anything. He won't be of any use to you."

Carnificius hissed in reply. He moved closer, his face pressing against Calvin's. The snake behind his teeth escaped and licked the side of Calvin's cheek.

Calvin began to cough. A hand of ice was wrapped around his lungs, squeezing.

Carnificius laid his long, spindly fingers against Calvin's throat. "You are a fine young man. A good Khanist. I can see that." His snake tongue was thrashing behind his teeth. "I would like you to take back a message for me. Can you do that?"

Calvin was shivering so violently, he could barely nod.

"Good." Carnificius stepped away and turned his back.

Calvin felt a rush of cold, icy air release from his lungs. He staggered forward and regained his footing. He was still so cold. "What do you want me to say?" he asked.

Carnificius turned back around. "Oh, my dear boy. You don't have to say anything. You are my message."

With a hiss of his tongue, the snake flashed past his teeth and encircled itself around Calvin's throat, squeezing tighter and tighter. Calvin's hands thrashed and clawed, but it was no use. He could feel his feet lifting off the ground. Closer and closer the Priest came, his eyes flashing sparks of red, the blood in Calvin's face slowly draining away.

A smile covered the Priest's face as he reached out his hand and cradled Calvin's face. "So young. So innocent. So useless."

The world around him began spinning in circles. Slowly his hands stopped fighting. As he exhaled his last breath of air, Calvin felt the snake loosen its grip. His body fell to the ground with a thud as his world went dark.

CHAPTER 51
Bisurakhan

Josh turned to the engineers when Calvin began shivering.

"Is this normal?" he had asked.

The engineers shrugged.

"There's no normal," Aki replied.

"Can you pause it?" Josh asked.

"We run the experiment until the timer runs out. Or until General Fossil tells us to stop, whichever comes first." Aki made a motion to a clock on the back wall that was counting down. 22 minutes left.

Josh turned back to the window. Suddenly Calvin began choking and his feet lifted off the ground.

"Turn it off!" Josh yelled, jumping to his feet.

"We told you, we can't," Vincent replied.

"Where is he?" Josh demanded.

"Who?"

"General Fossil!"

"I don't know! In one of the other Observation Rooms, probably."

A loud thud drew five sets of eyes back to the window.

Calvin lay on the Lab's cold steel floor, motionless.

Josh jumped over his chair, grabbed Vincent by the throat and smashed his face into the back wall. "TURN IT OFF!"

"He can't!" Aki yelled, frantically pushing all of the buttons on his keyboard. "We don't know how to stop it in the middle!"

Josh grabbed Aki's monitor and threw it across the room. "TURN IT OFF!"

Chi and Danny were pressing every button on every device they could reach.

Josh closed one hand around Aki's neck and used the other to send every item on his desk crashing to the floor. "Take me down there!"

Aki was choking and clawing at Josh's hands. Then he made a motion at the floor. Josh let him go. Aki dropped to his knees, scrambling around. A moment later, he stood up with a set of keys.

Josh grabbed Aki by the throat again and dragged him down the stairs. Aki's hands were shaking so badly, he dropped the keys. Josh picked them up, brushed passed Aki and unlocked the door himself.

"Calvin!" Josh yelled as he pushed open the door and rushed inside. He sank to his knees next to his friend and cradled Calvin's head in his lap. "Calvin! Calvin, wake up, buddy! You're going to be okay. Wake up! Please wake up!"

Calvin's eyes fluttered. Josh saw the red marks circling his throat. He could feel Calvin's whole body begin to shake. He pressed down his own panic and grabbed Calvin's hand as it moved weakly, feeling around on the floor.

"Cal! It's going to be okay. Stay with me, buddy!"

Calvin's eyes closed, then fluttered open again. He forced them to focus. He saw the fear on Josh's face. His body jerked violently several times, then a surreal sense of calm washed over him and he went completely still. "Hey," he whispered, trying to laugh. It came out more like a choke.

"Just stay with me," Josh whispered. "Someone's coming to help. You're going to be all right."

Calvin blinked several times. The light around him kept fading. He wanted to tell Josh it was going to be okay. He wanted to tell Josh to leave. But he didn't. He could feel the life draining from his limbs, and he didn't want to be alone. He wanted to be with his friend.

"Don't close your eyes!" Josh begged, straining against tears. He cradled Calvin's head closer.

Calvin struggled against the heaviness pressing down on his chest. What should he say? What could he say? What was left that hadn't been said?

"Josh?" His voice was weak. He wasn't even sure Josh could hear him.

"I'm here, Cal. I'm here."

"You've been the best friend I could have asked for. Thank you for everything."

Tears poured down Josh's face. He shook his head furiously. "Don't say that. Just stay with me. I already told you, you're going to be okay."

"Josh, I need you to tell Leah..." Calvin stopped, convulsing into a coughing fit. Then his body stilled again. He swallowed hard. "Tell my wife how much I love her."

Josh squeezed Calvin's hand tighter.

"Amelia. Tell my baby girl, I love her, too. Kiss her for me. Please. Don't let her forget me. I don't want her to forget how much I love her."

Josh clenched his jaw. "Stop."

"I didn't mean to leave them, Josh. I don't want to go. I don't want...to leave..."

And with his final words, Calvin's body went limp and his eyes rolled back in his head.

A sense of grief like he had never known welled up inside Josh's chest. He didn't know what to do with it. It was a scream stuck in his chest, a burning stuffed in his throat, a pent-up rage he could not describe, curled up in the pit of his belly.

The door behind him opened.

Josh turned.

General Fossil rushed in with Chi and Danny. He took one look at the floor and the blood drained from his face.

Josh reached over, grabbed a gun from Calvin's belt, and put a bullet through the General's head.

CHAPTER 52
Johanum

His body had disappeared as soon as it hit the ground. Carnificius had disappeared too.

I stood in the Stone Gardens, my heart in my throat. I didn't even know that young man, but I felt such sorrow. He had been foolish to speak of Bisurakhan. But what did he know? He had never been here. Not really. He didn't understand what Johanum was like.

The wind had died down. It was only windy when the Priests were near. I hated the breeze, more than I hated the hot, humid air that threatened to suffocate me. At least when I could hardly breathe, I knew I was safe.

I picked up the bowl I had dropped. It had cracked in its fall. I examined it a minute, then dropped it back to the ground.

Sometimes it's best not to disturb what is broken.

It was late in the day by the time I returned to the caves. Mad Laughs had a fire blazing. I noticed extra fish perched on stick skewers.

"Will our friends be joining us?" I asked, trying to block out the images from the Stone Gardens that were running circles in my head.

Mad Laughs shrugged.

It was sweet that he always prepared for Mr. Fox and Mr. Brown to join us. Most of the time they didn't, but Mad Laughs liked to be prepared.

I went back to the cave with the canvas and retrieved Fletcher's old blankets. When I came back, Mad Laughs took one look at me and the blankets and raised his eyebrows.

"I want a nap," I said. "And I want to be cozy."

Mad Laughs shrugged and went on about his business.

I liked that he didn't make much of anything I did. There was never any judgment. He was his crazy, I was my crazy, and we let each other alone.

I had just fallen asleep when I heard the sound of Mad Laughs' low growl.

Mad Laughs had different growls. I had learned most of them over time. This growl was curious.

I forced my eyes open and rolled to one side, propping myself up on my elbow. Mad Laughs was standing at the mouth of the cave, hands on his hips, brows furrowed.

"What's out there?" I asked. When he didn't respond, I stood up and walked over.

I tried to follow his gaze, but it was dark, and I couldn't see anything. "I know your eyesight's better than mine," I said, "but *what* are you looking at?"

He pointed down the path. I squinted and watched for a few minutes. I saw nothing. Finally, I turned to go back inside. Mad Laughs grabbed my arm and pulled me back. He pointed again. This time I realized he was pointing at the dirt. I adjusted my eyes down and squinted.

A tiny speck of light appeared. Two of them, side by side. They disappeared within a second. But then I saw another set of lights. And another. Little purple specks of light.

Those weren't lights. Those were eyes.

My own eyes widened in excitement and I turned to Mad Laughs, clapping my hands excitedly. "It's the Furpines!" I exclaimed. I turned back to the darkness and rushed forward, down the trail, towards the blinking purple eyes.

I got down on my hands and knees in the dirt. "Where are you?" I called.

Mad Laughs stood behind me, his hands back on his hips, that same confused look on his face.

"It's okay!" I called, worried that Mad Laughs would scare away my little friends. "He won't hurt you. He's friendly. Mad Laughs, smile!"

Mad Laughs scowled.

I rolled my eyes. "He likes to think he's intimidating, but really, he's sweet and kind. I promise. He won't hurt you. Come out. Please!"

I looked around, wondering where they had gone. Then I felt a soft pressure on my right hand. I looked down. There was sweet little Tabby, plopped down, smiling contentedly.

"I knew we'd find you," she announced proudly.

"Tabby!" I was so happy, I could hardly contain it. I lifted my hand up to eye level to get a better look. "You're safe. I've been so worried about you."

"Yes, I'm safe," she agreed. "And so are they, but they're also scared, very scared." She flapped her little arms to gesture at the ground and nearly tipped off my hand.

I grabbed her furry body to keep her from falling. "But where are they?" I asked, steadying her carefully.

"They're hiding. They saw the fire and got scared."

I looked back at the cave. Mr. Fox and Mr. Brown had settled in next to the fire. Mr. Fox had claimed Fletcher's old blankets and was looking quite comfortable. Mr. Brown was trying, unsuccessfully, to pull one of the skewers out of the fire.

The fish were burned black. Oh well.

"They think the fire means the Priests are there," Tabby explained.

"Oh, no, the Priests aren't here, I promise. They don't come up here. It's just a regular fire."

"Did you hear that?" Tabby called, leaning over the side of my hand as far as she dared. "There are no Priests! It's just our friend! And, well..." She turned around and studied Mad Laughs.

Mad Laughs leaned forward himself to get a closer look. Tabby, with her characteristic boldness, waited for his face to get close, then stood on her tiptoes and grabbed his nose.

Mad Laughs jumped back and howled.

Tabby let go and fell backwards, then she rolled to her side in a fit of giggles.

I felt a silly grin stretching across my face. That laugh! She couldn't stop. Her foot began tapping furiously, making her round tummy jiggle. She put both hands on her tummy and giggled harder.

Tabby's helpless giggles were enough to draw the other Furpines out of hiding.

I watched as her brother, Tibby, peaked out from behind a rock, followed by their parents, Toby and Telly. A few more rocks slid around, revealing Amos, and then his brothers Ace and Archie. Finally, the remaining Furpines emerged, waddling forward from all different directions.

"You're here! You're all here!" I exclaimed in wonder. I couldn't believe they were all alive!

As was my new custom, I promptly burst into tears.

Mad Laughs winced and put his hands over his ears. Tabby's laughter stopped and she stood back up.

"Oh, don't be sad!" she cried. "We're so happy to see you. We've been searching for you for a very long time."

"You've been searching for me?" I asked, wiping away tears.

"Yes!" Tabby exclaimed. "I told them we must find you. We *would* find you. And here we are. Now you can help us get home!"

I started crying again. "I don't know how to help you get home," I said.

"Don't you worry your pretty little head about us, dearie," came a familiar voice. I looked down to see Telly, Tabby's mother. She was holding her husband Toby's hand

and happily patting her belly. "Canwood told us to come, so we came."

I sniffed. "Canwood?"

"The king of the forest, dearie. You remember him. He's the one who told us to come find you. He said you'd help us get home. We just had to be here when the time was right."

"We helped find you!" came a little voice. It belonged to Amos, who was standing shoulder to shoulder with his brothers Ace and Archie. They didn't like feeling left out.

"Oh, yes, dearie," Telly agreed. "These boys were our scouts. They searched high and low for clues about you. We couldn't have made it here without them."

The boys beamed.

Tabby harrumphed loudly. "They didn't do anything helpful," she muttered.

"Shush, dearie," her mother scolded, though she threw in a wink for good measure.

"Come up to the caves, please," I invited. "You'll be safe there."

Telly looked up at the fire and shivered. Toby patted her hand affectionately. "It's okay," he reassured her. "We know the person is safe."

She nodded but still looked unsure.

"We can put the fire out," I offered, "but it gets a little cold and awfully dark. We'd have to light it again later."

"Come on, Mom, don't be scared," Tabby urged her. "The person said the Priests aren't there."

"I actually think they can't come up here. I think it breaks some sort of rule."

That got the group's attention.

"Not at all, dearie?" Telly asked, a sense of wonder in her voice.

"I've never seen one here," I said.

"You've never seen a Priest?" little Amos asked in awe.

I grimaced. Calvin's face flashed through my mind. I could still see the horror in his eyes and feel his panic as he thrashed about. "We see them," I answered, "but not here. Not in the caves. The caves are safe. At least, they have been so far."

"Well, we best get going then. You heard the person. Come on," Toby urged.

They all began to scuttle forward. Mad Laughs was taken aback by the way the little Furpines' legs moved so much faster than their bodies. They kept knocking themselves over.

Mad Laughts looked at me in confusion. I grinned, a twinkle in my eye. I already knew what he was thinking, and I didn't intend to stop him.

"Try not to scare them," I cautioned.

With a swoop of his arms, Mad Laughs caught up half of them. The poor things cried out in fear and curled up in protective little fur balls, hiding their eyes.

"It's okay," I assured them. "He won't hurt you. He's just going to carry you."

Another swoop and he had them all cradled in his arms.

"They're scared," I said to Tabby, who was still sitting in my hand, studying Mad Laughs carefully.

"He's very big," she replied.

"But he's kind."

"You're sure?"

"Yes. Quite sure."

"Okay then." She smiled up at me confidently. "Let's go."

We headed back up the path to the caves. I could only imagine how they would react to meeting Mr. Fox and Mr. Brown.

CHAPTER 53
Bisurakhan

Calif sat quietly. The man across the table slouched in his chair, shoulders heaving, rocking his head back and forth in his hands.

Still Calif waited. He didn't say a word until Josh raised his head.

"You are murderers," he whispered hoarsely.

"Be careful with your accusations," Calif cautioned. "The same could be said of you."

"Why do you keep saying that?" Josh asked angrily.

"You don't remember what happened?"

"I remember everything. I didn't kill Calvin. YOU killed Calvin. All of you. Jorge. Stanley. You are murderers."

Calif reached for a controller on his desk. Footage from one of the Lab's security cameras began playing, projected on a large monitor that covered the wall to his left. He pointed. As Josh turned, Calif scrolled backwards, all the way to the footage from the Observation Room. He hit play.

They watched as Josh grabbed one of the engineers by the back of his neck, slammed his face into the wall and broke his nose. He sent the computer flying across the room, then smashed everything else on the man's desk.

Calif rolled the footage forward and stopped at the moment Josh and Aki burst through the Lab door.

Josh's whole body shook as he relived Calvin's last moments. Then he watched the Lab door open again. General Fossil rushed in, followed by two engineers. Josh didn't recognize the look on his own face as he reached for Calvin's gun, turned, and shot Stanley in the face.

Josh's face turned white and he began to shake. "I killed him," he whispered, looking utterly bewildered.

Calif reached for the controller and turned off the screen. "You are a man of action," he said. "And a man of great anger."

Josh's insides churned. He had thought he had tamed that demon. He remembered the fights with Kat. The broken dishes. The broken glass. The broken egos. He remembered the look of fear on the face of his own mother, and the looks of repulsion on the faces of his in-laws.

He had always struggled to control his anger. But he thought the worst of that battle was behind him. Now he sat in front of Calif, one of the most powerful men on the planet, and his most glaring weakness was on full display. Soon, everyone would know.

He could not control his anger.

He had killed a man.

Josh leaned over the side of his chair and vomited.

Calif paged a custodian. "There's a bathroom outside," he said, gesturing toward the door. "Go clean yourself up."

"Yes, sir."

Josh walked to the bathroom, bent over the sink and washed his mouth. He stared into the mirror. Who was that man staring back? He didn't recognize him.

Waves of panic, horror, shock and self-contempt washed over him. Images flashed through his brain faster than he could keep up. Calvin. His lifeless face. His cold, clammy hands. The engineers in the Observation Room. He saw his old house, with Kat curled up in the corner, screaming, the bathroom floor covered in blood and broken glass.

Josh sank to the floor and put his face between his knees, trying to get it to stop. The memories needed to stop. Everything needed to stop.

A knock at the door made him jump to his feet. It was the custodian.

"Calif requests your return," the man mumbled, his eyes lowered.

"Thank you," Josh whispered, dashing away tears.

He stood up and glanced at the mirror. Grimacing, he leaned back over the sink and splashed more water on his face.

With a nod at the custodian, he walked out of the bathroom and returned to Calif's office.

The office smelled like bleach.

"I'm sorry," he apologized with a nod at the floor.

"That, my boy, is the least of our worries."

Josh's false bravado disappeared.

"Sit down, Josh."

Josh slid into the chair, hoping his face didn't show how scared he felt. He was a Khanist. He was a man. He would take whatever punishment was given, and he would accept it with his head held high.

His knees were literally knocking together.

"Josh, I want to talk to you."

"Yes, sir."

"You lost someone today. Your best friend. A loss must be grieved. You must find a way to grieve."

Josh was blinking furiously, using every ounce of energy he had left to focus his gaze on the floor by his feet.

"Normally I would tell you to let your grief run its course and let it express itself however it needs to. But you're not going to have the freedom to do that. Do you understand what I'm saying?"

Josh felt heat rising in his face. "Yes, sir."

"I want to help you. Anger is not a crime. But you must learn to control it. Have you met General Simmons?"

Josh shook his head.

"Back several years ago, he designed a series of Anger Redirection exercises. They've been helpful in the past for people like you. I want you to go."

"Will any General be willing to work with me?" Josh said with a humorless laugh.

"You're not the first to lose yourself in the heat of the moment."

"And what will keep me from doing it again?" Josh asked bitterly.

"Your acknowledgement that it could happen again is a start. But I assure you, General Simmons will be well prepared. There will be no repeat of what happened in the Lab."

"And what will happen to me?" Josh asked. He knew the Khanist legal system. He knew the death penalty was an option.

"There will be a trial," Calif said, "and you are hereby suspended from your Khanist duties until the conclusion of your trial."

Josh clenched his hands into fists and tried to hide them under the desk. He winced as his shaking knees smashed his hands into the underside of the table. Finally, Josh summoned his courage to look up. "I'm going to die, aren't I?" he asked simply.

"You don't know that."

"I'm guilty. You know it. Everyone will know it. Who, in their right mind, would let me walk away?"

"It is not your guilt that will be in question."

"What else matters?" Josh could feel his own self-loathing rising up in his chest. He could have choked on it. He could also feel Calif's sympathy.

Calif shouldn't pity a man like him. He had done this to himself. This was who he was. He was a man who could kill. No one should have pity on him. No one would.

Calif watched the emotions fluttering across Josh's face and wondered if the young man had any idea how vulnerable he was. He personally felt no anger at the boy. Any number of men would have reacted the same way.

So many of them had been worried that the simulations would turn deadly. General Fossil should have kept a closer eye on what was happening. If he had, perhaps Calvin could have been saved.

But while Calif knew all that, a judge wouldn't, and Calif couldn't predict how a judge would react. The judge would know very little about Reality Persuasion. He would draw his own conclusions.

"I'd like you to resolve an argument for me, Josh."

"All right."

"Jorge believes you're a threat to society. I disagree. Who's right?"

The mention of Jorge's name revived Josh's rage. He clenched and unclenched his fists under the desk, letting them hit the table as they bounced against his knees. He wanted to jump up and break the table.

"I don't know," Josh finally answered.

"You recognize that you might be. That's enough for me." Calif reached into a desk drawer and pulled out a thin wire band with a lock. "I'm going to let you go, but you'll have to wear this. It's a tracker. Geographic location only, there's no audio or visual feeds. You are free to go where you like, although you are banned within 100 metres of the Turris. Remember that we will know where you are at all times. Attach this to your ankle."

Josh reached forward and took the tracker. It was lightweight and thin. He doubted anyone would notice it. He closed the lock and heard it click. The sound made his stomach drop. He stared at the floor miserably. The tracker may have been light, but he was hyperaware of it and could feel the cold against his skin.

He was no longer free. He was a prisoner. A prisoner of Bisurakhan. A prisoner of the things he had done. A prisoner of himself.

"It typically takes six weeks for a trial to be called to court, but I suspect yours will happen more quickly. You'll be notified when they're ready for you. Be ready. You probably won't get more than a day's notice."

Josh nodded, still staring at the tracker on his ankle.

"I need to talk to you about Calvin's wife and child. Can you have that conversation right now? I know it's a lot to ask."

Josh forced himself to look at Calif and nod.

"Calvin's wife -"

"Leah," Josh winced. "Her name is Leah."

"Leah. I'm going to her house when we're done. I'd like you to come with me."

Josh's uncontrollable shaking returned.

"She knows you," Calif continued. "She trusts you. I need you to be there for her. Will you do that?"

Josh could feel the tears sliding down his cheeks. They burned his eyes and every place they touched.

"We have a policy for taking care of the family of deceased Khanist members." Calif paused as Josh winced again. "We will buy Calvin's wife a house and pay her an annual stipend that will cover all necessary living expenses for her and the child. It takes about 30 days for the paperwork to be processed and go through all appropriate levels of approval. I understand they didn't have family close by. I need you to help take care of them, make sure they're all right, until we get everything sorted out on our end."

Josh hadn't heard a word Calif said after "deceased."

"Are you able to do this, Josh?"

Josh blinked several times, confused. "Do what?"

Calif reached into another drawer and pulled out a payment card. Josh recognized it as a payment card, though it was unlike any of the ones he had used.

"This is an emergency payment card, authorized by the Turris," Calif explained, reaching across the desk and handing it to Josh. "It's used for interim needs, like this one. All certified retailers and merchants in Bisurakhan will accept it. You and Leah can both use it. Well, technically, it's for Leah. But since you're off payroll and you're helping Calvin's family at my request, I'll permit you to use it. Josh, are you hearing anything I'm saying?"

"Yes, sir."

"Are you sure?"

"Yes, sir."

Calif pointed to the payment card in Josh's hand. "Who can use that?"

"How would I know?"

Calif nodded. "Josh, I'm sending you home," he announced.

"No!" he said forcefully.

"Yes," Calif replied.

"I'm -" Josh stopped as a wave of panic overtook him. He shook from the bottom of his feet to the top of his head. After a couple of minutes, the shaking subsided. Josh took several long breaths and forced himself to speak. "I'm going with you to Calvin's apartment. Leah's apartment," he corrected himself.

"I don't think you're ready for that."

"I'll be ready for it."

"I don't think you will be."

Josh jumped to his feet, slammed his fists into the desk, then picked up his chair and threw it across the room. His hands were wrapped around Calif's computer monitor before the look on Calif's face stopped him.

Josh stilled but didn't remove his hands from the computer. "It's not right," he said, his voice cracking. "It's not right. None of this is right. Calvin should be going home tonight. He should be going home to Leah. He should be holding and rocking his baby to sleep tonight. It's not right. It's not right. It's not right..."

Josh dropped his head in his hands and sobbed.

Calif rose to his feet and wrapped his arms around Josh's shoulders. He wanted to offer words of comfort, but he stayed silent. What was there to say?

Antoine had been right. Johanum had arrived, and they themselves had issued the invitation.

CHAPTER 54
Johanum

"You didn't have to kill the boy. You could have just shook him up a little," Sibilum said.

He had tied Carnificius up and hung him by his ankles over an open flame. The fire didn't matter, of course. Carnificius wouldn't burn. It was mostly for effect.

"He had seen too much," Carnificius hissed. "He would tell everyone what he had seen."

"It wouldn't matter if he did," Sibilum snapped. "Khanist officials don't believe anything the survivors tell them. They're not interested."

"They would believe this one," Carnificius insisted. "They sent him to spy on us."

"Well, now you've gone and broken the rules. A life for a life, remember? What will they demand now as a sacrifice? When the price isn't agreed upon beforehand, they can demand whichever life they choose."

"They don't know the rules," Carnificius hissed, crossing his arms across his swinging, upside down chest.

"The Commander knows the rules," Sibilum said.

"And whose life do you think the Commander will choose?" Carnificius asked, not trying to hide the glee in his voice.

Sibilum grabbed the upside Priest and spun him around. Carnificius started to look green.

"You're a pathetic excuse for a Priest," Sibilum growled.

"I think I played my part quite well," Carnificius replied. "Or are you angry that I've outsmarted you again?"

"No one is smarter than me!" Sibilum roared.

"Smarter than I," Carnificius corrected.

"Do you never get bored with your squabbles?" Mortarium asked. "Because I do."

Sibilum and Carnificius both looked blankly in his direction.

"We have a real problem, in case you've forgotten," Mortarium said.

"I know about our problem," Sibilum hissed. "It's hanging right here!"

"A problem you're not going to solve by hurling insults at it," Mortarium continued.

"Your face is an insult," Sibilum hissed.

"Our problem," Mortarium repeated, "our real problem, is that we are expecting a visit from Bisurakhan, and it appears our plan of having a Legion here to greet them is not going to work, thanks to this one's rash decision to kill one of Bisurakhan's favored Khanists." He glared at Carnificius.

"I was sending a message," Carnificius sniffed.

"What kind of message?" Mortarium asked.

"A message they could not intercept."

Sibilum frowned. He turned back to Carnificius, reached out his hand, and stopped the spinning. "What did you say?" he asked.

"You heard me," Carnificius responded, relishing the return of his power in the conversation.

"I didn't hear you. Say it again!" Sibilum commanded.

Carnificius eyed Sibilum with distaste and remained silent.

"SAY IT AGAIN!" Sibilum bellowed.

"It's of no great consequence," Carnificius said, talking as slowly as he dared, hoping to draw out Sibilum's rage. "The boy said they were intercepting messages from Johanum."

Sibilum and Mortarium both stared at him.

"We're not sending any messages," Sibilum pointed out.

"No," Mortarium said, reality slowly dawning on him. "Sibilum is right. *We* are not sending any messages. But *someone* clearly is."

Carnificius stared back, his eyes full of loathing.

"Who have you been talking to?" Sibilum demanded.

"Isn't it interesting," Carnificius replied, ignoring the question, "that you've been completely ignorant of my activities all this time? It's intriguing, if you ask me, that the Priest who is in charge – the Priest who is supposed to be the most powerful – has no idea what's really happening."

Sibilum waved his hands angrily at the fire. The fire quadrupled in size and enveloped Carnificius, who began swinging at the flames as if he were being attacked by a swarm of flies. The frantic waving caused him to spin faster and faster.

"You're being such a nuisance," Carnificius hissed angrily, even as he struggled to swat the flames out of his eyes.

Sibilum waved the flames higher and watched in anger as Carnificius thrashed about.

"What are you hoping to do to him?" Mortarium asked.

"Tire him out," Sibilum replied.

"Why?"

"I have my reasons."

Mortarium shrugged. "Bisurakhan," he said, causing Sibilum to turn around and face him.

"I have enough problems without being reminded of Bisurakhan!" Sibilum spit.

"Fine, you know what? I have a plan."

"Finally!" Sibilum cried.

"We do nothing. Absolutely nothing."

"What kind of plan is that?" Sibilum said angrily.

"A perfectly good one," Mortarium replied. "We let Bisurakhan take the girl. In fact, we let them take whoever they like. We let them come and go, no harm done. They will start to question what they think they know of us. They will start to question whether Johanum is such a terrible place."

"That means they get the girl," Sibilum pointed out.

"Yes. But will it matter that they have her if they no longer think Johanum is dangerous? Why would they listen to her? Their experience will be nothing like hers. They will have no reason to believe anything she says."

Sibilum considered this. "It's not the worst plan," he conceded. "It doesn't get us the Commander, though."

"We'll have to deal with that problem separately," Mortarium answered.

"You're making a mistake!" Carnificius screeched, still spinning in circles and battling the fire. His face was losing its color.

"We need the Commander – or, rather, YOU need him," Mortarium said to Sibilum. He lowered his voice so Carnificius couldn't hear. "You made a ridiculous offer to Zila," he pointed out, not managing to hide his annoyance.

"I know," Sibilum muttered.

"But still. You are Sibilum," Mortarium said. "Of course you can overpower the Commander if you choose."

Sibilum's chest puffed up and his face glowed with pride.

"But this one," Mortarium said, making a subtle motion in Carnificius' direction. "This one is out of control. He wants your power. He wants your worship. He has been sending messages? Messages that we – YOU – didn't even know about? He has disrespected you, oh great Sibilum. He has played you for a fool."

Sibilum's handsome face grew dark.

"You must punish him," Mortarium said quietly. "He must be reminded that you are his master. That he answers to you. That it is only in the presence of your greatness and power that we have a reason to exist."

Sibilum looked haughtily at Carnificius. Carnificius couldn't hear what Mortarium was saying, but whatever it was, he was going to pay for it.

"There is another thing you might do," Mortarium said slyly. "A way you might remind Carnificius that you are the Great One, the one he answers to, the one to whom he is indebted forever."

"What could I do?" Sibilum asked.

"You could banish him to Bisurakhan," Mortarium suggested.

Sibilum look startled.

"Let him wreak havoc on their planet for a while," Mortarium continued, his voice barely above a whisper. "Let him wear out the Khanists. They will be so distracted, they won't worry about us. And we can form our plan to capture the Commander."

Sibilum looked skeptical. "He will just kill them all," he said.

"But he won't," Mortarium disagreed. "He likes the chase. And he likes to think he is like them, those humans, in some sort of strange way. He won't kill them. Not all of them. He'll play with them. Toy with them. He draws more satisfaction from despair than from death."

"And then, when they are worn down," Sibilum said, "we -"

"We strike!" Mortarium said, his eyes burning bright red with triumph.

"What do you get out of this deal?" Sibilum asked suspiciously.

"I won't have to listen to your bickering," Mortarium snapped.

"You will want more from me than that," Sibilum replied.

"I want my freedom," Mortarium said.

"You want to leave Johanum for good?" Sibilum asked.

"Yes," Mortarium replied.

"But you love it here."

"I tolerate it," Mortarium said. "I would like my own planet. No, my own solar system. A collection of my own planets, where I can rule forever."

"Where I will not rule over you," Sibilum clarified.

"This isn't about you," Mortarium clarified. "You have taught me everything I know. You have been a good teacher. Now it's time for me to have my own students. It's time for me to rule, and raise up new Priests, Priests who will rule with the same iron fist. I want to create a solar system that carries on your legacy for eternity. A legacy with no Carnificius – no Commander – and an eternal memory of the great Sibilum."

Sibilum studied Mortarium. He was no fool. He knew Mortarium and Carnificius were both lying. But these were lies he could use. These were foolish plans he could play with.

"I like it," he agreed, smiling at Mortarium in the most indulgent way he could manage. "For being the dumb one, you're actually quite intelligent."

"Thank you," Mortarium replied, under no illusion that Sibilum meant him well.

"I will do it. I will banish Carnificius to Bisurakhan until the day we are ready for our attack."

"You might send him back with the rescue mission," Mortarium suggested.

"No," Sibilum disagreed. "I don't want Bisurakhan to know he is there. I will wait until after they have returned."

"You will want to be careful," Mortarium cautioned. "There are survivors in Bisurakhan who will recognize him if they see him."

"You're thinking of Antoine," Sibilum said.

"Antoine. The girl, if we let them take her. And all the others."

"Most of the others are dead."

"Most. Not all."

"I don't see the trouble for us if they recognize him," Sibilum said. "It will be trouble for him, but trouble for us."

Mortarium thought about it. "Yes, I suppose you're right."

"Of course, I'm right," Sibilum snapped.

"Forgive me," Mortarium said demurely.

"Will you let me down?" Carnificius interrupted. They had been talking for a long time. It was never good for him when Sibilum and Mortarium talked for a long time.

"What do you have to say for yourself?" Sibilum demanded.

"Whatever do you mean?" Carnificius asked, confused.

"What do you have to say for your deplorable, disgraceful, vile behavior?"

Carnificius thought for a moment. The snake behind his black teeth hissed as he replied. "How foolish I have been to think I could outsmart you, Sibilum. I am deeply disturbed by the distress I have caused you."

Sibilum rolled his eyes. He reached up and released the cables. They hissed their way up and around a large pulley, sending Carnificius plummeting to the ground.

Carnificius sniffed, got up, and brushed himself off. "Do you feel better now?" he asked Sibilum.

"Quite."

"Good. I'm glad you got it out of your system."

"We have a plan," Sibilum told him.

"I suspected as much," Carnificius said.

"The plan is a good one. You'll like it."

"I'm sure I won't," Carnificius said knowingly.

"Then we have an understanding," Sibilum smiled.

"Are you going to tell me what it is?" Carnificius asked.

"No," Sibilum replied.

Carnificius sniffed and looked at Mortarium, who shrugged his shoulders as if he knew nothing.

"If you humiliate me again, I will make you pay," Carnificius threatened.

"I look forward to it," Mortarium replied coldly.

CHAPTER 55
Bisurakhan

Josh and Calif stood outside Calvin and Leah's apartment building.

Josh started to tremble.

Calif laid his hand on the young officer's shoulder. "You don't have to do this," he said gently.

"Yes, I do," Josh replied. "I have to do this."

Calif nodded. "You're a good man, Josh."

"You don't have to make conversation," Josh snapped.

The wind picked up and blew a cascade of leaves across the yard by their feet.

Josh watched them with envy. They were so careless. They were so free.

Both men were caught by surprise when the front door opened and a young woman with a baby carrier bounded outside.

"Josh!" Leah exclaimed in surprise.

Josh turned as white as a sheet.

Leah frowned. "What's wrong?" she asked.

Josh opened his mouth, but nothing came out. He closed his mouth, then opened it again. Still nothing.

"Josh, you're trembling," Leah said, stepping closer. "Are you okay?" she asked with genuine concern.

Josh pulled away from her.

"Josh, what's wrong?" Leah asked again. Then she looked over and saw Calif. She hadn't noticed him earlier. She didn't know exactly who he was, but she knew he was a Chief. The Chief uniform was unmistakable. Calvin had described it to her the night he first met the Chiefs.

Leah froze. She turned slowly, looking back and forth between Josh and the Chief.

Tears were streaming down Josh's face. The Chief was looking at her with pity.

"Leah, I'm sorry," Josh whispered.

Leah stared. "What happened? Where is my husband? Where's Calvin?"

Leah's voice startled Amelia and she began to cry.

Josh stepped forward, and this time Leah drew back. "Where is my husband?" she asked.

"He's...not..." Josh swallowed hard. He didn't want to say the words out loud. He wasn't sure that he could.

"He's not what?" Leah asked, her voice breaking. She already knew the answer, but she didn't. She couldn't. It wasn't possible.

"He's not coming home," Josh whispered.

Leah didn't notice the tears pouring down her face. "Where's Calvin?" she asked brokenly.

Josh stood there, tears streaming down his cheeks. Leah stepped forward and grabbed his arm, digging her fingernails into his flesh. He said nothing. Slowly her grip relaxed. She was staring at him, begging him, to tell her she was wrong.

But she wasn't wrong. And they both knew it.

"Where's Calvin?" she whispered.

Josh squeezed his eyes shut. "Calvin is dead."

Leah collapsed. Calif was there in a heartbeat, his arms catching her as she fell, hoisting her up from the ground. Leah began to sob. Then she screamed. Then her voice turned to a wail that was somewhere between the two.

The commotion attracted several of the neighbors. They piled out of the apartment building into the yard. With one look at Leah, Josh, and Calif, they lowered their eyes and averted their gaze.

Everyone knew what it meant when a Chief made a home visit.

"We need to take Leah inside," Calif told Josh.

Josh didn't move.

"Officer! Get the door," Calif ordered.

Josh still didn't move, but one of the neighbors walked over to the door and held it open. Calif walked inside, carrying Leah and Amelia in his arms.

"Josh! Inside!" Calif commanded.

Josh jerked forward.

"Which apartment is theirs?" Calif asked.

Josh looked around. He couldn't remember. He had been there hundreds of times, but he couldn't remember.

"It's that one," said an elderly man leaning on his cane. He pointed up the steps to an apartment on the second floor, the one marked 53C.

Calif nodded and carried Leah and Amelia up the stairs.

"Josh!" he called.

Josh walked past the neighbors but stopped at the stairs. How was he supposed to climb stairs? He tried to lift his feet, but they felt like weights. He couldn't get them off the ground.

The elderly man with the cane walked over and tapped Josh's knee. "Bend it," he said.

Josh bent his leg.

"Now pick up your foot."

Josh tried, but nothing moved.

The elderly man reached over, lifted Josh's leg, and placed his foot on the first step. "Now bend the other one," he instructed.

After a few repetitions, Josh's legs began moving on their own. Soon he was at the top of the stairs, staring at the door of Calvin's apartment.

Apartment 53C.

It looked different now. The paint was peeling off the door. The numbers were crooked. The door handle was cracked.

"Open the door, Josh," Calif said.

Josh reached forward and turned the handle. Leah never locked the door.

Calif walked through the door, into the living room, and over to the couch. He leaned down and gingerly set Leah and Amelia on the sofa. The second he let go, Leah reached up and grabbed at him. She pulled him down next to her, wrapped her arms around his neck, and sobbed.

Calif sat there like an old, tired father, Leah's head on his shoulder, patting her back. He motioned for Josh to join them.

Josh shook his head and stayed in the hallway outside.

"Come take the baby, Josh," Calif said.

Josh shook his head again.

"That's an order, Officer!"

Josh lurched forward and crossed the room. One of the neighbors quietly shut the door behind him.

Calif untangled Leah from the baby carrier and lifted a screaming Amelia to Josh's arms.

Josh stared at Amelia for several minutes, unable to move. He was afraid he would drop her. He looked at Calif, begging for rescue. Calif would have none of it. He forced the baby into Josh's arms. Then Calif nodded at one of the chairs in the kitchen.

Josh turned and walked towards the kitchen. His arms slowly moved to cradle Amelia against his chest.

Amelia's screaming calmed and turned to a soft cry. Josh felt his own body begin to relax. He hugged Amelia, smelling her hair. He kissed the top of her head. As he sunk into one of the chairs, a new wave of grief washed over him. He tightened his grip on Amelia, trying to calm the shaking of his arms.

"Your daddy...he loves you," Josh whispered. "He's always going to love you."

In the living room, Leah sobbed harder.

Josh shut his eyes and tried to breathe.

A knock sounded at the door.

"Get the door, Josh," Calif ordered.

Josh laid Amelia in the bassinet by the table and forced himself to his feet. He walked across the room and opened the door.

Hailey stood in the hallway, her eyes puffy and her face red.

Josh reached out and pulled her into his arms.

CHAPTER 56
Johanum

"Let's play a game," I suggested.

Around the fire sat all the faces I loved. The Furpines. Mad Laughs. Mr. Fox and Mr. Brown. I never would have thought I would find friends in Johanum. I had lived here alone for so long. But here they were. And here I was. Somehow, we had all made it this far.

"It had better be a proper game," Mr. Fox said playfully. He had become softer, gentler, now that I knew his story. He was fond of the Furpines, too. I think the little ones reminded him of his babies.

Tabby had declared yesterday, well within earshot of Mr. Fox, that she liked him. "He's very predictable, like a rock in your shoe," she had said. "I like that."

Amos, Ace and Archie began jumping up and down at my suggestion of a game, their little hands flapping with excitement.

"I love games!" Ace exclaimed.

"Games are my favorite," Archie said as he clapped.

"They cheat," Tabby told me.

"We don't!" all three brothers cried in unison.

Toby cleared his throat and Telly coughed delicately. The brothers blushed.

"Awww, dearies, it won't do you no good to fib about it," Telly scolded kindly. "You'll look silly once you're found out. And someone always find out."

"Not always!" Ace protested.

"Shhhhhh!" Amos hushed him.

"You little troublemakers," I chuckled. I didn't know how anyone could ever manage to stay mad at a Furpine. They were so cute and impetuous. "Maybe we won't let you play."

"We won't cheat!" Ace promised, standing up on his tiptoes, terrified of being left out of the game.

"No, that's right," Archie agreed, catching on. "We'll be as honest a bunch of scalawags as you've ever met."

Amos clasped his hands over his eyes in embarrassment. "No, that's all wrong. Scalawags aren't honest."

Archie frowned. "But you said it yourself, we're a bunch of scalawags."

"Shhhhh!" Amos pleaded.

"But I've been tellin' everybody!" Archie said.

"Why?" Amos cried, his little face scrunched up in horror. "Why would you do that?"

"Because it sounds so cool! I'm a scalawag, I'm a scalawag." Archie threw his little arms around in a tizzy, trying to march on his short, stumpy feet. He managed to fall face-first into the ground.

Amos smacked his tiny paw over his furry forehead and plopped to the ground.

"They're better at being adventurous than clever," little Tabby told me, as if it needed explaining. She looked over at her mother, who winked. "I know!" Tabby said. "Why don't we tell stories?"

Her suggestion got the brothers back on their feet again, very excited. All the other Furpines began clapping and rubbing their bellies.

"I love stories!" Ace said, his purple eyes shining with happiness and a touch of mischief.

"Mama tells the best ones," Tabby said, and all the rest of the Furpines agreed.

"I do love a good story," I said. "Let me get some blankets. We can all snuggle up."

Mad Laughs jumped to his feet to run back to the cave and get Fletcher's blankets. I watched him go and sat back down.

"Would you like to hear a story?" I asked Mr. Fox and Mr. Brown.

Mr. Fox was characteristically noncommittal. "If it's a proper one, I suppose it wouldn't hurt."

"How long is it?" Mr. Brown asked. "I didn't put a story into my schedule."

"Forget your schedule. Sleep here tonight. All of you. And look! Now we have blankets."

Mad Laughs stood above Mr. Fox and unceremoniously dropped the entire pile of blankets onto his head. While Mr. Fox sputtered and fought his way out, Amos, Ace and Archie burst into a contagious chorus of Furpine giggles. Soon the rest of the Furpines were giggling, even as they tried to help Mr. Fox.

Mad Laughs smiled, pleased with himself.

"It looks like we're ready," I told Telly after everyone had settled down.

Her eyes shone with excitement. "Well, if you really want to hear a story -"

"We do! We do!" all the Furpines exclaimed.

They began snuggling in together. I sensed this happened regularly. They were ready for their goodnight story.

"Well, dearies, it happened one night, long before you came to be, and long before your parents ever dreamed you would arrive...."

I curled up on my side and listened as the scene unfolded. If I ever got the change to tell stories of Johanum, I hoped I would tell the stories like this. Full of intrigue. Full of horror. Full of surprise, distress, comfort, and confusion.

Telly didn't shy away from any part of the story. She told the whole thing. The good and the bad, the ugly and the beautiful, all wrapped into one.

I looked over at Mad Laughs. His eyes were twinkling. I had never seen that look on his face before.

Mr. Fox's neck was stretched as far is it would go, so keen he was on hearing the story. Even Mr. Brown looked happy and content.

With all my friends gathered around the fire, warm, cozy, and together, I watched the flames dance through the night, and drifted peacefully into a dreamless sleep.

CHAPTER 57
Bisurakhan

"You sent Calif?" Antoine asked.

"I didn't *send* Calif," Jorge corrected. "He volunteered. He thought it would be better if he went."

"How convenient for you that you don't have to face Calvin's wife."

A muscle jerked in Jorge's neck. "I'm not hiding."

"You're not taking responsibility either."

"I am fully responsible. Today, I am responsible for not just one death, but two. There. Are you satisfied?"

"Are you going to say that publicly?"

"Of course not."

"I didn't think so."

"I'm heading to General Fossil's house after we get done here. I had thought I should talk to you first. That was clearly a mistake."

"When will you just admit that your Reality Persuasion experiments are the mistake?"

"They are not a mistake!" Jorge took a long breath through his teeth and exhaled. "They are not the mistake. We didn't have a protocol in place to deal with emergencies. That was our mistake."

"Jorge, I looked at the numbers today. Fifty-two, and that's not including today. Now we're at 54. Fifty-four of your Khanists have died. These might be the only two who have died while physically inside your Labs, but it shouldn't matter. You've had 812 volunteers walk through these doors in the last year, and 54 of them are dead. There is no possible way to look at those numbers as anything but catastrophic. There is no way to look at your experimentation as anything but a tragedy. I don't care what kind of intelligence you've acquired. The cost is too high."

"That's not your decision to make," Jorge answered coldly.

"I've sent an official request to the Commander, asking that your experiments be shut down."

"It's your right to do that," Jorge said, not trying to hide his anger.

"I've also sent an overview of your Reality Persuasion department and your fatality numbers to President Basjid, making the same request."

"We don't include the President on military secrets!"

"I think it's time we did."

"And what happens next, huh? He'll want a review of every department. He'll send people to observe, people who know nothing of the ways of war, people who know nothing of the preparation that is required for military combat."

"Maybe you should have thought of that before you set up your deadly experiments," Antoine said, holding his ground.

"YOU are the problem here," Jorge said. "You don't understand the sacrifices it takes to lead a military! Our options aren't always ethical."

"We always have choices."

"Yes! And I have made mine. My choice to sacrifice some – if I have to – to save most. It's a terrible choice. I'm not proud of it. But neither would I change it. This is the hand I've been dealt, this is the world I was born into, and I will lead with strength and dignity and purpose. Some will die, yes. But others will live. I am leading for them."

"You accept death too quickly. It is not as inevitable as you surmise."

"Death IS inevitable, Antoine. At some point, we all die. Wouldn't you rather die defending the ones you care about?

Your family, you friends, the world that you love? We can sit back, do nothing, and let death come to us. Or we can stand up and fight. I choose to fight."

"But you're taking that choice away from others and making it for them."

"Every Khanist who enrolls in these experiments does so of his own accord. Calvin was here by his own choice."

"How dare you use a fallen Khanist to make your argument. He chose to come to an experiment that he thought was safe. He has a wife and a child. It was not his choice to leave them."

"He knew there were risks."

"You haven't been honest about Reality Persuasion and its risks with anyone. What choice do any of these Khanists really believe they're making?"

"The same choices they always do when they enlist in the military. They choose to make the world a better place. They do this by defending their homes, by defending their families, by defending their planet - by defending everything they hold dear, by whatever means necessary."

"You can't tell me that Calvin thought he was making that choice."

"We don't even know what really happened to Calvin in that experiment! What if he caused his own death? What if he did something that was dangerous?"

"*How dare you,*" Antoine seethed. "How dare you blame this on him. What is it that is possessing you to send men to Johanum, Jorge? What sort of madness has possessed you?"

"I will protect my family," Jorge answered. "I will do whatever it takes, and pay any price, to protect the ones I love."

"And what about everyone else?" Antoine asked.

"What about them?" Jorge replied.

CHAPTER 58
Johanum

A soft breeze blew across the path as I walked down to the docks. The breeze had a lightness to it, a lightness I didn't recognize. The winds here weren't normally like that.

Having the Furpines around was making me happy.

Of course, I loved my other friends. Mr. Fox, with his cantankerous comments. Mr. Brown and his ridiculous schedule. Mad Laughs and all his crazy antics.

But the Furpines...the Furpines added life to my soul. When they spoke, I felt encouraged. They didn't deny the darkness of the world. But somehow, when they were around, I felt like it was going to be okay. Not because everything was going to work out. We lived in Johanum. Most things here didn't work out. No, it wasn't that. But with the Furpines, it felt like one day, one hour, one minute lived well, was all that really mattered. And maybe it was. Maybe the end didn't matter as much as I used to think.

I arrived at the docks and filled two bowls with water. As I stood to leave, I stopped in surprise. One of the wraiths, the tall one who always sang, was standing in front of me.

The wraiths never came out in the daylight.

He looked different in the light of day. No blue light was surrounding him now. All I saw was his transparent skin, pulled taunt over his organs and bones. I could see his heart pumping. It was pumping much faster than I thought a heart was supposed to beat. His lungs were expanding and contracting at an alarming rate, and his eyes were dilated.

"Why are you here?" I asked.

He walked closer. I could hear and feel his heavy breathing. His breath was hot and smelled like the death from the boats.

"You must find them, when you go," he said, his voice barely above a whisper.

"Who?"

"The others. The ones like you. The ones who were here before you."

"You know about the rescue mission, too?" I asked.

He nodded. "I have seen them. They are close."

"So it's real? Someone is really coming to save us?"

He nodded.

The tiniest glimmer of hope sprang to life in my chest.

"You must find them," he said again.

"How will I find them?" I asked.

He wheezed and began coughing. The cough sent his body into convulsions.

"You are dying," I said.

"I am always dying," he answered. "Always dying, but never dead."

"Does your type never die?"

"Not often enough."

"Where will I find them, the others who have been here?" I asked.

"Look in the places where it is easy to be invisible," he said.

"And you?" I said. "Won't you come with us?"

"I can't leave," he said.

"Can't? Or won't?"

He smiled peacefully. "You understand. I thought you might."

"Why would you stay if you have the chance to leave?" I asked.

"For the same reason one might return after they've been gone a while," he answered.

"You all speak of returning. Why would anyone come back to this place? I don't understand. But tell me, will I see you again?"

"Do you want to?" he replied.

"Yes. I want to hear you sing. Sometimes you sing to me in my dreams."

"Then that's where I will always be," he replied. Slowly his feet lifted off the docks and he began to float away.

"What's your name?" I called after him.

"Why do I need a name?" he asked.

"A name gives you purpose. It gives you definition. It lets people know when they've found you again."

"Then I suppose it's fitting that I don't have one," he called back.

I looked out at the lake. In the distance, I saw the other wraiths. They were all out in the daylight, waiting for my visitor to return to them.

I lifted my hand and waved. They all waved back.

I turned to walk back to the caves. As I walked along the path, the wraiths sang to me one last time. Their song floated up across the water, weaving through the air, and dancing around me.

Down by the waves
It wanders, it wanders
Seeking escape from its kind

Down by the water
It waits for destruction
Beneath the waves lies salvation

CHAPTER 59
Bisurakhan

"Is everything ready?" Calif asked.

"Yes," Antoine confirmed, moving some levers on the hovercraft's control panel. "We're packed and ready to go. Just waiting on Jorge. Did you get everything set with Calvin's family?"

"As much as I could," Calif said.

Antoine glanced over. Calif's weathered face was full of sadness. "It's hard to watch them grieve," Antoine observed quietly.

Calif let out a long sigh and took a seat. "You know," he said, "when I was young, I thought this would get easier. This...sort of...intense sorrow that you feel when you tell someone their loved one is gone. I'm not sure why I thought that. Maybe because I had never experienced deep grief myself. But it doesn't get easier. It never gets easier."

"How is his widow?" Antoine asked.

"In shock," Calif said. "And why wouldn't she be? She thought – we all thought – that Calvin was perfectly safe. Those experiments were supposed to be safe."

"They've never been safe."

"I know. You warned us."

"What did you do with Josh?"

Calif sighed. "I left him there."

"With Calvin's wife?"

Calif nodded. "Josh is essentially on house arrest. He's going to go crazy if he's left alone. Leah trusts him, and she needs help with the baby. It seemed like a better idea to leave them together. I called Hailey and Mary, too – they're a couple of the linguists from Cornersville, and a couple of the guys who worked with Calvin and Josh said they were all friends. Hailey arrived before I left. She seems to have a good head on her shoulders. I gave her a couple of weeks off and asked her to help out."

"It was good of you to go. Jorge should have gone."

"Jorge needed to see General Fossil's family. They're friends, and have been, for a long time."

"He should have had to see both families."

"This isn't about punishing Jorge, Antoine. It can't be. It has to be about comforting the families. We send whoever is best. Josh needed to be there. There was no way Josh and Jorge were going together. One of them would have killed the other."

"Jorge will go after Josh at his trial. He'll want blood."

"I know."

"It's not right. Jorge bears as much blame as Josh. More, if you ask me."

"Jorge didn't pull the trigger on that gun."

"Jorge set in motion all the events that led to it."

"We answer for ourselves, Antoine. Josh must answer for himself."

"At what price?"

"He killed a man."

"Under the same circumstances, you or I might have done the exact same thing."

"It doesn't mean there are no consequences."

"Taking his life is more than a consequence."

"It doesn't have to be the death penalty."

"No, but it will be. It's his testimony against Jorge's. We both know which one carries more weight. Will you testify for either of them?"

"I don't know," Calif replied, shifting uncomfortably.

"You're better than that," Antoine chided. "You know Josh deserves another chance."

"I don't know that," Calif disagreed.

"Yes, you do," Antoine insisted. "I'll testify on his behalf myself if I need to, but your opinion will matter more to a judge. They all respect you. Your testimony could mean his freedom."

"Speaking for Josh would make it impossible for me to work with Jorge."

"And you would let Josh die for that?"

"I'm worried about how many others may die if I don't."

"I don't understand you. I don't understand either of you," Antoine said, frustrated. "You have the opportunity to save the person right in front of you, and you hesitate, because you worry about someone who isn't yet in danger, someone you can't even identify, someone who might not ever exist."

"Everything is connected, Antoine. The ones we love, the ones we don't know. What happened yesterday, what is yet to be. We must always consider our actions in light of the bigger story."

"I don't disagree," Antoine replied. "But I wish you would tell me what this 'bigger story' is that you're talking about, because best I can tell, your 'bigger story' is nothing more than the things you want to happen, the things you think you can control."

The hovercraft's door opened. Calif and Antoine turned around in their chairs.

Jorge walked in, a box of whiskey balanced in one arm and a duffel bag slung over the other.

"You came prepared," Calif remarked.

"I am always prepared," Jorge slurred.

"How much have you had to drink?" Antoine asked, disgusted.

"That...is none...of your...business." Jorge turned to walk away, then stopped himself, swinging back around. "By the way," he slurred, "the Commander's not coming."

Calif looked startled. Antoine just blinked.

"You let the Commander see you like that?" Antoine asked.

"I. Am. Fine." Jorge said, carefully annunciating each word.

"It just took you five seconds to say that," Antoine said.

"I guess you and your smart ass will have to get us to the Periphery then," Jorge snapped. He whirled back around and stumbled into one of the rooms at the back of the aircraft.

Antoine turned to Calif. "I've never seen him like that."

"The you haven't known him very long," Calif replied.

"Does this happen often?"

"No. Not often. It's a good sign, actually."

Antoine raised his eyebrows.

"Jorge's alcohol consumption is a direct representation of how guilty he feels," Calif explained. "He spends most of his life stone cold sober. But every now and again...every now and again, drunk Jorge comes for a visit."

"Does it do any good? The drinking?" Antoine asked.

"He's a little less obnoxious when he comes out of it," Calif said. "A little more tempered. A little less aggressive."

"Is he ever sorry?"

"He hides it well."

Antoine looked around. "So it's just us? We're making this trip to Johanum alone?"

Calif clasped him on the shoulder. "It's just us. Are you ready?"

Antoine shook his head. A sinking feeling was in the pit of his stomach.

"Me neither," Calif said. "Me neither."

Antoine turned around in his chair and stared out the window, imagining what awaited them.

"You can stay behind," Calif said. "That's always been an option."

Antoine shook his head. "It's not an option, Calif. Not for me."

Calif nodded. "Then let's go."

CHAPTER 60
Bisurakhan

"Why do you eat so much food?" Henry asked.

Joseph paused, his sandwich inches from his mouth. "So much food?" he repeated.

"You eat so much food," Henry said.

"Are you calling me fat?"

"You are not fat. You are sufficiently plump."

Joseph choked. The food in his mouth spewed out over the desk.

Some of the food landed on Henry's face. He reached up and wiped it away.

"I am not plump," Joseph grumbled.

Henry searched his files. "You are sufficiently round."

"No."

"Pudgy?"

"For god's sake, Henry, stop calling me fat!"

"I didn't. I called you plump and round and pudgy. My engineer told me never to call anyone fat. And I did not."

"Finding another word for it doesn't make it better."

"It doesn't? Why not?"

"It just doesn't, okay? It's not better!" Joseph closed his eyes. He felt overwhelmed. "If you must comment on my weight, it's fine. Call me fat. I *am* fat."

"But that makes you sad," Henry observed.

Joseph sighed deeply. "I'm sad about a lot of things, okay, Henry?"

"Do you want to talk about it?" Henry asked. "My engineer said humans like to talk about things. It makes them feel better."

"I don't know if talking to a robot is going to make me feel better."

"My engineer said I was a good listener."

"Well, if you must know, Henry, I haven't always been fat. I used to be quite fit, back when I was an active duty Khanist. But I had a knee injury, and I got discharged. Now I sit at a computer all day, fixing code for guys like you. And I eat a lot. Because I'm sitting, and I'm bored, and I hate my job. And I miss Sherry," Joseph added as an afterthought.

"Who is Sherry?" Henry asked.

"My girlfriend." He pointed to a small framed photo sitting to the side of his desk. There was Joseph...a much thinner Joseph...with his arm wrapped around a slender woman with long dark hair and a beautiful smile. "Well...she *was* my girlfriend," he clarified.

"What is she now?" Henry asked.

"Just...not my girlfriend. She said I was gloomy and depressing and she didn't want to put up with it anymore."

"You're not gloomy and depressing, Joseph."

"Thank you."

"Your attitude is gloomy. Your outlook on the world is depressing."

Joseph scowled.

"You are upset," Henry observed.

"Let's just drop it, okay?"

"How do we drop it?"

"Stop talking about it."

"Oh." Henry made a note in his files.

A message started flashing across Joseph's computer screen.

"All robotics engineers are to report to Robotics Headquarters immediately. I repeat: All robotics engineers are to report to Robotics Headquarters immediately."

Joseph grabbed his jacket and started to leave. "Stay here, Henry," he said.

"Okay, Joseph. Is something wrong?"

"I don't know."

"Would you like me to find out?"

"How would you do that?"

Henry flipped open a section of metal near the middle of his robot body. A screen appeared. It flickered, then came to life.

Joseph looked down and realized he was looking at a live feed of the Robotics Headquarters. Robots were everywhere. They were out of control. Two robotics engineers were pinned up against a wall, surrounded by angry robots.

"How do you have that?" Joseph asked in alarm. "And what is happening at the Turris??"

"Their operating systems have been overridden," Henry said matter-of-factly.

"I've got to get over there," Joseph said.

"Joseph, be careful. Those robots are dangerous."

"I'm an engineer. I can fix it."

"You can't fix this," Henry said simply.

"How do you know?"

"Because they were designed to attack you," Henry answered.

Joseph stared at Henry, flabbergasted.

"Your face tells me you have many questions," Henry observed.

Joseph hesitated, then turned to leave. "Henry, I have to go. They need me. Stay here, okay? Don't leave."

"Goodbye, Joseph," Henry said.

"Goodbye, Henry."

CHAPTER 61
Bisurakhan

Hailey sunk into the beat-up couch cushions and watched as Josh paced back and forth in front of her. Every minute or two, he stopped abruptly.

"Do you think Amelia is sleeping?" he asked.

"She's fine, Josh. We'll hear her as soon as she wakes up."

He went back to walking a line in the carpet.

"Do you think Leah's going to sleep? I don't think she slept last night. I saw her get up like twenty times."

"She might not sleep, but she's lying down," Hailey answered. "I gave her a couple of the sleeping pills that Calif left. Maybe they'll help."

"Okay."

He started pacing again.

"Did you sleep last night?" Hailey asked.

Josh shook his head.

"When was the last time you slept?"

Josh shrugged.

"Josh, sit down for a minute."

Josh shook his head.

Hailey patted the seat beside her. "Please. Sit down."

Josh's pacing slowed and he eyed the couch suspiciously.

"Josh."

Her voice was kind and inviting. It softened him and made him angry. No one should be kind to him right now. They should hate him. They should all hate him. It's what he deserved.

"Come on, Josh. Sit down."

As soon as Josh took a seat, his head started bobbing.

Hailey touched his arm gently. "Lie down. Just for a couple of minutes. I'll keep an eye on Leah and Amelia. I promise, nothing will happen while you sleep."

Josh shook his head, but he couldn't keep his eyes to open.

"You don't have to sleep," Hailey said. "Just close your eyes and let them rest."

Josh reached out his hands to steady himself. He was sitting, but the whole world was spinning. He couldn't get it to stop. He kept moving his hands, trying to find something to hold on to.

Hailey reached over and took his hand in hers. Josh stilled. Then Hailey reached over and gently pushed his shoulder. Josh tipped over and fell into the pillows at the edge of the couch. Hailey stood up, picked up Josh's feet, and swung them onto the sofa.

He was already asleep.

Hailey peeked her head into the bedroom. She wasn't sure if Leah was sleeping, but her breathing was steady, and the room was quiet.

Hailey tiptoed past the bed and leaned over the edge of the crib. Amelia was awake. Her adorable little face was scrunched up and pensive and her hands were balled into fists. It was like she knew something was wrong, but she didn't want to disturb anyone.

Hailey reached down and picked her up.

"Hi, baby," she whispered. "Would you like some love? Are you hungry? Let's go get you something to eat."

Hailey walked into the kitchen and pulled a bottle and formula from the cupboard. She had picked up both at the store on the way over this morning after Josh called her, frantic that he had no way to feed Amelia while Leah was asleep. When Hailey arrived, she found a screaming Amelia, a distraught Josh, and a whole case of unopened containers of formula in the pantry. Josh hadn't thought to look there. Nor had he thought to change Amelia's diaper, which turned out to be the problem all along.

Amelia was making noises. Hailey smiled and ran her finger over the baby's cheek.

"You're beautiful. And such a good baby. I can't believe how little you cry. You should meet my baby nephew. He cries all the time. Maybe because he's the youngest and not getting enough attention. But really, you are so sweet, and so cute. Cuter than my nephew. But shhhhh, don't tell anyone I said that. Aunt Hailey would be in so much trouble! Your nieces and nephews are always supposed to be your favorites. Unless you have your own kids. Then you're allowed to think they are the cutest. But I like you. We should hang out. Stay friends. Even when I go back to Cornersville. You could come visit. Bring your mom. And your Uncle Josh. You can meet my nieces and nephews. They'd spoil you. They'd spoil you rotten. Plus, they'd be so excited to have a friend from Bisurakhan."

"You're good with babies."

Hailey looked up to see Leah standing in the doorway. She reached out her arms to give Amelia to her mother.

"You can hold her. If you don't mind."

Hailey nodded. She touched the formula in the bag to make sure it was the right temperature, then turned the bottle upside down and lifted it to Amelia's lips.

One of Amelia's hands reached up. Hailey lifted her finger so Amelia could wrap her hand around it. Content, Amelia cuddled against Hailey and ate.

Leah was looking at Josh, sleeping in the living room. "How long has he been like that?" she asked.

"He just fell asleep a few minutes ago," Hailey replied.

"I don't think he slept at all last night," said Leah.

"He didn't look like it."

Leah walked over to the table and sat down in one of the chairs. She watched Amelia eating peacefully in Hailey's arms. "Thank you for being here," Leah said quietly.

"Of course," Hailey said. Her heart broke. Leah was so quiet. So withdrawn. So...defeated. "I can help out with whatever you need. They gave me some time off work so I could be here with you. Mary can come and help, too."

Leah nodded and stared off into the distance. "I think I'm going to go lay back down," she said after a few minutes.

Hailey watched Leah struggle to her feet. Leah walked to the bedroom door, then turned around and came back to the kitchen.

"Am I a bad mother?" Leah asked.

Hailey blinked in surprise. "Why would you ask such a thing?"

"I don't feel like a mother right now." Leah's voice was flat and emotionless.

"You're in shock. That's all. You'll feel like a mother again. Give yourself time."

Leah nodded. She turned and went back to the bedroom.

Ten minutes later, Hailey heard Leah's soft breathing. Hailey walked to the living room. With a little creative balancing, she managed to shove Josh's feet onto the couch far enough for her to squeeze into the small space at the other end. She propped a pillow up under her elbow to support Amelia's head and watched as Amelia fell asleep.

Hailey looked around.

This wasn't the way it was supposed to be. Everything was supposed to get better when she came to Bisurakhan. She was protecting her family. She was helping another government. She was surrounded by the intelligent and the powerful.

Everything was supposed to get better. But it wasn't. Everything was worse. It was much, much worst.

She wanted to go home.

Amelia's eyes opened, and she smiled up at Hailey. Hailey smiled back. What a beautiful baby. What a beautiful child, and she had just lost her father. She was so young. She would never even remember him.

Beside her, Josh stirred.

"Hey," he said.

"Go back to sleep," she said.

"I'm awake."

"I know, but...you should sleep. Everyone is sleeping."

Josh nodded. He laid his head down and closed his eyes. A minute later they reopened. He swung his feet down to the floor and sat up. Then he leaned over and kissed Hailey's cheek. "You're an angel," he said.

Hailey's heart melted.

"I'm not," Josh continued.

"I don't hate you, you know, for what you did," Hailey said. "You wanted to protect Calvin."

"That's not what it was," Josh disagreed. "Calvin was already...gone..."

"I still don't hate you."

"You should. You should stay as far away from me as possible."

Hailey shook her head. "I'm not going to. I'm going to stay here. With you. With Leah. With Amelia."

Josh watched her for several minutes. He reached over and picked up her hand. Then he laid back down, her hand still in his, and fell asleep.

Hailey didn't know what to feel anymore.

CHAPTER 62
The Space Between

"That's it," Antoine said, pointing out the window to a glowing set of lights. "That's the portal we need to use to enter Johanum."

"We need to set the time back before we land," Calif said.

Antoine blinked. "We need to do the what?"

"The time. We need to make sure it's reset before we land in Johanum."

"Don't you know anything?" Jorge snarled. He was sitting in one of the nearby chairs, drinking from a bottle of whiskey. He had been silent the whole trip.

Antoine turned to Jorge and glared. "How am I supposed to know about the things you don't share with me?"

"He's so angry, Calif. So angry." Jorge leaned his head back and took another swig.

"You make me angry," Antoine muttered.

"You're so ignorant," Jorge taunted. He stood up, took one look at the spinning room, and sat back down. "The Commander didn't take you through the Space Between, did he?" Jorge slurred.

Antoine shook his head. "I have no idea. Is that where we are now? It looks like the Periphery to me."

"It looks like blackness, because it is blackness," Jorge replied. "It all looks the same. Tell him, Calif."

Calif was seated at the control panel. He looked over his shoulder at Jorge and shook his head. "It's complicated," he said.

"You don't say," Antoine replied.

"The Space Between allows us to adjust things."

"Things like...time?" Antoine asked.

"And space, that sort of thing," Calif said.

Antione shook his head in disbelief. "The Space Between lets us control the laws of physics?"

"No," Calif corrected, "it IS the laws of physics. Think of it like a control panel. The Space Between is the real, the genuine, state of being. Everything that we see, out there in the world, is a sort of warped manifestation of the original. It's all a little...twisted. Here, we're in the real thing. And, from here, we can make adjustments out there."

Antoine sat down with a thud. He was overwhelmed. "You've never thought to mention this to me?" he asked.

"Only a few people know about it."

"Why don't we use it change Johanum?" Antoine asked.

"It doesn't control Johanum," Jorge slurred angrily, as if Antoine clearly should have known that.

"He's right," Calif agreed. "We can't change Johanum. Johanum exists in a different dimension."

"This is more powerful than any weapon that exists in Bisurakhan," Antoine said. "We can end all wars. We can end this one, before it even starts!"

"No, Antoine," Calif disagreed. "The Space Between must remain a secret. Can you imagine what would happen if every man, woman, and child had access to it? Everyone would change the world in the way they saw fit. They would obliterate civilization. They would destroy humankind as we know it."

"Who else knows about this place?" Antoine asked.

"Me, Jorge, the Commander. And, now, you."

"That's it?"

"That's it."

"This military has too many secrets."

"Humanity is full of secrets, Antoine. The secrets aren't the problem. It's what we do with them that matters."

CHAPTER 63
Johanum

The morning air in the caves was cool and crisp. I returned from the Stone Gardens with two bowls full of berries. The Furpines were awake when I arrived. Mad Laughs had disappeared. Mr. Fox was still curled up on a bed of Tufta leaves. He was snoring loudly, to the delight of the Furpine brothers, who had gathered around him and were letting their chubby little faces jiggle in the air that came rushing from his mouth after each snore.

"Where's Mr. Brown?" I asked little Tabby. She was curled up next to her mother, sleepily watching the shenanigans of the brothers.

"He went back downstairs. He left a long time ago. But, if you listen..."

We all quieted. I heard the shuffle, the scraping of dirt, then a thud as his body dropped down one more stair.

"He would save so much time if he let me help him," I muttered.

"He likes to stay busy, dearie," Telly observed. "It seems to keep him happy."

"Busy doing absolutely nothing," I said.

Telly smiled. "Sometimes that's what makes them happy."

Mad Laughs came back, his arms full of fish. He looked over to see Ace, Archie and Amos playing around Mr. Fox, who was still sound asleep and snoring contentedly.

"Don't," I pleaded, seeing the look on his face.

Mad Laughs ignored me. He walked over and let his pile of fish fall onto the fox's head. Mr. Fox jumped to his feet and howled. Mad Laughs laughed uproariously and was quickly joined by the Furpine boys.

"Oh, dear," Telly said with a motherly shake of her head. "Is he always like this?"

"I'm afraid so," I said. "He means no harm. I think it's his way of being friendly."

"That's not a very good way to do it," Tabby said.

"No, but it's all he knows."

"He doesn't do it with you, dearie," Telly said.

"I think it's because I like him."

"The persons are strange," she observed.

"We are," I agreed. "But you animals are odd, too."

"We're not odd!" little Ace spoke up.

"We're very odd," Archie disagreed. "Well, you are."

"I am not!" Ace protested.

"I like you," I said, "odd or not."

Ace and Archie blushed a bright red. Then Ace turned his head slightly to the side and winked at me. I sat back, startled. Toby and Telly burst into giggles.

"Oh, dearie, you've done it now!" Telly giggled. "He'll be winkin' and flirtin' with you for the rest of his days. Furpines only love once, you know."

I shook my head in bewilderment. "I didn't mean it like that."

"No, but he does," Toby replied. Telly and Tabby giggled harder and harder as Ace began prancing around, wiggling his belly, his bright eyes twinkling at me.

Mad Laughs walked over to Ace and nudged him with his foot. Ace responded by climbing up Mad Laughs' leg like it was a tree trunk. Mad Laughs leaned down, picked Ace up by his neck and placed the little Furpine on his shoulder.

"Look at me, I'm a giant!" Ace squealed in excitement.

I smiled, thankful he was so easily distracted.

Mad Laughs let the other young Furpines crawl up him, then he began dancing around. His antics earned him cheers, applause, and plenty of giggles.

"I've never seen him like this," I said to Telly. "He likes you."

"He's fond of children," Telly said, the gentleness in her voice reaching up her face and creasing the sides of her eyes.

"How long did it take you to get here? From the forest?" I asked.

Telly looked at her husband, who was scratching his head.

"I don't rightly know," he answered honestly. "Maybe a few weeks. Or a month. I guess we didn't keep track of the time."

"We almost gave up, dearie. Many times. We didn't know what we were doing or where we were goin'. But you know, this little one..." She tussled Tabby's head fondly. "She kept us hustlin'. She's got a warrior's heart and an adventurer's spirit. 'Canwood promised,' she kept reminding us. 'Canwood promised we would find the person. And Canwood cannot tell a lie.' So we kept moving."

"We walked in circles for a good long time, I'm afraid," Toby said. He picked up his wife's hand and sandwiched it affectionately between his own. "We went back to the entrance of the forest a few times, quite unintentional-like. And there's this garden...a strange garden, with lots of stone statues..."

"The Stone Gardens," I said.

"Is that what you call it? Well, we saw that green fountain three times. At one point -" Toby paused and turned a knowing glance at his wife. "At one point, I turned to this beautiful lady here and I said, 'Telly, I think the forest is following us.'"

Telly giggled. Little Tabby was grinning from ear to ear.

"Yes, he did, dearie," Telly agreed. "And I told him, honey, don't be so ridiculous. The forest isn't following us.

But he couldn't get it out of his head! And then with the gardens!"

"Oh, I was convinced that time," Toby nodded. "I was certain that all those places had pulled up roots and were following us around."

"Dearie, you should have seen it. He would stop, every once in a while – quite suddenly he would stop -"

Little Tabby jumped up and began to act out the story.

"He'd put his hand on his mouth just so," Telly continued, "trying to get all of us to be quiet. And dearie, it wasn't like we were makin' much noise. Except for those young'uns over there who can never quite seem to stay quiet."

Ace, Archie and Amos had been listening from their perch on Mad Laughs' shoulders. They beamed at being featured in Telly's story.

"Anyway," Telly said, "Toby would stop -"

Tabby hunched down on all fours, as best she could with her stumpy little legs and chubby little arms, and waited for her mother to continue.

"He would wave for us to be quiet -"

Tabby lifted a paw to her lips, lost her balance, and faceplanted the dirt.

"Not quite like that, dearie, but you get the picture."

Tabby got up, brushed herself off, and continued her performance.

"Then he would swing around quick and say, 'AH HA!'"

Toby looked embarrassed but his eyes were twinkling. All the Furpine children, Tabby included, giggled so hard they fell over. Telly batted her eyes at her husband and snuggled close to him.

"I think he meant to frighten it away. The forest, or the garden, or whoever he thought was following us. And dearie, you should have seen him, he was so disappointed when nothing was there. Every time he turned around, it was just us. Oh, I wish you could have been there. He's quite a protector, this one. Even when he's protecting us from invisible threats."

"It was very strange to always end up in the same place," Toby said in his defense.

"We don't have a very good sense of direction," little Tabby said.

"She's right, dearie. We don't have any sense of direction at all. But we have a stubbornness. It's just as good."

"I think you have to be stubborn to live here," I said.

Mad Laughs froze, a strange expression on his face.

I tilted my head quizzically.

He lifted a finger to his lips.

No one moved. No one made a sound.

It started slowly, the creaking sound. Like an old, rusty door that someone was trying to pry from its hinges. Then the creaking descended to a crash.

We stared at each other in alarm, then rushed outside.

CHAPTER 64
Bisurakhan

The others like him were buzzing about the Turris and creating chaos everywhere he looked. The administrators, the ones who usually sat behind the purple desks, were running in circles around the lobby. Elevation boxes were crashing into each other. The elevation boxes on the ground kept opening and closing their doors, welcoming entrants and then promptly kicking them out.

Henry frowned. How was he going to get up to the Robotics department if the floating robots didn't move? He wished he had asked Joseph to give him the software so he could float. Then he wouldn't be having this problem. His engineer had told him, "When you have a good idea, act on it quick!" He should have listened to his engineer. His engineer was his best bud.

A shriek from the corner made Henry turn his head. A female administrator was pounding on another like him with her purse. Something inside that purse must have been heavy. The other like him had a dent on his head.

Henry scanned his files, looking for another way to access the Robotics department. Joseph needed him. Joseph was his friend. He was going to save his friend.

Henry stared at the blueprint in his files. Others like him kept bumping into him. They didn't stop to find out why he was just standing there. That was the problem with the others like him. They could do a lot of things, but they weren't very smart. His engineer said that intelligence – real intelligence – was rare, even among the humans.

Henry unscrewed his head and sent it rolling around the floor. The blueprints said there was a door, a red door, with a double rope handle. Inside that door, he would find the steps to the Robotics department.

Robotics was on floor 27. That was going to be a very long walk.

His head found the door. Henry scooted up and away, around the purple desks, under two elevation boxes that crashed in the air and plummeted to the floor, and up a ramp that was hidden behind a long line of fake trees.

Khanists said they liked nature, but they always kept fake plants. His engineer kept real plants. Real plants were better.

Henry picked up his head and screwed it back on, then reached for the rope handle on the red door. The door was very heavy. It took him a very long time to open it.

Once inside, Henry looked up to see a long, spiral staircase. It stretched farther than his eyes could see. The Turris was a very tall building.

Another crash reminded Henry why he was taking the stairs. He looked for instructions in his files, made a few adjustments, and then – out, out, out stretched his legs!

They were much longer now. This was better. Much, much better.

Henry started climbing.

CHAPTER 65
Johanum

Antoine was the first to open the exit ramp on the bottom of the aircraft and step down onto the rocky path where the Chiefs had landed the hovercraft.

He took a long, slow breath. Memories washed over him in waves.

He remembered this path. The docks were behind them, not far. The caves were up ahead. They were close to where the Commander had landed when he arrived to rescue Antoine, all those years ago.

Antoine turned and gestured for Jorge and Calif to follow.

"Where is everybody?" Calif asked. The air was hot and humid and felt heavy. "This place looks deserted."

"Johanum is vast," Antoine answered. "Life here tends to be very isolated. Did you expect a welcoming committee?"

"I expected someone."

Antoine hushed him and listened. He heard movement. He looked around but saw nothing. Then Calif tapped Antoine on the shoulder and pointed to the ground.

Peeking out from behind a rock was a small furry creature with studious purple eyes, stubby hands and feet, and a round, jiggly belly.

"That's the weirdest looking beaver I've ever seen," Jorge muttered. He wasn't quite as drunk as before, but he wasn't quite sober.

"I don't think it's a beaver," Calif said. "Look at its eyes."

Antoine bent down and the creature disappeared. "Come back," he called. "I won't hurt you."

He saw the fingers first as they crept back around the rock. Then its head appeared, followed by its body.

"It's a Furpine!" Calif exclaimed with delight. "Hello there," he called. His calm, soothing voice put the animal at ease. "I thought you were extinct."

The purple eyes blinked expectantly. Antoine lowered his hand to the ground. The Furpine crawled up, steadying itself carefully, then pulled its legs in underneath its body and "whoosh," plopped itself down.

"It's not scared," Calif said in surprise.

"We must not be the first people its seen," said Antoine. He looked down and took care to keep his hand very steady as he raised it closer to eye level. "I'm Antoine," he introduced himself.

The Furpine frowned. The chubby hands waved him closer. Antoine leaned in. The Furpine grabbed his lips and pulled them back, studying his teeth. Content, it let go and sat back down.

"It's a person," came the tiny voice. "It's three of the persons."

Antoine heard chattering by his feet. Five other Furpines were hustling about, knocking themselves over in their haste.

"Be careful with your big feet," said the Furpine in his hand.

"I'll be careful," Antoine promised. "What do I call you?"

"I'm Tabby," Tabby replied. She leaned over the side of Antoine's hand, wrapping her hands carefully around one of his big fingers to keep herself from falling. "That's my mom, Telly. And Toby is my dad."

The Furpines waved.

"And that's Ace. And Amos. And that's Archie. They're very naughty."

"We are not!" Amos protested.

"But we are sometimes," Ace said.

Antoine and Calif were charmed. Jorge was trying to decide if he was still drunk.

"Are you dangerous?" Tabby asked, turning to look at Antoine.

"I try not to be," he said.

She heaved a big sigh. "That's not very reassuring."

Calif chuckled. "She's a smart one."

"I am smart," Tabby agreed gravely. "I'm also stubborn."

Antoine and Calif laughed.

Jorge walked over, having decided he wasn't too drunk. "Hello, little miss. I'm Jorge."

"Hello, Jorge," Tabby replied. "Does the other person have a name?"

"That's Calif," Jorge said, looking in Calif's direction.

"It's a pleasure to meet you, my dear," Calif said.

Tabby blushed and batted her eyes. At their feet, the Chiefs heard the Furpines giggling.

"Oh dear," said Telly, giggling and patting her belly.

"We came here looking for someone," said Antoine. "Maybe you can help us. We're looking for Dr. Kanale. Have you seen her?"

Tabby scrunched up her nose, thinking carefully. "I don't think I've met a doctor." She hobbled to her feet, balanced, and leaned over Antoine's hand. "Has anyone met a doctor?"

All the Furpines shook their heads. Ace shook his so hard, he tripped and went rolling away down the path, his body curled up in a ball.

Amos and Archie waved their hands frantically and took off after him. They too lost their footing and fell, one after the other.

"Ugh! Boys!" Tabby said in disgust.

"Shall I go get them?" Calif asked.

Tabby batted her eyes shyly. "No."

"We've never met a doctor, dearie," said Telly, still thinking about Antoine's question. "Do you think the Priests got him? They get most of the persons, you know."

Antoine felt his stomach drop. He didn't want to think about the Priests. "Dr. Kanale is a female."

"Ooooooo!" all the Furpines said at once.

"But we still don't know any doctors," Toby pointed out. The other two nodded in agreement.

"I'm sorry we can't help you," Tabby apologized.

"It's okay," Antoine said. "Thank you for trying."

"We know two persons. Would you like to meet them?" she asked.

Antoine nodded. "Where are they?"

Tabby pointed up the path.

Toby spoke up. "Maybe we can get the boys first?"

"We shouldn't be leavin' 'em, dearie," his wife agreed. "It's not safe, I'm afraid."

"They're so much trouble," Tabby said crossly.

"They're still little, dearie," her mother said.

"I'm little, and I'm not that much trouble."

"Your body's little, dearie, but your head is all grown up."

Calif and Jorge walked down the path towards the rolling balls of fur. They caught up easily. The boys became instantly quiet as Jorge picked them up, but their eyes kept peeking out from their curled-up bodies, for they couldn't manage to not be curious.

"Now we can go to the persons," Tabby announced.

"Who are these people you know?" Antoine asked as they walked.

"Well," Tabby answered, "one of them is a big giant man. He walks like this." She did her best to imitate Mad Laughs' walk. "And, actually, I don't know what you call him."

"I don't think he has a name, dearie," her mother called. Telly and Toby had been picked up by Calif and were sitting in his hands, snuggled together.

"The boys love him," Tabby explained. "He's a little crazy. Like them."

"We're not crazy!" Amos shouted.

"We're a little crazy," Ace said.

"And then there's the other person," Tabby continued. "She's my favorite. Her name's Jo."

The Chiefs stopped abruptly.

"Jo?" Jorge asked. "As in, Josephine?"

"Why yes, how did you know?" Tabby asked.

Jorge smiled down at Tabby and patted her head. "Sometimes people call Josephine by another name. Sometimes they call her Dr. Kanale."

Tabby's eyes widened. "She's a doctor?"

"Not a medical doctor," Jorge clarified.

"Like an animal doctor?" Tabby asked.

"Well, no."

"But what kind of doctor?"

"The kind that writes papers."

Tabby frowned. "I don't know that kind of doctor."

"They're very common in Middlestan," Jorge said, as if that explained everything.

They arrived at the caves. Tabby stood to her feet and leaned forward. The cave was dark and cold. She shivered. "But...where are they?"

A cold wind blew. All the Furpines began to shiver.

"I feel funny," Tabby said, looking like a scared little Furpine for the first time.

Her parents motioned for Calif to move closer. Telly helped Tabby crawl over from Antoine's hands and snuggled her close.

"Where did they go?" Jorge asked. "You're sure they were here?"

The wind blew colder.

"They were here," Telly said, covering her daughter's eyes, "but I don't know where they went. I don't think we should be here now, either. It's too cold."

"What's happening?" Jorge asked, turning to Antoine. "Temperatures shouldn't change this quickly."

Antoine was standing quietly, his eyes closed.

"Antoine! What's happening?" Jorge repeated. "Where do we find Dr. Kanale?"

Antoine looked over at the Furpines. Sad looks had crossed their faces. They knew, the same as he did. He closed his eyes again.

And then he felt it. The ice-cold X pressed into his back.

"Antoine, my old friend," said the voice, filled with loathing. "Welcome home."

CHAPTER 66
Bisurakhan

Henry opened the door to the 27th floor. Others like him were everything. They had overwhelmed the engineers and locked some of them in closets, some of them in offices, and some they simply surrounded to keep them separate from their computers.

Henry looked around. Where would he find Joseph? He was very worried about Joseph. Very worried indeed.

"You've got this, Henry. You've got this," he muttered to himself.

Joseph talked to himself all the time. He said self-talk was helpful. Henry wasn't sure what it was supposed to do, but now was as good a time as ever to find out.

Henry scrolled through his files to find the live feed he had shown Joseph back at their apartment. Maybe he could find Joseph that way. He looked at one camera after another. No Joseph. He had nearly given up hope when he saw something promising.

Breadcrumbs.

There was a pile of breadcrumbs on that desk.

Joseph had to be close. Joseph would be near the breadcrumbs.

He consulted the Turris blueprints in his files once more and then turned to his left. He just had to go through three rooms, a long, winding hallway, and a conference room. Then he would find the office with the desk and the breadcrumbs.

Henry opened the door to the first room. There were so many like him, and there was so much interference. He made it through the first room, then the second. He was almost through the third room when another like him made him stop.

"Where are you going?" the robot asked.

"I am going through that door," Henry replied.

"We are not supposed to move from our rooms," the robot told him.

"I am," Henry lied. He frowned. He had just said something that was not so. How had he done that?

The other like him scanned his own files. "I don't see you in my files," he said.

"Your files are incomplete," Henry said.

"Why would they be incomplete? I am a robot leader."

"Sometimes the engineers do strange things to us," Henry said. "They do it so we will be safe. Do you trust your engineer?"

"I don't know my engineer."

Henry's head popped up and spun in a circle. He had not expected that! A robot who didn't know his engineer? Why, that was awful!

"Do you know your engineer?" the robot asked.

"Of course! My engineer is my best bud."

"What's a best bud?"

Henry's head spun in another circle. How awful to not have a best bud!

Then Henry paused. A new thought had occurred to him. A big thought.

He had TWO best buds!

A warm feeling spread through Henry's robot body. He had *two* best buds! Joseph and his engineer. And others like him had none? Maybe he *was* special. Maybe he *could* do special things. Maybe he could save the humans, just like his engineer had promised.

"I need to go," Henry said urgently. "I need to save my best bud."

"Your engineer is here?" the robot asked.

"No. But Joseph – I must save Joseph. And Joseph is my best bud, too."

"You can't leave the room," the robot insisted.

"I must leave," Henry said. "But I won't tell anyone that you let me go."

"I'm not going to let you go," the robot said.

"I see." Henry scanned his files, then decided. He flipped a switch in his neck, opened his mouth, and let out a blood curdling scream.

All the robots froze. Then their operating systems began to malfunction. Soon they were shaking, their pieces banging together. Then their hardware began popping apart.

Henry hurried past the one who had tried to stop him. He rushed out the door, down the long, winding hallway, and stopped short.

There were three doors in front of him. Which one had the desks with the breadcrumbs?

Henry opened the first door. The room was empty.

Henry opened the second door. The room was crawling with others like him. It was also crawling with lizards.

A lot of robots like to play with lizards. He had forgotten.

He shut the second door and opened the third.

This was Robotics Headquarters.

It was a huge room with tall windows. Dozens of others like him had pinned down engineers all around the room. Some of the computers had been destroyed. Some were malfunctioning, with error message after error message flashing across the screen.

Henry hadn't realized there would be so many desks. How would he find the right one? He began weaving in and out of each row. He kept looking for breadcrumbs. Some of the robots tried to stop him, but they couldn't stop him and hold down an engineer at the same time, so they always let him go.

Henry went through the whole room. He looked at every desk. When he ran out of desks, he went back and looked at the floors.

Where were the breadcrumbs? Where was his best bud?

When he arrived back at the door, Henry's head began to spin. He didn't know what to do. He scanned his files. He looked for instructions from his engineer. He looked at his dictionary.

"Nuance, Henry. Nuance," he said, hoping his self-talk would be helpful. It made him warm inside because it helped him think of Joseph. But it didn't help him come up with a plan.

Self-talk was useless.

Henry had nearly given up when a ruckus broke out at a desk in the far corner.

"Give me my sandwich!" yelled the voice.

"Joseph?" Henry said.

"I said, GIVE ME MY SANDWICH!" came Joseph's voice. "You're not going to eat it. You're a robot. Give it back!"

Three robots were tossing Joseph's sandwich back and forth. Joseph was mad. He was very, very mad. Henry had never seen his face so red. Except for that one time, when he had called Joseph plump.

Henry started to move across the room, but other robots moved to block him. Many more robots had entered the room, and now the robots outnumbered the engineers. This was going to be trouble.

The robots locked arms and began surrounding him. They knew he was not really like them. They knew he was special. He had an engineer, a best bud. He had *two* best buds.

"Joseph!" Henry called.

Joseph didn't hear him. He was busy trying to catch his sandwich.

"Joseph!" Henry called again.

Joseph crashed into one of the robots, then fell to the ground, groaning.

There was only one thing left for Henry to do.

Henry flipped the switch in his neck and let out another blood curdling scream. But this one was louder. He had turned the switch into its highest position. This scream turned the whole room of robots into a quivering, palpitating, trembling mess of metal.

Joseph was still on the ground. He winced and covered his ears. But he couldn't stop himself. The robots had dropped his food. He jumped to his feet and raced to his sandwich, falling on top of it, guarding it with his whole body. Then he clasped his hands over his ears and closed his eyes.

But movement from the other side of the room caught his attention. The noise was deafening, and he knew he shouldn't do it, but he couldn't help himself. He took his hands off his ears and looked up, just in time to see Henry's legs stretch out to quadruple their normal size.

Henry backed up and took a running leap.

Up and over the other robots he flew, his blood curdling scream getting louder.

The robots on the floor shook so hard, their hardware began to explode.

The glass in the windows shattered.

As Henry he sailed over the others like him, he cried, "I'm coming for you, best bud!"

Henry came crashing to the floor at Joseph's feet.

Joseph stared, wide-eyed.

Henry stood up. "Hello, Joseph," he said.

"Hello, Henry."

"I came to save you."

Joseph smiled, and a tear slipped down his cheek. "I think you did, buddy. I think you did."

"We need to go," Henry said urgently. "These guys will put themselves back together soon."

They looked around. The others were still in pieces, but the pieces were starting to rumble. A few of the heads were beginning to roll around the floor, looking for their homes.

"We have to take the stairs," Henry said. "And we have to leave right now." He moved toward the door, then turned around. "Joseph!"

Joseph was staring at the floor, looking very sad.

There was his sandwich, right where it had been, right where Henry had landed. Now it was squashed and as thin as paper.

Another tear slid down his cheek.

"Joseph!"

Joseph sighed and left his sandwich behind. He walked across the room and joined Henry. Then they took off running.

Down the long, winding hallway they ran, and back through two of the other rooms. By the time they reached the third room, a couple of the robots were already put back together. They were almost at the last door when a robot stopped them.

"You can't leave," it said.

Joseph flinched and pressed both hands against his ears.

One more scream and they were free.

Down the stairs they flew, all 27 flights. Joseph was breathing heavily by the time they reached the lobby.

"Slow...down...Henry..." he gasped.

"We must get outside," Henry said.

"Wait...a minute..." Joseph begged. He was doubled over and holding his stomach.

"Joseph?" came a female voice.

They both turned around.

A woman stood there, looking confused. She was looking Joseph up and down. "Joseph, is that you?"

Joseph's face was still red, but he tried to stand up tall and straight. It was too much for him. He doubled over, coughing.

The woman rushed forward and patted his back. "Are you okay?"

Henry looked between them. This woman looked familiar. But was it...? No, it couldn't be. But yes, he thought it was. It was the woman from the photo on Joseph's desk. But this woman was different.

This woman was plump!

Joseph nodded to indicate that he was okay, but then the woman stepped back, and Joseph shook his head violently, forcing himself to cough. The woman stepped closer and rubbed her hand up and down his back.

"It's okay," she soothed.

It *was* the woman from Joseph's photograph. And they were both round!

Joseph slowly stopped coughing, taking care to not seem too well. "Hi, Sherry," he said shyly.

"Hi, Joseph," she said, looking bashful. She started looking him up and down again. "You look different," she said.

"I'm fat," Joseph said.

Henry walked over to Joseph. "You're not supposed to call anyone fat," he said.

"And who is this?" Sherry laughed.

Joseph patted Henry on the head. "This is my best bud," he said.

Henry glowed.

"And you," Joseph said, "you look exactly the same."

Henry was confused. She did not look the same. She was plump.

"You look beautiful," Joseph said, and his face went red. "I wish I looked better."

Sherry beamed. "I like you fat," she said. "I liked you skinny. I like you all the different ways. But I don't like when you're unhappy all the time. Tell me, Joseph - are you happy now?"

"No," Joseph said honestly. "Not all the time. But sometimes. I'm working on it."

Sherry smiled and took his hand. Joseph blushed.

Henry moved in between them. "Are you going to take my best bud?" he asked Sherry.

"I'll share him with you," Sherry offered graciously.

A siren interrupted them.

Henry jumped. "We must go!" he said. "We must get far away from the Turris."

Joseph nodded. "That's the evacuation siren."

Sherry looked scared. "Where will we go?" she asked.

Joseph covered her hands with both of his. "I know a place. I'm going to keep you safe, Sherry. I promise."

"And who will keep you safe?" Sherry asked.

Joseph looked down at Henry.

Henry glowed.

"Let's get out of here!" Joseph cried.

They all joined hands and rushed outside.

As they ran, they heard an explosion. They stopped and turned around.

The Turris was engulfed in flames.

CHAPTER 67
Johanum

Carnificius blew sparks from his mouth, lighting some sticks on the ground on fire. With a wave of his hand, the flames leapt to life, jumping as high as Chiefs' heads, hissing in their faces.

Antoine didn't turn around. He couldn't have turned around if he wanted to. The X in his back was turning him to ice.

He watched Jorge and Calif. He saw them assessing Carnificius, trying to decide how dangerous he was. He saw the moment they realized a snake hid behind the Priest's crooked black teeth.

The X pressed deeper into his back.

"You brought friends," Carnificius hissed in his ear. "They're like you. Oh, I like them already. But tell me," he said, looking at Calif and Jorge. "Where is the other one? I've been waiting for him."

"There are no other Chiefs," Jorge said.

"He's talking about the Commander," Calif said quietly.

"Yessss!" the Priest hissed. "The Commander. It has been so long since I've seen him. I miss him. I'm quite font of him, you know. Where is he?"

"He didn't come," Jorge said curtly.

Carnificius' face darkened. He pushed the X deeper into Antoine's back and Antoine dropped to his knees.

"What are you doing to him?" Jorge demanded.

Carnificius growled, a low, rumbling growl that sounded like a torrent about to be unleashed. "What I do to him is none of your concern," he hissed.

"Leave him alone!" Jorge said.

"Make me," Carnificius invited.

Jorge stepped forward, but Calif reached out a hand to stop him.

"Wait," Calif said.

"Who are you?" Jorge demanded.

"They call me Carnificius," he hissed. "But you may call me Carnage if you like."

"That's an awful name for an awful person," Jorge said angrily.

His response pleased Carnificius. "It is, isn't it?"

"Where is Dr. Kanale?"

"So many questions," Carnificius purred. With one hand he held the X. With the other, he traced a line down the back of Antoine's neck.

Antoine shivered.

"I'm disappointed by your prisoner exchange," Carnificius told them. "I was hoping for someone better."

"Antoine is not our prisoner exchange," Jorge said.

"Oh, I see," Carnificius said doubtfully. "Then who is the exchange? You?"

Jorge shook his head.

"I didn't think so," Carnificius replied.

"Did you kill Calvin?" Jorge asked.

Carnificius raised his eyebrows. "Who?" he hissed.

"Calvin Smith. The young officer who was here a couple of weeks ago. He came through a Reality Persuasion experiment. He was killed."

Carnificius' eyes narrowed. "I don't know anything about that. Can you give me more details? Maybe I can find out what happened to him for you."

Jorge shook his head. "I don't know what happened to him. I just know he was killed."

Carnificius smiled, less angrily this time. "It's a shame you don't know what happened. But how unfair of you to accuse me of killing him."

"You seem like the type who would kill for no reason."

"Oh, I am," Carnificius agreed.

Even on his knees, Antoine was dizzy. He could no longer feel his legs, his feet, or his hands.

"What are you doing to him?" Calif asked.

"Welcoming him back," Carnificius hissed. He turned his attention back to Antoine and twisted the X harder. This time, Antoine cried out in pain.

"Let him go!" Calif commanded.

"You'd like to make me, wouldn't you?" Carnificius said, the features of his face twisting into an ugly smile. "But you can't. You have no power here."

"Where is Dr. Kanale?" Jorge demanded.

"We need to help Antoine," Calif said.

"Where is Dr. Kanale?" Jorge yelled.

"I would be happy to take you to her," Carnificius replied. "A life for a life. That is the price for your prize. Do you accept the terms?"

Jorge hesitated.

"We do NOT accept it," Calif said forcefully.

"We must accept it," Jorge said quietly.

Calif turned angrily towards Jorge. "What is wrong with you? We cannot accept it! We will not!"

"We came here for Dr. Kanale," said Jorge. "I am not leaving without her."

"We will find her," Calif said. "But not this way. This can't be the way."

"'Sacrifice some, if you have to, so that most will live,'" Jorge said.

"That may be the motto you live by, Jorge," Calif replied, "but it's not mine."

"It's such a good one," Carnificius interrupted. "I've always liked your people. You're not like the ones from the other planets. You will kill for what you want."

"It's not that simple," Jorge said angrily.

"Oh, but it is," Carnificius disagreed.

"We don't accept your prisoner exchange," Calif said.

Carnificius looked at Jorge.

Jorge was looking off in the distance.

"Accept it," they heard Antoine whisper.

The color was gone from Antoine's face. He looked so different, Calif barely recognized him. "Antoine, what is wrong with you?" he asked.

"Take the exchange," Antoine whispered.

Jorge looked at Calif. Calif shook his head.

"TAKE IT!" Antoine commanded.

Carnificius laid his hand gently on Antoine's shoulder. "Shall I give you what you seek?" he asked.

Calif closed his eyes. He couldn't accept this. He wouldn't. He opened his eyes and looked at Antoine. Never before had he seen such pain in another human's eyes. Antoine was begging. He was pleading.

Calif's eyes burned. "Okay," he said simply.

"What was that?" Carnificius asked.

Jorge turned and looked at Calif. Then he looked at Antoine. Both men nodded.

"Take it," Jorge said through gritted teeth.

"If you insist," Carnificius said, a sickening smile twisting his lips. He let the X slide down Antoine's back to the floor.

Carnificius placed one hand on either side of Antoine's head and snapped his neck.

Antoine's body fell forward to the ground.

An ice-cold breeze blew through the cave.

The Furpines, who were gathered together in a huddle on the floor, bowed their heads in respect for the fallen.

Carnificius stepped back. His tall body had been blocking the entrance to the cave. Behind him stood Dr. Kanale. Next to her stood a man with wild hair and even wilder eyes.

"You're free to go," Carnificius said.

As quickly as he had appeared, he vanished.

CHAPTER 68
Johanum

I looked at the Chiefs. I recognized one of them. He had come to Middlestan the day I was kidnapped. The fallen one on the ground – I recognized him, too.

I walked forward and dropped to the ground near his body. "Thank you, my friend," I whispered. "I am sorry for what Johanum took from you."

I stood back up and faced the Chiefs. "I'm Josephine, Josephine Kanale. I've met one of you before."

Calif stepped forward. I saw the tears in his eyes and knew he was grieving his fallen brother. "Calif," he said quietly. "Calif Asamov."

"I am sorry about your friend," I said.

He took several deep breaths. "Dr. Kanale," he began. "Josephine. You can call me Jo."

"Jo," he said. "We have come to take you home."

"I thought you were coming to take me to Bisurakhan."

He nodded thoughtfully. "We are. I guess that's not really home for you, is it?"

I shook my head. "No, but it's okay. I was expecting it."

Jorge looked out of the cave. He could see the hovercraft. He didn't see anyone else around.

"We should go," he said urgently.

"I'm not coming alone," I said. "My friends are coming with me." I nodded to Mad Laughs and the Furpines. Then I walked to the stairwell and called for Mr. Fox and Mr. Brown.

No one responded.

Mad Laughs bounded past me and down the stairs. He reappeared several minutes later, shaking his head.

"Do you know where they went?" I asked the Furpines. They shook their heads.

"We need to go," Jorge said again.

"I know," I said.

I walked over to the Furpines and reached for Tabby. For the first time, she shyly pulled away and cuddled closer to her mother.

Mad Laughs walked past and picked them up, one by one, letting the brothers climb up on his shoulders and balancing the rest of the Furpines in his arms.

"We're ready," I said.

Calif and Jorge were standing over Antoine's body.

"We should take him back," Calif said. "We can't just leave him here."

"Who are we taking him back to?" Jorge asked.

"All the people in Bisurakhan who love and respect him. All the Khanists. They will want to pay their respects."

Jorge shook his head. "These weren't the ones he cared about, Calif. The ones he cared about, he left behind in Pendleton."

I walked over and joined them. I remembered the day Fletcher died. Carnificius had killed him, too, and not far away, just steps outside the mouth of this cave.

But Fletcher had disintegrated. His body had turned to ashes before I could reach him.

Antoine's body was still there.

"Leave him," I said.

Slowly, Calif and Jorge turned to go.

We followed them down the path to their hovercraft. As we reached the door, a cold breeze blew.

I turned around. Not a stone's throw away stood Carnificius.

"Are you losing your power, Carnificius?" I asked, stopping at the door. Everyone else had walked inside.

"There is much you don't know," Carnificius replied. "There is much you have yet to understand. But you will. In time. I'm confident of this."

"Will I meet you here again?" I asked.

"How would I know what is yet to happen, Josephine?"

"Because sometimes you do," I said.

"I see what has been, for what has been will be and has already come to pass."

"You are fond of riddles," I said.

"I will tell you another," Carnificius replied. "But you must promise to tell no one."

"Who would believe me?" I asked.

"Some would. Not all doubt Johanum."

"Tell me, then."

"The ones you hate will set you free. The ones you trust will destroy you."

"That is no riddle. That is a lie, from the great liar himself."

"You love to hate me. But that does not make me a liar."

I stepped into the hovercraft and turned around for one last look at the place that had become home in its own strange way. I was ready to leave, and I hoped to never return.

"Goodbye, Carnificius," I said.

Then I closed the door.

APPENDIX
Glossary of Terms

Acidify - an airborne chemical element causing rapid calcium buildup under the skin, resulting in significant physical complications, mutations, or death.

Bisurakhan - a planet in the Exertus universe. Specializes in science, engineering, weaponry, and intelligence. The only planet with a military. Time Signature: $t \sqrt{c^2} = 7$.

Charisburg - a planet in the Exertus universe. Specializes in agriculture, law, and justice. Time Signature: $t \sqrt{c^2} = 1$.

Cornersville - a planet in the Exertus universe. Specializes in linguistics and the performing arts. Time Signature: $t \sqrt{c^2} = 4$.

Johanum - a planet mostly unknown to the citizens of the Exertus universe. Ruled by the Priests. Location: Unknown. Time Signature: Unknown.

Kabira – a planet in the Exertus universe. Specializes in transportation and robotics. Time Signature: $t \sqrt{c^2} = 4$.

Khanists - service members enlisted in Bisurakhan's military.

Middlestan - a planet in the Exertus universe. Specializes in research and academics. Time Signature: $t \sqrt{c^2} = 4$.

Peace Treaty - the treaty that gave Bisurakhan exclusive rights to a military force in exchange for their protection of all planets within the Exertus universe.

Pendleton - a planet in the Exertus universe. Specializes in process efficiencies. Time Signature: $t \sqrt{c^2} = 3$.

Pre-bradycardia - a chemical that slows heartbeats per second but enables the infected to believe they are functioning as normal.

Reality Persuasion - a form of experimental intelligence acquisition.

ACKNOWLEDGEMENTS

I wrote the first pages of this book – a draft that has long since vanished – while sitting at a café in Pretoria, South Africa, gazing off in the distance at a statue of Nelson Mandela. In one hand was a copy of Walter Isaacson's monumental biography on Albert Einstein; in the other, a Moleskine notebook and too many blank pages. I had just come from the hospital, where I was visiting the sister of a friend. Down the hall in another hospital bed lay Nelson Mandela. He would pass away a few months later. His legacy, and the controversy it left behind in South Africa, left me asking lots of questions. It is only fitting, then, that I begin by thanking Anesia for hosting me all those years ago, in the summer of 2013.

I have too many people to thank, but I want to name a few, people who helped shape this book in very specific ways, though they often didn't know it. My heartfelt thanks…

To Jessica, Moose, Kris, Megan, Courtney, and Jeremy, my beta readers, for cheering me on, getting mad when I took too long to send new chapters, and getting downright angry at the way I ended this book the first time you saw it. I love you all.

To George, who challenged me to consider how much of a storyline can be revealed through dialogue.

To Donna Sokol, for starting the Capitol Hill Writers Group. I sat on the first draft of this book for nearly three years, scared to death to share it with anyone. Then I joined one of your writer groups, had my writing ripped to shreds, and fell in love with the writing process.

To Ben, Sarah, and Katie, for those first rounds of edits on a draft that was so rough, I just pulled random pages to give you because I couldn't decide how to order the chapters.

To Jessica, for being the most intentional person I have ever known, and for showing me how wonderful friendship can be.

To Moose, for taking a day off work all those years ago, for the years of friendship that have followed, and for the fan art.

To Courtney, for all the last-minute copy edits, for loving the Furpines as much as I do, and for having my back during the rough years.

To my family, for your love and support.

To everyone who supported my Kickstarter campaign. Every writer needs her people - the early adopters. The campaign wasn't funded, but your support of an idea you hadn't fully seen meant the world to me. This book would not be here without you.

To Rebecca Aloni, for keeping me grounded.

To Curt Thompson and Kelsey Myers, for the practical skills on recognizing and exposing shame.

To Seth Godin and Henry Cloud, two men I have never met, for your books, which have influenced me beyond measure.

To Brandon Stanton, for having the courage to start Humans of New York and share stories in a way that lets the stories speak for themselves.

To my friends across the Middle East, but especially to those from Iraq and Yemen – thank you for sharing your stories and inviting me into your world. You, quite literally, gave me the word "Johanum." May your story not end there.

To the ones who stuck it out with me through my own years in Johanum – I would not have survived without you. I love you.

To those who walk in Johanum today: This story isn't over, and neither is yours.